The Stockholm Syndrome

Also by Jonathan Havard

Blood and Judgment

The Stockholm Syndrome

JONATHAN HAVARD

W H

Heinemann : London

William Heinemann Ltd
10 Upper Grosvenor Street, London W1X 9PA
LONDON MELBOURNE
JOHANNESBURG AUCKLAND

First published 1986

ISBN 0 434 31395 5

Photoset by Deltatype, Ellesmere Port
Printed and bound in Great Britain by
Mackays of Chatham Ltd
Chatham, Kent.

To Beth and our family

Oh, East is East, and West is West, and never the twain shall meet,
Till Earth and Sky stand presently at God's great Judgment Seat;
But there is neither East nor West, Border, nor Breed, nor Birth,
When two strong men stand face to face, though they come from the
ends of the earth.

Rudyard Kipling

Under conditions of siege, a bond of affection, sometimes amounting to intimacy, can develop between criminals and hostages, directed against the forces of law and order outside. In 1973, an escaped convict and his companion took over a bank in the Swedish capital, holding many of the staff as hostages. Such was the intimate relationship built up between captors and captives that, after several days, gunmen and hostages walked out together so that no harm should come to either.

Acknowledgements

When writing about a branch of medicine of which one has had no personal experience, the easiest research method is, overtly or covertly, to pick one's ex-colleagues' brains. Dr Felicity Davies and Mr Peter Griffin of the Dialysis and Renal Transplant Units at Cardiff Royal Infirmary are two doctors who willingly allowed me to benefit from their considerable skills in this way and I gladly acknowledge their most generous assistance. In similar fashion, I would like to thank Mr Craig Otley of the Civil Aviation Authority for his help in giving me an insight into the fascinating world of Air Traffic Control.

PART ONE

Prologue

They stood behind their respective seniors halfway through a teaching ward round; Helen, her mass of black hair pinned up beneath a tiny laced cap, ready to react to any whispered instructions from the Ward Sister, he hovering at the Consultant's shoulder like an heir apparent. He listened, acutely embarrassed, as the Consultant witheringly exposed a flinching medical student's ignorance of human anatomy. He struggled not to show his distaste as he listened to the pompous little man pumping up his ego in front of the other, sniggering students. From his position behind his Chief, he smiled compassionately at the crumpled young man, shrinking within the short white coat which bulged with a student's impedimenta of stethoscope, notebook, torch and patella hammer. He made a mental note to take the student aside afterwards to go through the anatomy with him once more, help rebuild his confidence.

The surgical team progressed erratically up the long, Nightingale-style ward and back again to the door. With little more than a cursory nod to his Ward Sister, the Consultant left, giving the Registrar time to whisper but three words to the Staff Nurse.

'Half past eight?'

Helen's reluctance was obvious but he had a way with women. A bit shorter than average, he had coarse, untidy hair, dark enough to make him look in permanent need of a shave; not the sort of man other men would have thought attractive to women. Though his features, when relaxed, had an almost weary mien, he had a ready smile for anyone, male or female, junior or senior, which made him popular with all strata of hospital staff. His hard drinking did nothing to dull his quest for personal success which he pursued with a stubborn singlemindedness that had brought him higher qualifications in both medicine and surgery very young. He had found the secret of switching off a frenetic social life the moment it posed a threat to his career, and Helen had no illusions that she too, at the first sign of slowing him down, would soon join the line of discarded women that milestoned his steeply upward path.

It was nearer quarter to nine when, standing near the Casualty entrance, impatient for that first drink, he saw her walk towards him down the long, stone-floored corridor. He hadn't minded waiting, moving to and fro in the early evening flow of minor human debris, appreciating that unique attitude of blasé expectancy shown by the staff of the main Casualty Department for a teeming city on pay night. The sound of her footsteps was regular and even, not the skittish variation in pace of some of the excited probationers who had come his way, the tiny, capricious steps that went with the giggles and the flirtatious teasing. Almost as tall as he, Helen had her hands thrust into the pockets of a plain but expensive looking raincoat.

'You're late,' he smiled with mock severity. 'Come on; I'm dying for a beer.'

She didn't move with him immediately and he had to turn round and come back to her.

'Come on,' he repeated. 'What's the matter?'

'Do we have to go?' Helen tried to smile but only succeeded in frowning. The truth was that she loathed the Black Lion. Everyone knows that each hospital has its local where young doctors and nurses, even occasionally senior staff, meet after the stress of caring for the sick and dying, to enjoy themselves, let their hair down. The 'Black' was the Royal Infirmary's local but, unlike the locals of novels and stage, it was cheap, grubby and paint-chipped. Helen always came away feeling grimy and cheapened.

'Wouldn't you rather come round to the flat?' she asked, knowing it was futile to ask. 'I've got the whisky you like.'

'And miss Stan's farewell? You can't be serious. One of my oldest friends decides to call it a day and you expect me to miss the party? Come on.' And he started for the door again.

When he had to turn a second time there was no hiding his irritation. Helen saw it and began to walk reluctantly towards the door also.

'Just one drink, love,' he said. 'Just one. You can't really expect me not to wish Stan good luck, now can you? But we won't stay late. Promise.'

It was raining heavily. Though the 'Black' was no more than 150 yards away, they had to dodge amongst the ambulances in the Casualty yard and stand back while another swept in, its flashing lights reflected in the wet shiny tarmac. By the time they had got to the 'Black', Helen's hair glistened with rain and she felt the wet discomfort of a mud-spattered ankle. She braced herself against the hot, damp, noisy atmosphere as he opened the door, saw his huge grin in response to the sudden upsurge in sound as they saw him come in. Helen struggled to a smile that she knew she would not be able to sustain all night and eased her way in after him.

The 'Black's' snug was accepted by the locals as a room the Infirmary's young doctors and students called their own. A bare, square room with wooden benches screwed to three of its walls, a meagre coal fire in a small black fireplace in the remaining wall adding to the stifling heat. When the room was full, at least some of the squalid decor was hidden from view by the mass of young, healthy bodies but, from where Helen found herself sitting, there was nothing between her and the withered husk of Annie McGuire.

'What can I get you, Helen?' He had come back to her from the crush that had enveloped him as soon as he had entered. He had already drunk half the pint that someone had put in his hand.

'Can I have an orange juice or a tonic or something like that?' Helen asked.

'Orange juice?'

'Yes. If you don't mind. I don't feel much like drinking tonight.'

He pulled a face as he fought his way to the half-door with its shelf which opened into the back of the public bar. He watched the landlord serve a huge man in a sweat-stained T-shirt, taking money from a pay packet that would never find its way into any domestic budget. While he was away, Helen did her best to ignore Annie McGuire's winks, nods and knowing, vacuous smiles. Annie Mac, known to generations of Casualty Officers at the Royal; Annie and her friend, to be found every night in the 'Black's' back room, sitting silently side by side, their glass of stout in front of them, the carrier bag for the flagons, carefully folded on the floor behind the skin and bone ankles in their thick, wrinkled stockings. Helen had helped strip her once, drunk, cut and blasphemous. Helen knew the filth of the underclothes beneath that threadbare coat, the matted hair beneath the turban hat. She was glad to stand up and turn her back on her as he came back with Stan.

'Helen, my love.' Stan's kiss and embrace were clumsy as he had a glass in each hand and was already unsteady on his feet. He'd started early. 'You look absolutely gorgeous.' Long past tasting what he was drinking, he took a gulp from the glass that had been thrust on him by an anonymous hand. Even so the strength of the drink made him catch his breath. 'Christ,' Stan said, 'that's a corker,' and, in the same breath, turned to Helen again, raising his voice above the noise. 'When are you going to make an honest fellow out of this chap, then?'

'That'll be the day, Stan,' Helen laughed, anxious to change the subject. 'We're going to miss you, you and Lucy. Is she here?'

'Oh yes. Brave little woman's somewhere over there.' Stan waved vaguely across the room. 'We're going to miss this place too, don't mind admitting it.' He belched politely. 'But there it is; if you can't get the exams that's it, isn't it? Nothing you can do about it then. We can't all be geniuses like our friend here,' and Stan jerked his thumb sideways.

They both smiled affectionately in the direction the thumb pointed and he accepted the smiles as homage due to someone with his own particular world at his feet. Stan, his best friend, a man of action, a good practical surgeon but with no temperament for the books. Stan, who just couldn't flog his way through the basic sciences again to get his Primary. All that practical ability going to waste. He wondered what would happen to him. The place wouldn't be the same. And Helen – he smiled his thanks for the drink handed him by the student his Chief had torn to shreds that morning – just like Stan had said, absolutely bloody gorgeous. 'Pure blue ice,' that's what they'd said she was. 'Haven't a prayer,' they'd said. 'Honestly, old boy; if I'd gone an inch further, I'm bloody sure she'd have hit me; nearly froze my fingers off.' Well, he could tell them different now. Yet, for all his experience and her virginity, somehow she had made him grow up a little, become less 'one of the boys'. He felt good with her, not just randy, but – good. They talked; they laughed. And, without consciously trying, she was making him take a long hard look at himself, be more honest with himself. He scanned the scene around him. It was a sham, that's what it was, a sham, and he was part of it. He knew himself to be a passionate, caring man. He loved his job, cared for people; all he lacked was the simple honesty to show it, hiding his fear of embarrassment behind the facade of a hard-drinking womaniser.

Moving abruptly, as if a decision had been made, he put his hand round Stan's shoulder.

'Right, Stan. Let's make this a night to remember.'

An hour later Helen and Lucy were confronted by two men, flushed and excited.

'Come on, you two,' Stan ordered. 'On your feet. One last drink at the County. Can't go without saying goodbye to them.'

The County Hospital, ten miles away in a distant suburb, had been where Stan had striven to keep his foot on the surgical ladder for the past two years, and no cries of protest from Lucy nor dumb, appealing looks from Helen were going to spoil Stan's enjoyment of his last night on the staff.

'But Stan's drunk,' Helen pleaded as he took her arm to cross the road to the Infirmary's car park, a fine drizzle making them blink, as if fighting back unwanted tears. 'He's not fit to drive.'

'He'll be all right,' he answered, full of bravado. 'Knows the road like the back of his hand. He ought to; he's driven it often enough these last two years.'

He opened the back door of the aged Ford to let Helen in and climbed in beside her, laughing as Stan fought to get the engine started.

'Not to worry, love,' Stan turned to his wife. 'A couple of years in Abu Dhabi and you can have whatever car you want.'

By the time they reached the dual carriageway, Stan began to focus a little better through the arcs swept by the two juddering windscreen wipers and he felt himself getting into his stride.

'Stan, you're driving too fast,' Lucy said, frightened.

'Rubbish, woman. If we don't get there soon they'll have all gone to bed. I'd better take the short cut.'

With a squeal of tyres, Stan pulled the car off the dual carriageway and into a minor road.

'Oh no, Stan; it's so narrow.'

Helen sat bolt upright alongside him, one hand braced against the seat in front of her, and, grinning confidence and reassurance, he put his arm round her shoulders and drew her towards him. Stan saw the movement and switched his gaze from the road to the rear view mirror.

'What's going on in the back there? Nothing, I hope, that . . .'

'*Stan*.'

There was a terrified urgency in the one word from Lucy that made him hold Helen closer and try to force her head down. The next few seconds were a mosaic of sounds and flashes as the car sped through the police accident signs and lamps. He had snatched views of dazzling headlights through a rain-flecked windscreen, a wall flashing alongside them, the tailboard of the broken down lorry with its yellow diagonal stripes, and finally the sight of Stan, taking his hands from the wheel to cover his face.

The first thing, the next thing, was the smell, a filth of dust and oil and petrol and blood and vomited beer. He could hear little except for dripping sounds, the occasional metallic creaking and faint moanings from the darkness in front of him. He felt no surprise at not being in pain. He found he could move his head and arms but his legs were trapped, painlessly, beneath the front seat.

Helen. He felt in the blackness and found her raincoat, her arm. Feeling for her face, his hand traversed her chest and he felt her rapid, shallow breathing.

'Helen, are you all right?'

There was no reply.

Futilely, he cried for help into the fear- and remorse-filled darkness and it seemed an age before there were voices outside and wavering torch-lights, an age during which he had ample time to plead with some faceless God to turn the clock back and give him another chance. In the stabbing beams of lights, he could make out Helen's shape but he could see nothing of Stan or Lucy and their moanings had now stopped. He felt the wreckage shake as someone tried unavailingly to open the back doors and he heard wailing police sirens getting closer. Suddenly his eyes hurt as the police car's headlights flooded in.

Helen was conscious. She tried to speak to him but made no sound. The blackness of her hair only accentuated the pallor of the face it framed and she looked at him with eyes no more than dilated, black discs, thin-rimmed with blue. She was still staring at him, as if in accusing disbelief, when her mouth gaped in a feeble, silent scream as, in her terminal agony, she aborted his three-month foetal son, the secret she had so wanted to share with him.

1

Dai Stud stretched, scratched his head and then his backside, lifting the baggy corduroy of his trousers up and down as he did so. He still wore a thick pyjama jacket and his hand moved to the gaping buttons to rasp across the hairs on his chest. He broke wind.

'That's better,' he muttered to himself, appreciatively.

He waved as a figure passed across a window above the stables. He didn't notice the bare rotting wood in the window frame, the piece of hardboard replacing one of the tiny panes.

Who in his right mind stayed in bed on a morning like this, however much he might have had to drink the night before? He took a deep breath and looked out over the remains of the Castle, over the crumbling, stratified cliffs, south over the muddy, tide-ripped water of the Bristol Channel. His focus shortened to sweep proudly round his shambling kingdom. Two sides of the stony, grass-tufted yard in which he stood were occupied by weather-beaten, red brick stables, tiles now missing from their sagging roofs, the rusting boot of a large, ill-used car projecting from the dilapidated shed at one end. Behind the shed a pile of stable manure steamed gently in the early morning sun, an upturned wheelbarrow resting against it. On the third side of the yard stood the large caravan, propped up on breeze blocks, its only evidence of twentieth-century facilities being the telephone wire that looped to the stable roof and on to the post in the lane outside. That this was home for himself and Jessie was witnessed by the old fridge, mattress and broken chairs, strewn around the caravan to be pecked over by the clucking hens and raucous cockerel. The chickens scattered noisily as an evil-looking, cross-bred border collie bitch emerged sleepily from the caravan door to slink devotedly to her master's feet. Dai took another deep breath as he smelt the bacon. He felt his chin and decided he'd give everyone a treat today and have a shave.

'Morning, Hannah,' he smiled at the girl who had just come down the bare wooden steps from the loft and out into the yard.

'Morning, Dai,' she replied, smiling back at him as she walked the length of the stables, a bridle in her hand and a saddle supported on one hip.

Dai Stud turned the palms of his hands upwards. 'Bloody marvellous morning, isn't it?'

'Sure is, Dai.'

To look at Dai Stud, no one would have recognised the son of the late Dr Nathaniel Davies, doyen of the local General Practitioners. Dai could just remember going up to the Castle with his father after it had been converted into a convalescent home during the war. He could just recall the soldiers in their thick blue suits, white shirts, red ties and heavy army boots, sitting in the sun outside the Cutty Sark, high above the sparkling sea. Dr Davies had had trouble with his son who had been thrown out of medical school, forced out of National Hunt racing by injury and had finally spent months on skull traction after breaking his neck at a point to point. As a last desperate effort, just before he died, old Dr Nat had bought the stables and fifteen acres from the absentee landlord who was pulling down the Castle and selling up.

It was shortly afterwards that Jessie Ellis moved in. No one could remember exactly when; the place just seemed to attract stray animals.

She had alternately wheedled and goaded Dai into trying his hand at running the land as a smallholding. When he tried and failed, everyone thought he'd sell out to the developers who had built on the adjoining land, but Dai and Jessie had been united in telling the accountants what to do with their money. And then Mason, the scrap merchant, had bought the Manor and Dai had taught his daughters to ride, had looked after their ponies for them. Mason hadn't minded Dai giving other kids rides on his ponies and before Dai knew where he was he had a pony trekking business on his hands, buying ponies of his own. Children seemed to trust him, feel safe with him. And then had come the day he had always dreamed of. He looked across the yard at the sleek heads of his brood mares, in such pampered, elegant contrast to the disarray around them, and the black, restless head of his stallion, Tempest. He watched Hannah reach up lovingly to put a bridle over Tempest's head. She had the narrow hips of a boy and he knew the firmness of those breasts, the nipples showing through the thin T-shirt. Jessie had seen the scratch marks that had crisscrossed Dai's face that morning, a few hours after he had drunkenly climbed those wooden stairs.

'Nothing doing, was there?' Jessie had spat at him, the sizzling frying pan threatening in one hand. 'Didn't fancy you, did she, you old ram? I could have told you that and saved you the trouble, you randy old sod. Here; eat your breakfast.'

And so Hannah had become another of those strays that had found refuge with Dai.

'Want some breakfast?' he called.

'No, thanks, Dai.'

'Bacon smells pretty good this morning.'

'Not hungry.' She opened the half-door and slid in alongside the excited animal, crooning to him as she ran her hand along the long, powerful neck. She swung her heel to kick the lower half of the door shut just as Dai came over to hang his pyjama-clad elbows over it and rest his chin on his hands.

'What's the matter with you, girl? You're never hungry. You don't eat a thing.'

There was no reply, only the sound of the stallion's hooves on the cobbles and Hannah's coaxing as she leaned her tiny frame against the horse's flank to move him over. Tempest pushed back and pressed Hannah against the wall. Dai Stud saw her wince and heard her gasp as the saddle she was carrying dug into her side. He saw her wince again as she tried to throw the saddle on the horse's back and fail.

'Here; let me do that for you,' Dai said, moving to open the door only to stop when he saw the look on her face. He saw her grit her teeth as she threw the awkward harness up and over, this time successfully.

Dai wondered about Hannah taking that great stallion for his exercise. She looked so bloody frail. Out in the fresh air all day but never seemed to have a speck of colour in her cheeks. And, towards evening, she looked as if she was all in, absolutely exhausted, driving herself to overcome fatigue that she should not have shown at that age. He shouldn't really let her ride that horse. She never wore a hat; just that hair down over her shoulders. But she could handle a horse, no doubt about that. Where the hell she'd come from he had no idea; but, by God, she could ride. He'd seen her take jumps he'd have thought twice about even back in his younger days. And God knows where he'd get help like her again; all she seemed to ask was a roof over her head and her keep.

He stood back to watch Hannah lead Tempest out of the stable. She gathered the reins, reached with the other hand for the saddle, towering above her, and, in swift movements, mounted him. She bobbed easily in the saddle as the stallion sidestepped towards the gate, tossing its head, making the harness jingle.

'You watch out, d'you hear?' Dai called after her. 'That horse is a handful. You take care now, d'you hear me? You're not to take him down the cliff path.'

The only answer was a brief wave of her tiny whip over her shoulder as she disappeared through the gate on to the lane outside.

Dai shook his head slowly as he watched Hannah go, his mind going back – how long was it now? must be more than a year – to when he had found her, crouching behind those bales of hay, those blue eyes wild and watchful, her body tensed for flight like a sprinter in his blocks. He had stood in the doorway blocking any chance of escape but had failed to get a word out of her until he had yelled for Jessie. Between them they had managed to get out of her that her name was Hannah, that she had no family, that she was living rough in Swansea and was on her way to London. They had got her to take some food, but only when it was taken over to her in the stables like the stray, lost animal she was. She'd slept in the loft and he'd come home a few days later to see her and Jessie carrying an old bedstead and worm-holed dressing table up the loft stairs. Hannah had disappeared for days at a time when the police had called. So had Dai. He'd been happy to leave the police and those snooping Social Security bastards to Jessie. He smiled. He wondered why Jessie had so little time for the police, the hardest of whom seemed to wilt from the effect of the raw edge of her tongue. Gradually they had lost interest in just another kid living rough after finding she was of an age when she could, quite legally, walk out of care. Equally gradually, Hannah had begun to clean herself up, look more sleek, her hair glistening like a stray cat who begins to eat regularly. They had found her a mirror and a calor gas heater, though Dai had complained of the fire risk, and she had begun to help around the yard, groom the ponies and muck out. As the weeks had gone by, she had started to take the pony treks if Dai had a hangover.

But where she had learned to ride like that, they would never find out.

Irritation suddenly made a thin line out of Dai's normally generous mouth. Why the hell had he tried to take advantage of her that night? He wished he hadn't; he'd been so pissed. She didn't seem to hold it against him but, my God, how she'd fought.

'Are you going to stay out there all morning?' Jessie appeared at the caravan door to deliver her invitation to breakfast.

'Coming,' Dai grinned as he turned and followed her in. It had crossed Dai's mind several times whether he should do the right thing and marry Jessie but had always decided he didn't want to run the risk of ruining their relationship.

Where the lane went close to the cliff edge, nothing survived winter's southwesterly gales to leave any suggestion of a hedgerow. Inland of the lane was an old dry wall, much in need of repair, but between the dusty track and the cliff edge was an expanse of grass where, later in the year, Dai would charge motorists to sit with their thermos flasks, staring over the Channel to Lynmouth and Ilfracombe. With no semblance of fear, Hannah took Tempest to within a few feet of the cliff's edge, having great difficulty in holding him as he felt the grass beneath his hooves. She tried to stand in the stirrups to get a better view of what had been the private beach below but she found that it hurt her. She shivered. It was no use; the tide was too far in, still lapping around the untidy boulders that lay at the bottom of the crumbling cliff. But she could tell from the beach that it was ebbing. She would have to go the long way round to the stretch of sand that went on and on as far as the estuary, but the tide would be out when she came back. Dai had only said, 'Don't go down the cliff path.' He hadn't said, 'Don't come up it.'

Gradually, descending all the time, Hannah came to that stretch of main road where she would have to take to the grass verge before cutting down behind the hotel to the beach. Some of the early morning commuters made no allowance for the slim girl, fighting to control such a big horse anxious to have its head, and Hannah's arms began to ache. She found she was sweating, the armpits of her shirt wet and clinging. Other drivers slowed down and she would have acknowledged the courtesy if she hadn't needed both hands. Few failed to notice the pair, the frail girl in jeans and T-shirt in such contrast with the powerful animal, the colour of his coat matched only by her hair.

She felt wretched. She felt detached and remote from the surging noises of the cars as they passed. For a moment she thought she was going to faint. She tried to smile at two of the hotel's kitchen staff who had come out into the lane to admire them going by. Normally she would have looked down on them almost with pity. To think they had to go back into that barracks of a place while she, in a few moments, would fly on Tempest's back. Normally she would have felt special. Today she just felt ill; worse than usual. She was used to that awful lethargy that she had to fight so constantly; the feeling of weakness that terrified her. The thought that she couldn't be free; might have to depend on others; owe people. She wished that pain in her side would go away. Suddenly, she was engulfed by a premonition that something awful was going to happen to her.

Once on the beach, she crouched and eased the reins, one hand now each side of the mane that began to whip back in her face. The sand beneath them sped by and she was conscious of blurred faces as two early morning walkers stood back in admiration. For a moment the rush of air made her feel better but the premonition returned as if she had only momentarily outrun it. In defiance rather than fear, Hannah dug her heels in and the stallion stormed into a full gallop.

Nearly two miles of open beach raced beneath the long strides until the stony mouth of the estuary slowed the horse to a trot. Hannah turned the horse's head and drove him as furiously as she could back once more, the spray hissing upwards in clouds as the hooves splashed through the streams that ran down the beach from the outcrops of rock to the sea. They were still galloping as they passed below the hotel. There was still no sand uncovered by the receding sea when they reached the headland, but the horse, its chest heaving, its nostrils flared, slowed to a walk as it took to the water, to splash its way round to the small beach beyond. The reins hung loose from Hannah's hands as she grasped the pommel to prevent herself from falling off. Her head drooped, her mouth open as she gasped for breath. She clawed at the neck of her shirt as if struggling for air and was only just conscious enough to realise that the horse was heading for the cliff path. Trying to gather up the reins only resulted in her falling forward around his neck.

'Jesus Christ, girl. What the hell have you . . .?' Dai Stud's outburst was at the sight of his beloved stallion coming into the yard, its chest still heaving and smirched with sand, its neck sweat-stained and chafed, but he stopped, open-mouthed, as he saw Hannah. He raced to the horse's side only just in time to break her fall as Hannah slid to the ground.

'Jessie! Jessie!' Dai shouted, despairing as he tried to hold her, giving a little cry as he failed to stop her head strike the ground with that unique sound of skull on stone.

'Jessie!' he bellowed, looking round to see her hurrying towards him. Without a word, Jessie brushed him aside and knelt on both knees to take Hannah's head gently in her hands.

'What happened?' she snapped.

'I don't know. She came in now and just fell off.' He looked up at the horse, wringing his hands. 'Jesus. Looks as if he's been ridden to hell and back. Oh, my God,' he watched as Hannah moved her head, her eyes rolling sightlessly, her pupils wide and as black as her hair, 'she's dying.'

'No, she isn't, you daft ha'porth. She's fainted. No wonder, going without breakfast like that. Go and get a pillow and a blanket. Go on.'

When they had her head resting on the pillow and had tucked the frayed blanket around Hannah, Jessie stayed kneeling over her while Dai undid

Tempest's girth and slid his saddle off. He threw a blanket over the sweating back and led him to his stable. He walked back to where Hannah lay and gave a little groan as he looked down at her.

'What d'you think, Jessie?'

'I rather think this is a bit more than a faint. I think we'd better get some help.'

'Help? What d'you mean, Jessie?'

'An ambulance, you old fool. Go and ring for an ambulance. Go on, hurry.'

2

Sayyid Yousef bin Hamad al Wahaibi had never been in Britain before. He had been obliged to change planes at London Heathrow once or twice before but one could hardly count that. Of course he had heard of Wales but he knew about as much about the country as a Welshman would know about some Middle Eastern state. Certainly, he had no idea that the early stillness of a May morning could be so breathtakingly different. He crossed Avonport's wide promenade, deserted at that time of the morning except for a pair of elderly joggers, painfully ignoring the magic that was around them. Yousef looked at his watch. It was not yet seven o'clock. 'They should be in bed,' he thought, smiling to himself. 'Making love is good exercise too.' He watched the juddering backsides inside the shapeless tracksuits and shook his head. Not that, relative to his surroundings, Yousef himself, in his well-cut but indefinably foreign clothes, looked any less incongruous. Immaculately dressed, his tight black curls and heavy moustache carefully groomed, he had checked out of his half-empty hotel at first light, impatient at the somnolent inertia he had had to overcome to settle his bill. He leaned his forearms on the upper bar of the old-fashioned, cast-iron railing and marvelled at the view across to Mumbles

Head, reflected in the waters of Swansea Bay, the few ripples that skimmed over the glassy surface hissing their way gently into extinction. Yousef, a sensitive man, shivered slightly with a vague feeling of expectancy, looked once more as if taking a mental still photograph, and walked to his car.

A few minutes later, as he drove westward beyond the end of the promenade, he had his first glimpse of the hospital. He drove the steel-grey Mercedes with an easy assurance, but at the roundabout, where the approach road to the hospital turned to the right and up a long grassy slope, the inevitable banks of direction signs demanded his concentration and his first view of the buildings was a fleeting one. Even so, he was impressed.

In low gear the car purred up the gentle incline of the hospital's approach road, a narrow tarmac strip between wide open expanses of well cared for turf. He came to another, smaller roundabout, again with its multiplicity of directions. He smiled at the sign pointing to the right towards the Consultant Staff car park in the prime position in front of what looked like the Ward Block. Bearing left, he passed in front of the ambulance bays outside the Casualty Department, a weary driver climbing into the cab of an ambulance while his colleague slammed and bolted its rear double doors. To get to the hospital's general car park, Yousef had to drive around the corner and in front of the main entrance. As he did so, he passed groups of night staff, their usual chatter dulled by fatigue, heading for the Nurses' Home 200 yards away, where they would shut out the sunshine and hope they were not too tired to sleep. One or two were not too exhausted to react to the handsome young man in the throbbing sports car, with a straightening of the shoulders, a twitch of a cape.

Avonport's District General Hospital was brand new, opened less than a year before. Royalty, everyone agreed, had done a thoroughly professional job of it, had shaken all the right hands, said all the right things. There had been just one problem – the name. The Area Health Authority had argued long and bitterly over whether it should be called St David's Hospital or Ysbyty Dewi Sant, a problem solved at the opening ceremony by using the names alternately. However, everyone was quite sure, no more so than the local inhabitants, that it would be years before it was referred to as 'The General', the name still affectionately reserved for the crumbling old workhouse that St David's had been built to replace.

Dissent had been rife during the planning stages, mainly centred around the location. Who on earth decided to put it way out there on Druid's Common, right on the western outskirts of the town, nothing beyond it but the golf course? Why couldn't they leave the Casualty Department where it should be, right in the middle of the town? And Outpatients – who in their right mind would put an Outpatients Department so far out, out where they'd have to lay on buses for the patients? And visitors; what about visitors? It had all been so much more convenient in the old General.

But criticism had melted away once the staff had settled in. How on earth had they managed to cope in that old place? Here there was so much feeling of space.

Yousef reached into the car's glove compartment and took out a compact but intricate camera. He opened it, checked all its functions with deft, practised movements and snapped it shut again. His left hand, thrust once more into the compartment, emerged with four or five rolls of film which he tipped into his jacket pocket. Another roll was inserted into the camera, his eyes flickering back and forth through the windscreen as if he hardly needed to look at what he was doing. He put the camera in the other jacket pocket, got out of the car, locked it and looked round.

The new hospital was a large T-shaped building, the longer downstroke of the T being five storeys high, the cross-stroke three storeys. Only one or two structures of any size, like the Nurses' Home and the boiler house, the mortuary and post-mortem room, were separate from it. From where Yousef stood beside his car, he looked straight at the main entrance in the centre of the three-storey wing. To the right of the main door and occupying all the ground floor down to the corner round which the ambulance had been parked, Yousef recognised the Casualty Department, unmistakable with its neon and electric lights still shining blue and yellow through the windows. To the left, as yet showing no signs of life, was the Outpatients Department. Of the other two floors, Yousef could not be too sure. On the one side they looked to him rather like offices while, on the other, his first guess was the Pathology Department. Although this part of the hospital faced northwest and was in the shade of the early morning sun, he took out his camera and took several exposures, with more of the rapidity and expertise of a press photographer than the hesitant care of the amateur.

For a moment he stopped, turning his head to listen to a distant bell that must be an ambulance or police car. The sound was foreign to him, the thrill of excitement that crept up his back the same the world over.

He turned and looked away from the hospital to the northwest. Apart from the Nurses' Home, half left of him, there was nothing between him and the golf course, nothing beyond that but marshland until one came to the giant steelworks, blue-green hills providing the final backdrop. Adjusting the focal length, he raised his camera again, taking panoramic views in a series of clicks and whirrs.

Yousef was walking around the corner, back in the direction in which he had arrived, apparently satisfied that there was nothing he had missed so far, when he heard a distant squeal of the ambulance's tyres as it negotiated the large roundabout at speed. As it accelerated up the long slope to the hospital it gave a final short burst on its siren to let the Casualty Staff know it was nearly there. It had been Yousef's intention to be as inconspicuous as possible but the ambulance acted on him like a magnet, drawing him towards whatever fragment of human misfortune it contained. It is doubtful if the driver and his mate noticed Yousef as they dashed for the back of their vehicle but they didn't fail to show their irritation when he stood close alongside as they maneouvred the stretcher so gently down on to the low trolley. The rough-looking woman who stepped out of the ambulance behind the stretcher, also showed her hostility to what she saw as some bloody foreigner, standing there gawping.

If she had not been so worried about Hannah, Jessie Ellis, a perceptive woman for all her rough tongue, might have seen that Yousef was more than a mere morbidly interested onlooker. There was nothing of the voyeur's look of vicarious pleasure as he stood looking down at the ashen face, all that could be seen in the mass of blankets. He stood as if he were part of the scene, as if he were no stranger to the situation. His face showed no excitement, nothing but quiet compassion and understanding, and the young girl, with what vision her semi-conscious state permitted, saw it and drew strength from it. She gave a faint smile before her eyes closed once more. Yousef just had time to stretch out and touch the blankets around Hannah's head, like some silent benediction, before the ambulancemen pushed the trolley towards the Casualty entrance and Jessie shouldered him out of the way.

'Bloody vulture,' she spat as Yousef managed to snatch one photograph before Hannah disappeared into the building.

The flexible, transparent doors swung shut with a noise somewhere between a slap and a thud and Yousef returned methodically to photographing the hospital and its surroundings. By the time he had got round to the front of the long, five-storey Ward Block, there was a trickle of day staff arriving and he began to feel conspicuous, stationary as he was in the middle of the irregular flow. He was impressed by the uncompromisingly modern architecture, the sheer face of the building being broken only by two vertical rows of balconies, corresponding to the two fire escapes he had seen to the rear and dividing the block into three sections. At ground level and beneath each row of balconies was a door. It was obvious the architects had made sure the patients would have full benefit of the view out to the southwest and Yousef, pausing to reload his camera for the third time, could understand why. The view from the hospital's elevated position was even more magnificent than from where he had stood on the promenade. The rolling grassland of the old common led down to the coast road, the long beach beyond broken only by the sloping, stratified curve of Graig Ddu reef, exposed now at low water to hook out viciously in the direction of the giant ore ships, anchored and low in the water, waiting for the tide to take them into the steel works hidden from view away to the right.

It was with a feeling of anti-climax that Yousef walked round the far end of the hospital to come full circle to his car once more. The surroundings there were so dull and flat and uninteresting that Yousef almost forgot that this, too, was important and needed to be recorded. It was necessary to have views of the whole of the hospital's perimeter, pleasant or not. He disciplined himself to take photographs of the municipal car park, enormous enough to cope with the influx of day trippers from the industrial valleys on a hot August day, a vast expanse of black tarmac that divided the hospital from the nearest private houses. He squinted into the low sun and made a mental note that he had better take additional shots of the car park from a different angle later. He took as much care to obtain the best angles on the dreary, low-grade farmland that extended behind the hospital, back as far as the main east–west trunk road. His final shots had been of the end of the building, another fire escape zigzagging its way down to a small door which, he saw, also provided entrance to the Pharmacy

Back at his car, he sat in the driving seat but with one leg still out through the door. He emptied his jacket pockets, piling the camera and rolls of exposed film into the glove compartment which he closed and locked. He began to get out of the car but hesitated and looked at his watch. It was not yet eight o'clock. He withdrew his leg and closed the door; another half an hour or so and the hospital would be that much busier, making it easier for him to move around without being questioned. He was still searching for something of interest in the previous day's newspaper when a bright red Triumph Spitfire heralded its arrival with the roar of a leaking exhaust. A large young man extricated himself and, without stopping to lock the car, hurried through the open main entrance and wheeled right towards the Casualty Department. Plainly, to Yousef, this had to be someone called in to see that pale, deeply shocked young girl, and he spent a few moments imagining the phone call, the language, the missed shave, the longed-for breakfast. The image of that pallid face appeared again. It had to be massive haemorrhage to do that. He had seen the air hunger. But why? There had been no sign of external bleeding. Ruptured ectopic pregnancy perhaps? Seemed a bit young for that but one never knew, these days. So where? Well, it wasn't his problem; some other poor bastard was going to have to sort that one out.

Shortly after 8.15 a.m. his patience ran out. He locked the car and walked through the main entrance. He strove to walk at a pace slow enough to give him time to look around and remember, but not so slow as to make anyone ask what he wanted. He need not have worried; no one took the slightest notice of him. Looking to the right from the main entrance hall only confirmed what he already knew – it led to the Casualty Department and there were signs of intense activity inside. To his left was an outpatient waiting area, a few patients already sitting there, looking hopefully to register their early arrival with two clerks, busy at a glass-fronted desk. He walked straight across the waiting hall and, as he had expected, through into the long wide corridor that stretched ahead throughout the whole length of the Ward Block. Though he would be able to get all the details later from Salem, he wanted to see the place for himself. Salem could help him make diagrams later but he must get a feel of the place, look for snags. The X-ray Department occupied both sides of the corridor through 'A' Block and Yousef stopped as long as he dared at the intersection between it and 'B' Block, long enough to note the pairs of lifts, facing each other. He had a mental picture of similar lift gates facing each other across each landing above. Odd, he thought; seven buttons but only five floors and the basement. Probably access to the roof and the winding gear. His eyes ran over the list of wards alongside the row of buttons. He made no attempt to memorise the names, many of which he could not even pronounce. He would get a list later.

Yousef passed through the next section, 'B' Block, flanked on the right by administrative offices and, on the left, by the Departments of Ultrasound and Oral Surgery. At the intersection between it and 'C' Block, Yousef paused with a small grunt of satisfaction. While lifts were in identical positions to those between 'A' and 'B', one of them, one of the pair facing him, had no ward names opposite its row of buttons but, painted in thick capitals across its door, the words 'Theatres Only'. So the theatres were somewhere in that 'C' Block, somewhere at the extreme end of the building. He couldn't tell yet on what floor but that, for the moment, was irrelevant.

He was so engrossed in his thoughts that Yousef didn't see the silver-haired woman approach him from the far end of the main corridor, a row of multicoloured pens protruding from the top pocket of her white coat, a plastic name tag identifying her as the Chief Pharmacist. She opened her mouth to ask if she could help him but Yousef, recovering rapidly, gave her such an engaging, steady-eyed smile that it threw her into confusion and she changed her mind.

He moved on down the final section of the main corridor through 'C' Block, hearing the clatter from the hospital kitchens on his left. To his right, the Hospital Administrator's and Senior Nursing Officer's rooms led, finally, to the Hospital Pharmacy. He looked through the doorway at the end of the corridor and saw the bottom of the fire escape he had seen from the outside. He turned and retraced his steps to the main entrance hall, underlining in an excellent memory all the salient points once more.

Without further hesitation he turned and approached the clerks in the Outpatient Appointments desk. He stood opposite one of them, patiently waiting for her to stop writing. Beryl Bates, blowzy, good-natured provider for three young daughters and an unemployed husband, didn't look up.

'Yes, love. What can I do for you?'

The cultured American accent to Yousef's reply made her head jerk up in surprise. What she saw made her jaw sag and her face blush, something that didn't happen too often to Beryl these days. A pair of crystal-green eyes rendered her helpless as Yousef treated her to one of his Omar Sharif smiles, with the inevitable results.

'Pardon me, ma'am, but perhaps you could help me? I believe you have a friend of mine working here; a Dr Salem?'

'You mean our little Dr Abdul? Yes, he works here.'

St David's still hadn't quite outgrown the size where everyone who worked there became, whether they liked it or not, members of one huge, complex family.

'In the Ear, Nose and Throat Department, I believe you call it?'

'That's right,' Beryl answered, feeling perhaps she should apologise for such an old-fashioned nomenclature. Her mouth went quite dry at the thought that she'd called him 'love'.

'How would I get to find him?' Yousef asked, conscious that the girl alongside had stopped writing to listen.

'Well,' Beryl squinted at the large clock in the hall, 'I don't think he'd be on the ward yet. Probably still having breakfast. Would you like me to ring him for you?'

'Please don't bother, ma'am.' Yousef was at his most charming. 'If you'd be so kind and tell me how to find him. He is expecting me.'

Beryl leaned forwards and pointed across the hall.

'Out through that door on the left. Down the main corridor past X-ray.

You'll see some lifts on the left, in the hallway between 'A' and 'B' Blocks. Take any one up to the top; the button without the name. The Resident's quarters are on the roof. Anyone will tell you from there.'

'I'm obliged, ma'am.'

Yousef turned away. Now he knew the reason for the extra button.

'Don't look now, Ber,' Beryl's partner turned laughingly towards her, 'but your tongue is still hanging out.'

A deep growling sound came from the back of Beryl's throat.

'There's one fella who could park his boots under my bed anytime.' She laughed. 'I'd put my Fred in in part exchange for him like a shot. Just imagine working somewhere where people like that . . . Hey, steady!'

She broke off as she saw Yousef, just about to go through the door, reel back, almost falling. The cause of the impact was a thick-set, red-headed young man, his shoulders hunched as he hurried from Casualty to X-ray. 'God, I'm sorry,' he said. 'Absolutely my fault.' He hurried on, repeating over his shoulder, 'So sorry.'

Yousef rubbed his shoulder ruefully where it had absorbed most of the young man's momentum, gave a small, forgiving wave of his hand and disappeared from Beryl's view.

3

There was no doubt in Roger Morgan's mind that there was a time and a place for everything, and that included making love. The place was in bed, the time, early morning, infinitely preferable to the hasty, dutiful thrashings of two people already exhausted by a long day's work with nothing to follow but inky sleep. Far better the nuzzling, gradual awakening, both physical and sensuous, with time afterwards to lie back, totally relaxed, and contemplate breakfast.

And the portents that morning had been particularly favourable. It had been Sian who had started proceedings, running her hand over his chest, biting his ear.

The clamour of the telephone a few feet from that ear could not have come at a worse time. For a few gasping moments they tried to ignore it, but failed. Roger stretched out a hand if only to knock the phone off its stand but couldn't quite reach. In many walks of life they might have pressed on in the knowledge that, sooner or later, it would stop, but Roger, at twenty-eight, had been in the junior ranks of the hospital service long enough to know that the phone didn't ring at that time in the morning without good cause and that this was one telephone that would not stop ringing.

With a groan he rolled away, to take the phone in one hand. His other hand he put on Sian's shoulder as she turned on her side, her lower lip pinched between her teeth. He waited for his heaving chest to subside before putting the phone to his ear.

'Yes?' He snapped out the word.

'It is Patel here, Roger. I am sorry to be ringing you so early in the morning.'

The only reply he got was a bad-tempered grunt, though Roger saw from the bedside clock that it wasn't that early; it was about a quarter to eight; time to get up anyway.

'I have to ask you to come in without delay, please.'

'It had better be good, Sundram. You've no idea what you've just interrupted.' Roger was still breathless enough for Patel to grasp his meaning.

'Roger, you are embarrassing me. As I said, I am so sorry.'

Roger smiled. He could almost see Patel bowing on the other end of the phone. Nice chap; always so correct. And good too. No doubt about it; if you had a good Indian, then he really was good. Roger knew that his father-in-law thought the world of Patel, trusted him implicitly. If Sundram said something was urgent then it probably was.

'What's the problem, Sundram?'

'Young girl, about seventeen, eighteen, I think. Said to have fallen off a horse about an hour ago.'

'Said to have?' Roger asked.

'That is what a very rough lady who came in with her is telling me but I am doubting it. There are no bumps or bruises that I can find.'

'What does the girl say?' Sian swung her legs out of bed and reached resignedly for her dressing-gown as she heard her husband begin to take a professional interest.

'She is too shocked to say. She is not remembering much.'

'And what do you think, Sundram?'

'I am thinking she has a ruptured kidney.' Patel's voice was quietly confident. 'She has passed very little urine, only a few drops, but it is heavily bloodstained and there is a fullness in her loin. I think I am also feeling a mass in her abdomen but it is very difficult. She is very tender and guarding.'

'Which side?' Roger asked.

'Right.'

'Could it be liver?'

'I don't think so.' Patel's voice took on a slightly appealing note. 'Please, Roger, I think we need an urgent IVP before I am ringing your father-in-law.'

'OK. Will you get in touch with the duty Radiographer?'

'I have done that already.'

Roger threw back the bedclothes as he asked his final question.

'What time did they dig you out then?'

'I haven't been to bed yet. We have been very busy.' There was neither complaint nor pride in his voice; merely a statement of fact. 'Please be quick, Roger. This young girl is very ill.'

When Roger eased his bulk out of the battered Spitfire, his ears were ringing from the noise of the blown exhaust. Rushed though he was, he still had time to appreciate the grey 380 SL nearby. Another time and he would have walked around it admiringly, looked inside it if there hadn't been that lucky devil sitting behind the wheel.

He ran into the main entrance and turned right into Casualty. As he was going in, the Superintendent Radiographer was coming out, a large flat cassette under his arm.

'Morning, Ray. What are you doing here? I thought you left this sort of thing to the youngsters.'

Roger got no reply, merely a martyred look.

'What have you got there?' Roger pointed to the cassette.

'Ten-minute film. The control is up on your viewing box.'

'Right.' Roger hurried on into the depths of the Casualty Department. He could put up with Ray Upnorth's dying swan act as he knew he could rely on first-class films first time. No hanging around for infuriating retakes. It wasn't difficult to find the cubicle where Hannah lay, he simply followed the scurrying nurses. As he rounded the screens he saw the jumble of drips and bottles, sheets and tubes, with monitors flickering in the steady glare of striplights. Roger saw Patel supervising the House

Surgeon putting up another intravenous line and noted the length of the tube the House Surgeon held. It took him back just those few years to when he, as a raw beginner, had tremblingly put up his first central venous line. He nodded as he saw Patel look up and then he had his first clear view of Hannah.

'Christ.'

He spoke only the one word, turning to hurry away to his room where, he knew, he could be of most help. Roger Morgan was not noted for his tact. It was one of the reasons why he had chosen a branch of medicine away from the bedside. Not that his bluntness meant he did not care, and this fact usually attenuated the wrath of his seniors when it fell to them to smooth some patient's or administrator's feathers. A powerful young man, he had a temper to match his red hair and it was the opinion of the cognescenti at the local rugby club that it might still prove the only bar to his wearing a red jersey one day.

As Roger Morgan walked out of Casualty, back to his room, he left Patel, a small white paper in his hand, whispering encouragement to a hesitant House Surgeon as he gingerly fed inch after inch of plastic tubing into one of Hannah's arm veins. Minutes afterwards, he entered Roger's room, standing back politely to allow the Radiographer to enter first. They found Roger leaning forwards, gazing intently at the control film as he pulled his white coat over a broad pair of shoulders.

'Nothing much on the control, Sundram,' he said, not taking his eyes off the viewing box. 'I think I can see your mass on the right side.' His index finger drew a rough circle on the film. 'If that is it, it's a bloody great thing. Let's have a look at the ten-minute, Ray.'

Ray Upnorth slid the film under the clips at the top of the box, leaning forward beside Roger Morgan to shake his head. Patel, small, neat and good-mannered, stood behind them.

'Bugger all,' Roger said. 'Nothing. No sign of any excretion either side.'

'Perhaps this would explain that.'

Patel's slightly apologetic tone made the other two men turn their heads. Patel was holding a pathology report form towards them and Roger took it from him, glanced at it and gave a small shout of astonishment.

'Good God!'

'It's only just come back from the lab. Fortunately the technician was still here from the last case we were having,' Patel explained.

'Well, that explains why there's no excretion,' Roger said, 'but why so high? I can't remember a blood urea as high as that, can you?'

'It is certainly very high indeed,' Patel agreed.

'But, I mean, she shouldn't be . . . How the hell does she manage to be conscious with that level? She ought to be comatose if not dead.'

Patel shook his head wisely from side to side. 'She must have been uraemic for a long time, gradually getting worse. I agree with you, Roger; this cannot be a sudden thing that is happening. She could not possibly be getting so uraemic in so short a time. It must have nothing to do with her injury.'

They fell silent as each of their minds followed their own individual paths, guided by their skills and interests. The silence was broken by Ray Upnorth.

'D'you want me to take any more films, Dr Morgan?'

'No thanks, Ray. Waste of time. But don't go for a minute,' Roger added as Upnorth turned to leave.

'I must go and ring your father-in-law now,' Patel said but Roger stopped him too.

'Hang on, Sundram. There's one more thing I'd like to do.' He turned to Upnorth. 'Ray, d'you think you could get the ultrasound along to Cas as quick as you can? She's a bit too ill to move her down to the Department. Can you do that?'

Upnorth nodded and hurried out, a decision made without reference to Patel who felt the girl was ill, needed exploring by his Chief, and the sooner the better. Patel felt sure he knew what Roger had in mind and didn't approve. Once again he sensed the unspoken arrogance of someone who knew he must be more likely to be correct because he had trained in Britain and not in Delhi. But you don't go quarrelling with your boss's son-in-law, wherever you trained.

'You would not be thinking of a nephrostomy, would you, Roger?'

Roger looked irritated that this quiet little man had read his thoughts.

'I certainly think she would benefit from an ultrasound.'

'She is very ill, Roger.'

'I know; I know. But she'll be all the better for another unit of blood. And it won't take long. In any case, the old man is going to be that much happier if we can confirm a kidney on the other side.' He poked a finger in the direction of the viewing box. 'Because, frankly, I can't see any renal shadow on the other side on those films.'

'I accept that, Roger,' Patel generously conceded the point but his face remained anxious, 'but I hope you are not thinking of doing a nephrostomy.'

'I think she would benefit from a scan,' Roger's voice was firm but he could not look at Patel as he answered.

'Because, if you are,' Patel's voice was equally firm if quieter, 'then I am asking you to ring your father-in-law first.'

Roger Morgan was of equal rank to Patel, that of Registrar in Radiology. Unlike Patel, however, he was only in St David's for six months, part of a post that rotated amongst several hospitals but was based at the local teaching hospital. His professor had taken it for granted that he would want to work in the hospital where his father-in-law was one of the senior surgeons, particularly as he too had similar interests. But it had its snags. Sian's old man was a bloody good surgeon, no problem about that, no reason to be embarrassed talking to the boys about his work. It was just that he was so difficult to get to know. He'd love to get him into the Rugby Club one night, get him pissed, see what made him tick.

It still made Roger's flesh creep to think back to the day the two families first met; the local Consultant Surgeon and his solicitor wife and the brickie and his missus. He remembered how awkward his father had looked in the huge house and rolling garden, almost as out of place as Sian's mother and father had looked in the stone-built two up and two down on the return visit. Though, in all fairness to Sian's old man, Roger suspected that he and his father, given a couple of pints on their own, would probably get on famously. But his mother-in-law? No chance; no unbending there, drunk or sober.

'Well, let's go and see,' Roger said gruffly as he led the way back to the Casualty Department.

Ray Upnorth had already manoeuvred the scanner in amongst the paraphernalia surrounding Hannah when Roger reached the cubicle and sat beside her. He smiled gently at her.

'I'm just going to run a scanner over your tummy, Hannah. No needles, no jabs, I promise you. Quite painless. I know your tummy's very tender so I'll be very gentle but you tell me if I hurt you, OK?'

'Don't worry, I will.'

The reply was no more than a whisper but, even so, there was a hint of defiance carried in it and a flicker more of life in her eyes.

'That's the girl.' Roger looked up at the Staff Nurse, a stethoscope round her neck. 'How is she?'

'Better. The last couple of units seem to have done wonders. Her pulse pressure is much better.'

'Passed any urine?'

The Staff Nurse silently shook her head.

'All right then.'

Roger poured a few drops of liquid paraffin over Hannah's upper abdomen and lower chest after the nurse had carefully preserved a young girl's modesty with a folded towel over her breasts. With infinite gentleness, Roger, with hands that had ripped a ball from the depths of a maul on a rain-lashed Stradey Park, spread the oil over the smooth, tense abdomen, searching Hannah's face for any sign that he was hurting her. He began by scanning her left side, away from her obvious disease, sweeping the transducer transversely and vertically across the oily skin. Patel watched over his shoulder as sweeps of patchy grey filled the screen, broken only by irregular patches and serpentine tracks of jet black, rather as a Lancaster navigator must have gazed at his radar screen over Hamburg. Hannah scanned their faces just as intently.

'Nothing there,' Roger muttered over his shoulder. As he did so, he pointed to where the echoes from the left kidney should have been. 'I didn't think so on the straight film.' He made a few more passes with the scanner to confirm it for Patel. 'There, you can see, the colon is displaced backwards to take its place.'

'What does that mean?' Again the tiny voice carried determination.

'Nothing,' Roger smiled. 'Just admiring the pretty pictures of your insides. If you were a bit fitter, I'd let you see. I'm just going over to the other side now, Hannah. I'll try not to hurt you but I may have to a little to get a good picture.'

Hannah winced, bit her lip and closed her eyes as Roger moved over to scan over the mass distending her right side. His words became clipped as if making mental notes of what he was seeing.

'Fluid; large collection of it. Hydronephrosis without doubt. But, see there? The echoes are not uniform. There's blood or pus in there too. Blood, I imagine. I agree with you, Sundram, it's renal. Bleeding into a massive hydronephrosis, I reckon. I'd like to scan her prone but that's out of the question, isn't it?'

Patal nodded. 'What about around the kidney?'

'Yes. Bleeding around the kidney too, I reckon. Nearly finished,' he said as Hannah moaned faintly. 'Just a quick look for her ureter.'

He slid the transducer almost to her right groin and searched again.

'There it is. Dilated right down to the pelvis but no bladder to speak of and no calculus. We'd have seen that on the straight film anyway.'

He stood up. 'That wasn't so bad, was it, Hannah? We'll be back in a minute. Mr Patel and I are just going to have a final look at your pictures.'

In one of the far cubicles, out of earshot, Roger and Patel faced each other.

'Bleeding into a massive, probably congenital, hydronephrosis. The trauma needed would be trivial; a sudden twist might do it.'

'Agreed,' Patel said, his tone inferring gently that he had decided that long before, back at his first examination.

'But you now know that she has no left kidney, or at least none worth shouting about. Probably congenital absence. That you didn't know before,' Roger said forcibly.

'That is most important,' Patel conceded.

'So,' asked Roger, 'what's to be done?'

'We must ring your father-in-law at once, while her general condition is staying better. He will decide.'

'There's something to be said for a nephrostomy,' Roger began. 'She has only one . . .'

'No.'

'It would not rule out surgery later, when her blood urea is down and she's in better nick.'

'You will also be running the risk of making things much worse. The pain she is having, that means tension in that mass, tension that is almost certainly stopping the bleeding at the moment. If you are relieving that tension with your tube you are also running the risk of starting the bleeding again. No, I cannot agree to you doing this thing unless a Consultant is present.'

Roger could see the logic of Patel's argument and, in his heart, knew that he was right. 'All right. You ring him. You're probably right, Sundram. Let me know when he comes in, would you?'

An inner burst of disappointment urged him through the main hall on the way back to his room, colliding, as he did so, with a man also heading for the door into the main corridor, almost knocking him to the floor.

'God, I'm sorry,' he said. 'Absolutely my fault.' He hurried on repeating over his shoulder, 'So sorry.'

4

'Rhys, you are pathetic, you really are,' she said, viciously, meaning each and every accentuated syllable of a sentence that was simply the continuation of a bitter row temporarily set aside during a night of fretful sleep.

Rhys Wyn Owen, Consultant Surgeon, father of Sian, sat up in bed and looked bleakly at Alexandra Mary Owen, senior partner in the firm of McCartney, Tibbs and John, Solicitors, and mother of Sian. She had just walked into the bedroom, fully dressed and immaculately made up. He glanced across at her bed, already made; she must have done that while he was still asleep. Alex looked furiously at her husband. She looked at the rumpled bedclothes, the creased pyjama jacket, the top button missing. Why didn't he get up, look alive, for God's sake?

'I'm sorry,' he said. 'I just forgot.' He leaned his head forward and Alex nearly screamed as she watched him stretch for that ritual scratch between his shoulder blades.

Alex had dressed and made up in the adjoining room and Rhys looked wistfully through the open door. It had been Sian's bedroom, the tiny figure in the bed the bond, almost the only bond he had now come to accept, between Alex and himself. Now the room was virtually Alex's dressing room. She couldn't bear Rhys watching her dress any more, sitting up in bed, his head moving back and forth, back and forth, like some Centre Court spectator. Now she merely appeared, often before he was awake, professionally smart in her suit and blouse, standing her full height in her black Kurt Geiger court shoes. The only thing that was missing was the 'Hands off' sign around her neck.

'Were you really that keen to go?' he asked, wondering why he was inviting the inevitable reply and, now, that look of open dislike.

'What a stupid question to ask, Rhys. You know how keen I was.'

'Yes, I suppose that was a rather daft thing to say,' Rhys replied, glad to see his wife go down to breakfast and allow him to get up in peace.

He knew that Alex had a point. It was he who had been mean and selfish this time and he suspected his motives had been no more than downright spiteful. Avonport's Grand Theatre was old and small, its red brick stained and crumbling, its entrance steps concrete and uninviting, straight off a back street pavement. But inside, it was intimate, with faded plush and tip-up seats and acoustics the envy of flashier orchestral halls for a hundred miles around. It thrived. And tonight there was to be a performance by the Welsh National Opera Company. The WNO sang at the Grand quite regularly – it was always a sell-out – but tonight was to be a gala performance which called for dinner jackets and evening gowns. Tickets had been at a premium but he could have got a pair if he'd tried. He knew enough people. But it would be hopeless now.

Owen squirmed in the bedclothes as a feeling of guilt passed through him. He knew that, if it had been a symphony concert, he would have made the effort. He loved music, but purely as an assault on his emotions. Not for him the academic appreciation of sonata form or counterpoint. He simply allowed the music to work on him, building up a bitter-sweet sadness within him that, amid the applause in which he often felt too strung out to join, so personal was the experience, left him with a lump in his throat and eyes so full that he feared they would be obvious to Alex, clapping her hands so enthusiastically besides him. He liked to attach his own feelings and passions to the music he heard and resented the interpretations of others, so often unconvincing, thrust on him at the opera. Added to his antipathy to opera had been his reluctance to dress up and plunge into that milling throng. He didn't enjoy the crush and it embarrassed him to have the usual fit of coughing when he tried to raise his quiet voice above the din. But, in fairness to Alex, he should really have made the effort.

He glanced at the bedside clock. Just after eight o'clock; not too bad on a morning when his first official commitment was a ward round at ten o'clock. He swung his legs out of bed, walked into the bathroom, closing the door behind him, and passed urine. Before stripping off his pyjama jacket, he stared at his image in a coldly unsympathetic mirror. Those bloody eyes – his hair was still thick with little evidence of grey but those eyes made him look half-pissed most of the time – ran in the family. He'd seen a photograph of his grandfather – same eyes. Methodically, mechanically, he washed and shaved. Dropping his trousers, he glanced instinctively at his silhouette in the mirror before stepping into the shower.

Downstairs, Alex sipped her coffee. She still couldn't understand the man. How could he be so competent, so decisive in his job – and she knew he was – yet such a . . . such a . . . wimp at home. Alex stamped her foot in vexation, listening meanwhile to the sounds of Rhys flushing the loo, emptying the handbasin and turning on the shower, timing to milliseconds the intervals between the whole sickeningly predictable routine. He really had been pathetic over those tickets. There would have been no difficulty if he had only tried, or if it had been the BBC Welsh Symphony or the Hallé. He'd have got tickets for those all right. He'd have sat there, all up-tight so that he could hardly speak, as if he was the only one who mattered, the only one who felt, understood, as if the whole bloody orchestra had been playing just for him. Alex paused in her thoughts to drink again but found her cup empty and cold. He knew how she loved the opera, the colour, the movement, the warmth. Not that she disliked symphony concerts, but opera was different. Things happened. There was life. And it was to be a gala performance too, with such a good company. The foyer would be full with people shuffling patiently towards the stairs, with gowns to look at and handsome men in dinner jackets. She was still an attractive woman; she'd seen men look. Alex stood a little straighter, tucking her white silk blouse in with one hand. And there would be all her friends in the bar in the interval; all that friendship and noise and bustle. If Rhys went on the way he was going, they'd have no friends left. There might even be a judge or two there. The two Circuit Judges who lived in the area, she knew to be opera buffs and certain to be in the bar at the interval and, who knows, perhaps the Hon. Sir Malcolm Gedridge might also decide a gala performance of the WNO warranted his patronage. It would do her ambition to become Avonport's first female Recorder no harm to continually remind the local judiciary of her presence. Tonight's opera would have been a golden opportunity. And Rhys had forgotten to get tickets.

Ten minutes later Rhys was making himself some toast, walking around his wife as she stood motionless, staring through the kitchen window. Alex broke the silence. She felt she had to say something.

'What have you got on today?' A question asked in the tone of someone who already knew the answer and wasn't really interested in it anyway.

'Ward round this morning. I think I may have got a fistula to do this afternoon. I'm not sure. What about you?'

'I'm in County Court all day. An action for damages. Starts at ten but I must call in at the office first.'

'That's nice,' Rhys began. 'I know how much . . . '

But Alex had already put her cup down, left the kitchen and was striding across the living room to where the telephone was ringing.

'Yes?' There was a pause as she listened to the unmistakable accent, then, 'Hold on a moment; I'll get him.' She held the phone at arm's length in Rhys's direction and, with no attempt to cover the mouthpiece, said, 'It's your Indian friend.'

She handed the phone to her husband and returned to the kitchen to wash the few dishes. By the time she had finished and was preparing to leave, Rhys had replaced the receiver.

'Trouble?' she asked.

'Not really,' he answered, 'but I'll have to go. They've admitted a young girl who's bleeding badly. They think it's probably a ruptured kidney. She sounds pretty ill.'

'But you're not on call today, are you?'

'Up until nine o'clock.'

'What's the time now?' Alex looked at the clock. 'Quarter to nine. You won't be able to operate on her till after nine. You won't be on call then. Why not let Johnnie do it?'

'Doesn't work like that. She was admitted while I was on call so she's my patient.'

'Can't you tell Johnnie you're tied up?' she asked, knowing Rhys was far too honest an old devil to do any such thing.

'No,' Rhys replied testily. He imagined Terence Johnson cancelling a few private consultations to operate on someone who had come in on Rhys's intake day. 'If you remember, I'm supposed to be the local urologist around here as well as a general surgeon. I'm supposed to do these cases.'

'You're too easy-going, Rhys,' Alex said, not unkindly. 'You let people run all over you.'

'No I don't,' Rhys snapped, almost adding, 'And for Christ's sake go to work and leave me alone.'

'See you this evening,' Alex said, but Rhys only nodded.

It did not take him long to drive into hospital. They lived in one of the large white detached houses surrounded by a rolling, salt-scorched garden, overlooking the sea a few miles to the east of Avonport. It was too big for them now but perhaps, one day, there would be grandchildren and it was so convenient for the beach. The mortgage had seemed horrendous when they had moved in, and combining their considerable incomes to pay it off had been one of their few mutual interests. That and Sian, for whom Alex had shown her love with that degree of good sense and justice that she felt was necessary to compensate for Rhys's irresponsible tolerance. It had been a time when Rhys had gradually enjoyed more harmony in the hospital than in the home, finding in the other surgeon, Bill McGrath, an amiable, easy-going colleague, only too happy to let Rhys develop his own interest in urology. Within their limitations they had been contented years until money, politics and personal ambition had taken a hand.

Money played its part in the form of a charity run by local entrepreneurs who enjoyed the limelight, and politics in the form of Plaid Cymru asking embarrassing questions in the House about the 1200 patients 'murdered' throughout the UK each year by a Government who did not provide adequate facilities for renal dialysis. This had coincided with the adoption throughout Wales of a scheme whereby potential donors agreed to their names being kept on computer rather than carrying donor cards – less than 5 per cent of those who signed cards carried them – and the sudden upsurge in donors had required the establishment of another transplant unit. Personal ambition had arrived in the form of Terence Johnson, appointed to carry out the transplants. It had soon become obvious that the new surgeon had seen transplantation only as a means to a Consultant appointment. A hard-working extrovert, his readiness to run the renal unit had waned as his interest in private practice had waxed. He had found in Rhys Owen a man whose main interest was urology and who had been at that stage in his career where he had felt his work was becoming repetitive. Rhys also had seen in the dialysis unit a chance to exercise his considerable ability in matters medical as well as surgical. Without any formal recognition of the fact, it had become accepted that Rhys ran the Renal Department while Johnnie Johnson had applied his talents where they seemed most effective; making money.

Alex had been furious.

It was shortly after nine o'clock that Owen drove into one of the spaces reserved for the Consultants in front of the Ward Block. More than half the spaces were now occupied and he had a short walk to get to the Staff Entrance where he found Patel waiting for him.

'Morning, Patel.'

'Good morning, sir. Sorry to be bothering you.'

'That's all right,' Owen said, 'She sounds a pretty sick girl.'

'Oh, she is indeed, sir. I have taken the liberty of sending her straight up to theatre. I thought it would save time if you are agreeing that she should be explored.' Patel's manner was polite and modest but there was an underlying firmness that Owen had come to trust.

'Certainly sounds as if she needs to be explored from what you say.'

He had reached the intersection with the main corridor and was heading for the theatre lift when Patel courteously headed him off.

'Would you like to see her X-rays and ultrasound before going up, sir? They are in Dr Morgan's office,' he said, turning left up the long main corridor.

'Perhaps I'd better,' Owen agreed and they walked the length of the middle section, Owen exchanging nods and smiles with all manner of staff on the way. 'Tell me honestly, Patel; how do you get on with this damned ultrasound? X-rays – all right – we all consider ourselves experts, don't we? But these ultrasound pictures, can you make head or tail of them? Damned if I can.'

Patel made polite noises of disbelief as they turned into the Radiology Department. With a perfunctory tap on the already open door, Rhys walked into his son-in-law's office. Roger stood up and smiled.

'Morning, Roger.'

'Morning.'

It was difficult. Roger Morgan was not a man to call another man 'sir', Rhys Wyn Owen was not a man a Registrar called 'Rhys', and he could hardly call him Dad.

'Got you out of bed a bit too early this morning, did they?' Rhys laughed.

'A bit.' Roger smiled ruefully. It went through his mind to make some crack about what he'd been doing to Rhys's daughter at the time but he thought better of it. 'Still, that kid really is rough. I don't mind then.' He pointed to his viewing box. 'Those are the films such as they are; just the control and the ten-minutes. We didn't take any more after we knew the blood urea.'

'That really was something, wasn't it?' Owen muttered as he leaned forward to peer at the two films, his eyes narrowed to slits. 'I found it difficult to believe when Patel gave me the result over the phone.'

'Fantastic. Amazing that anyone with a blood urea like that could be still conscious.' Roger stood back, saying nothing more.

Again, it was difficult. He was a full-time radiologist but his father-in-law had been in the business now for a long time and urologists liked to read their own X rays anyway.

'Can't see a renal shadow on either side,' Rhys said, almost to himself, then, slightly louder to include Roger and Patel. 'Sure, she's got the mass on the right side, but one can only assume it's renal. It could be a mass in something else obscuring the renal shadow.'

'I don't think so.' Roger sounded adamant.

'I didn't say I think so,' Rhys said, quietly, 'just that it could be.'

Patel shifted from one foot to the other in the ensuing silence.

Owen turned to Patel. 'I think we've got to take it that she has no left kidney. No chance she's had a nephrectomy in the past?'

Less polite colleagues would have taken the question as a slur on their clinical examination.

'Oh no, sir. She has no scars anywhere.'

'She's got no left kidney on ultrasound.' There was youthful certainty in Roger's statement.

'Ah, yes. The ultrasound.' Rhys smiled. Here was something he was going to be in no position to contest. He had stood over Roger, watching him scan many times. He had had Roger explain the mottled shadows on the stills until he had convinced himself he could see what Roger was talking about, but put an unreported picture in front of him and he knew he was too old to ever come to terms with them. 'What do they show?'

'Absent left kidney, mass in the right.'

'Fluid or solid?'

'Fluid.'

No equivocation.

Roger spread the films on his desk but Rhys didn't bother to look. There didn't seem much point. Such a dogmatic statement hardly left room for discussion. Rhys looked at his son-in-law and, for the first time, wondered whether he liked him. He thought so. He had no real reason to dislike him unless one always dislikes the man who has taken your only daughter away from you. There was no doubt that he was good at his job, but he was cocky with it. Rhys had been good at that age too but had he been as cocky as that? Perhaps so, without knowing it, but he didn't think so. He hoped it would never come to a trial of wills.

'Dr Morgan was thinking about a percutaneous nephrostomy, Mr Owen.'

Patel's remark might have had the same effect as throwing a rat into the ring between two terriers, but the quiet assertiveness of Owen's immediate response ruled out any chance of bitter argument.

'No.'

Owen noticed the resentful frustration on Roger's face. He relented. Roger should be given the chance to put his case. 'I see your point, Roger. Severely uraemic patient, solitary kidney and all that. But, from what Patel tells me, she's had a major bleed as well and, if she's going to bleed again, I'd rather she did it in front of my eyes where I can do something about it. What do you reckon the fluid is?'

'Blood,' Roger said, resentment obvious in the one word as Rhys began to win his argument. 'And not just in the kidney. There's a damn great perirenal extravasation too. I think she has probably bled as much around her kidney as into it, probably more. The echoes from the mass are those of fluid but they're irregular. There's either blood or pus in there and all the clinical picture points to blood.'

'Quite,' Rhys agreed. 'So, really, we are operating for haemorrhage, not renal failure at this stage. I can always leave a tube in there as a nephrostomy if I think that's the right thing to do, but I think you will agree that I must stop her bleeding first.'

'I quite agree,' Roger answered and wondered why the man couldn't be as persuasive, as quietly authoritative at home, why, as soon as he stepped over his own doorstep, he became so gutless.

And Rhys felt he'd been hard on the boy whose only crime had been to be young and keen. He must be getting to be the crabby old bastard he had sworn he would never become. He tried to make amends.

'I'm sure your nephrostomy has a place, though. The last one you did for me did very well. I'd like to watch you do your next one. Would you give me a shout?'

'Yes, of course,' Roger replied.

Rhys turned to Patel. 'Come on then. We'd better get moving.'

Rhys and Roger smiled at each other before Rhys left. When Rhys and Patel reached the theatre lift, they found Paddy Moore standing there, a plastic bag of blood in each hand, looking up as the numbers over the gates lit up in succession. He turned and, on seeing Owen, his face split in a friendly grin.

'Morning, Mr Owen.'

'Morning, Paddy.' Rhys nodded at the bottles of blood. 'Those for this young girl?'

'Yes, Mr Owen. Poor mite is really clapped out. Such a shame. Such a gorgeous looking kid.' He stood back deferentially as the lift doors opened to let Owen and Patel enter. He followed them, lifting one hand still holding the precious blood, to press the top but one button, the muscles of his forearm below the short sleeve of his theatre tunic rippling the large dagger tattooed in the overlying skin. Paddy Moore was one of the Theatre Technicians. He was not the Senior Theatre Technician; that he would never be, not with his reputation. Dark and swarthy, his hair was sleeked down with grease to shine with a grain like a gramophone record. Thin and wiry, his cheek-bones protruded, skull like, between lively eyes and a large, mobile mouth. His frame was slim and wiry in spite of his drinking and he was a tireless, cheerful worker, never off sick, always the first volunteer for overtime, virtues that caused the theatre staff to close ranks around him at the first sign of the police or a debt collector. Owen knew him to be totally reliable in theatre but would hardly seek the company outside the hospital of someone with such a notoriously vile temper when drunk.

The lift delivered them out on to the top floor landing and Patel and Paddy followed Owen as he turned sharp left and through the swing doors into the theatre's corridor.

'Where is she, Paddy?' Owen asked.

'In the Recovery Room, sir. They put her in there until you've seen her.'

Without another word, Owen did what was generally forbidden; he walked directly into the Recovery Room without first passing through the Surgeons' Room and changing. With no more than a nod to those standing around, he approached the theatre trolley with its jumble of pillows and sheets, taking care to avoid the tubes and wires that radiated out from the human shape beneath the coverings. Owen's face automatically took on that smile of quiet confidence that is *de rigueur* in a surgeon on such occasions, whatever inner feelings he might be experiencing. A nurse moved a sheet so that he could see Hannah clearly. In a moment, the smile was wiped from his face by stark horror as he was suddenly transported back in time, back to the rear seat of a car where he had gazed in impotent terror at just such another beautiful, pallid face, framed in such stark contrast by the strong, luxuriant tresses of black hair, and from which blue eyes appealed. Rhys heard once more the dripping, creaking noises, smelt again the filth of blood, petrol, dust and beer. It was as if everything that had happened in the years between – consultant appointments, Alex, Sian, small-time ambitions, local jealousies – had been irrelevant, merely a time-lapsing limbo between the two pictures of that face, that hair, those eyes. He stretched a hand towards the shrouded face and heard his own voice. The one word, 'Helen', was uttered with dream-like tenderness but was distinct enough for Patel to show his surprise.

'Hannah, sir. Her name is Hannah.'

Rhys shook his head slowly as his dry lips closed and his mouth thinned out with a new-found determination. To him, Helen lay there. He had been taken back to that moment when, in one moment of obscene violence, the greater part of his life had stopped. And now, he had been given hope, a second chance. He was going, at last, to expiate that guilt that had dragged at all feelings of success and joy during the years between. He felt a first, tiny thrill of excitement as he saw the silent scream of horror on the face so deeply etched in his mind change to a gutsy smile and a defiant jut of the jaw as, near to death, Hannah looked up at him.

5

'What position do you want her in, Rhys?'

Peter Parfitt's head appeared around the changing room door just as Owen was thrusting one foot down the leg of his white operating trousers, separating the layers with a brushing sound. One of St David's team of Consultant Anaesthetists, Peter Parfitt was a slight, neat, economical sort of man. If every individual is given a fixed quantum of nervous energy to dissipate in one lifetime, he seemed destined to live to a great age. Totally unflappable, sparing with his emotions, seeming to have all the time in the world for whatever he was doing, he accepted Owen's ambiguity in predictably languid fashion.

'Don't know yet, Peter. I'll decide when I come in. Is she ready?'

'Yep. On the table. What d'you think you'll have to do?'

'Won't know that until I get in, Peter. Sorry to be so vague.' Owen hopped on one leg, almost losing his balance as his foot stuck at the lower end of the trousers.

'That's OK, but she's ready when you are.' Parfitt's head disappeared and the door swung to behind it.

Owen was faced with a decision, one he would finally make only minutes before the event, even though the pros and cons had begun circulating round his brain from the moment Patel had given his tentative diagnosis over the telephone at home. While talking to Roger in the X-ray Department, the question of which position to place Hannah in on the operating table had been bubbling away beneath the surface. The same had gone for other decisions he knew he might have to make, conflicting factors being supplemented constantly by data fed into his brain by Patel, by Roger Morgan, by forms thrust at him with lists of figures, by black, white and grey shadows on transparent film or opaque paper. He had to allow for Patel's diffidence and Roger's assertiveness in the value he applied to their opinions, anxious as they both were in their own ways to influence him. Owen had wondered what might have happened if Roger had been the senior, an older, experienced Radiologist dealing with a young, inexperienced surgeon. Conversely Patel's diffidence could be almost as dangerous. Owen had muttered something, almost inaudibly, while in the lift, about the possible value of putting a needle into the peritoneum to see if Hannah had bled there, only for Patel to inform him, in apologetic tones, that he had already done that and had found no more than a little bloodstained fluid.

It was less than half an hour since he himself had examined Hannah. The clinical details that he had assimilated through his hands, eyes and ears were taking longer to settle into their positions of relative importance, influenced as they were by the emotional impact that Hannah had had on him. He would always have examined a desperately ill young girl with great tenderness but he had handled Hannah with reverence, almost praying that he would not find anything that would rule out any chance of success. He had seen the vague fullness in the right side of her abdomen. He had put the flat of his hand on the white skin, first on the left, where he had felt nothing, then on the right side where he had sensed the huge mass in her flank, confirmed it by gently sliding his left hand under her loin to feel the mass bulging backwards also. He had listened briefly with a stethoscope and heard nothing.

There were no other factors to take into account now. A few minutes more, the time taken to finish dressing, pass urine and walk that short distance from changing room to operating theatre and he would have to make the decision. No one else was going to do it for him. Should he operate on Hannah with her lying supine on the table or lying on her left side in the so-called 'kidney' position? If he opted for the supine position he would find it much more difficult to deal with any trouble in her right kidney, particularly if he was faced with major haemorrhage from the renal vessels. The incision would, however, allow him to confirm whether any left kidney existed, and also allow for any misdiagnosis – he could deal with almost anything he might find through that incision. Conversely, if he put Hannah on her side, Owen would have the best chance of coping with anything in the kidney, but if he found her right kidney to be normal and the mass to be in her peritoneal cavity and inaccessible, he would experience that sinking feeling of despair that goes with the discovery of a major surgical misjudgment. In the lateral position, he would also find it extremely difficult, probably impossible, to evaluate her left kidney. If Hannah had not been so ill, he could have done something else to find out whether she had a left kidney or not – put a cystoscope into her bladder to see whether she had an opening into it from the left kidney – but Owen had judged that this would simply add to the length of an operation where the less time she spent under the anaesthetic, the better.

The time had come to work out the equation. As he walked down the corridor he concluded that there really was only one result. As he crossed the operating theatre, conscious of several faces looking at him expectantly, he said, 'Left lateral position, please, Peter,' in a tone that, to anyone who didn't know better, implied a decision arrived at with mathematical certainty.

Owen always liked to position the patient himself. There was nothing worse than operating on someone badly positioned and, if he found himself in any such difficulty, he preferred to have only himself to blame. This meant that he had frequently to take the strain of humping enormous masses of anaesthetised flesh, but there was no such problem with Hannah. With the help of Parfitt and Paddy Moore, he put his arms under her, lifted her as if she might break in his hands, and turned her on her left side. Paddy, equally carefully, flexed her left knee to keep her stable. To get to her kidney, Owen would have to explore in the narrow angle between her rib-cage above and the bony crest of her hip below, an angle he could make wider by elevating a narrow metal bridge which ran across the table beneath her. Her young, supple spine bowed as, cautiously, he turned the handle to raise the bridge, but he stopped well short of its maximum height for fear of rupturing the mass which now presented itself all too plainly.

As Owen went to scrub up, Patel and the House Surgeon, already scrubbed and gowned, took over and painted and draped the operation site. The pale slim body with its grotesque swelling disappeared under the green sheets except for the rectangle of skin that shortly would be so skilfully mutilated.

Owen was still pulling on his gloves when he returned to the table. He smiled at the Theatre Sister.

'Hello, Sister. How are you?'

'Very well, thank you, Mr Owen.' Sister Ferguson smiled back.

A totally unnecessary pleasantry under the circumstances but, in reality, a simple recognition by a sensitive man of the existence of a most important member of the team.

'All set?' Owen looked towards Peter Parfitt.

'Sure,' Parfitt replied. 'As good as we'll get her, I think. She's got a tachycardia that I don't seem to be able to do much about. I don't think she's got much in reserve. But she's a fighter beneath it all. I get the impression she's a pretty tough kid.'

The incision that split open under Owen's scalpel oozed watery blood that was reluctant to clot. Normally he would not have proceeded until this bleeding was under control but, after making a token, ineffectual effort, he snorted with irritation and began to deepen the incision through the muscles, already resigned to the fact that this was going to be a very bloody affair and that the wound probably wouldn't stop bleeding until he had sewn it up again. The blood obscured the operating field and Owen struggled to keep his irritation within bounds as, with scalpel, scissors and the distracting force of two hooked fingers, he opened the wound so that yellow fat, more watery than usual and flecked with small bruises, protruded from end to end, thrust forwards by the pressure in the mass below. As if testing the pressure in a child's balloon, Owen squeezed the mass gently once or twice between his fingers and thumb. He asked Sister Ferguson for scissors and Patel instinctively picked up the sucker, both realising the moment of truth had come. With a confident movement, Owen snipped open the thin but tough layer of tissue that invested the kidney. He had expected the gush of fluid, welcomed it as a confirmation of the diagnosis and choice of operation position. Even so, the force of the ejected fluid took him by surprise and he stepped back smartly as some of the fluid splashed at his feet. He did not operate wearing a plastic apron, disliking the clinging sweat beneath, and a warm wetness on the inside of his left thigh told him he had not stepped back quickly enough. Owen waited patiently as Patel sucked what fluid he could from the small hole the scissors had made, then enlarged the opening fully and cleaned away the clots from the untidy, irregular cavity that remained around the huge, dilated kidney.

'Gently,' Owen muttered as Patel stabbed into the depths alongside the kidney with the rigid sucker. 'We don't want to start it up again if we can help it.'

He ran his hand over the tense, shiny kidney, caressing it one moment, prodding it with a fingertip the next.

'Have to chalk this one up for ultrasound, I suppose,' he said to Patel. 'Got it dead right; a massive hydronephrosis full of blood clot. Can't feel much kidney tissue as yet,' he added gloomily.

'However,' Owen took a deep breath and settled his stance, spreading his legs a little as if to withstand whatever the next few minutes might have in store for him, 'we can't leave her like that. We've got to do something. We've got to open that sac and evacuate that clot. Then, if there's no sign of any fresh bleeding, we'll put a nephrostomy tube in and get the hell out of it. Right?'

He looked across at Patel who nodded without raising his eyes from the wound.

'Right then.' Owen picked up a forceps in his left hand and held his right out towards Sister Ferguson. 'Same scissors again, please, Sister.'

Snipping through the glistening bag did not produce the dramatic effect that might have been expected. Patel was quick to insert the sucker's nozzle into the hole that Owen had made but, in a moment, the sucker handle vibrated noisily. Patel withdrew it to find it blocked with blood clot. He pinched the offending clot off between finger and thumb and the sucker whooshed back to life.

Owen enlarged the hole he had made, put two fingers in and began to ease the blood clot out into a dish that Sister Ferguson held for him, leaning over in front of Patel to do so. Before the dish was half full, Owen's mouth hardened in disappointment beneath his mask as he saw the tell-tale bright red streaks of fresh blood amongst the fragmenting clot. His movements became more urgent and he enlarged the hole he had made as the proportion of bright to dark red increased rapidly. By the time he had removed all the clot, Patel was using his sucker vigorously to remove the fresh blood that welled up from the depths of the kidney without any one identifiable, localising source.

Owen took a pack, inserted it into the cavity, clenched his right fist and applied it firmly to the pack. He put his head back and uttered one word, loudly enough to act as a safety valve, blowing off disappointment and frustration, quiet enough not to be offensive to those around him who understood his feeling.

'Shit.'

He knew that he had a few moments' respite, a time to collect his thoughts and avoid any hasty, ill-judged decisions. Even so, time was limited as Patel was already busy, sucking away blood that was oozing around the pack, his face as inscrutable as ever. Owen looked at the others standing around the table, Parfitt's Registrar putting up another unit of blood, Parfitt himself standing, his arms crossed over his chest, totally in control of himself and his machines. Paddy Moore, hovering behind Parfitt, saw Owen glance at him. His face lit up with a smile, eager and anxious to help, capable of doing very little spontaneously but ready and willing to do anything he was told. Patel, a young surgeon who had faced enough lesser crises to appreciate the loneliness Owen was feeling. He saw his House Surgeon playing abstractedly with a short, discarded length of catgut, his apparent unawareness of any drama being, perhaps, an unintentional tribute to the way his Chief was coping with it. Finally, Sister Ferguson, poised, as skilful a Theatre Sister as Owen could ask for, her eyes flickering back and forth between Owen's eyes and the bloodstained wound in Hannah's side.

Owen placed a curved needle in its long holder alongside the wound, ready to hand. With a long artery forceps in his hand he nodded to Patel who rapidly removed the pack. For a few seconds, he held the points of the forceps over the site of the bleeding but found no spurting artery to grasp, just a pool that rapidly filled and welled up in spite of Patel's efforts. Another pack was inserted for a few minutes and removed rapidly. Owen tried to put a few running stitches where he thought the bleeding was worst, only to see Patel move the sucker outside the flaccid, oozing sac.

'I am afraid it is bleeding from the hilum, sir.'

Owen turned the kidney over and there was a rush of blood from deep in the wound.

'Give me a pedicle clamp, please, Sister; quickly.'

With both his hands in the wound, working purely by touch, Owen put the clamp in one rasping movement around the kidney's pedicle. He stood back, leaning on Hannah's hip, staring into the wound as Patel sucked it dry again.

'That is stopping it, sir.' Patel said quietly, encouragingly.

'Hm; but what do we do now?' Owen's question had only one answer, one that neither Owen nor Patel was, as yet, prepared to put into words.

'If she had a normal left kidney there would be no problem,' Owen said. 'I wouldn't hesitate. I'd take it out.'

'I don't think there is much functioning kidney there, sir.' Patel explored with his finger the paper-thin wedge of tissue that was all that remained of Hannah's kidney, so thin that he could feel the edges of the clamp through it. 'I really don't think there is any chance of that functioning again.'

'But it would be nice to leave her with even a small amount of renal tissue if we can.' Owen straightened up. 'I'm going to have one more go.'

Five minutes later they were back in the same position after futile attempts to staunch the ever-increasing torrent that had lost Hannah the best part of another pint of blood. Without a word to anyone, Owen tied a ligature around the pedicle beneath the clamp, tied and divided the ureter, and threw the floppy, slithering obscenity into a dish. He hung his head as if in shame.

Peter Parfitt tried to say something that wouldn't jar.

'Well, you know what they say, Rhys; better a live problem than a dead certainty.'

'Perhaps you're right, Peter.' Owen tried to smile. 'How is she?'

'Pretty rough; but she should make it. The sooner we get her dialysed, the better. Would you like me to fix it?'

'Please,' Owen replied tiredly. 'You only need to give Maggie a ring.'

'I'll do that as soon as we've finished here.'

'Thanks.'

No further word was spoken as Owen closed the wound, every movement down to the last skin stitch heavy with the feeling of defeat. In later, less despairing moments, Owen would accept that he could have done no more, that he had looked for a miracle. In his mind's eye he had seen a healthy, black-haired, blue-eyed girl walking towards him again, holding out her hand. His heart ached but, slowly, his sadness and despair gave way to a grim determination. It would happen. He would make it happen. Peter Parfitt showed his surprise as he saw Owen beat the air with a fist clenched inside a glove still covered in Hannah's blood. He had been given a chance of redemption and nobody would stand in his way, nothing would be allowed to snatch it from him.

6

The Lamb and Flag was situated at the midpoint of a narrow Avonport backstreet that connected two other narrow Avonport backstreets. Squeezed between empty warehouses and facing seedy cafés and dirty bookshops, it did not look out of place in its surroundings and rarely enticed the passerby who wasn't that desperate for a drink. Once through the black, wooden swing doors, however, and there was warmth, polished brass and solid mahogany. A few legal prints looked down on red, plush seats in small, intimate alcoves and the price of the beer was high enough to keep the vagrant riff-raff of that part of Avonport at bay. Through the back of the bar, on seven rickety, oilcoth-covered tables with wooden, uncomfortable chairs, the best food in South Wales, confirmed by Egon Ronay, was served by a couple of grumpy old women. But, between the hours of six and seven-thirty, despite its surroundings, the Lamb and Flag owed a great deal of its prosperity to the legal profession. Convenient to the Crown, County and Magistrate's Courts, not far from Courtenay Road with its gold-lettered, frosted glass and brass plates, it was accepted as the lawyers' pub.

Alex Owen was the last to leave the office. She made sure the burglar alarm was set before she slammed the front door behind her. She climbed into her car, pulled on her safety strap and turned the ignition key until the warning lights glared and flickered at her. But something prevented her from starting the engine and she stared as if mesmerised by the glowing red squares, her thoughts in turmoil. Her mind still raced on the high that a day in court invariably induced, but, sitting alone, she also felt the emptiness. She wanted someone to talk to, someone to share the afterglow of her success, provide the approbation for which she inwardly cried out. Alex and Rhys had got to that stage where she never told Rhys of her problems and he never mentioned his. Even if she could bring herself to tell Rhys about her day in court, he would not understand; or was it that he was the last person in the world to whom she could admit a weakness, profess a guilt? Alex had pictured herself amongst the evening chatter in the Lamb and Flag, modestly acknowledging the ribald congratulations of her peers, perhaps accepting the offer of a drink from some impecunious young barrister. But now the Dunbar file would always seem a bit grubby – the judge had seen to that. In a fit of pique, she kicked her foot against the accelerator pedal. Without knowing why, she tugged at her ignition key, unclipped her safety strap and got out of the car, flinging the door shut behind her.

The Lamb was probably the only pub that Alex would ever contemplate walking into alone but, within minutes of her pushing through the doors, she was half sitting on, half leaning against, a bar stool, enjoying a barrister's facile flattery, while her articled clerk made sure the barman put ice and lemon in his boss's glass of Coke. For half an hour, she tried and failed to drown her excitement in the flow of good humour that surrounded her. She squirmed restlessly, finding it difficult to maintain an apparent interest in the friendly triviality of her chatter to the two young men, her eyes darting over their shoulders at any sudden movement beyond. She was physically excited. This was more than the usual over-run of adrenalin after a court appearance. There were sexual overtones that she found intriguingly uncomfortable, a tightening within her that gave her a restless sense of premonition. She realised that Rhys had never produced such feelings in her – she would not have allowed him to do so even had he shown the inclination. Rhys's initial sexual attraction, with his apparent vulnerability, his rather romantic melancholy, had never provided an adequate foil to her direct, no-nonsense, physical assertiveness, fading rapidly as she began to feel contempt for his total disinclination to oppose her natural sexual instinct to dominate. As their mutual physical attraction had frayed to breaking point, it had never occurred to Alex to find a sexual challenge elsewhere, simply finding refuge in flinty, ambitious workoholism.

A sudden movement near the door attracted her attention once more and, this time, held it throughout that lull in the conversation that occurs when any stranger walks into a room crowded with close friends. Arrogantly sure of himself, Gordon Baxter threaded his way through the crush to stand before her.

'Congratulations, Mrs Owen. You did well today. To the victor the spoils, eh? No hard feelings, I hope?'

'Thank you. Of course not,' Alex said. As she introduced Baxter to her two friends, she saw him concentrate on each for a second, a man who never forgot a name or a face.

Baxter turned to the barrister. 'Is there anything illegal or unethical about accepting a drink from your opponent after the trial is over?' he smiled.

'Not that I know of.'

'In that case, Mrs Owen, what can I get you to drink? Is that Coca Cola?'

'Yes.'

'And you like that stuff?' Baxter feigned incredulity.

Coming from Baxter, even banality seemed like a challenge.

'I'm driving,' Alex said, smiling, 'but I think I could stand another one.'

The two other men politely declined Baxter's offer of a drink, said a few words which neither Alex nor Baxter heard, and seemed to melt away, leaving two elegant, forceful characters facing each other.

There had been no real need for him to appear in the County Court that day; it had been a small matter of a few thousand pounds which his lawyers had advised him to settle out of court. But it had been personal. Duggie Dunbar, that good-looking Scouse git of an electrician from one of his companies, Baxter Switchgear, had been sent to his home at ten in the morning to mend a kitchen switch, not to electrocute himself somehow at four o'clock in the afternoon. Knowing his wife's little weakness, Baxter could well imagine how, alone in the house, she had spent most of that six hours. The bastard had been lucky to get away with just a curled up finger; it would have served him right if he'd topped himself. Baxter had realised that an award for damages had been inevitable; he had just wanted to do all he could to make sure Dunbar got the minimum possible. He had stayed to hear the Judge stress that he was awarding the maximum damages that were within his powers to award in that court, a ruling that had been given in quick, detailed phrases that had left Baxter with the feeling that the whole process had been a farce from beginning to end. That had not been all. The Judge had made one or two remarks to the plaintiff's solicitor which were almost asides, just too quiet and legalistic for Baxter to catch, but producing fascinating effects in the solicitor, bringing a flush to her face and an ill concealed look of guilt as Dunbar had tried to thank her. However, all such thoughts had been driven from his mind as he had recalled how the plaintiff's solicitor had slowly, mercilessly, taken him apart, leaving him, in the eyes of the court, the archetypal miserly, vindictive employer.

And it had been the long, admiring, challenging look that Baxter had given her before stepping down from the witness box that had convinced her that he would come for her again. He had not looked the man to leave the matter there. What had started as a mere matter of money had become something personal, and she was certain that Baxter would not accept defeat, particularly at the hands of a woman.

'I suspect you enjoy winning, Mrs Owen,' Baxter began.

'My friends, even some of my adversaries, call me Alex,' she smiled. 'Yes, I enjoy winning. Doesn't everyone? Don't you?'

'I certainly don't like losing. I'm not used to it. Don't believe in it.'

'So it's been a bad day for you; I'm sorry. Perhaps we'll both be on the winning side next time.' Alex found herself choosing her words as carefully as if she were in court.

'Not all bad,' Baxter argued.

'Losing £5000? That's not a bad day?'

'What's five grand?' Baxter said, shrugging his shoulders.

'Oh, come on,' Alex said. 'Even people like you can't go losing £5000 every day.'

'I expect my accountant will find some insurance policy that covers that sort of thing.' Baxter sounded as if he had long since dismissed the money from his mind. 'No,' he said, slowly. 'If, by losing £5000, I have had the pleasure of meeting you, I don't think I have come out of it too badly. As I said, the day has not been all bad.'

Alex flushed and was glad to turn away to say goodbye to her clerk as he left. Baxter took the opportunity to admire the curve of Alex's thigh and the thrust of her breast as she twisted her shoulders. When she turned back he took up the attack once more.

'And what do you mean – people like me?' he demanded, but gently. 'Money, d'you mean?'

'No, I don't,' Alex replied, beginning to enjoy herself, relishing an argument.

'Yes, you do,' Baxter persisted. 'And if you think I'm rich, it means you think you're poor; and you're not.'

'Of course we're not poor.'

'Then it must be because I'm richer than you,' Baxter said, happy that the conflict was not over after all, perhaps might only just be starting.

'Rubbish,' Alex retorted.

'Then what is it?' Baxter drained his glass. 'Look,' he said. 'Let me get you a decent drink.'

Alex pushed her unfinished drink away from her.

'All right. A brandy, please.'

'Anything with it?'

'No.'

'Right.' Baxter pointed towards an empty alcove. 'Go and sit over there and, when I've got the drinks, you can tell me what's different between us apart from how much money we've got.'

Alex derived a certain pleasure from being told where to go and sit. Rhys would have asked her where she wanted to sit, claiming he had no preference himself. She watched Baxter taking his change from the barman with as much human contact as collecting it from a fruit machine. She smiled her thanks as he sat opposite her.

'And how's Rhys?'

His question took her by surprise. 'He's fine, thank you.' The look of surprise slowly gave way to understanding. 'Of course. I'm sorry. I should have remembered. I thought there was something when I saw you in court today. I remember now – the photograph of you and Rhys at the opening of the Dialysis Unit. How stupid of me. I should have remembered.'

'You weren't at the opening.' His remark was a simple statement, but Alex's feeling of guilt turned it into an accusation.

'No. I'm afraid Rhys and I live in two different worlds – from nine to five, that is,' Alex hastened to add. 'Come nine o'clock in the morning and we go our separate ways.' She made sure the inquisition was not going to be one way. 'And Mrs Baxter? What does she do?'

'Not a lot.'

'I'm sorry,' Alex said, feeling somehow she should commiserate.

'Tell me,' Baxter said, as if they had talked about his wife long enough. 'Are you always as aggressive cross-examining a poor witness?'

'Aggressive?' Alex was genuinely surprised. 'Was I aggressive?'

'If you weren't, I'd love to be around when you are.' Even though he was engrossed in the early sexual sparring, he could not prevent his prominent, restless eyes from flickering in response to the slightest movement or upsurge in laughter around them.

'Didn't seem to bother you much,' Alex said. 'There was nothing personal, I assure you.'

'Now that does bother me,' Baxter was quick with his reply, switching his eyes back to hers, daring her to stare him down as she had in court. 'I'd rather hoped there was.'

Alex found that difficult to counter but, within minutes, they were both sitting forwards, intent on each other, talking animatedly, obviously, to anyone but a fool, no Darby and Joan out for an evening drink. Alex had nearly finished her second brandy and the early evening drinkers had given way to the menu-reading sherry sippers, when the pint glass slopped some of its contents on to their table and they became conscious of the figure towering over them.

Alex and Baxter looked up to see Duggie Dunbar leering down at them. It was obvious that the brewers had already benefited from the plaintiff's new-found wealth. After watching his solicitor walk away from him in the court room, Duggie had spent some time in the waiting room, hoping to catch Alex on her way out. He had been still a little hazy over what had gone on in court and he had sat on the hard bench, trying to marshal his thoughts. Of one thing he had been reasonably sure; he was £5000 better off than he had been the day before. He had more or less gathered that from all that legal gobbledegook the judge had spouted at the end. And he was sure Mrs Owen had confirmed it for him afterwards; come and see me next week, she had said. So why the long faces? Surely it had been grounds for at least a handshake? He would not have been averse to giving her a hug; a powerful-looking woman, Duggie thought. He would have liked to have bought her a drink, but he could see that might be a bit difficult. But to just walk off like that, that was bloody odd. She'd seemed to be so pleased with herself up until the time the judge spoke and then, if he'd given the maximum he could, why get so upset? What had the judge said? Or perhaps she was just a bad-mannered bitch anyway.

Duggie had finally given up waiting, had left the court and headed for the nearest bar. There had been nothing he would have liked more than to have got happy drunk, buy everyone a drink, yes, even Baxter – after all, he had felt perhaps he owed Baxter a drink – and he had tried different drinks in different bars with different companions. He was not a vicious man but now, the more he drank, the angrier he got. The angrier he got, the more direct his thoughts became. He now heard the Judge's ruling clearly enough not only to hear the words but the intonation also. 'This court'. Why had he stressed 'This' court? He was sure he had. It hadn't been all that obvious; the Judge hadn't shouted it out or anything like that. In fact, Duggie would not have thought twice about it if his solicitor had not been so bloody toffee-nosed about it afterwards. What had the bitch been up to then? Because there had been no doubt who the Judge had been looking at when he'd said it.

His tortuous deductions had led Duggie ultimately to the lawyers' pub, where he now stood, swaying gently, at their table. Though his mind was clear, he was having difficulty in focusing as he looked from one upturned face to the other. His mouth felt like rubber when he tried to speak.

'Having a bit of a party, are we?' He tried to sneer but he failed to control his facial muscles sufficiently. 'Must say, it's very kind of you to be celebrating for me like this, but you must let me buy you both a drink.'

Duggie's 'What can I get you?', Alex's 'No, thank you', and Baxter's 'You're drunk' were simultaneous.

Duggie looked down on Alex.

'Like to buy my solicitor a drink. No law against that, is there?'

Alex shook her head and smiled, nervously. 'Another time, maybe, Mr Dunbar, but I have to drive home and I have already had two of these.' She raised her glass before drinking the last few drops. She looked at her watch. 'I must be getting home.'

'Running away from me again, are you?' Duggie's second attempt at a sneer was somewhat more successful. 'Like you did in court? Tell me. What was the hurry? You didn't even give me the chance to thank you.'

'I do apologise, Mr Dunbar. I'm afraid I was a little preoccupied at the time.'

'You mean about what the Judge said?'

Alex realised suddenly that, inside that intoxicated head, there was a clear and very angry mind. The flush already on her face deepened to extend blotchily down her neck beneath the silk collar of her blouse. She tried to stand up but Duggie didn't move and she was obliged to sit again, looking appealingly across the table at Baxter.

'Where's your car?' Baxter asked.

'At the office.'

'Seems bloody funny to me.' Duggie now leaned his thighs against the table to steady himself, his broad Merseyside accent drawing attention from the tables around. 'You've just cost him 5000 quid and here you are, out drinking together. What's going on? Could it be, Mrs Owen, that you are celebrating your win today – ' again he jabbed his finger towards Baxter ' – or is he celebrating the fact that he got away with just 5000?' Duggie's eyes sluggishly narrowed to slits. 'I don't suppose you two were in cahoots, were you?'

Duggie took an unsteady pace backwards as Alex stood abruptly. Baxter also stood, his face congested, his eyes wet and protruding.

'Dunbar, you'll apologise to Mrs Owen for that remark.'

Duggie looked Baxter up and down and laughed. 'Get lost, sunshine. You don't own me any more. Get your big fat arse and your big fat wallet out of here before I put my foot up them.'

Alex took Baxter's sleeve in her hand and guided him through the door. Duggie jammed the door open with his foot as he watched them cross to Baxter's Jaguar, parked with the near side wheels over double yellow lines.

'And if you make a habit of parking like that, you'd better find yourself a good solicitor an' all,' he shouted triumphantly after them.

Alex sank gratefully into the deep leather seat, feeling secure once more as wealth and power closed around her. She nodded as Baxter asked, 'Where's your office? Courtenay Road?' the only words spoken until the Jaguar came to halt behind the XR3i. Alex made no effort to get out and Baxter switched the engine off. She continued to stare through the windscreen as Baxter turned on his shoulder to smile at her.

'You shouldn't let people like that get to you,' he said. 'Don't take it so seriously.'

'People like them?' Alex's laugh had little humour in it.

Baxter laughed with her. 'You know what I mean. But he has got to you, hasn't he?' Baxter watched the corners of her mouth go down as she nodded. For a moment he thought she was going to cry but then realised his mistake. He was not dealing with that sort of woman. It was anger and frustration that dragged at her mouth. If she was going to burst into anything it would be fury, not tears.

'Then why?' Baxter began to work it out for himself. 'Dunbar got as much as you could get him and yet, after what the Judge said, he's not pleased, not pleased at all.' He paused, thinking hard. 'That means he feels you could or should have got more for him. But you couldn't, not in – Ah!' Baxter slowly nodded his head. 'Not in that court. That's what the Judge said, didn't he? In this court, he said. And friend Dunbar has put two and two together as well. Correct?'

This time it was Alex's turn to nod her head.

'But, if it had gone to the High Court, he might have got more, is that it?'

'Perhaps a little. His final disability is not very great, but you know how much they seem to award these days.'

'However,' Baxter spoke slowly, 'that would have meant briefing a barrister and you would have had to take a back seat, out of the limelight?'

'Got it in one,' Alex answered, bitterly.

'Well, for God's sake, don't let that worry you. People like Dunbar, they just don't know how to look after money. I'll give him six months and that five grand will be gone, you take it from me. Another thousand would only have lasted a couple of months longer. And you can take that disability with a pinch of salt too. Bet you anything he's taking his Social Security and moonlighting like hell on the side. Don't worry about him.'

What Baxter had intended as genuine words of comfort elicited no visible response from Alex. She continued to stare, tightlipped, at the back of her car. Puzzled, Baxter's brow furrowed until his features became moulded, this time not only by understanding, but by surprise and admiration. The first time he touched her was to beat rhythmically with his finger on her arm as he said, 'You're not concerned about our friend Dunbar at all, are you?'

Alex reacted quickly if a little half-heartedly. 'That's not true. I do feel a bit guilty that I didn't take his case to the High Court. If you hadn't been so damn vindictive and settled out of court, the case wouldn't have arisen anyway.'

'But that's not what's really bothering you,' Baxter persisted, leaving his hand gently on her arm. 'So, if you were not that concerned about Dunbar, and you certainly weren't worried about taking the money off me, who were you concerned about? That only leaves the Judge. You – ' he began patting her arm again, cupping his hand to add weight as his conviction grew ' – were upset because you got a wigging from the Judge or just about as much of a wigging as a Judge gives a solicitor in court like that. Right?'

When Alex turned her head, there was a small conspiratorial smile in her eyes and mouth. 'You should have been a bloody detective,' she said.

'They don't pay enough,' Baxter said, still searching her face with quick, darting eyes. 'Now why should you be so upset about that?'

'D'you think I should enjoy being told off by a Judge?'

'You? I don't think it would bother you too much.' Baxter made it sound like a virtue of which he could become quite fond. 'I think we are rather alike, you and I, and that sort of thing would not bother me. So why?'

'Because,' Alex smiled, enjoying the sensation of relief at finding someone who would understand, 'the Judge will talk to another Judge, and that Judge will talk to another Judge, and that Judge . . .' Alex disengaged her arm to indicate an endless series of judges stretching into the distance.

'And how would that affect you?' Baxter asked. Getting no reply, he set about answering his own questions once more. 'Because you harbour ambitions in that direction yourself. You wanted that case in the County Court. I remember now, my solicitor was surprised. When he advised me to settle, he warned me it would probably mean being taken to the High Court. But you wanted that case for yourself. Well, well.' He sat back against the door to take a long, cool look at her. 'So we're ambitious, are we? Not just beautiful, but ambitious with it.'

'There's nothing wrong with that, is there?' Alex spat the words out on the wave of relieved tension.

'Not one bit,' Baxter answered. 'Not one bit.'

7

Hannah felt lousy. She could find no better way of describing it. Her side was still painful, especially if she coughed or moved suddenly. She didn't feel hungry – she hadn't felt like food for months – but what they were giving her to eat was awful. She had heard of hospital food but this was ridiculous. They kept telling her it was a special diet because of her kidney troubles but it was so dull. She couldn't see herself ever eating it. And thirsty. She was so thirsty.

Half propped up on pillows, she turned her head and looked around the small operating theatre, taking in the jumble of trolleys, dishes, rows of syringes in their plastic packets, a glass-fronted cabinet displaying rows of frightful looking instruments, most of them also wrapped in plastic. There were bottles containing clear fluid with labels on them. Unlikely to be pop but, the way she felt, she'd drink anything. They were so mean with what they gave her, writing down each miserable drop on a chart at the end of her bed. And there was nothing she could do about it – yet. Wait until she could get out of bed, didn't keel over every time she tried to stand up, just walk a few steps to a tap when no one was looking. She wasn't going to stay as thirsty as that for ever. Beneath the surgical mask they had put over her nose and mouth, she ran the tip of her tongue around her lips, trying to moisten them. She laid her head back on the pillow and read the name on the operating light. Carl Zeiss – she wondered where the hell Carl Zeiss was now.

Hannah was improving, still a very sick girl, but improving. There had been no more bleeding but she was still very anaemic, something that was going to remain a very real problem for Rhys and his team. Rhys had not only been thinking of the kidney's usual function when he had mentioned his anxiety to leave even the smallest piece of kidney tissue at her operation. Her kidney, damaged as it was, was still a source of one of the blood-forming hormones and her anaemia was going to be difficult to correct without it. She was going to need repeated blood transfusions with all the problems that brought in the way of antibodies and an overload of iron. The main reason for her feeling unwell, however, was her severe uraemia, the accumulation of those waste products that should have been filtered off by the kidneys. It was called uraemia because the level of urea in the blood was the easiest to measure but it was only one of many substances, some of them as yet unidentified, that might well be making Hannah feel so ill.

In the Intensive Care Unit, after her operation, Hannah's slide down that slippery slope to eternity had been halted and she had been transferred to Rhys's ward to begin the long drag back up to what quality of life they could offer a spirited, rebellious young girl with no kidneys. Peritoneal dialysis, the removal of waste products by inserting tubes into her abdominal cavity and perfusing with fluids of carefully balanced solutions, had clawed her back from the levels that would have spelt certain death and reduced the toxic effect to the point that her character began to show through once more.

'What are you going to do to me then?' she asked, as the nurse, a long hooked forceps in each hand, began to take sterile covers off trolleys to reveal rows of instruments.

'Mr Owen is going to do a small operation on your arm,' Staff Nurse Rees explained. She moved over to the table, leaning her hip against it, holding the tips of the forceps away from her as she looked down on Hannah. 'Nothing terrible, *cariad*. Just another stage in making you feel fit and well again.'

'It'll have to be some operation then. I feel lousy. When's he coming?'

'He won't be long. He's a very busy man, you know.'

The Staff Nurse went back to her trolleys, turning her back on Hannah as if, looking at Hannah's pale face, she was suddenly ashamed of her rosy cheeks and vigorous good health.

'What's your name?'

The simple, direct question came from the table behind her. She turned and smiled at Hannah.

'Nansi.'

'Nansi what?'

'Nansi Rees.'

'Are you married?'

'I was. Now, will you let me get on with my work?'

The Staff Nurse turned her back once more and there were a few moments of silence before the next question came.

'Nansi, do you like men?'

'Do I like what?' There was laughter and astonishment in the nurse's face as she turned yet again.

'Men.'

'What an incredible thing to say.'

'Well, do you?'

'Well . . .' Nansi Rees hesitated.

'I don't mean sort of husbands and fathers and things like that. I mean men,' Hannah persisted.

'Yes, I suppose so,' Nansi laughed. 'Yes, I suppose I do.'

'I don't. I'm never going to get married,' Hannah said, savagely. 'I hate men. And women,' she added after a few moments' reflection.

'Now I know you're crazy,' Nansi said. 'You can't go round hating everybody, a pretty girl like you. You must love someone.'

'Well, perhaps two . . .'

She broke off as Rhys Owen walked in, his white theatre clothes hanging loosely on him.

'Good afternoon, Hannah. How are you today?' he asked.

'Rotten,' she answered, pouting.

'Good.'

'Good?' Hannah looked surprised. 'Good, did you say?'

'Yes.'

'Why?'

Rhys looked at the Staff Nurse and winked. 'I'm sure neither you nor Staff Nurse Rees is old enough to remember the words of that old song, "It ain't wot you say, but the way wot you say it." Is that right, Staff Nurse?'

'I'm sure it is, Mr Owen.'

Hannah just pulled a face. She looked directly at Rhys but pointed her finger at the Staff Nurse.

'Did you know her name is Nansi and she likes men?'

The Staff Nurse had worked on Rhys's dialysis unit for a long time – she was one of the nurses with whom he always felt at ease – but, with their mutual burst of laughter, he looked at her with sudden interest. He saw her flush as he said, 'I happen to think that is a particularly beautiful name. With an i or a y?'

'I.'

'Even better.'

'Why don't you call her Nansi, then?' Hannah asked Rhys, frowning, 'if that's her name? Why do you call her Staff Nurse?'

'Because it wouldn't do for Consultant Surgeons to be so familiar with Staff Nurses,' Nansi answered for him. 'Now will you behave yourself?'

Hannah thought she could squeeze one more remark in.

'Why? Does he ever tell you off?'

Nansi looked at Rhys, smiling appealingly.

'Mr Owen. When you've finished the fistula, d'you think you could take an inch or so off this young lady's tongue?'

Hannah's head fell back on the pillow to watch Rhys and his Staff Nurse chatting quietly as they stood, shoulder to shoulder, scrubbing up. That was as much talking as she could manage without becoming totally exhausted. As they crossed back to the table, Rhys asked, 'Now then, Hannah, are you right- or left-handed?'

'Right. Why?'

'Because we want to do this operation on the other arm.'

'What are you going to do then?'

Rhys cleaned Hannah's left forearm and hand, finally painting it with pink antiseptic dye. As he arranged the sterile drapes that Nansi handed him, he explained, 'I'm going to do a little operation on your wrist to make the veins stand out more. Then, when they're nice and big, we'll teach you to manage your own treatment; save you coming into hospital all the time.'

'How d'you mean?'

'We'll teach you to put needles in your veins and connect them up to your own machine. That's why we wanted to know whether you were right-handed or not.'

Hannah stuck her tongue out in disgust under her mask. 'Sounds filthy,' she said. 'I'll never do that.'

'Yes you will.' Rhys turned his head to thank Nansi who was edging a stool beneath him with her foot as he sat, his knees disappearing under the table. Nansi pulled her trolleys around her and stood at the table, her thigh and hip brushing Owen's shoulder. Hannah had made him aware of the attractive woman to his left and he felt her warmth.

Silence settled over the small theatre as Rhys infiltrated the skin, just above the wrist joint, with local anaesthetic. What he was about to do was considered a minor operation, but, minor or not, it was important for Hannah that it was performed correctly. Although it didn't take long, it was a tricky little technique to learn and Rhys liked to fashion his own fistulae rather than have a succession of juniors learning on his patients, only to move on elswhere.

'What are you two doing down there?' Hannah's head and neck craned forwards and Rhys had to restrain her from raising her head to look at it. 'What's that?'

'That's a vein.' Rhys put a fine probe under the flat, collapsed, blue tube and lifted it out of the wound.

'Yuck; it looks disgusting,' Hannah said.

'Well, you did ask,' Rhys grinned. 'You don't have to look.'

'And what are you going to do with that?' Hannah persisted, finding she was not strong enough to hold her head forwards any longer.

'Join it up to an artery, if I can find it,' Rhys smiled.

'Charming,' Hannah spoke to her reflection in the lamp above her. Exhausted by her effort at chirpy defiance at the people who had so much control over her, Hannah dozed off in the warm, somnolent atmosphere, lulled by the subdued, intimate conversation between the two heads bent so closely over her wrist. Slightly louder, brisker words roused her once more.

'Good,' Rhys said, straightening his back. 'I think that should do.'

'Did you find it after?' Hannah asked.

'Find what?'

'The artery.'

'Yes, no problem,' Rhys laughed. 'D'you want a look at it before I stitch it up?'

'All right,' Hannah said bravely, lifting her head once more.

'There it is.' Rhys pointed with his probe. 'That's where the join is; it's called a fistula.'

'Yuck,' Hannah said but her gaze stayed steady as Rhys put his finger above and below the fistula. 'What are you doing that for?'

'Feeling for a thrill.'

'A what?'

'A thrill. When the blood from the artery leaks into the vein, you can sense the jet of blood going up and down the vein and I'm never happy until I can feel it. But yours is fine. No problem.' Rhys picked up a stitch for the skin while Hannah's head fell back again.

'Funny way to get a thrill,' she muttered as a wave of nausea washed over her. The hard rubber ridges of the operating table's cushions cut into her wasted buttocks and she longed for fresh, salt air, the sound of Tempest's hooves. She thought wistfully of the days when to spend a penny meant no more than to walk into a loo and pull her pants down. Now she fumed at the illness that was going to shackle her to one of those frightening machines. 'But then, I suppose you've got to be a bit of a sadist to be a surgeon.'

'Hannah!' There was very little allowance for Hannah's illness in the severity of Nansi's tone, but Rhys shook his head good-naturedly at her. How was she to know that this patient was allowed anything, that he had it coming to him, in a way welcomed it.

'Enjoy your job, don't you?' Hannah's eyes were now closed.

'I do.' Rhys paused before putting in the last stitch.

'Well then. Like I said, you've got to be a bit of a sadist to enjoy cutting people up, haven't you?'

The poker face that Rhys's features instantly assumed was, to Nansi, as much a reaction to hurt as if Rhys had winced. His immediate silence was as eloquent as if he had made some biting riposte, and she felt the sadness about him as he bundled up his swabs and handed them to her. There was still no word from Rhys as Paddy Moore came in to wheel Hannah back to the ward. Nansi made no effort to clear up.

'A cup of coffee, Mr Owen?' she asked, quietly.

'Yes – yes, thank you. I'd love one.'

'Go in Sister's room then. She's not on today. I'll bring you one in.'

'Just so long as you'll join me, Staff.'

'Of course, Mr Owen. I won't be a moment.'

When she walked in, a mug in each hand, Rhys was lounging in a chair, the legs of his ill-fitting theatre trousers pulled up to show hairy shins above his socks. He accepted a mug from her with a smile and Nansi took a chair facing him across the tiny room, sitting sideways on its edge to prevent her tight, thin skirt from riding up.

'She's still a very sick girl, Mr Owen.' Nansi's voice was soothing.

'She is, Staff, yes.'

'How d'you think she'll do?'

'Difficult to say exactly.' Rhys slipped back into reverie until inherent good manners jerked him out of it. 'We can but do our best.'

It was the answer Nansi would have expected, but there was an unusually determined note to his voice that she did not miss.

'D'you think you'll ever teach her to dialyse herself?'

'Oh, yes,' Rhys was quick to reply. 'Don't take any notice of what she said in there. She's a survivor. Those veins will take six to eight weeks to mature, so we won't be able to start her off on her own until then, but she'll do anything to survive, that one, believe me.'

'But she'll never be able to dialyse herself at home, Mr Owen.'

'No?'

'No. You know where she lives?'

'Vaguely. Pretty rough, is it?'

'Oh, terrible.' Nansi took Rhys's empty mug from him, hoping that talking as she did so would prevent him using the event as an excuse to leave. It excited her to see him settle back in the threadbare chair, showing no sign of being anxious to get away. She made a conscious effort to keep a surging pleasure out of her voice. 'She's living out in Dai Stud's place.'

'Dai Stud?' Rhys repeated pensively.

'That's what they call him. Davies his real name is. His father used to be a GP in Avonport many years ago; looked after me when I was a baby apparently.'

'Of course; that's right. Wasn't there something in the *Echo* about him the other night?' Rhys raised his eyelids, enjoying the intimacy. 'Weren't some of his neighbours objecting?'

He suddenly realised what an attractive woman Staff Nurse Rees was, with her mask pushed down beneath her chin and that generous mouth so ready to smile. He remembered the incident now, remembered chuckling as he read about it. The row of new gardens backing on to Dai's land had not had time for the privet, beech and cupressus to grow high enough to hide Tempest's cavortings with the brood mares which were allowed to run free with him. As a result, much to Dai's delight, there had been complaints that Tempest's potency had disrupted several of the local Tupperware parties and that coffee mornings were being forced into the gloom of drawn curtains.

'I remember now,' Rhys laughed. 'The goings on on his land have rather upset the local housewives, I believe. Is that where Hannah lives?'

'Yes.' Nansi was still laughing. 'That's the horse that Hannah was riding when she was injured. What Dai was thinking of, letting a slip of a girl ride a horse like that, I don't know. Have you any idea how she came to be living there, Mr Owen?'

'None. In fact, it's very difficult to find anything out about her background.' Rhys moved, making himself more comfortable. Nansi saw the movement and slid backwards into the depths of her chair. 'She has no parents, no family at all, as far as we can find out. All we know is that she was in care in Swansea and kept on running away, living rough. In the end they seem just to have given up trying to find her when she'd reached the age when she could walk out anyway.'

'But she can't go back to that place of Dai's. She could never have a machine there. Have you seen the place?'

'No,' Rhys admitted. 'We haven't sent anyone out yet to look at it. There'll be plenty of time for that. I thought I might go myself this time.'

'Don't bother.'

'As bad as that?'

'It's filthy, Mr Owen. Dai and his – ' she searched for the word '– woman live in an old caravan and Hannah sleeps in one of the barns.'

'But they seem very fond of her. I had to see the woman – what do they call her, Jessie? – after Hannah's nephrectomy.' Rhys chuckled at the recollection. 'She really put me through it.'

'Oh, yes,' Nansi conceded. 'They're probably the nearest thing to parents that Hannah is ever likely to have but it's a hopeless set-up.' She looked closely at Rhys. 'You don't look all that concerned.'

'Well, no; not at the moment, anyway. The first thing is to get her fit.'

'And transplant?'

'Yes.'

It was the first time the question, the decision, the answer, had been put into words.

'How soon?'

This time the only answer Nansi got was the downturn of his lips and the shrug of his shoulders. His eyes seemed to close a little as he receded from her. He felt at ease in her company; for once he didn't have the overpowering desire to protect his feelings, withdraw all means of contact that might prove painful. If he had mentioned to Alex the questions that had been etching themselves deeper and deeper into his conscience over the last few days, she would have brushed them aside, calling him too sensitive by far, telling him not to be so stupid, to do what he thought right for Hannah and not to worry about it. One of the reasons he felt so at ease with Nansi in the work-worn intimacy of the tiny room was that he was in no doubt what her reaction would be if he were to allow her warmth and friendliness to lure him into dropping his defences. He had seen her open-hearted attitude to his patients, her instant change of mood, dictated by the patient's needs, as she busied herself from bed to bed, from machine to machine. Put the same questions to her, the same doubts, and he imagined her smile, just saying those few words that would coax him to her, encourage his confidence. But they were still, would still be tomorrow, no more than surgeon and nurse having a coffee together after a fistula operation. Rhys's thoughts would have to remain his own.

There was still a long waiting list for kidney transplants. The demand always outstripped the supply. The increase in donors that had followed the computer project had been transient, a short-lived bonanza. The potential donors who had signed donor cards but then never carried them had been equally reluctant to commit themselves to some cold, impersonal data bank. The shortage had not been helped by TV documentaries that had created in viewers' minds pictures of surgeons snatching kidneys from donors whose total death was still in doubt. Patients were still dying waiting for kidneys. Their progress up the order of priority was not a smooth, orderly one; there was no question of first on, first off. Owen never brought pressure to bear on any member of a patient's family to donate a kidney but, if a relative came forward and the kidney matched, that patient did not have to wait long. Otherwise, the main factor involved remained the compatibility of the kidney that became available. But the waiting list was so long that it happened frequently that the precious kidney matched more than one patient. At such times, other factors had to be taken into account in the final choice, criteria that could not be fed into any impersonal computer that would come up with a cold, comforting, clinical decision. It usually fell to Owen to cast the final vote and he wondered just how far he could trust himself to exclude his personal feelings should a kidney become available that matched Hannah's tissue type.

'I don't think anyone would begrudge any priority you gave to Hannah, Mr Owen.' The crooning Welsh lilt to Nansi's voice sounded like an absolution. 'She is so young. She has so much to live for.'

Rhys, startled, wondered whether her remarks had been accidental or whether she had really read his thoughts.

'Well, of course,' he answered hurriedly, 'there is a lot to be said for her having her transplant sooner than later. As you say, she's young, very active, with a pretty rebellious personality that wouldn't augur well for the discipline of dialysis two or three times a week. Can you imagine her sticking to a restricted fluid intake?'

Nansi shook her head decisively.

'She's not', Rhys went on as if glad to hear himself speak the words, 'one of your steady, middle-aged Civil Servants, nine to five job, catching the five to eight every morning. And it's not as if one would be giving her life at the expense of a man like that, would it?'

Nansi watched his anxiety to rationalise what he knew he was going to do sooner or later, bring an intensity to eyes from which he seemed to do his utmost to shut out all vestige of expression, as if he were afraid of the consequences.

'What I mean is, I can find you figures that show that a cadaver transplant doesn't do much better than long-term dialysis. And, I mean, a cadaver kidney is all that Hannah can hope for; there's no real chance of anything else. So it's only quality of life we're talking about, isn't it, not life itself?'

'Of course not, Mr Owen.' Nansi had an overwhelming urge to touch him, hold him.

'I mean, Hannah has nowhere to go, has she? She has no home. There's nowhere around here for her to go. She would have to stay in some institution or other and she would die if she ran away again and lived rough. She might as well be in prison – and can you imagine that girl behind bars?'

8

Yousef brought the Mercedes to a halt in almost the identical spot to that where he had parked nearly a fortnight before. He turned the engine off and looked around. The car park was fuller than on the previous occasion but now it was past nine o'clock and there was a constant stream of people entering the main doors. He took a deep breath as if marking the beginning of some new adventure, opened the car door and got out. He reached back into the car to grasp a long white coat and stuff a stethoscope into its pocket. He walked purposefully through the entrance hall, into the main corridor of the Ward Block and into the lift. He pressed the button for the third floor. He smiled broadly at the nurse who travelled up with him but hesitated for a moment while he found his bearings after emerging on to the landing.

'Thank you,' he murmured to the nurse as she held the door to the Urology Ward open invitingly for him. 'Where can I find Sister's office?'

To get to the Sister's office, he found he had first to pass, on his right, the untidy bustle of a Dialysis Unit in full swing. The door to the office was open and he walked in. He saw first a tall, fair girl in a white coat sitting with her back to the wall, intent on an open file in her lap. The Ward Sister sat, her head sunk into her shoulders as she rested her elbows on her desk, her cap pinned to dark, short-cropped hair.

'Good morning, Sister.' It flashed through his mind what reaction he might have expected had he greeted her American counterpart like that. 'I'm Yousef.'

'Oh.' Sister Vaughan looked up, surprised and confused at the American accent. 'Good morning.' She stood up and shook the hand this very handsome young man had just thrust towards her.

'I've come to work for Dr Owen for a month or so.' He had thought hard whether to say 'for' or 'with'. 'I take it I'm on the right ward?' he asked, knowing with absolute certainty he was.

'Yes,' Sister Vaughan answered, not thinking to introduce herself. 'He should be here about ten o'clock; does a ward round every Monday morning. This is Dr Drury.' She waved across her desk.

Without closing the file balanced across her knees, Clare Drury slowly extended a hand and, as he leaned forwards to take it, Yousef found himself being coolly sized up by a very level pair of grey-blue eyes.

'Good morning. Welcome to Avonport.'

Her languid voice was in keeping with her movements.

'Good morning, Dr Drury. You must be Dr Owen's Registrar?'

''Fraid not.' Her smile was friendly. 'Just a humble SHO. I was Mr Owen's House Surgeon six months ago and I'm holding the fort while his Registrar is away for six weeks. He's only just gone; taken his annual leave all in one go. They tend to do that.' She smiled suddenly. Perhaps she should not have said that. Perhaps he would consider himself 'one of them'.

'What you mean is that, for the next six weeks, you're boss round here, that so?'

'I wouldn't know about that,' Clare Drury laughed. 'What I do know is that I'm absolutely terrified. I just don't see myself getting through the next six weeks at the moment.'

'You certainly don't look terrified to me,' Yousef smiled.

'You'll be all right, girl.' Sister Vaughan's Welsh accent vied in intensity with the American. 'Rhys will look after you. It's not as if you were with one of the others. There's never any problem about calling him in, is there? In fact, I sometimes think he is happier in hospital than at home.'

'Yes, but not for every appendix.' There was nothing sham about Clare

Drury's anxiety. 'What am I to do if I'm stuck with a really nasty appendix at two o'clock in the morning?'

'If that happens, perhaps you would allow me to help you out.'

Sister Vaughan came round from behind her desk, her hand outstretched, as if formally accepting Yousef into the family. 'Let me have your coat, Dr . . . Mr . . . ' She hesitated. 'I'm sorry, but what do we call you?'

'Yousef,' he laughed. 'Yousef will do fine, Sister. I don't think you would cope with the rest.'

As Yousef pulled on his white coat, transferring his pen to the top pocket, Sister Vaughan hung his jacket behind the door.

'There. It will be quite safe there, Yousef.' She was surprised just how easy it seemed to call him by his Christian name; there had been Registrars to whom she had not done that after two years. Perhaps that gorgeous American accent had something to do with it. 'I'm afraid we don't have a separate room for junior staff on this ward. We all have to muck in here. Where are you living? Are you in Resident's?'

'No, Sister. I've only just arrived but I hope to find myself a furnished apartment near the . . .'

Yousef broke off as a stocky, curly-headed man hurried in, his white coat flapping, his hands and arms a jumble of folders, syringes and small glass bottles.

'Sis, be a sport and give me a hand, would you?' From his accent, he might have been born in the same street as Sister Vaughan. 'How the hell Rhys admits patients at nine o'clock and then expects me to have them all written up by ten, I don't know.'

Alun Jones, Owen's House Surgeon, gave a friendly grin and a brief 'Hi' as he was introduced to Yousef.

'Just give me a hand with the bloods, Sis; that's all I ask. The nephrectomy's as fat as hell.'

Yousef and Clare Drury smiled at each other as Ward Sister and House Surgeon disappeared into the corridor, chatting volubly. Yousef sat down opposite her.

'You're not Welsh,' he said, more as a statement than a question.

'No, I'm English. I come from a place called Malvern.'

'It's going to take me a little time to learn the different accents,' Yousef said.

'I wouldn't worry about it, though perhaps I should give you one word of warning.' She gave a short laugh. 'You can get away with mistaking an Englishman for a Welshman – he may not appreciate it very much but he's unlikely to actually strike you – but never, never, for God's sake, mistake a Welshman for an Englishman.'

'Thanks for the warning; I'll keep that in mind,' he laughed before becoming serious once more. 'And you are going to do surgery?' he asked.

'Yes.' There was an immediate defensive tone in the word, a trace of defiance in her look. Yousef smiled inwardly, resisting the temptation to raise both hands and say, 'All right, all right.'

'It's a long haul,' he said, considerately.

'Because I'm a woman?'

This time he did put his hands up.

'Now who mentioned about you being a woman?' he asked.

Clare relaxed, smiling. 'Sorry.'

'I just meant that it's a hell of a lot of work and I imagine the competition is as bad here as in the States, even for a man. When you are as beautiful as you are, they are all going to think you won't stay the course but get married. It's got to be tougher, hasn't it?'

Clare lowered her eyes, disturbed by the compliment, but still there was defiance in her reply.

'That's why I'm here where I can do some practical surgery rather than go to the Teaching Hospital as Mr Owen advised me to. Here I can find out at an early stage whether I'm up to it; in the teaching hospital I'd only be sixth in the queue for the next appendix. In that way you can take years to find out you've made a mistake and then it's too late to be a success at anything else.'

'That, I must say,' said Yousef, impressed now with a mind as well as enchanted by a face, 'sounds very clear reasoning indeed.'

'For a woman, d'you mean?' Clare asked, her voice, this time, full of banter.

'For such an attractive lady, yes.'

It was a laughing, slightly flushed SHO that Owen saw first as he came through the door followed closely by his Sister and House Surgeon. The sight brought a smile to his face which remained as the tall, dark young man rose from his seat and introduced himself.

'Good morning, Dr Owen,' he said. 'I'm Yousef. I sincerely hope you were expecting me. Professor Steele; he rang you?'

'Yes, of course. I'm so pleased to meet you. Welcome to Avonport.' They shook hands. 'You've met everyone?' Owen waved his hand.

'Yes, thank you, I have.'

Owen had completely forgotten about the chap until Sister Vaughan had met him in the corridor and told him that a younger version of Omar Sharif was waiting for him in her office. Then he remembered some London professor ringing him, telling him that an Arab surgeon wanted to spend a month in Avonport, wanted to learn how to set up a dialysis and transplant unit. He also remembered the lofty tone of voice that had implied 'Why the hell he's picked your unit, I can't for the life of me imagine.' In fairness, it had also gone through Owen's mind, 'Why Avonport?' and it had pleased him to think that someone at least had heard of them. He had looked forward to the visitor coming; perhaps he might be the first of many. Fame at last.

'I hope you will enjoy your stay with us, Joseph.'

'Yousef.'

'I beg your pardon?' Owen asked, looking a little bewildered.

'Yousef. It is pronounced Yousef,' and there flickered across the handsome features a fleeting hint of something that burned fiercely beneath.

Smiling broadly, Owen took a piece of paper from the desk, laid it flat and patted it. 'Now then, there's only one way to settle this, get it right from the start. Write your full name down there so there can be no confusion.'

Yousef took the pen from his pocket and printed his full name, Sayyid Yousef bin Hamad al Wahaibi.

'Oh, my God,' Owen laughed. 'You're Yousef, all right? Yousef,' he repeated, slowly, stressing the pronunciation.

'That'll be fine by me, Dr Owen.'

'Mr Owen.'

'I beg your pardon?' It was Yousef's turn to look perplexed.

'Mr . . . that's how we pronounce Surgeon in this country.'

There was a meeting of minds in the laughter that followed.

'So, why are you here?' Owen asked and Yousef felt four pairs of eyes gazing at him inquisitively. He had prepared a ready answer that had little to do with the truth.

'I've come to learn how to set up a dialysis unit and how to transplant kidneys.'

'Why? Or perhaps I should say "why us?" ' Owen asked.

'Because I have been told you started your unit here from scratch; is that true?'

'Yes, quite true.'

'So you would know all the snags, all the difficulties of working with limited means.'

'Limited means?' Owen showed his surprise.

'Not all Arabs drive round in gold-plated Rolls-Royces, Mr Owen. There are such places as poor Arab states, you know.' He shrugged his shoulders. 'All right, so poor is a relative term. We have a limited amount of oil but we have to be careful how we spend our money.'

'And you are from . . .?' Owen tried to suggest he only wanted confirmation of what he knew already but Yousef smiled knowingly as he replied.

'Shahin.'

'Ah, yes. Shahin.'

It was equally obvious to Yousef that Owen had no idea where that was but was far too polite to say so.

'I wouldn't be at all surprised if you hadn't heard of us, Mr Owen. We have rather been out of the limelight for some years, ever since we – ' he caught himself in time ' – ever since you left us, when we gained our independence. We were one of the smaller patches of red on your school atlases not so long ago.'

'Oh,' Owen said, suspecting suddenly that perhaps he should tread warily, 'but, forgive me, the American accent?'

'That's easily explained,' Yousef put his pen away in his pocket with slow, deliberate movements as if indicating that the inquisition had gone just about far enough. 'I was educated in America. I grew up there, graduated from Stanford. I had a surgical practice in Charlotte, North Carolina, for several years before I returned to Shahin.'

Owen already had sufficient rapport with this rather proud, upright young man to sense that it would be intrusive to push his questioning any further. There would be other times.

'Well then, Sister.' He turned, clapping his hands. 'Let's see what we've got on the ward to show Yousef, shall we? Anything interesting in? That great fat nephrectomy, did she come in afterwards?'

Sister Vaughan fell in beside Owen to walk down the corridor. Alun Jones followed behind with Yousef and Clare Drury bringing up the rear.

'I really don't know whether we shouldn't send these people home, Sister,' Owen opened the ward door for Sister Vaughan to walk through. 'Refuse to operate on them until they have lost a couple of stone.'

And so, another surgical ward round began, typical of a multitude that must have been starting at about the same time up and down the country. The group moved from bed to bed, first in the Urology Ward and then, across the landing, in the General Surgical Ward, jostling with each other in the confined space as they stood back for Owen to pass. It gave Yousef time to take a long and searching look at the man who was, quite unknowingly, central to his plans. His assessment of Owen would be crucial – it was essential he got it right – and, to Yousef, first impressions were important. He watched and listened, absorbing the novel sensation of practical surgery in a new country. The basic principles, he knew, would be identical whether it was Charlotte, North Carolina, or Avonport, but there would be a difference of style, of manner, of relationships, that would be unique to Great Britain, perhaps even to this part of Great Britain. He saw Owen take no more than a few moments with one patient, getting no closer than the foot of the bed, sitting on the bedside locker with another, smiling, using a voice and a few words in Welsh that were totally in tune with the patient, sometimes shaking the man's hand before leaving. Yousef was drawn to a man who could coax a smile, even a laugh, out of someone who, as Yousef could see from the notes, must have been in agonising pain. And he appreciated the respect that Owen plainly commanded from his staff. His House Surgeon might call him Rhys in his absence but there was no hint of such familiarity to his face.

Nor was the assessment all one way. The ward round also gave Owen his chance to size up a man about whom he knew almost nothing. There was no doubting his charm. He already had Sister Vaughan eating out of his hand, no mean achievement in so short a time. And that his influence was not solely on women was shown by Alun Jones's reaction as Yousef inquired about this patient and that X-ray. And Clare – someone to warm Owen's heart every time he looked at her – what of her? Perhaps it was the confirmation of Owen's instinctive affinity with this stranger that he felt no resentment as he saw them, so fair and so dark, side by side. There was still the small matter of ability and experience. Owen was not quite sure exactly how active a part it was intended Yousef should play on his unit. Nothing had been mentioned by the Professor but Owen could hardly see Yousef standing and watching patients being dialysed for a month, perhaps assisting at the periodic transplant. It was no accident, therefore, that, throughout the ward round, Owen asked Yousef to comment on his patients, asked him how they would handle similar problems in the States, even, at times, framing his words as if he were asking Yousef's advice. Together they stood in front of X-ray viewing boxes, peering at shadows, or bent over case notes, their fingers running down lists of figures and typewritten reports.

They were back across the landing, through the Dialysis Unit and back into the Urology Ward itself when Owen saw the smile on Yousef's face. He stopped and the two men faced each other.

'Why the smile?' Owen asked.

'I was just wondering whether I had passed.' Yousef replied.

There was a pause while Clare and Alun Davies searched Owen's face for his reaction; then all four laughed.

'I'm sorry,' Owen said. 'Was it so obvious?'

'I haven't been grilled like that since I graduated.'

'You must forgive me, Yousef, but usually there has been some sort of interview before someone like yourself starts working here so that we know roughly what we are getting. I'm not too sure whether you've come purely as an observer or whether we're allowed to get some work out of you. Prof. Steele didn't say. But I'm sure you'll appreciate how careful we have got to be.'

'Please, Mr Owen, I want to work. No offence, but I just couldn't stand round watching for a month. I promise I won't take on anything I don't feel competent to handle, I have a full, temporary registration in this country and I've joined a Defence Organisation. I'm raring to go.'

'That's fantastic,' Owen said. 'Perhaps Dr Drury has told you; my Registrar is away for six weeks and she's holding the fort. I rather suspect she's feeling a bit shaky so perhaps you wouldn't mind holding her hand from time to time.'

'I can't think of anything I would like to do more, Mr Owen.'

'And I'll put enough of the cold stuff your way to keep you happy. Good.' Owen sounded well pleased. 'In that case, just let me introduce you to Hannah and then I'll leave Dr Drury and Dr Jones to show you round the Unit.'

Hannah heard the burst of laughter from her bed. Although her single room was way down towards the end of the ward corridor, her door was always open and she heard the group of doctors come into the ward. Only doctors made that sort of noise. She could not hear what they were saying but she recognised Alun Jones's laugh and Rhys's voice. But the other voice she could not place; it sounded strangely distinct. They had stopped and she pictured the group, vague figures in white coats, a knot of happy, healthy people amongst the uniformity of courageous ill health all around them. Hannah stormed inwardly with jealousy. She was as jealous of anyone who took their good health for granted as she was fearful of the brave, smiling acceptance of debility shown by the patients she saw learning to dialyse themselves. The thought that she was to become 'one of them' horrified her. She would rather die. She resented the long-term patients who put their heads round her door, their faces shining with encouragement for her. Hannah wondered what they thought when all they met was a snapping, almost snarling rebuff. It just seemed to make them even more determined to succeed in welcoming her into their fold. Hannah knew she could never do that. She would be healthy, healthy enough to kick herself free from the suffocating care of an institution that she found even more restrictive than the professional love of foster mothers, or she would be dead.

Hannah had that indefinable attraction that brought male members of staff to the foot of her bed to smile their affection, however vile her mood, but her spiky defiance was seen by many of the female staff as evidence of how spoilt she was becoming – 'Needs her bottom smacked, that one,' had been the opinion of more than one weary night nurse – but it was obvious to all that she meant something special to Mr Owen, and all sorts of allowances were made to please him. The only company into which she seemed to blend was that of Jessie and Dai. The three of them seemed to close ranks against the nurses and doctors alike. Dai, his face gleaming – he had never washed and shaved so regularly in his life – beamed wider and wider the more abusive Hannah became. 'It's a good sign,' he would say to Jessie as the rusting Granada banged and ground its way home, 'means she's feeling better, more her old self.' All three would glare in open hostility as a Staff Nurse whisked away the 'proper food' that Jessie had brought in for her, hoping she would overlook the contraband titbits hidden away in the corner of her locker. But no one could take from Hannah the priceless gift that Dai, quite unknowingly, brought with him – the smell of fresh air and horse manure.

From her bed in the window, high on the third floor, with only the operating theatres above, she only had to prop herself up a little and sink her right shoulder into her pillows and she could gaze out over Swansea Bay. She could watch the constant comings and goings of ambulances, buses and cars as they swung past the roundabout and up the slope to the hospital. Beyond the road, she could see a stretch of sand, its surface left wet and shimmering by the ebbing tide, just as she knew it would look a few miles up the coast. She knew exactly how that beach would feel and sound under Tempest's hooves. She had tried, many times, with eyes tightly closed, to recreate every step, every pound of the hooves, every sound of the waves on one of those mornings when Tempest had given her what no human could, breathtaking escape. Each time, her imagination had run away too fast, try as she would to slow it down so that she could recapture each moment. She had estimated just how long each stage of one of the gallops had taken, the walk down those stairs, rickety step by rickety step; the heaving and pushing needed to saddle a restless stallion; the tightreined impatience along the cliff top; the liberation of the gallop. Then she had striven, using the slow motion clock on the wall, to stretch her imagination over the same period but, to her dismay, always failed. It was after just such a period of aching sadness that she had opened her eyes early that morning, to see a young man running along the beach – not jogging, but speeding with the rhythmic strides of an athlete.

For the first time in many years, Hannah had cried.

And then a resurgent spirit had made her sit up. With a jutting chin, she had drawn the back of her hand across a snivelling nose and had dabbed at her eyes with her pyjama sleeve.

'And that's one lot of fluid loss that's not going down on that bloody chart,' she had muttered to herself.

Hannah heard the voices get closer, saw Owen come through the door.

'And this,' he said, looking over his shoulder, 'is Hannah.'

Hannah looked at the man who followed immediately behind Owen. Her eyes wavered for a moment to register Clare and Alun Jones but soon returned to stare at Yousef with unsmiling intensity.

'Who are you?' she asked.

Owen turned to Yousef before he could reply. 'One word of warning, Yousef,' he smiled. 'Watch out. Don't get too close. The lady bites.'

'Yousef?' Hannah said. She looked directly at him. 'That's a funny sort of a name. Where do you come from then?'

'I am an Arab,' Yousef smiled indulgently.

'You don't sound like an Arab,' Hannah retorted.

'Oh? And how exactly should Arabs sound?' Yousef asked while Owen nodded his approval of Yousef's natural adaptation to a patient's mood.

'Well,' said Hannah, caught off balance, 'well, sort of – Arabian.'

She was glad of the chance to change the subject in the ensuing laughter and she turned to Alun Jones who had slipped the loose pyjama sleeve on her left arm upwards and was running his finger up and down the inside of her arm.

'Enjoying yourself, Dr Jones?'

Alun Jones only grinned.

'How are they coming?' asked Owen.

'Beautiful, sir.'

'Beautiful,' snorted Hannah and then listened, pouting, as Owen and Yousef, with Clare and the House Surgeon listening and learning, launched into a discussion of the superiority of the fistula over the Quinton-Scribner shunt. Within a few sentences the two men were oblivious of their surroundings, argument and counter-argument oscillating between two well-matched brains. Owen, feeling unusually excited, finally, reluctantly, paused.

'Yes,' he said, leaning his head back as if anxious to take a longer view of Yousef. 'Yes – I think we should get on famously.' He looked at his watch. 'God,' he said, 'I'm late. I've been talking too much.' He turned to Clare Drury. 'Perhaps you'd show Yousef round the rest of the unit, Dr Drury, and give me a ring tonight, let me know what's on the list for tomorrow?' With a parting 'Goodbye, Hannah. Be a good girl and behave yourself,' he was gone.

As the others went to follow him, Yousef turned and smiled at Hannah.

'Be back to see you real soon, Hannah. Fill you in about us Arabs, if you'd like.'

'If you feel you must,' Hannah answered ungraciously, but there was the hint of an appeal in her face that belied her words – and Yousef was not blind to it.

9

The following day, Yousef walked slowly through the Dialysis Unit, watching the end stages of another crowded session. It had been a busy day and all six cubicles had been in use. All the patients would have attended promptly at eight in the morning but, anything from six to nine hours later, they would leave in ones and twos. Some were already quite expert at setting up their machines. These would be sitting back by nine o'clock, reaching with their free arm for the paperback, crossword or magazine that would help them endure the drudgery of the next six or eight hours, while the less brave or the less technically adept would still be shakily priming the pump or timorously prodding a needle into that frighteningly large vein. Hovering constantly over them would have been the Departmental Sister, cajoling, bullying, encouraging anxious beginners not to panic when a red light blinked or an alarm bell shrilled its warning, but to stop – and think – and cope. As Yousef went from cubicle to cubicle, he found that some patients had already freed themselves from the machines and tubing that, like some man-made placenta and umbilical cord, had given them a few more days' precarious life. These were cleaning their apparatus of blood and fluid stains until they were spotless, though Yousef noticed that, life-saving though the machines might be, there was none of that affectionate attention lavished by some teenage motorcyclist on his gleamingly lethal obsession.

Yousef felt uneasy that he had spent the whole day in the operating theatre with Owen. It was not that he would have preferred to have been on the Unit – he wasn't really that interested in dialysis. He knew there would be many more opportunities for him to join them in their weary vigil in the month to come. But it would have been wiser for him to do so. He was meant to be studying the running of a Dialysis Unit and he had started off by spending the day watching Owen operate. It really had been rather stupid of him. Not that anyone seemed to have thought it strange. Owen had obviously enjoyed his company. He had probably felt too flattered by Yousef's undivided attention to think it strange that Yousef had shown no burning desire to start on the Unit as soon as he could. But he must be more careful. He must show more interest in the Unit, in the dialysis and the pumps and the membranes. He must ask the Sister whether they used tubes or sheets or hollow fibres – make himself sound keen and knowledgeable. He must check on the notes he had made before he came, try and remember what he had been taught. He had better not go to theatre again for a few days. He must not allow his anxiety to assess Owen's surgical skill to become obvious.

He was leaning over to say a few words of encouragement to a patient with an hour's dialysis still to go when he heard his name spoken.

'You must be Yousef.'

The voice was firm and friendly but, for a moment, Yousef could not decide whether it was male or female. He stood up and turned to see a smiling face and an outstretched hand which he took in his.

'I'm Maggie; Maggie Rix. How d'you do?'

Yousef saw a square, healthy looking woman in her early sixties, with straight, grey hair and no trace of makeup; her eyes sparkled behind a thick pair of tortoiseshell NHS glasses. Under her white coat she wore a plain jumper and skirt and comfortable-looking flat-heeled shoes. Her only adornment apart from the tiny gold cross at her throat was a plain gold wrist-watch with a black leather strap.

'Finding your way around, are you?' she asked.

'Thank you, yes,' Yousef replied. 'Everyone is being most kind.'

'You're an American.' Maggie Rix's statement was forthright but kindly.

'And you're British,' Yousef countered.

Maggie put her head back and laughed.

'How did you guess?' she asked.

'Only the British could make an incorrect statement with such authority,' Yousef replied. There was still a smile on his face but now he didn't sound as if he was altogether joking and Maggie sensed it.

'But surely, you've got to be American – I mean – with that accent?'

'I am an Arab.'

Maggie heard the suppressed fervour in his voice and tactfully changed the subject.

'Mr Owen told me you were going to spend some time with us. If I can help in any way, you've only got to shout.'

'That's real kind of you, Maggie. May I call you Maggie?' Yousef was back to his charming self as he waved his hand at the activity all round him. 'Is all this your baby?'

'Oh, I just help; Mr Owen's the boss. He really got this place going but he couldn't possibly do the surgery and run the day-to-day stuff as well, so here I am. He got me the job and I'm grateful to him for it – nine to five, mostly – five days a week with just the occasional problem on the weekend – suits me well. Rhys came to see me. He'd heard I had just come back from abroad – I was a Junior Lecturer in Medicine when he was a student – and offered me the job. Of course, I jumped at the chance.'

'Where did you work abroad?' Yousef asked.

'Oh,' Maggie made it sound of little consequence, 'I spent a short time in South America but mainly Abyssinia, Southern Sudan, Eritrea – places like that.'

'So you've lived in the desert too,' Yousef said, wistfully.

'Oh, yes, rather.'

Yousef smiled at the heartiness of the reply.

'Now, how can we help you?' Maggie Rix went on as if anxious to get back to practical matters. 'What d'you want to know?'

'I guess, sooner or later, I'll have to get down to the boring administrative side of things – you know, Maggie – which machines to buy, types of membranes, how to get trained staff, that sort of thing. But first, I would like to spend a day or so here, seeing the process from start to finish, find out the patient's side of it.'

'That's no problem,' Maggie said. 'If I can stir my old bones in time, I'll meet you here at eight tomorrow morning. Sister will probably have a fit, but never mind. Then you fire the jolly old questions as hard as you like and I'll do my best to answer. That suit you?'

'I'd appreciate it, Maggie. Thank you.'

'Not that I play a vital role around here exactly,' Maggie said, digging her hands deep into her pockets as if in frustration. 'Dialysis is essentially a nursing procedure. I feel as if I'm around most of the time just because the patients expect to see a doctor in charge. If you're wise, Yousef, you'll take more time over picking your Unit Sister than anything else. All I ask is that you don't pinch ours.'

'Something tells me you're too modest, Maggie. What exactly is your job?'

'I'm transplant co-ordinator. Sounds grand, doesn't it? I go round trying to organise everyone when a kidney becomes available.'

'And what does that entail altogether?'

Maggie Rix leaned her head to one side, looking sceptically at Yousef.

'Honestly, Maggie; treat me like a medical student. I promise you, I know little or nothing about the subject.'

Maggie explained to him how they frequently had as much as twenty-four hours' notice of a kidney becoming available, and it was her job to ask the donor's hospital to carry out brain stem tests by midday. She then arranged for the surgical team to go and 'retrieve' the kidneys which were flushed through with hyperosmolar citrate solution and then stored in ice. Kept like that, they were 'good' for at least twenty-four hours. Back in Avonport by teatime, tissue typing and crossmatching was carried out by the tissue typists, using the spleen which had also been taken from the donor. The results were usually ready by the early hours of the morning and the patient selected and brought into hospital in time for his transplant early the next morning.

'Not much of the old dashing around in aeroplanes and fast cars any more.'

'Very rarely,' Maggie laughed.

'But, at the end of it all, someone has to be around to make the final decisions, not only as to who gets a kidney, but who gets even as far as being dialysed.'

'True,' she said, carefully.

'I'm sure that can't be easy at times.' Yousef was not going to let Maggie retire behind a defensive silence. He felt instinctively that she was an honest, caring person who would say nothing rather than tell a lie. 'And you do have to select your patients for dialysis, don't you?'

Maggie nodded. 'Unfortunately,' she smiled, sadly, 'it's not the sort of thing for which you can run up a waiting list.'

'And, if you do not have enough machines, you have to select?'

'Yes. I suppose the only answer is to have half a dozen machines in the corner surplus to requirement.' Yousef saw the wrinkles around the outer canthus of her eyes concertina in a smile, as if still squinting in tropical sunshine. 'Fat chance of that, of course, however hard we try. And we do,' Maggie added, passionately, 'we really do. Ask Rhys to show you the correspondence file.'

'I take it it all comes down to money in the end,' Yousef said.

'That's right. But we've got to be fair. Money is not unlimited. We tend to do well for a while if there's been some scandal and the media gets hold of it. But then they move on to something juicier and we tend to get forgotten again for a while. Some reporter finds that a couple of people have died waiting for coronary bypass surgery and that's in the news for a couple of weeks and those boys get a bigger slice of the cake for a while just to quieten things down. Then it will be the turn of spina bifida or the nursing of autistic children. Conditions in our Victorian mental hospitals, that's always a hardy annual if they can't find anything else. We just wait for our turn to come round again.'

'And, in the meanwhile, you are left with the problem of selection.'

'We share the load, really,' Maggie said. 'Some of them don't get as far as hospital; the GPs do the selection. Other times the General Physicians do it for us.'

'But, inevitably sooner or later, you would have to do some selection,' Yousef gently persisted.

'Yes,' Maggie admitted, 'that's got to be true. After all, they reckon about three and a half thousand people up and down the country get renal failure every year and only something over half of those get treated; there's no way you can escape those figures, though – ' she defended her Unit to the last – 'we have been very lucky here recently. It is some time now since we had to turn anyone down.'

'But, when you do, you have to find some excuse for doing so, am I right?'

Again Maggie nodded.

'What sort of excuses?'

'Oh,' Maggie shrugged her shoulders, 'age, I suppose is the commonest; diabetes, spina bifida, any multiple pathology.'

'Age, that's important?'

'As things stand at the moment, yes, I'm afraid it is.'

'So,' Yousef hesitated as if he were choosing his words more purposefully than before, 'what chance would, say, a man in his late sixties have of being put on the dialysis programme, let alone getting a transplant?'

Maggie got the feeling that all the previous discussion had been no more than a preamble to this last, strangely specific question. There was a puzzled frown on her face as she shrugged her shoulders philosophically. 'With the present shortage of machines, he would certainly be on the borderline; any older and he'd be very lucky to get a machine.'

'And the other end of the age scale? I've read of children in this country being turned down for dialysis because their parents were alcoholic or inadequate.'

'Not in this part of the world,' Maggie responded briskly but then lapsed into silence as they both stood still, almost as if in honour of those who had been turned away to die. Maggie looked at her watch.

'I'm off,' she said, stretching her back. 'Time for feet up and a cup of tea, I think. Care to join me?'

'Another time, perhaps, Maggie. I've promised to have a chat with Hannah.' Yousef nodded in the direction of the Urology Ward beyond the Unit.

'Ah, yes; Hannah.' The eyes twinkled behind the thick lenses once more. 'Seems to have a fatal attraction for the men, that young lady.'

'I promised to go back and see her,' Yousef explained.

'Yes, yes,' Maggie nodded, sagely.

'She's a very sick girl.'

'She certainly is that, Yousef,' Maggie became serious again. 'The sooner we get a kidney for her the better.'

'Why do you say that?'

'Well, we have some strange people on dialysis, as you can imagine. We even have one or two gypsies who live pretty rough, ride horses and so on. But Hannah; she's such a wild young thing, not just physically but spiritually. The sort of youngster who would choose to be either healthy or dead and would have no fear of facing the latter if need be. No; to my mind she's a non-runner as far as long-term dialysis is concerned. I don't think we'd ever get her out of hospital. I think you'll find that Rhys won't let her out of hospital, not for a day. Once out and I don't think we would ever see her again.'

'And what are the chances of a kidney?' Yousef asked.

Again the expressive shrugging of the shoulders that begged the question.

'Come on Maggie,' Yousef chided. 'No one else can hear you. You must have some idea.'

'Honestly, Yousef, I'd love to be able to answer your question, but it really is difficult. Kidneys are scarce these days and Hannah is, theoretically, on the end of a very long waiting list.'

'Theoretically?' Yousef raised an eyebrow but, this time, Maggie would say no more and Yousef was too polite to press her. 'When a kidney does turn up,' he asked, 'who decides who gets it?'

'Rhys, ultimately.'

'Just him?'

'More or less. Obviously it depends on the degree of match; he talks that over with the lab people. And then he often talks it over with us – ' she waved her hand in the Sister's direction ' – Sister and I know just about everyone on the dialysis programme around here now; certainly know them better than Rhys does. But, at the end of the day, if the kidney happens to match perhaps two or three patients equally, that's another unpleasant decision he has to make. Still, that hasn't happened yet as far as Hannah is concerned.' She looked at her watch again. 'We'll cross that hurdle when we come to it. See you in the morning, Yousef. I hope you enjoy your stay with us. Goodbye.'

Yousef walked briskly through the open door into Hannah's room, his mouth already shaping the words that he knew would be the first thrust in a verbal fencing match. Abruptly, he raised himself on his toes as he saw her sleeping. He tiptoed to the window-sill where he sat, his back to the early evening sun. For a while he sat and looked and marvelled at young beauty that transcended disease and the obscenity of the machine alongside her that alone kept her alive. Even in sleep, there was a firmness about her lower lip that kept her mouth in a determined curve. Not for Hannah the slack-mouthed gape of oblivion even when propped up on her pillows. Her pallid frailty as she lay between the white sheets contrasted with the strong black plaits of hair, one over each shoulder, which the nurses had tied with bows of white cotton bandage. He was just making a mental note to get her some ribbon when he saw her eyeballs begin to move beneath her pale lids as her arms and legs jerked erratically, making the plastic tubing dance and rattle. Her forehead furrowed and she gave a little cry.

'Hannah.' She did not wake when Yousef called her, so he stepped to the bed and gently shook her shoulder. 'Hannah.'

She woke, her eyes frightened and restless, and it took her a moment to recognise where she was and who was leaning over her. In an instant, her defences were up.

'What do you want? What are you doing here?'

'I've come to see you, as I promised.' Yousef went back to the window. 'You were having a nightmare.'

'I wasn't,' Hannah answered.

Yousef pointed to the machine. 'You're having a long session today; why's that? Have you been a bad girl again?'

'It's that Sister.' Hannah stuck her tongue out in the direction of the door. 'She's got it in for me.'

'I find that difficult to believe,' Yousef said.

'Yes, she has. She weighed me this morning and just because I had put on a couple of lousy pounds, she told me I had to have two hours extra today. That woman is a sadist.'

'No, she's not,' Yousef laughed.

'How d'you know? You've only been here a day. She'd suck up to you anyway. You should hear the nurses going on about you already. "Oh, isn't he nice," ' she mimicked. ' "Have you seen his car? And his clothes? Isn't he dishy?" They all want to know whether you're married or not.'

If, in reality, this had been an oblique attempt to find out for herself, it was not successful.

'And I don't suppose there's the slightest chance you've been fiddling the fluid intake?' Yousef pretended to look severe as he pinched his upper lip between finger and thumb.

'What's it like to have a moustache?'

Yousef's jaw dropped in surprise.

'Hannah, you really are the most extraordinary person – what do you mean?'

'Nothing. Just what's it like?' She twitched angrily at a stiff and aching arm.

'D'you mean to say you've never been kissed by a boy with a moustache?'

'Yuck. I hate men,' Hannah said, trying to eject from her memory the bristling chin rasping against her cheek as she had fought off Dai's drunken assault. 'Do all Arabs have moustaches?'

'No, of course not.'

'What do all Arabs do then?' She turned awkwardly on her right side, flicking one plait of hair over her shoulder with her free hand, fretting at her inability to see his face clearly against the low sun. Yousef detected a softening in her manner as if her illness was not the only thing that wearied her, as if she was feeling the strain of keeping everyone at bay, as if, behind that staunch defence, she longed for someone she could trust enough to share her thoughts. 'What I mean is, all Welshmen are meant to sing, all the Irish fight, all – ' she searched for a final example '– those little men in Switzerland make money. What do Arabs do? Dig up oil and get filthy rich, I suppose.'

'Some do,' Yousef agreed. 'Too much for their own good, some of them. What do all Arabs do?' He repeated Hannah's question slowly, his eyes closing slightly as he suddenly remembered what Clare Drury had told him about Hannah's injury. 'I thought everyone knew what all Arabs do; they capture beautiful young girls and carry them away into the desert on the backs of their Arab stallions.'

'Do you have an Arab stallion?' Hannah asked, dreamily, inviting him to lie if need be.

'No.'

'Oh,' Hannah pouted, disappointed.

'I've got a string of them,' Yousef laughed, enjoying the delight that burst on Hannah's face.

'You're kidding,' Hannah said, wide-eyed. 'You've got to be joking.'

'No, I'm not joking,' Yousef said, softly.

Hannah nestled her cheek into the pillow, pushing the thick cotton down so that she could still see Yousef. To Yousef she looked like a small child demanding a fairy story before going to sleep.

'A whole string of them?'

'Well, not all stallions, of course. Mostly mares. And they don't belong to me. They belong to the nation. We are very lucky in Shahin; we have a Sultan who loves horses. He calls them our only luxury. It is a national stud and he has made me responsible for it. In fact, one of the last things I did in the States was to buy a stallion and take him home with me.'

'And do you ride him?' Hannah asked, breathlessly.

'Whenever I have time.'

'What do you call him?'

'Damani.'

'That's a funny name.'

'It means gazelle. It's our word for a gazelle.'

'Is it fast?'

'It gallops like the wind. Not even the Saudis have a horse to catch it.'

'My Tempest would.'

For a while, Yousef managed to take Hannah away from smothering disability as she listened to him talk with a love and passion she understood. For the first time in months she forgot how ill she felt, became oblivious to the plastic tubes and hard mattress, as Yousef helped her dream about the only love she had ever felt she could safely bestow. Open-mouthed, she listened as Yousef told her of the five mares given to Mohammed by his followers from a breed that went back long before the birth of Christ. He talked of their stamina and intelligence and was extolling their fine, silky hair when Hannah broke in.

'Our Tempest is a thoroughbred, you know.'

'I'm sure he is, Hannah. And I wouldn't be a bit surprised that, if you went back far enough, you'd find some Arab in him somewhere; after all, they are thought to have been brought to this country in about the third century. Just think,' Yousef laughed, 'My Damani and your – what did you call him, Tempest? – they might be related from all those hundreds of years ago.'

'Would you like to see him?' Hannah asked, excitedly. 'I'm sure Dai wouldn't mind.'

Yousef did not get the chance to answer. Before he could do so, a nurse put her head around the door.

'Phone call for you, Mr Yousef.'

'For me?' Yousef looked surprised.

'Yes; in Sister's office. It's theatre.'

The head disappeared.

'Bitch.'

'Hannah, you mustn't speak like that.'

'Well, she is. D'you have to go?'

'Of course. But I'll come and see you tomorrow and you can tell me all about that rotten old horse of yours.'

'Promise?'

'Promise.'

Yousef left Hannah snuggling into her pillows, a small smile on her face as if she had a secret; as if now, suddenly, she had something to look forward to again. In Sister's office, Yousef found the internal telephone lying on the desk. He picked it up, the feel of the instrument and the sound of the voice it carried strange to him.

'Paddy Moore here, sir; theatre orderly. Dr Drury's compliments but would you be kind enough to come up to Main Theatre for a moment?'

'Of course, Paddy.' Again the easy, friendly use of the Christian name. 'What's the problem?'

'I wouldn't know exactly, sir, but I think she'd appreciate your opinion on something fairly urgently.'

'I'll be there in two minutes.'

Finding no lift waiting on the landing outside, Yousef ran up the stairs to the Theatre suite on the floor above. Without hesitation he pushed through the doors and headed for the changing room. He knew the layout now like the palm of his hand. Owen had operated all morning and most of the afternoon, Yousef spending most of the time looking over his shoulder. Both Clare Drury and the House Surgeon had acted as assistants and there had been no invitation to Yousef to scrub and help. He had found standing and watching more tiring than operating but it was not only to ease his aching back and legs that he had walked around the entire Theatre complex, looking into every room, seemingly interested in the view from every window, disarming any glances of surprise from the staff with a frank-faced smile. His opening of the door at the far end of the corridor and his few steps out on to the fire escape had drawn a frown of disapproval from a passing Sister.

In the changing room, he found Paddy Moore putting out some theatre clothes for him.

'Thank you, Paddy. That's very kind of you.'

'Sir.'

'Any real panic in there?'

'Not really, sir. I think she's just got herself a little bit out of her depth, if you know what I mean.' Paddy's face broke into the understanding smile of someone who has worked in theatre for a long time, someone who has seen it all before. 'Only just starting, you'll understand, Mr Yousef. Feeling a bit lost though she's trying her best not to show it.'

Yousef was still tying his mask as he crossed the theatre. He sensed the tension. Everyone was standing very still, saying nothing, as if whatever had been going on had ground to a halt. He walked up behind the House Surgeon to look over his shoulder at the patient and Clare Drury beyond. He saw her eyes appeal above her mask, imagined the anxious smile behind it, as she took a wet, bloodstained swab away from a small wound in a thin, loose-skinned abdomen.

'Spot of trouble, Dr Drury?' he asked, making it sound as light and as matter of fact as he could.

'Well, I don't think so.' Clare tried to make it sound as if she could have coped really if he had not been around but, seeing that he was . . . 'It's just that something has come up that I did not altogether expect.' She showed him the swab.

'What's the history?' Yousef asked.

'Old girl of eighty-two, two-day history of right-sided abdominal pain, nothing else. Always been very fit. Very tender with guarding in the RIF. Slight temperature. I know she was a bit old but, I must say, I thought she had a classical appendix.'

With nothing but friendliness in his voice, Yousef said, 'And now you're learning, very early in your career, that there is no such thing. What exactly have you found?'

'Well, nothing.' There was now a slight tremble in her voice. Probably she would have been able to control it better if Yousef had been sarcastic or arrogant. 'Just this.' Clare held the swab nearer to him.

He looked at it carefully, sniffed at it. 'That looks like infarction to me. There's got to be something gangrenous in there. That's not fresh bleeding.'

'Her appendix is normal,' Clare said, trying to feel that she was still contributing something.

'No chance she's obstructed?'

Clare shook her head. 'She's hardly vomited and her X-ray doesn't look obstructed.'

'Bit old for twisted ovarian cyst,' Yousef mused and was careful to make his next question sound like a joke, 'and I'm sure you've looked for a strangulated femoral hernia?'

Clare smiled as she nodded.

'And that's a MacBurney incision, obviously.' Yousef said.

'Yes.'

'Hm.' Yousef looked at troubled grey eyes. 'She needs a paramedian, doesn't she? Have you ever done a paramedian?'

'No.'

'Would you like me to give you a hand with one?'

'Yes, please.'

Two syllables were enough to convey the note of relief. By the time Yousef returned to the table, scrubbed and gowned, the House Surgeon had disappeared and Clare had taken his place. As he pulled on his gloves, Yousef gave the anonymous nurse a friendly nod before turning to the anaesthetist.

'How is she?'

'This is Dr Kumar, Yousef; Anaesthetic Registrar,' Clare interrupted.

'Hi,' Yousef said, brightly. 'Is she all right?'

'She is well, thank you. Very tough old lady. These stringy ones often are.' A pair of dark eyes smiled from behind gold-rimmed glasses. 'I am not worrying about her.'

Yousef turned his attention back to the patient's abdomen. With his right index finger he poked up, down and across through the small opening Clare had made. He shook his head and made another, longer, vertical incision near the midline. With gentle assurance, he removed the excess fluid and traced the length of her bowel.

'Zilch.'

The word echoed strangely in a British operating theatre. He put his hand in the patient's pelvis.

'Nope; nothing there either. Very strange. You certainly know how to pick them, don't you, Dr Drury?'

And Clare began to feel a little better.

His hand was searching the upper abdomen when a look of surprise lit his face. 'Well, I'm damned,' he muttered.

'What's that?' Clare asked.

'Just look at that.' Yousef produced a black, rounded sausage in the palm of his hand as if slowly disclosing a small, defenceless animal to a child. 'Would you believe that? A gall bladder.'

'I can see it's a gall bladder but what's wrong with it?' There were puzzled creases in the skin around Clare's mask.

'It's gangrenous due to torsion. I've only ever seen one before. How about that?'

'What are you going to do?' Clare asked.

'Take it out; at least you're going to take it out.'

'Me?' Clare's voice rose in surprise and sudden anxiety.

'Yes, you,' Yousef laughed.

'But I can hardly take out an appendix yet. I can't do a cholecystectomy.'

But Yousef was already halfway round the table to swap places. 'Don't worry; you'll be surprised,' he said.

Clare crossed to where she had stood originally and Yousef took up the role of assistant. Gently, coaxing Clare into tentative, cautious manipulation, he got her to look closely at the gall bladder, see which way it was twisted and to carefully untwist it until it hung free on the end of the long fold of tissue that held it to the undersurface of the liver. He explained to her that it was this long fold that had made the twist possible and that, although a rarity, it was commonest in old, thin, visceroptotic women. He showed her where the twist had caught up the artery to the gall bladder, blocking it and causing the gall badder to become gangrenous.

'Like I told you, it's now probably the easiest cholecystectomy you'll ever do,' Yousef said encouragingly as Clare took up the scissors. He showed great patience in the next twenty minutes in helping her perform an operation he could have done in five. He taught her where to look for and identify the bile duct and showed her the safest method of tying off the artery even though he knew it was already blocked. Oversewing the cut edge of the suspensory fold was simplicity itself. Clare sighed deeply as if she had held her breath for the last twenty minutes.

'Yousef, that was smashing. Thank you so much.'

'My pleasure, ma'am.'

He stayed to help her close both wounds, leaving a drain in the smaller incision, but left her to suture the skin herself. He was sprawling in a chair but sat more upright as Clare came into the Surgeons' Sitting Room. He looked at her admiringly. She had that sort of figure that made her theatre clothes, taken at random from a pile, look like *haute couture*. Even so, there were wet stains under both armpits and the hair that tumbled as she pulled off her theatre cap was streaked with sweat.

'I'm most grateful, Yousef; I really am.'

He raised one arm. 'You're welcome, Clare. Only too glad to help. There you are; you can now tell everyone you've done your first gall bladder.'

'I don't imagine they're all quite as easy as that.'

'Not exactly, no,' he smiled.

They both looked up to see Paddy Moore standing at the door.

'Cup of tea, Dr Drury?'

'Thought you'd never ask, Paddy.'

'And you, Mr Yousef?' There was undisguised respect in Paddy's manner now.

'I guess so, Paddy. I imagine if I don't get to like tea, I could die of thirst in this country quicker than in the desert.'

When Paddy was out of earshot, Clare looked anxiously at Yousef.

'How do I explain the two incisions to the patient? What if she asks?'

'My dear girl, that is not the last time you or I will do that. It's a calculated risk you were taking in the patient's interest. She probably won't ask but, if she does, tell her you had to make that hole to put the drain in. You'd have had to put a drain in anyway. Don't worry about it.'

The light was failing when the night staff arrived to find Clare and Yousef still sitting, quietly sharing an empathy not entirely arising from a common love of surgery. Yousef helped restore Clare's confidence with stories of his own frightening mishaps when he was beginning, reassuring her that it was a stage that all surgeons had been through. He told her that surgery would become a drug of addiction to her, that one moment she would be giving it all up and then, the immediate crisis over, she would experience that blissful feeling of having two feet on the ground after being convinced she was certain to drown.

'It's better than making love,' he said, looking straight at her.

'There, sir, you have the advantage of me,' she retorted, smiling, but was unable to hold his stare.

'Charming,' Yousef murmured.

'What's that?' Clare asked.

'I was just wondering how long it was since I saw a beautiful girl blush. You just don't see it these days.'

He laughed delightedly as the blush only deepened.

They were tired and Clare felt her dress clinging to her back. She felt a wreck but she was in no hurry to leave. She was fascinated by his hands, restlessly playing with a pen, slim and fine-boned but, unlike similar hands in a Westerner, with their backs covered in a mat of fine, black hair. Yousef was so easy to talk to. She knew that, if it had been Patel who had come to her rescue, he would have done the operation himself and would have been too reserved to stay and talk afterwards. He would have politely left her to feel a failure. Even if Patel had stayed, she doubted whether she would have sat there so long in that cold wet dress.

Yousef smiled to himself too as he wondered if he would be taking so much trouble over this surgical ingénue if she were not a beautiful, fair English girl but some hairy, male graduate from Athens or Cairo.

'Are you married, Yousef?'

They had reached that degree of rapport that rendered the question free from invasive curiosity.

'Yes, I am.'

'Is your wife over with you?'

'No, she's still in the States.'

'And d'you have any children?'

Across the dimly lit room, Clare could see the shadow cross Yousef's face.

'Yes. Two.'

'I'm sorry, Yousef. It's no business of mine but I got the impression that you live in the Middle East now.'

'That's quite true, Clare. My family is still in Charlotte and I now live in Shahin.' He waved his hand as he saw Clare begin to protest once more. 'I would feel happier if you knew, Clare. I intend to spend the rest of my days in Shahin. I could never go back to work in the States now – Shahin is now my home. But my wife wouldn't stay – she's an American – says she couldn't face bringing the children up there, but I don't think she would stay anyway. And I can see her point. I don't hold it against her for a moment. And so –' he moved his hands in a gesture of helplessness as he paused. '– we're not divorced, not legally separated, we're – ' he hesitated ' – just apart.'

'I'm sorry, Yousef,' Clare said, softly. 'You must love your country very much to make that sort of sacrifice for it.'

And Yousef's reply had the resonance of some religious oath.

'I do.'

10

It was towards the end of a ward round that Owen received the phone call. Usually the tour of his patients would have been over some time before but he was luxuriating in the atmosphere that now surrounded his firm. He was enjoying sharpening his surgical wits against the young, agile brain of someone who was already very experienced. Yousef had, politely and deferentially, manoeuvred him into corners with his arguments, making Owen reconsider basic concepts of his daily practice that he had come to think of as sacrosanct. Yousef had revitalised him, made him enthusiastic again about a discipline that was in danger of becoming humdrum. It only added to the alacrity with which he drove to hospital, more than happy to exchange the scratchy boredom of his home life for the challenging excitement that Yousef had brought with him. Owen was already regretting the short time that Yousef would be with them; he would be loath to see him go.

It had occurred to Owen that, for someone who had come to study how to set up a Dialysis Unit, Yousef seemed somewhat disinterested. It was true that Maggie had told him that Yousef had spent the day with her. It was equally true that Yousef had discussed with him some of the administrative and financial problems of setting up such a unit but there had been none of the fire and enthusiasm he showed when arguing out some general surgical problem. But there had been no doubting Yousef's enthusiasm when Owen had carried out a renal transplant late the night before. There had been no controlling the look of appeal on Yousef's face which Clare had seen, and she offered him the chance of being first assistant.

During the operation, he had honoured Owen's concentration and kept silent except for the few inevitable and essential muttered sentences; but, afterwards, obviously impressed by what he had seen, Yousef's questions had been quickfire and pertinent, never argumentative; almost as if they had been rehearsed for just such an occasion. They had talked until the early hours but Owen, calling to see the patient the next morning before beginning his formal ward round, had found Yousef, as immaculately shaved and dressed as ever, hovering around the bedside, taking blood, searching anxiously in the bottle for those cherished drops of urine.

What Owen was probably enjoying most, however, was his patriarchal role. He took great pleasure from being in the company of such wholesome young people. It was made all the more pleasurable by the obvious respect they paid him, even Yousef who had known him for so short a time, something he felt no longer existed in his real family life. On the other hand, he would have happily given up his role of revered elder to be transported back in time, to become one of them again. With a heart-aching pang he realised that no longer now, with any stretch of the imagination, could he consider himself one of them. A few years earlier and he might have got away with the idea that they were younger contemporaries, but not now. A generation gap seemed to have appeared overnight. Had he been in Avonport so long? He now looked at them more as gifted children, clustered about him around a patient's bed or operating table. Alun Jones was not going to scale any great academic heights but he was an honest, cheerful, good-looking youngster. As to Clare and Yousef, it did not require Owen's considerable degree of sensitivity to detect how close they had become. It warmed his heart to see the pair, so elegantly similar, so culturally different, as they talked, so intent on each other at times as to be oblivious to his presence.

The message that Owen was wanted on the phone was delivered to him with all due protocol. The nurse who brought the message would not have dreamed of speaking to Owen direct. Her whispered message to Sister Vaughan was transmitted to Owen during the next gap in his discussion on the diagnosis of the acute abdomen with Clare. When Owen picked up the phone, the GP on the other end did not have to identify himself; it could only be one person with that soft, almost breathless Hebridean accent. Like so many of his compatriots, Ian Stuart had come down to the South

Wales valleys in the mid-thirties when times for a lowly paid assistant in General Practice were almost as hard as for those in the community they served. He had married the local chemist's daughter and had stayed, childless, to outlive all his contemporaries. Now, well into his seventies, his practice had dwindled to an aged but devoted few, still happy to slide sideways along a hard bench surrounding the damp-walled waiting room, their only appointment system being the ping of a desk-top bell.

'Good morning, Dr Stuart. What can I do for you?' Owen asked, brightly. He had a soft spot for this gentle, erudite old man who now never ventured beyond the valley of his adoption.

Owen, his face screwed up in concentration, had to place his finger in his other ear to shut out the ambient sounds in his attempt to hear what Dr Stuart was saying. He caught a few words here and there – 'nice old fellow' – 'not diabetic' – 'awful lot of pain'. From experience he knew it would be fruitless to ask him to speak up; that, within seconds, the voice would be almost inaudible again. A couple of infuriating searches along steeply inclined streets in slanting rain had taught him the importance of writing down the address correctly – trivia such as the patient's name or diagnosis, he would find out for himself – and he asked Dr Stuart to repeat the address a little louder.

'9 Balaclava Crescent? All right, Dr Stuart, leave it to me. I'll go and see him on the way home this evening.'

To get to Balaclava Crescent, Owen drove down to the roundabout below the hospital and along the coast road and promenade towards the centre of Avonport. There was no other way to go – except for the golf club meandering amongst the dunes beyond Druid's Common, the coast road ended at St David's. He turned left into the straggling shopping centre with its disparate windows and patchy renovation. He headed north under the ugly, stained concrete supports of the long flyover that carried the main east–west dual carriageway. Another two miles and he was already funnelling into the cleft of a narrow valley, streets climbing away steeply on either side from the one main road to divide and subdivide amongst the terraced houses that traversed the lower mountainside.

All seventy-four houses of Balaclava Crescent stretched in a row, as straight as a die, at the foot of Mynydd Bychan. The steep gradient of Incline Row had brought a growl out of the Saab and the engine note fell as it turned into the Crescent, Owen, one arm and shoulder out of the window, struggling to read the numbers on the doors. His task was made easier by the fact that there were houses on one side only. On the other side only a children's park separated Balaclava Crescent from the rocky, bracken-mottled barrenness of the mountainside. He found number nine near the far end, where the houses stopped short of the tipping system of the old Pentre colliery. The pylons, cables and buckets had gone, as had the Pentre itself, now just a flattened out area in an obscure Welsh valley hoping to catch the eye of some Tokyo industrialist, but the tip was still there, a menacing black keloid scar, too big to grass over, too small to demand removal. Owen's Saab looked incongruous amongst the other cars parked irregularly along the gutter. He turned the engine off and looked at the playground, its grass being both cropped and fertilised by a few tattered mountain sheep, its paths no more than tracks worn bare black by generations of children's feet. He saw the swings, the slide, the carousel, and smiled quickly at a smell instantly recalled. He heard again the frightening confusion of a ring of untidy children holding hands, shouting 'Fight, fight', remembered vividly the first occasion in his life when faced with something he knew he must not run away from, felt again the numbing pain of a bully's knuckles, tasted once more the bloodied nose.

In two strides Owen crossed the front garden demarcated by a low stone wall bearing the stumps of the wrought-iron fence that had gone to make a Churchill tank. The front door, separated from its right-hand neighbour by no more than a column of faced stonework, was open. He stepped into the tiny hall and tapped on the inner door with its Prince of Wales feathers etched into the frosted glass panel. There was no answer. He turned the knob, opened the door and, hesitantly, pushed his head and shoulders through.

'Hello.'

This time there was a faint response from somewhere within the shadowy interior. Owen walked in and closed the door behind him. 'Hello,' he said again as he poked his head into the first door on the left, only to be glared at by huge faded pictures of Gladstone and Disraeli hanging guard over a gleaming harmonium. The next door was closed. Owen tapped on it and opened it to be enveloped in a billow of hot air pungent with tobacco smoke.

'Come in, doctor *bach*. Come and sit down.'

Before sitting down, Owen crossed to shake the hand of the old man sitting to one side of the fire.

'I'm Mr Owen. I'm a surgeon from the hospital. Dr Stuart has asked me to call and see you.'

The old man smiled and nodded. He pointed with his pipe to the seat on the other side of the fire and then went back to puffing and staring intently at the coal that glowed red through the steel bars. As Owen sank into the old armchair, he heard and felt the layers of old newspaper covering the broken springs beneath the thinned out cushion. On the wall above the old man's head hung a trophy case enclosing a faded red jersey and a velvet cap, its piping ravelled and tarnished.

Owen sat back, enjoying for a moment the warm peace. He looked at the old man who seemed totally unembarrassed by his presence and in no hurry to talk, almost as if he would be grateful if Owen did no more than just sit there. To someone who did not know the community, the old man's reticence would have seemed awkward, even ill-mannered. But to Owen, all the clues were there to be seen or heard, the blue-black coal scars on the back of the hand that held the pipe, the gash across the forehead tattooed in coal dust, the forced expiration and the wheezing he could hear across the room. The man did not have enough breath for more than a few words at a time. Owen saw the right leg, thin through the trousers of an old pin-striped suit that had once been Sunday best, propped on a low stool in front of the fire. The foot was covered in a woollen slipper, a bandaged big toe protruding from a hole cut in it. It was a picture he had seen only too often. He knew exactly what was to be found under that bandage. He leaned forward, taking a pen and small filing card from his inside pocket.

'We'd better start from the beginning,' he smiled. 'What's your name?'

'I'm not deaf, doctor,' the man said quietly without reproof.

'I'm sorry.' Owen felt he should have learned by now; not all quiet old people are deaf. The man had gone back to contemplating the fire and Owen had to repeat the question to get an answer.

'Morish; one r and an h,' the old man added as if anticipating the inevitable.

'And your Christian name, Mr Morish?'

'Stanley; Stanley Mametz.'

'Mametz,' Owen repeated. 'That's interesting.'

The man nodded and smiled but put his pipe back in his mouth as if that was enough for the moment, and he was slow to remove it when Owen asked him his age.

'If I'm spared until the autumn, I'll be sixty-nine, doctor.'

Owen looked at the thin white hair and thought he looked eighty. 'And what's the trouble?' he asked, appreciating the stupidity of the question.

Again the pipe was used as a pointer. 'Toe,' he said. 'Very painful.' He nodded wisely as if he was sure Owen would understand.

'Any trouble with the other foot?' Owen asked.

'No. Bit cold in the night, you know.' He began to smile but the unusual amount of talking brought on a fit of coughing that shook him mercilessly for a while. When the spasm was over, the old man gave him the rest of the smile the coughing had interrupted.

'Let's have a look at it then, shall we?'

All the old man could do to help was to lift his foot off the stool briefly as Owen removed the slipper and bandage. For him, lying or bending down were things of the past. A shiny, hairless foot was revealed, blotches on the skin the colour of boiled lobster, the black of the patch on his big toe surrounded by fiery red. Owen made a show of feeling for the pulses at the ankle. He tried to replace the bandage and was making a mess of it when he looked up to see the old man grinning at him.

'Never could put a bandage on,' Owen admitted and was rewarded for his honesty with a wheezing laugh that ended in another bout of coughing. Owen sat back in his chair and they contemplated each other, Owen feeling a comfortable empathy he would never have experienced in a private consultation with some puffed-up local industrialist or cash-paying tax dodger.

'What are we going to do with you, then?' Owen asked.

Morish shook his head as if he did not know, then, with a grin, put his head back and drew the stem of his pipe across his throat like a knife.

'I don't think we need go quite as far as that yet,' Owen laughed. He looked around the room, saw the fruit on the sideboard, the daily papers piled beside the fire, the scuttle full of coal. The softwood table had been scrubbed spotless. 'Who looks after you?'

'Daughter. Good gel,' and again the knowing shake of the head. He looked at the clock ticking his life away on the mantelpiece. 'Should be home soon.'

'I really would like to have a word with her,' Owen said, rising half out of his chair. 'Perhaps she could . . . '

Without knowing why, he stopped, then sank back into the uncomfortable chair, suddenly feeling at peace. For a few moments, he said nothing while Morish returned to his quiet contemplation as if he were much more inclined to have Owen's quiet company than any decision about his foot.

'That your jersey?' Owen asked, pointing to the cabinet on the wall.

Morish took the pipe from his mouth and turned his head briefly as if to confirm which jersey it was that Owen was talking about. He nodded and there was pride in the curve of his lip as he bit on his pipe once more.

'When was that?' Owen asked.

'Just before the war.'

'At the Arms Park?'

Morish nodded.

'What position did you play?'

'Prop.'

'How many caps did you get?'

The only answer Owen got was a bubbling laugh and a raised index finger.

'And I didn't quite finish that,' he said. 'Broke my ankle five minutes before time. Never played again.'

'That would have been – ' Owen paused, thoughtfully '– let me see. That would have been in the days of Tanner and Vivian Jenkins. Windsor Lewis; was he still playing then?'

'Played against them all,' Morish said, proudly, 'except they were the toffs, of course.' He laughed. 'The backs were mostly the college boys, not like us donkeys up front. But good boys, yes; good boys, all of them. I was tackled by Claude Davey once,' he added, as if describing how he had been blessed by the Pope.

They were still comparing modern rugby with the old man's era when they heard the kitchen door open and felt a bustling atmosphere replace the murmuring tranquillity. Owen stood up as the cause of the transition hurried into the room. He saw the dark hair, the high-necked jumper under the navy ski jacket, the single gold chain around her neck, but it was only when he saw the amusement in the brown eyes and the softness of the mouth that he recognised her. He had never seen Nansi Rees out of uniform before.

'You?' he said in astonishment.

'Yes, me, Mr Owen,' she replied, mimicking his surprise. 'I'm sorry I wasn't here when you arrived but I missed the bus and had to wait for the next.'

'But . . .' Rhys simply waved in Morish's direction as he sat down once more.

'My father, Mr Owen.' She took her jacket off and threw it on the table. She crossed to stand behind her father's chair, his face softening as she stroked his hair. 'Yes, this is my old nuisance, aren't you, Dad?' The old man's face beamed. 'I don't know who's more trouble, this one in here or those two in there.' She nodded at the wall and Owen simply looked puzzled. 'I've got one old child in here and two young ones in there.' Again she nodded at the wall. 'I live next door, Mr Owen.'

'I see,' Owen said.

'He's no trouble really,' Nansi said, now kneeling between them in front of the fire, rearranging the bandage with a few skilled movements. Rhys felt an intense impulse to put his hand on her head, to smooth the thick, dark hair where it fell forwards to cover both cheeks. She looked up and laughed at the expression on Owen's face, totally misinterpreting it. 'I know, I know, Mr Owen. There's no need to look so disapproving. Perhaps we can have a chat about that toe later.'

She stood up, straightening her tight jumper, and amused wrinkles appeared around her eyes as she saw Rhys's confusion as he struggled to look anywhere but at her thrusting breasts. She had sensed already while at work, that she was getting to him behind that apparently emotionless calm. Now, in the warm, un-uniformed proximity, she knew she had not been mistaken. She knew that, given the right circumstances, she could, with a few soft words, a few gentle touches of lips and hands, brush that facade aside and find herself overwhelmed by what she was sure she would release. And a surge of pleasurable longing brought a flush to her face and neck as there dawned in her mind the certainty that it was going to happen.

'I usually make a cup of tea for Dad about this time, Mr Owen, before I make the children's tea; you'll stay and have one with us, won't you?' The appeal in Nansi's voice was augmented by that in her father's face as he paused in knocking out his pipe against the bars of the fire.

'I'd love one,' Rhys said, sitting up, 'but I must take my jacket off. I find it rather warm in here.'

'Dad feels the cold, don't you, *cariad*?' She turned towards her father. 'Like your fire all the year round, don't you?'

As Nansi busied herself making the tea in the kitchen, the two men reverted to talking rugby but, as the older man, with long pauses between short sentences, spoke of the rugby played by men in long baggy trousers and short haircuts, Owen's mind wandered to picture Nansi relaying a fire every day of the year, coping with an invalid father and two young children while holding down a full-time job. All he had ever seen was the bright, warm-hearted nurse, never wondering what happened to her outside the hospital. He had never visualised this warm, loving atmosphere, never thought of Nansi as the provider. There had been no mention of a husband.

Owen was asking Morish just how he had broken his ankle, which hospital he had gone to, how it had been splinted, when Nansi came back into the room for a moment, swirling boiling water round a large brown teapot.

'It's my mother you should have talked to about that, Mr Owen,' she said, anger in her voice. 'She'd have told you a different tale. There's no need to look like that,' she said to her father who was shaking his head apologetically to Owen. 'You tell him what really happened. You tell him about the three months off work with no money coming into the house.

And where were your fine rugby friends then, eh? Big hero when you got your cap, weren't you? All over you in that club, weren't they? And what happened afterwards?'

She gave a snort and disappeared into the kitchen again.

'Don't understand,' the old man winked.

'Understand.' The word echoed from the kitchen as Owen heard the teapot being emptied violently into the sink.

Rhys thought it diplomatic to change the subject when Nansi came back in, carrying a tray.

'I was interested in your father's Christian name.' He could hardly call her Staff Nurse in her own home. 'There are quite a few Verduns round here, I've even had a Mons and an Ypres, but never a Mametz before. I imagine that was Mametz Wood?'

'That's right, Mr Owen. Dad's eldest brother, Stanley, was killed on the Somme in 1916. That's right, isn't it, Dad?'

Her father nodded through the clouds of smoke as he relit his pipe. '9th RWF. Good regiment. Lost a lot of good boys; aye, indeed.' He went back to staring into the fire as Owen and Nansi inevitably reverted to hospital gossip, about Hannah's tantrums, the handsome new American Registrar and was there going to be a romance between him and Dr Drury.

It was with true reluctance that Owen got up to leave. The subdued, intimate conversation in the warmth of the fire had lulled him to the point that he was in danger of putting his head back and falling asleep.

'I must go.' He shook the old man's hand. 'I'll come and see you again shortly.'

'Thank you, doctor,' Morish replied with no reference to the pain that still pierced his foot. He politely chose not to notice Owen's semaphore to Nansi that he would like a word with her outside. In the tiny hall, they stood so close as to embarrass Owen and, on the doorstep, they could imagine the neighbours' curtains twitching.

'Come in the car a moment.'

As the doors slammed behind them, they turned on their shoulders to face each other. As they did so, a squall of rain lashed the windows with tropical suddenness.

'Now then, Staff Nurse Nansi Rees.' Rhys tried to look severe, but even mock severity was difficult with lips like that so close.

Nansi laughed and put her hands up. 'All right, I know, I know. It's all wrong, what I'm doing for Dad. But, really Mr Owen, what else am I to do?'

'You know perfectly well you should stop him smoking like that. That's the first thing you should do, especially with that chest of his. And then that foot, cooking it in front of the fire like that, with that thick slipper on.'

'I can't stop him smoking, love him,' Nansi said, softly. 'It's the only thing he's got left in life and he can't be with us much longer, can he?' Her eyes filled up as she saw Rhys nod. 'I give him whisky as much as I can afford but he's been very lonely since my mother died. You're not thinking of doing anything about it, are you?' She looked anxiously at Rhys.

'No. Taking his toe off wouldn't help; it wouldn't heal and any other amputation would mean above the knee and his chest wouldn't stand that.' Rhys saw her lower lip tremble. 'We'll take him in if it gets too difficult for you.'

Nansi shook her head violently, unable to speak for a moment.

'Why don't you move him in with you?' Rhys asked. 'Surely that would be much easier for you?'

'No. He'll die besides his own fireplace; that's the least I can do for him. He hardly goes to bed, poor dab, he's in so much pain. Just sits in that chair. He's no trouble really.'

She laid her head back against the seat and closed her eyes as if sinking into the comfort and security of another world, a world she knew she would have to leave in a few speeding minutes. For a few delicious moments there was no grinding routine of laying fires, making breakfasts, meeting school bus deadlines, staying cheerful for others' benefit, toiling up Incline Row with her supermarket yoke. Rhys was happy to sit and gaze at a smooth, rounded cheek and inviting lips. He saw her eyes open and the humorous, worldly smile return as she ran her finger down the steaming window.

'I bet everyone's wondering what's going on in here,' she laughed. 'If I don't go soon, Mr Owen, you'll have to marry me.'

Rhys laughed with her as she made the opening for the question that hung in his mind.

'And what about your husband; what would he say to that?'

'My Iestyn? I don't think he'd mind. Very keen fisherman, was my Iestyn. Two years ago, he and a mate of his went out fishing one evening in a small boat off the Mumbles and were never seen again, Iestyn, his friend or the boat. Seems the tide was very strong and they think they probably capsized. Seemed funny somehow; we didn't even have a funeral.' She laughed bravely at the sadness on Owen's face. 'With two kids under ten, you don't think I'd go out to work, do you, if I had an old man to kick out of bed in the morning?'

'But how do you manage? I mean, the two children, your father?'

'Well, the answer is that I couldn't if it wasn't for the job on the Unit. I couldn't do it if I was still working in Theatre as I used to. We lived in Swansea and I was a Theatre Sister in Singleton up until my Iestyn was drowned,' she explained. 'It's been a godsend, having the weekends free. I take all my holidays during the school holidays and I have a sister married to a farmer in Brecon who takes them for weeks at a time in the summer. We manage. But the main thing is living in a street like this. They're as nosy as hell – they will have got you and your car down to the last detail already – but there's one blessing; I know no harm will ever come to the kids if I'm ever late. They can walk into any one of these houses as if it was a second home.' She fell silent for a moment. 'That's not to say I wouldn't like to get away at times – just for a short while.' The brisk, cheerful manner returned. 'I'd better go if I don't want to be hauled up in front of the Deacons on Sunday,' she laughed, 'sitting in a car with a stranger for so long – and in broad daylight too.'

And Rhys could find no excuse to make her stay.

It took him some time to turn the car in the narrow road after Nansi had got out, running to find shelter in the porch against the rain which had now settled into a steady drizzle. He leaned forwards to wave to her through the misted windscreen. He drove home slowly, feeling the emptiness of the still warm seat alongside him.

11

Rhys tried to reverse the Saab into the space but it just wouldn't go. He heard Alex's cluck of annoyance alongside him. When he had failed to get into the previous space, she had told him they should have brought her car.

'Would you like to get out here and go in, while I find somewhere to park?' he asked.

Alex's reply was a tight-lipped shake of her head. Rhys pulled out again, uncomfortable in what he called his Sunday suit. He had actually got as far as putting his sports jacket on when Alex had seen him and exploded.

'I'm not going with you in that.'

With bad grace he had changed, chafing at the thought that he did not have the guts to stick to his guns.

He hated these Sunday lunchtime drinks. Some he hated more than others. The one he hated most was Johnnie Johnson's. They were involved in a rota of such parties where most sighed with relief when their turn was over and they could relax for a couple of months, until the same group of people descended on them again, greeting each other as if they had not seen each other for years. Johnnie was the exception, enjoying his own parties, holding at least two to Rhys's one, apart, that is, from those to which Alex and Rhys were not invited.

After Johnnie had been on the Staff at Avonport for a short while, it came as no shock to his new colleagues to discover that he had married money. They had bought the Old Rectory in a small village in the Vale of Glamorgan, with long windows down to ground level and opening on to rolling lawns and a tennis court, the swimming pool discreetly hidden behind the old house in the privacy of the walled garden. A long drive wound past the tennis court. Even so, by the time Alex and Rhys arrived, the parked cars, which included one chauffeur-driven Rolls, extended out into the lane. When Rhys finally parked his car and they walked back to the house, there was mud on their shoes.

Clarissa Johnson seemed to have the knack of circulating brightly round all the groups in the huge, high-ceilinged dining and drawing rooms and yet always being on hand to welcome her guests in the hall, her clear, incisive voice echoing amongst the antique mahogany. Rhys wondered whether they had taught the art formally at Cheltenham. Rhys was very fond of Clarissa. Beneath that shell of elegant triviality, Rhys sensed an honest, hard-headed woman whose intelligence was wasted in the sort of life she gave every impression of enjoying.

Rhys was still wiping the mud off his heels while Alex and Clarissa exchanged pecks. Alex stood back and watched as Rhys walked into Clarissa's outstretched arms.

'Good morning, Clarry.'

'Rhys.' Clarissa's voice rang out as her arms enfolded him and Rhys changed his mind; he was glad he had come. Rhys was the sort of man hostesses seemed compelled to hug. He had been enveloped in blousy softness, seeing at close quarters layers of makeup and eye shadow that only accentuated the thick-skinned wrinkles, and he had also felt, from pressures applied by more lissom frames, those subtle invitations to what was available.

But Rhys knew he had nothing to fear in Clarry's embrace and didn't shrink from the firm friendliness of her body hug. They stood back and looked at each other.

'Clarry, you look as gorgeous as ever,' Rhys smiled.

'And you look as sexy as ever, you old devil,' Clarry answered. 'How do you do it?' She turned in Alex's direction. 'You'd better watch out, Alex. That's one hell of a sexy husband you've got there. I give you fair warning, you'd better not leave him alone with me too often.'

'Promises, promises,' Rhys laughed as Clarry's quick eye detected strain in Alex's smile.

'Press on and get yourself a drink,' Clarry said as she directed them towards the drawing room, 'while I see who this is coming in. I think you know just about everyone.'

At the door to the drawing room there stood a man in a short white coat, a silver salver supporting glasses of champagne in his hand. Alex took a glass without looking at him and walked into the room beyond. Rhys screwed up his face apologetically.

'Any chance of a beer?' he asked.

If the man felt any irritation, he had been trained not to show it.

'Yes, of course, sir. It may take a moment but I'll bring it in to you.'

Rhys smiled his thanks and passed on, feeling as much as hearing the noise he had come to hate more than any other. He fought down the spasm of horror that the sound of a room packed with drinkers still stimulated in him. A few heads turned momentarily towards him but none stayed to welcome him. He saw Alex, talking vivaciously, appearing to have picked up the tempo of the party almost immediately. He wandered hesitantly into the centre of the room, feeling awkward without a drink in his hand, adrift in the sea of banality that swirled and eddied around the groups. He met Paul Hattersby coming in the opposite direction. A big, solid man, his florid features set in a broad, understanding smile, Hattersby was Avonport's senior Consultant Pathologist. Born and bred in West Wales, he had two passions, pathology and fishing, and Rhys was surprised to see him there and not in his cottage on the banks of his beloved Teifi.

'Morning, Paul. What the hell are you doing here?' Hattersby looked relieved to find a soul-mate in this inane crowd who seemed to know very little about either pathology or fishing. 'I thought you'd be down west this weekend.'

Hattersby grinned ruefully.

'Seems I overdid it a bit last weekend. Couldn't get a family exeat this week. Actually, it's not a bad time to store up a bit of credit. Water's very low at the moment and I didn't get a bite last weekend.' He saw the drink that Rhys was handed and asked if he, too, could have a beer. 'And how are things with you?'

'Fine, thanks, Paul.'

'That uraemic girl you operated on a week or so ago, the one with the ruptured kidney – ' they slipped into talking shop as effortlessly as a good driver changing gear ' – that was interesting, wasn't it? How's she doing?'

'She's better,' Rhys answered.

'Amazing. Perhaps you don't know, but the boys in Biochem keep a sort of Guinness Book of Records – highest and lowest levels and things like that – and that girl had the highest urea and creatinine in anyone who has survived so far. Did you see the blood chemistry when she came in? – ' he did not give Rhys a chance to answer ' – yes of course you did. Isn't it amazing how the level of consciousness . . .'

For a moment, Rhys was happy to let Hattersby ramble on enthusiastically as he suddenly took notice of Alex. He was surprised at a small, cold ache that gnawed in his chest, enough to cause a pinching up of his eyes and cheeks. Alex was standing in the adjoining group but, even so, he could not hear what she was saying above the clamouring voices around. Alex was always an animated talker at these affairs, she could hold her own with anyone, but, this time, there was a difference. It was so obvious to Rhys that he even looked around, slightly anxious, to see if anyone else was watching her, but everyone seemed vociferously unaware. He looked at Alex again, mumbling something as he did so just to keep Hattersby talking, and saw her – a word kept surfacing in his brain which he could not bring himself to use, it sounded so trite – saw her glow. She looked radiant. It was more than a flush; the glass in Alex's hand was empty but Rhys knew she would have drunk very little. It wasn't anger or irritation; he'd seen that often enough to be able to recognise it instantly. It had to be excitement that had produced that look, an excitement he had never seen in her before. Her eyes did not waver from someone opposite her, someone Rhys couldn't see from where he was standing, and, as she listened to whatever that person was saying, her mouth, usually so resolutely firm, was softer, more appealing.

'Did you get my report on the kidney?' Rhys had to bring his attention back to Hattersby who was stretching out both hands to accept his beer. 'Or what was left of it, perhaps I should say.' Hattersby paused to drain a third of his tankard in large, forthright gulps. 'That's better. As I said, there wasn't much left to report on.'

'I know. But I must say, it broke my heart to take it out. You know she had only the one?'

Hattersby nodded. 'But that one was never going to function again, Rhys. You shouldn't feel too badly about it. I couldn't find any obstruction in the length of ureter you sent me. I reckon she must have had some congenital lesion at the lower end. You hadn't got a hope there.'

'All the same, Paul, I'd like to have kept a bit of renal tissue. I reckon we're in for a hell of a time with her anaemia.'

'I take your point, Rhys, but . . .'

'Don't you fellows ever stop talking shop?'

Owen turned as he heard Johnson's voice. A few more banal remarks and he and Hattersby found themselves in the same circle as Alex. Rhys caught Alex's eye and saw a flash of defiance as if signalling that this was her world, this was where she was happiest, that there was a limit to how far he could hold her back. He looked across from Alex to see to whom she had been speaking. It was Gordon Baxter. With the corners of his mouth turned down in the sneer that had come with the acquisition of great wealth, he stood alongside Johnnie Johnson, the smiling host, the two of them looking like slightly variant casts from the same mould. Rhys looked at their clothes and suddenly felt ready-made. He might as well have worn the damned sports jacket; at least he would have felt more comfortable. They had silently joined the circle for some while before Baxter finished joking as to whether he could still afford to run his new Jaguar XJS after what Johnson had recently charged him for a certain minor operation. When he finally paused, Johnson pointed to Owen and Hattersby.

'Gordon, have you met these two characters?'

Baxter shifted his glass of whisky to his other hand as he shook hands with Hattersby. He nodded with a friendly smile as he shook Rhys's hand.

'Yes, of course. We've met before. How are you, Rhys?'

Owen muttered something before lapsing into silence with a near-scowl on his face. There were some people Rhys resented using his Christian name on such short acquaintance and Baxter was certainly numbered amongst them. He had met him but once before when Baxter, Chairman of the local charity, had officially handed over the first of the dialysis machines in the flicker of Press cameras. He hadn't liked him then and he felt the emotion return and deepen.

'How's the boat, Rhys?' Johnson asked with the practised ease of the perfect host, plucking out a subject at random to fill a hiatus.

'You sail?' Baxter asked without giving Rhys a chance to reply, and Rhys had the sensation that Alex was watching him apprehensively.

'Yes, but not very seriously.'

'Where do you keep your boat?'

'Swansea marina.'

'That's nice. Very convenient for you.' Baxter's manner was kind with no hint of patronage. 'What d'you sail?'

Rhys's reply was mildly apologetic and he saw Alex's mouth tighten.

'Oh, nothing very grand. A little 19-foot Prelude. I find it very handy singlehanded. I'm not in the same class as this fellow here.' Rhys nodded in Johnnie's direction. 'Nothing as grand as that.'

'A Prelude; yes, I think I've seen one,' Baxter said and, this time, failed to hide the condescension in his voice. 'It looks a jolly nice little boat.'

'We're both out of our class here, Rhys,' Johnnie smiled, jabbing a thumb towards Baxter. 'We're talking to a man with a Nicholson 39 down on the Hamble.'

'Perhaps you'd care to come down and have a sail sometime?' Baxter smirked. 'The firm's Cessna is at Swansea airport; doesn't take long then.'

'Thanks,' Owen replied, 'But I'm afraid I'm going to be rather busy for the next month or so. I'm off to the Middle East.'

His timing had been perfect. Even Baxter could not hide his surprise.

'Going where?' Alex asked.

'Middle East; Shahin to be exact.'

'What on earth for?' They might have been alone at home to judge by Alex's tone.

'They want me to advise them on setting up a Dialysis and Transplant Unit. Yousef has asked me to go back with him.'

'Oh, God; not that man again. How long are you going for?'

'Month; six weeks.'

'Paying you well, I trust?' Baxter broke in.

'Haven't really asked,' Rhys admitted lamely. 'I'd be happy to go for my expenses. I'm overdue for a holiday.'

'Typical.'

Alex's scathing tone made no allowance for the others standing around them but it became brisker as she steered the conversation off at a tangent. Rhys felt as if he had been discarded, as if his visit to Shahin was not of real interest. He had pain in his belly as hunger and resentment took hold. His beer tasted of silver polish. His resentment was not based on what he thought of Baxter so much as what he imagined Baxter thought of him. He saw no reason to feel threatened. He ran his eye over the thin, faded blond hair, sleeked back with no parting to cover as far as possible the balding patch Rhys felt sure was round the back. Baxter's rather watery eyes were prominent, never still for long, his nose in keeping with the midday whisky in his hand, while the blood alcohol level of the occasional Cessna pilot flashed through Rhys's mind. Rhys's scathing survey finally took in the flabby jowl and the burgeoning paunch that was almost hidden by a Savile Row cutter's art. Having decided that he didn't envy Baxter his money, Rhys could find no good reason why Baxter should mean anything to him, why he should dislike Baxter so much; but he did. Slowly, he became aware that he was being included in the conversation once more.

'Gordon's got this idea for solving your dialysis problems,' he heard Alex say. 'Tell him, Gordon.'

While Rhys wondered how Alex knew so much about Baxter's plans, he was obliged to stand back and be lectured on what he should do. They should set up a private Dialysis Unit at the local nursing home, install a Rentakabin and train a few of the nuns. Baxter was to explore the possibility of renting or leasing the machines direct from the manufacturers. They would charge a fee and, in the case of NHS patients, bill the Health Authority. After all, already there were non-profit making units, run privately under licence for the NHS, so why not profitably run units? There was no reason why they shouldn't work side by side. Baxter reckoned the NHS charged overseas visitors anything up to £130 per dialysis – he was sure he could undercut that. There must be patients developing renal failure who were already on private insurance schemes; Baxter thought they could certainly provide rather more comfortable conditions for them. And if, at the end of the day, some of the patients had to pay something, if the relatives had to club together a bit to help out, wasn't that better than just letting old Aunt Mary die? There was more money around these days than people realised. If people couldn't afford it, then there was no big deal; Aunt Mary would only die just as she was doing now.

'And, of course, you would make a profit,' Rhys added the postscript.

'Sure; a small one,' Baxter admitted. 'And you.'

'Dirty word, I'm afraid,' Alex muttered.

'And, of course,' Baxter's face lit up as if he had just had another brilliant idea, 'with your new contacts in the Middle East, you would be able to keep the unit going with wealthy Arabs. I can see them now, a long line of sheikhs flying to Cardiff Airport. Take all the trade away from the London boys.'

'Balls.' Hattersby laughed quietly as he watched Alex's and Baxter's reaction to Rhys's retort. 'The only reason Arabs would have for coming over for dialysis would be with a view to transplant. Can you imagine the unions allowing a patient to be transferred from a profit-making organisation into my Unit for transplant, taking precedence over an NHS patient? They'd go mad, and quite rightly too.'

Baxter's eyes squinted as he seemed suddenly to take a great interest in his glass of whisky. When he spoke, his words were quite distinct despite their softness.

'I've been giving that some thought too. I believe it's not difficult to find some Indian lawyers who are co-operative over the matters of affidavits and that, given a going rate of about £2–4000 per kidney, it is possible . . .'

He did not get to finish his sentence as Rhys took a step forwards, jerking with fury.

'If you think I would ever transplant a kidney from some poor woman in some Bombay back street who needs the money to feed her kids . . .' Rhys could not find the words through his anger.

'Just a thought,' Baxter replied, as calm as Rhys was furious. 'I take your point, even though some might argue whether anyone who has never gone without a meal in his life has the right to dictate to a starving woman what she can or cannot do with her own kidneys. But there is one more question I would put to you. You run the Unit here and, obviously, you would be the first choice in any private venture. If, however, you were to say "no", how would you feel if we were to ask Johnnie here to run it for us?'

There was total silence as they all looked at Rhys. Rhys knew he could never run such a unit, could never be involved in anything alongside a man like Baxter. Yet he could see the point that Baxter had made – it could result in some patients getting dialysed, even transplanted, who were not now. He felt bitter that he could think of no vital evidence that would damn the project outright. He could find no compelling argument why such a scheme could not be a success. And, if he did not take part, as he knew he could not, could he bear to see Johnnie making money out of the surgery he had managed to wriggle out of under the NHS?

'All I can do is wish you all – ' he looked directly at his wife as if bidding her farewell ' – every success.'

As they began to leave, Rhys was still alongside Paul Hattersby as they shuffled down the hall. Rhys muttered out of the corner of his mouth, 'What operation did Johnnie do on that guy then, Paul? D'you know?'

'Yes,' Hattersby grinned. 'I reported on the specimens. Vasectomy.'

They giggled like schoolboys sharing a secret.

'That figures,' Rhys sniggered.

'And I'll tell you something else for nothing,' Hattersby whispered in

Rhys's ear. 'I happened to see the notes. The wife's half of the consent form wasn't signed.'

Rhys drew his head back in surprise to see Hattersby give him a mammoth, slow motion wink.

After a silent journey home, their Sunday lunch was late, lonely and loveless. There was sadness rather than malice or spite in Alex's voice as Rhys picked up *The Sunday Times*.

'Rhys, I don't know what is to become of us; I really don't.'

And, for the first time, Rhys found he didn't care.

12

There had been a period, when Sian had been young, when Rhys had enjoyed those precious holidays of clattering skis in the thick body atmosphere of crowded cable cars, the sweaty descent, the unclipped boots, the gassy beer, the biting winter sun warm on closed eyelids. Alex had liked her skiing straight, uncomplicated, fast, rising after the occasional tumble to laugh as she blew the snow from her face. Rhys had preferred his pistes to be steep and frightening. His descents had been a series of turns as near to perfection in style and technique as his ability would allow, any fall a prelude to self-recrimination. As a result, Alex and Rhys had met at the top and bottom of slopes, rarely staying happily together all the way down. And Sian's chatter about her ski class had kept them going through the evenings.

But Rhys no longer looked forward to holidays, Bank Holidays in particular. Always on call on a Monday, he could not go anywhere – not that he would have wanted to. In addition, the difficulty of getting patients to come in just before or just after a Bank Holiday amounted virtually to the loss of almost a week's work. The hospital would be half-empty, half-staffed. The normal bustle would be replaced by a depressing, enervating calm. And, this weekend, Rhys would be alone.

'Come on, Alex. Get a move on or you are going to miss your train,' he shouted up the stairs. 'It's gone eight o'clock already.'

There was no answer but, minutes later, Alex hurried down the stairs, her arms full of feminine disarray. 'Don't fuss, Rhys. You know you always get us there half an hour too soon. There was no need for you to take me. I could have got a taxi. Shouldn't you be on your way to hospital by now?'

It all added to the feeling of tension. Alex's question did not quite carry the tones that implied concern that he was doing something that he shouldn't, purely for her. The intonation suggested more the wish he was in hospital and not prolonging something they both found painful. If Rhys had not been around, Alex could have let her excitement show, not struggle to give the impression that she did not really want to go.

'I don't really know why I'm bothering,' she said and Rhys smiled inwardly at the lie. He too wondered why he was there, adding to his misery. Far better if he had gone to work like any other Friday morning, let her get her taxi, shut himself away from that face, that look of excitement that had nothing to do with a Law Society function and a couple of days with Auntie Di in St Albans. Try as she might, Alex could not damp down the exhilaration inside her that she knew Rhys would sense. 'The meeting will probably be very dull and the dinner worse. I probably won't know a soul there, but I feel I should start to go to these sort of things. One gets so out of touch here in Avonport.'

'It'll do you good, Alex,' Rhys smiled. 'You'll enjoy it, you see. Who knows whom you might not meet.' He found himself hurrying to add, 'And Auntie Di; you've always said she's your favourite. You've always got on well with her, haven't you?'

'Di's great. I really feel I should go and see her. She's not on the phone but I'll give you a ring from somewhere. And I'll be home sometime on Monday evening. I'm in court on Tuesday morning.'

'Fine,' Rhys said, picking up her case, feeling as if he were speaking lines from the first rehearsal of the local drama society.

In the car, there was a short period of a strange, perverse sort of intimacy, almost as if Rhys were taking Alex to hospital for some major operation from which it was not certain she would return. Rhys did not have to spell it out to himself – the precipitate interest in a London meeting where none had existed before, the sudden desire to see her Auntie Di again – all the words were there in the back of his mind, too torturing to bring into sharp focus. And Alex knew that Rhys could not bring himself to play the outraged husband, feeling, in his heart, that it was to a great extent his own fault, his inability to love her, try as he might. She had come to accept that there was a part of this emotional man that was dead, incapable of reacting even as he watched her go to a man he patently detested. There was gentleness in her face and voice as she turned towards him. She almost put her hand on his arm.

'What are you going to do with yourself?' she asked.

'Me? I thought I might go for a sail tomorrow. Weather forecast is good and the tides are right. Sian's asked me for Sunday lunch and I'm on call on Monday – probably get something to eat in hospital. I'll be fine. Do you want me to meet the train?'

'No. I'll get a taxi.'

Outside the station, Rhys got Alex's case out of the boot and handed it to her. There was rather more affection than usual in their kiss but no real warmth or inclination to linger. Rhys struggled to say whatever husbands say when seeing their wives off to a meeting in London but his 'enjoy yourself' sounded cruelly inept.

He watched her back disappear into the station. He remembered seeing relatives off on trains as a child, a formal occasion with platform tickets, awkward conversation above the hiss of steam, whistles and green flags. Thank God he didn't have to go through that this time.

Without knowing exactly why, Rhys, on entering St David's, made his way directly to the Urology Ward, the preliminary ritual of donning a white coat short-circuited by a mind abstractedly looking for warmth and comfort and affection. He still had his car keys in his hand as he walked into Hannah's room. Without a word, he crossed, as all her visitors seemed to do, to sit on the radiator with his back to the window. If he was looking for softness and sympathy, he had come to the wrong place. It was one of Hannah's dialysis days. She was just beginning a long stint and was not in the best of moods. Although she had not expected to see him, particularly dressed so informally, surprise was just another emotion she felt proud to hide.

'When am I going to get out of this place?'

No polite preamble, just rebellion.

'I can't stick this much longer.' She shook her arm, setting her tubing a-dance, making Rhys lean forwards urgently.

'Careful, Hannah, or you'll dislodge your cannula and then you'll have Sister on your track.'

'Don't care,' Hannah pouted. 'When am I going to get out?'

'About thirty years,' Rhys smiled and immediately regretted it.

'Don't joke. It's no joking matter.'

And Rhys cursed his frivolity. He had been at the game long enough now not to make a stupid remark like that. How could anyone imagine what it was like for a young girl like Hannah to lie tethered to a machine all day and watch others of her age enjoying themselves on the beach? Perhaps there had been something to be said for his ward in the old General, the only view from its window a sheer brick wall. 'It depends,' he said.

'What sort of answer is that? Depends on what?'

Rhys hesitated. If he was not careful, Hannah was going to force him to put into words what was perhaps better left unsaid. He was going to say things which she could twist into promises. How was she to know what she represented to him; the chance of atonement, the way to peace within himself once more, perhaps even the ability to love again? The single feature that prevented Hannah from becoming Helen's perfect image, radiant good health, Rhys knew could be restored only by a successful transplant, and, in his longing to see that beloved face again, he must not promise anything he could not deliver.

'On when we can get a kidney for you.'

'How long will that be?'

'Hannah, I have no idea.'

'Yes, you have.'

He shook his head. If only he could force himself to be realistic, he would see Hannah as just another on an endless production line of human frames that had simply lost the ability to secrete urine, but all he could see was Helen and, all reason shattered, a voice told him what he must do. He must grab the next suitable kidney for Hannah, find some excuse and to hell with those who may have been waiting longer. So he would lose some of the respect of his staff who would know exactly what was going on but, the voice assured him, he was sufficiently in credit to stand the loss; he could replenish his stock gradually over the years. Everyone knew there was some kind of special relationship between him and Hannah – it would not come as a complete surprise if they were asked to close their eyes should she suddenly jump up the waiting list.

'There is such a thing as a waiting list, you know, Hannah.'

'Yes, I know,' Hannah persisted, 'but how long?'

'Unless you have got someone in the family generous enough to . . .'

'You can forget that,' Hannah broke in. 'Haven't got any family, as you well know.'

'. . . you have to wait for a suitable kidney. And then, when one turns up, it may be compatible with any one of two or three of you. Then we have to decide who to give it to.'

'Who decides?'

'We do,' Rhys replied, firmly.

'And what would my chances be?'

'You will get a kidney sooner or later, Hannah; but I can't promise you the next suitable one.'

'How do you decide?'

'It's very difficult, believe me.'

'Playing God, d'you mean?'

'You've been watching too much TV,' Rhys smiled.

'What would be against me, then?'

A red light on the dialysis machine blinked its warning, and Rhys watched as Hannah corrected the fault with a few deft movements co-ordinated with all the confidence of youth. She was not going to let the incident change the course of her questioning and she looked at Rhys again.

'Well?'

Rhys answered hesitantly, not wanting to hurt her.

'Well – the life you lead, Hannah; living rough like that.'

'What's that got to do with it? Nobody's business how I choose to live, is it?'

'But it doesn't help. Be reasonable.'

'I am being reasonable. It's your reasoning I don't understand. Why should the way I choose to live my life have anything to do with whether I get a kidney or not? Tell me.'

'Think of it this way, Hannah. Try and put yourself in our shoes. If there was an endless supply of kidneys, there'd be no problem. Nothing would please us more than to be able to put kidneys in everybody, anybody, as soon as they were fit. But they aren't that plentiful and so we have to make a choice. Now – ' Rhys paused and thought for a moment before suddenly pointing at Hannah '– you are the surgeon, right? You have to decide. You have one kidney and two possible recipients – patients for transplant – all right?'

Hannah nodded, her face a picture of total concentration.

'They are both the same age, young students, but one is hard working, reliable, fine future predicted for him; the other is already a heavy drinker, maybe into drugs, everyone convinced he will be back on the bottle as soon as he is able. Now, you are the surgeon, Hannah. Who do you give the kidney to?'

'I don't drink,' Hannah growled, and Rhys took her answer as the only concession he was likely to get from her.

'We have, of course,' Rhys went on, 'an even more immediate problem than finding a kidney for you.'

'What's that?'

'Deciding where you are going to stay while you are on dialysis. You can't possibly go back to that place you were living in; it's totally unsuitable for dialysis.'

'How d'you know?'

'Because I've been there, had a good look at the place where you sleep.'

'What were you doing, snooping round there?' Hannah became restless in her anger. 'Did Dai and Jessie know you were there?'

'Of course they did. I had a long chat with them. They are two very fine people.'

'The only two people in the world who really love me, that's what they are. What have you been saying to them?'

'I didn't say anything they didn't agree with; in fact they had worked it all out themselves. They are just as anxious not to lose you, though – ' Owen grinned broadly ' – I can't imagine how anyone in their right mind would want to live with you, the way you talk to people.' His grin broadened even further as Hannah stuck her tongue out at him. 'They agreed you couldn't go back to that old hay loft and their caravan is too small for three. They don't have enough money to build, so Dai had decided. He was going to sell his land, just keeping enough to build himself a small bungalow.'

Hannah became agitated, for once at a loss for words.

'But the land . . .? How would he . . .? The horses . . .? Tempest . . .?'

Rhys waited for all the possible consequences to filter through Hannah's mind. As the realisation of what her illness could mean to Dai and Jessie gradually quietened her, he remembered with envy the shoulder-to-shoulder solidarity he had witnessed in that humble draughty caravan. Jessie had been the undoubted spokeswoman, Dai Stud nodding to her every statement.

'You needn't worry, Hannah. I soon talked them out of that. I explained that they could never get anything suitable built in time. But don't you – ' Rhys wagged his finger at Hannah ' – don't you ever do anything to let that couple down, d'you hear?'

Hannah's eyes filled and she swallowed loudly, a setting that, in any other patient, Rhys would have used as an opportunity to leave, but he enjoyed the ensuing silence, broken only by the clicking and purring of the machine. In the intimacy of the silence, Rhys had to fight down a desire to hint to Hannah at what had crossed his mind on the journey back from his interview with Dai and Jessie; fleeting mental glimpses of Hannah in Sian's old bedroom, even perhaps some sort of legal, long-term arrangement. But all such visions had been wiped clean at the thought of broaching such a subject to Alex, trying to explain why, out of the hundreds of patients that passed through his care each year, he should choose to bring home someone she would see only as a wild, untamable stray.

'And where are you off this weekend?' Hannah asked abruptly, as if anxious to change a discussion at which she was coming off second best.

'Nowhere special,' Rhys replied.

'How dull,' Hannah snapped disparagingly.

Rhys suddenly felt inept, as if, in some way, he was letting Hannah down. He tried to justify himself.

'I think perhaps I'll go for a sail tomorrow.'

'Oh . . .' Hannah changed mood and position exactly as she had when Yousef had talked of the horses. 'Can I come with you?'

Rhys laughed. 'No. Perhaps when you are a little better. If you behave yourself.'

'How big is it?' Hannah asked excitedly.

'My boat? Oh, very small,' Rhys laughed again. 'Only 19 foot.'

'Sounds big to me.'

'Not really.'

'Does your wife go with you?' Hannah asked, and saw the pain.

'No.'

'I've watched them from here,' Hannah said, wistfully. 'They look gorgeous. What's it like?'

'Sailing? Wet and expensive.' Rhys saw again that he had said the wrong thing. She didn't want slick, bogus answers but romance that would lift her above the aching arm and sore backside. On something like this, she wouldn't even mind if he were to lie a little. 'But it's worth every penny. It can be unbelievably beautiful and, of course, pretty frightening at times.'

'Do you go out in any storms?' Hannah dug her head into her pillows as if she wanted to hear tales of great adventures and, for the first time, Rhys had a glimpse of another Hannah, a dreamy romantic like himself, peeping from behind the snide defence of the rebellious, insecure teenager.

'No. I don't do that sort of sailing.' Rhys laughed but could follow Hannah's line of thought. Her body might be tethered to a sickbed but her spirit saw herself battling against all possible combinations of wind, sea and tide.

'I imagine it can be almost as exciting as riding a horse,' Hannah's voice became dreamy.

'Far more,' Rhys said.

'Couldn't be,' Hannah defied him, daring him to try and convince her.

'I've crewed a couple of times,' Rhys said, 'on one of these racing cruisers and, when you are going to windward in a bit of a blow with a bit too much sail up, or when you are running before the wind with a great big coloured spinnaker up, believe me, that can be like riding on the back of a wild animal.'

'Honest?' Hannah's eyes were wide.

'Honest.'

Hannah lapsed into silence as she tried to picture the scene while Rhys wondered, once more, whether Helen would have gone sailing with him – she went everywhere else with him.

'Will you sail it round for me to see?'

'Oh, I don't know about that.' Rhys shifted his feet nervously, his eyes evasive, regretting for a moment the picture of the intrepid sailor he had been painting of himself. 'I don't normally sail as far round as this. It's quite a small boat, you know.'

'Please,' she pleaded. 'Let me see your boat. It's not that far, is it?'

'Eight, nine miles. I don't usually go that far on my own.' He watched disappointment spread over Hannah's face. The tides were just about at their biggest; at mid-tide there would be anything up to four knots of tidal stream under him. In theory, if he timed it right, he could damn near drift there and back, let alone sail or motor. And it would give Hannah something to look forward to. 'Well – no promises but keep an eye out for me, let me see, say about one o'clock tomorrow.'

'Smashing,' she said. 'You can go now.'

13

When it came to sailing Rhys had but two regrets, that he had come to it too late in life and that he had no sons to sail with him. Sian had gone on the sailing course in Salcombe with him, her dutiful interest in the little cruiser

Rhys bought evaporating with the appearance of Roger. The hefty young man had tried to find favour with his future father-in-law by sailing once with him only to suffer the shame of being heartily sick within spitting distance of Mumbles Head. Alex had told him he should do what everyone else did, buy a share in a bigger boat, he had the money, and when Rhys had decided he would rather not, she had washed her hands of the whole affair.

He looked around Swansea's marina and decided it was time to go. It was just before half-tide on the flood and Rhys had planned to be off Avonport at high water, one o'clock. He looked a little speculatively at the outboard motor – he had had a struggle with it the last few times; he really must take it off and get it serviced. He smiled at it, patted it, apologised to it out loud when it started first pull. He cast off, reversed out of his berth and joined the queue at the lock. He was one of the last in before the gates closed behind them.

'Here, Rhys. Catch.'

The voice was female and friendly. Clarissa Johnson's face smiled down from the bows of the *Fulmar*. He caught the rope and made fast as the water level began to fall. Rhys had forgotten to get his fenders out but found that Johnnie already had two expensive-looking monsters protecting his gleaming hull. Clarry looked lean and fit as she leaned over the side.

'On your own, Rhys?' she asked.

'Yes. Alex is in London for the weekend.'

'Where are you off to?'

'Thought I'd just go as far as Avonport – get back on the tide.' He tried to make it sound offhand.

'For God's sake, Rhys, don't you see enough of the place? Why don't you come with us?' The invitation was spontaneous but utterly genuine.

'That's kind of you, Clarry,' Rhys turned his head for a moment to say 'Good morning' as two youngsters, sheathed in red and black, appeared alongside their mother. 'But some other time perhaps.'

'No problem, Rhys. We've got plenty of grub. We've kept our old mooring in the river. Tie up to that and we'll pick up your boat on the way back.'

'Yes, come on.' The children's voices were as welcoming as their mother's.

But, how do you explain about a promise made to someone you have sworn never to fail a second time? He imagined Hannah, looking from her window, the hours going by. He pictured their next meeting. Not that he would have gone with the Johnsons if there had been no promise to Hannah; he knew that. He would not have enjoyed getting his happiness secondhand from a man he did not like, the man who had just emerged from the cabin.

'Morning, Johnnie. Your crew are trying to get me to jump ship. Where are you going?'

Johnnie Johnson managed to smile and pull a face at the same time as if he were not entirely master of his own ship or his own fate but was thoroughly enjoying the experience.

'We thought we'd battle round against the tide to Oxwich or Port Eynon and anchor – let these two – ' he nodded to the two children ' – try out their new diving gear and then catch the ebb. I thought Dale, maybe Fishguard; they haven't been through the Sounds before. They want to go to Ireland though I keep telling them I don't think there's going to be that much wind. But they're dying to do their first night passage and I was daft enough to promise them.'

'When d'you reckon to be back?' Rhys asked.

'Sometime Monday.'

'Ah,' said Rhys, finding his excuse. 'I'm on call on Monday.'

Rhys could not be sure whether it was genuinely a last effort to get him to change his mind or whether Johnnie could not resist the final flourish as he offered to make a link call to Bill McGrath through his VHF and ask him to cover Rhys on Monday. It didn't add to Rhys's good humour either to struggle to restart his outboard while listening to the *Fulmar*'s diesel throbbing alongside him. One of the first out of the lock, Rhys had not gone far down river before the Johnsons glided past, towering over the *Prelude*. Out of the river, a quarter of a mile ahead, the *Fulmar* set sail. Rhys watched Clarry lean over the rail, one hand on the shrouds, the other waving goodbye. There was loneliness in eyes and mouth as Rhys waved briefly back. He wondered how such a wonderful girl as Clarry could be happy with someone like Johnnie; or could it be that, deep down, he, Rhys Wyn Owen, did not really dislike Johnnie so much as envy his style, his success, his apparent ability to do everything well?

At the starboard hand buoy that marked the end of the dredged channel, he switched off the hammering engine and sighed at the silence. With the gentlest of offshore breezes, he had no difficulty in leaving the tiller to hoist the main and genoa and, within minutes, the little boat had slotted into a broad reach, making way comfortably ahead of the strong following tide. The sky was cloudless, the air warm for the end of May, and Rhys felt a subdued excitement. So far, so good. He could well find that he was off Avonport sooner than he had planned, with a strong tide still running. He'd seen boats anchored off the bay in front of the hospital but it was not a popular spot, the jagged spur of Craig Ddu ever menacing. But he had promised Hannah and, with an offshore breeze, Rhys could see no real danger as long as he did not stay more than half an hour or so over slack water.

Within sight of Avonport, he had made such good time that he furled the genoa to delay his arrival. Approaching the sandy bay overlooked by the hospital, he gave the outer end of Craig Ddu a handsome margin before closing the shore, turning into wind and dropping the anchor. He felt his heart racing as he watched the boat carried broadside by the tide, hardly a breath of wind now to ripple the sail. By the time he was sure the anchor had held, he found his mouth dry. He had the sudden fear of no wind to sail away with and an engine that might not start. For a while, he crouched in the cockpit, hovering over the engine, alternately checking the transit bearing of a point on the beach and the far end of the hospital Ward Block, and watching the wake of the tide over the stern. Gradually, the streaming water died away and the craft began to swing lazily. He dropped the mainsail in a slithering rush. Longing for a cup of coffee, he faced the hospital and waved both arms above his head. He could count the windows and knew exactly which one was Hannah's. But he was too far away to see her and he stopped waving after a while for fear someone might think him in trouble.

His first drink was from sheer necessity. He ate his sandwiches and savoured another mug of coffee, slowly relishing each mouthful. The beach was crowded, the sound of children, shouting and screaming their happiness, carried clearly across the water. A dark head detached itself from the joyful chaos at the water's edge and Rhys watched its progress as it made its way towards him. A brawny pair of arms and shoulders hauled themselves over the transom, supporting a dripping, bearded face. A few cheerful, friendly remarks and the fragment of human contact was over. Rhys envied the man's slow powerful crawl. He suddenly felt tired. He fetched his lifejacket from the cabin, propped it against the bulkhead as a pillow and stretched out on the cockpit locker to stare at the immaculate sky. Rhys had read somewhere that bird life along the coast became hushed at slack water, almost as if nature was holding its breath, and the confused sounds from the beach became muted, seeming to blur into a subdued murmur.

The act of shivering woke Rhys, that and the feeling of movement in the boat. He looked over the side towards the beach to find nothing but open sea. Startled, he looked over to port to see the hospital, the grassy slope, the beach, the milling crowd, all still bathed in the same sunny stillness. The boat had swung on its anchor and Rhys felt the insistent nudging of the tide. Fighting off the dull-wittedness that came from sleeping at midday, he saw the tide streaming from the stern. His eyes lifted to follow the direction of the stream towards Craig Ddu. He had forgotten that, so close inshore, he would have the first of the ebb. Time to go. He looked at his watch, but his mind, now turning over too fast, did not register the time. He consciously made the effort to regiment his thoughts. What the hell; it was a glorious afternoon, the sea flat calm, children were enjoying themselves no more than a few hundred yards away, what wind there was was still off shore. Stop fussing and get the mainsail up first.

Rhys felt better when he saw the sail fill but, even as he watched, it flopped back lazily in the fitfully light air. There would be no question of sailing out of the bay, he must motor. It was at the cursing stage, as he thrashed at the recoil starter, that something else first competed for his attention. He had now flooded the engine and, in less urgent circumstances, he would have reconciled himself to waiting and trying again later. Insiduously, through his fury, the feeling grew that the shouting and screaming from the beach was clearer, more demanding. His preconditioned mind interpreted the sounds as evidence that he must now be dragging his anchor and drifting towards Craig Ddu. A quick look to confirm the fact surprised him. There was nothing to suggest he had drifted. The beach and Craig Ddu were still as far away, the beach still as crowded. Except there were now some figures, Lowry-like in the distance, trying to clamber along the slimy, sloping rocks of Craig Ddu, slithering in their haste, shouting, screaming, pointing.

Part of him knew that it was him they were shouting at, a part that the rest of his conscious being strove to deny. He looked all round as if some other boat might have appeared magically, someone to whom he might transfer the sudden clutch of fear in his belly. He made a few more futile attempts to start the engine as if hoping that, while he grunted in his efforts, things would have changed; that, when he looked up again, those menacing figures on Craig Ddu would have gone, the scene transformed back to a happy Bank Holiday beach. But it was not so. It was the same with the toy inflatable. He had seen the orange and yellow globule of colour long before he could bring his mind to accept the stimuli streaming back from his retinae. As the tide accelerated the fragile bubble along the edge of Craig Ddu, further and further away from loving, clutching hands,

Rhys could no longer turn a deaf ear to the screams of the child that soared above the background confusion like the solo instrument in some macabre concerto. The youngster, his small hands clenching desperately at the circular tube filled, so proudly, with the power of a father's lungs, now saw the man in the boat as his only saviour and turned his full attention on Rhys, his mouth a black, circular cavern even as he drew breath to scream again.

Rhys, his tongue too big for his mouth as he tried to swallow in his nervousness, looked towards the engine and smelled the flooding petrol. The inflatable had now passed across his stern and was going away from him towards the tip of Craig Ddu as it hooked back towards them. Rhys couldn't stand helplessly by. He must do something. He must be seen to be doing something. He ran to the bows, ducking under the shrouds, and gasped as he hauled in the anchor, dropping it in a tangle of chain and warp on the foredeck. Back in the cockpit, he found the tide was already taking him, stern first, towards the reef. He had no more control over his craft than the child had over his. An eddy in the current swung the bows gently and Rhys paddled the rudder frantically to help it round. With the bows at least pointing in the right direction, Rhys pushed the boom over but it promptly swung back. Holding the tiller extension, he sat out as far as he could, heeling the boat to bring the boom jingling over his head. He snatched a glance at the inflatable and saw it heading inexorably for the undulating water that marked the rocks just under the surface. Another glance up at the sail and he knew he would never reach the child in time. He was not making enough headway to save himself from Craig Ddu let alone pluck some child from the sea.

For a trance-like moment, he floated against a background of blue sky and sea, mesmerised by the happy sounds of children mindlessly enjoying themselves a few hundred yards away. He remembered somebody saying once that wind might blow you on to a reef but that tide would always carry you round. It certainly seemed to be proving correct for the inflatable as it now swirled along the reef, bumping from rock to rock, gyrating the bundle of terrified misery it carried first this way, then that. A transient puff of breeze gave Rhys a little steerage way and his heart lifted. He was in two minds whether to leave the tiller to raise the genoa when the fitful breeze died away again, but not before he had clawed his way a few yards seawards. He was still going to strike the reef but now, at least, it was going to be much nearer its seaward tip than Rhys had feared. He knew he had no time to lift his keel but he was wondering whether even raising it partially would help when he saw the inflatable race round the reef's far end, spinning viciously as it snagged the last of the rocks. In a splashing blur of movement, the boy lunged at the last fragment of solid ground before miles of open, tide-ridden sea and, in a confusion of arms and legs, disappeared. Rhys closed his eyes, heavy with defeat and a sense of impotent failure. When he opened them again, it was to see the inflatable speeding away, freed now from Craig Ddu's embrace. A moment later and there was a grinding judder that sent Rhys sprawling on to the cockpit floor. As he fell, Rhys felt the sickening crack as the tiller, scything viciously as the rudder struck the reef, caught him behind one ear. He lay helpless, half-stunned, as the graceful little boat ground and scraped, rattled and flapped, twisted and jerked its way along the gouging, torturing rocks until, in a moment, all was peace and gentle, gliding serenity once more. He dragged himself upright and, totally disorientated, searched again for the inflatable.

The sight of the small dark head, just above the water, one elbow hooked in self-preservation over the edge of the frail, yellow buoyancy, the other hand grasping the string-like lanyard, forced a sob into Rhys's throat. The sob never found expression in sound, however, as Rhys, suddenly overcome with fury, suppressed it and found release in positive, passionate action. Raging inwardly at his own ready compliance, his pathetic willingness to bend to circumstances, he hauled on the mainsheet, jamming it taut, fixing the boom amidships, bringing an immediate semblance of order to the boat. Next he turned his fury on the engine. With the throttle wide open and ignoring the choke, he put his shoulders behind the pull. In a cloud of blue smoke, the engine screamed into life and Rhys, in no mood to worry about stripping the gears, determined only to give the engine no chance to die on him, rammed the lever into forward drive. As the little boat shot forwards, Rhys tumbled again, grazing one elbow, the pain from which he would not feel for some hours. On his feet again, he grasped the tiller and headed for the inflatable. At full throttle, he rapidly overtook it, passed it and turned into the tide. His mind and movements frenetic, whipped along by the anger he felt at his own ineptitude, he was not prepared for the speed with which the two closed. A frantic grab over the side, the sight of wide, beseeching eyes in a white face, and the chance was gone, the gaudy blob spinning away in his wake once more. And years of training, experience and self-discipline finally came to his aid. What was he always teaching his juniors? 'Do it slowly, do it once.' And, after his initial inertia, he had been threshing around like a first year SHO with a bleeding appendix. He took a deep breath and consciously dropped his shoulders. With one hand on the tiller, he managed with the other to open the cockpit locker, lift out the boat-hook and hold it in readiness over the side. As he turned into the tide the second time, he gingerly throttled back as far as he dared to reduce the closing speed. Now totally in command of himself and able to concentrate mind and eye, he found no difficulty in picking up the white lanyard that ran along the inflatable's side. Without taking his eye off the boat-hook's tenuous hold, he felt for the engine's gear lever and put it in neutral, only to hear the engine splutter into silence. No second chances now. As he moved to the side, he almost lost his hold on the boat-hook as the child's frantic grab at its lower end detached it from the inflatable and reared the end Rhys was holding almost vertical. Thrusting his head and shoulders between the guardrail and cockpit coaming, Rhys stretched a hand towards the wet white skin, grasped a child-thin upper arm only to have it pulled away as the lad tried to reach towards Rhys. As, with a flopping splash, the youngster fell back to float face down, Rhys made a grab at dark hair and missed. Heaving himself further over the side, Rhys's hand slid down the cold spinal curve to hook his fingers in the waist of bright red swimming trunks. This, he knew, he would never let go. His other hand plunged beneath a thigh, brought an ankle above water. As he heaved on trunks and ankle, gasping at the effort of lifting even such a child from the water, the lad's head, lolling on a flaccid neck like some old rag doll, was last to emerge, frothy bubbles in the water cascading from his mouth and nose. Rhys decided not to risk losing his grip by bringing him over the guardrail and finally delivered a cold, inert body beneath the wire and, bumping and slithering over the seat, on to the cockpit floor.

For a moment, he slumped on to the cockpit seat, gasping for breath, his heart thumping. But it was not over yet. The young lad had the stillness of coma, his chest motionless, his eyes staring fishlike along the cockpit floor. The difference was that Rhys now moved with assurance, an amateur no longer. He turned the boy on his back, the thin body nigh cold as death. Kneeling, Rhys put his ear to the chest and heard a slow but strong heart-beat. On his feet again, Rhys, with a grunting heave, lifted the boy by his ankles until the flopping, bumping head came clear of the floor. Rhys grunted his satisfaction as two small jets of frothy, dirty water spouted upwards from his nostrils. Hampered by the boom, he strained to keep the boy upturned until no more water flowed from his nose and mouth, then laid him flat once more. The cockpit floor was so narrow that Rhys found difficulty in reaching the blue slimy lips with his and he felt the nausea as he tried to force his breath into a spongy, bubbling void. After two or three of Rhys's long, forced expirations, he felt the head beneath him move, then had the mouth beneath his snatched away as the boy made his own stridulent search for air. Rhys watched the pupils contract as life and incoordinated movement came back to the eyes. The boy began to cry, wild and animal-like, his arms and legs flailing as bright red blood sluiced away the last traces of his cerebral anoxia. As Rhys lifted him by his armpits to comfort and control, he felt the numbing pain of a small, hard fist as it caught the corner of his eye. Eventually, full consciousness that he was safe sent youthful arms and legs locking around Rhys, a sodden, whimpering head burrowing into his neck. It was then that Rhys saw the Inshore Rescue boat, the small dot in the distance rapidly increasing in size, the roar of the outboards soon blotting out the child's shivering sobs.

The *Prelude* rocked as a big man, expanded to comfortingly enormous proportions by waterproofs, safety harness and lifejacket, stepped from the Atlantic class inflatable in one practised movement and made fast. Crowded together in the small cockpit, ducking and weaving to avoid the boom, few words were spoken as Rhys handed over his charge. He did not part with the boy readily. He kept his hand in touch with the thin, vulnerable body as long as possible. No fellow creature had ever held him so close, never before had he been so tightly embraced by sweet innocence. He resented the man, towering over him, to whom the child had transferred his helplessness.

After a few clucking noises to the child against the background of the second lifeboatman's intonation into his crackling VHF, the man lifted a steady, green-eyed stare at Rhys.

'You all right, Mr Owen?'

'Yes, I'm OK.'

As if determined to prolong his contact with the boy as long as he could, Rhys ducked into the cabin to emerge with a thin tea towel and an old sweater. He did what he could to dry the boy's torso as he lay in the man's arms and engulfed the boy in the sweater. The lifeboatman let him do it as if he understood.

'Right; I'll get him aboard and I'll be back.'

Minutes later, the boy, still shivering violently, was safely aboard the rescue boat, shrouded in a thick blanket and already taking an interest in a bag of sweets that had appeared as if by magic. He stared across at Rhys as if he had never seen him before. The *Prelude*'s cockpit filled with the man's bulk once more.

'Now, how about you?' he asked, his voice having the firmness of another man used to making decisions in his own world.

'I'm all right,' Rhys answered, suddenly feeling rubber-kneed, a little light-headed.

'Can you get back all right? Do you need some help? We can bring someone out to give you a hand. No problem.'

Rhys shook his head, not trusting himself to speak as a lump rose in his throat. The man lifted his head, looked around.

'Bit of a breeze now. Should be all right, but we'll keep an eye out for you.' He smiled. 'We'll get one of the boys to come out and give you a tow if you look like missing opening time.'

He saw no answering smile on Rhys's drawn, tired face and his voice took on a softness surprising in such a big man.

'You did well today, Mr Owen. That isn't easy, you know; not even for us pros. Take care now on the way back and then I'd suggest a bloody great whisky and early to bed.'

The man was back in the rescue boat and casting off before Rhys could force words through a constriction in his throat.

'How d'you know my name? I'm sorry, I don't . . .'

A huge grin lit the man's face as he cradled the boy between his knees.

'How could I ever forget you, Mr Owen. You did my piles five years ago.'

No one waved as the craft heeled away in a roaring, hissing arc.

14

Gradually, Rhys felt the dragging weight of anti-climax as he walked up the pontoon, through the marina's gate and across to his car. Though his steps were springy, his mind racing, by the time he sat behind the steering wheel, he found himself near to tears of petulant exasperation. Slowly, reason brought to earth his flying thoughts, calmed the fine, high tension tremor that was agitating him from head to foot. In time, he was able first to smile, then laugh out loud at his foolishness.

His memory of the sail back had been blurred by fantasy. Mental pictures of his hero's return had flickered before his eyes like the jerking frames of an old silent movie. The RNLI man had said they'd keep an eye out for him – he'd seen himself escorted up the river. The boy must be back in the family fold once more – Rhys had felt the mother's tears on his cheek. News of the rescue must have got back by now – there would be eager hands to help moor his brave little boat with its proud scars. Sweet reason finally told him that sort of thing only happened in TV soap operas – his only human contact on the return journey had been with a drunken fishing party in the lock. But it would have been nice.

He braced his arms against the steering column and pressed his head against the rest. God, he was hungry. And tired. And he suddenly felt fitter, stronger, than he had for years. He clenched his fists and beat them against the wheel. He contracted all his muscles into a near-orgasmic shudder that forced out a grunt of animal pleasure. Hungry, tired and fit – was there any better feeling? Like the end of a long day's skiing. And a sense of refurbished pride. Gentle, easygoing, tolerant, compassionate, he knew this was how his friends and colleagues saw him. He enjoyed the smiles of affection the reputation earned. But he had come to wonder whether the characteristics which, at times, he made conscious efforts to cultivate, had rendered him truly soft, effete, emasculated. He had often wondered whether that opinionated assurance in his own ability that had characterised his youth, had truly died with Helen or whether it was simply suppressed by his feeling of guilt. Was he wearing some kind of emotional hair-shirt in perpetual mourning for Helen until he could find some form of atonement? Was this charade that he was happy to play out, some kind of loving tribute? That day, he had found out. That day, when the chips were down, he had found the plain guts to impose his will on events, not simply allow himself to be blown along by them. For a while, blind fury had dug his self-respect from under the shell of morbid self-pity with which he had surrounded himself over the years. No doubt he would retreat behind that shell again tomorrow but, that day, that night, he felt great. But, who could he tell?

His home, he knew, as he slotted the Saab into the holiday evening, family saloon traffic, would be as empty as his car, only bigger. He headed for the hospital. When he walked into the Urology Ward, he found the Sister was off duty for the weekend. The harassed young Staff Nurse, while she smiled and raised an eyebrow at the bruise below Rhys's left eye, had no time for a Consultant, dressed in jumper, open-necked shirt and slacks that reminded her of the holiday that was going on in the outside world. She had a report to write and drugs to check. And Hannah was fast asleep. Rhys stood smiling at the frown that puckered those dark eyebrows even in sleep. He glanced through the window at Craig Ddu and the water before tiptoeing out of the room.

'Hullo, Dad. Come in.'

Sian stood aside and Rhys stepped into the hall to stand politely as his daughter closed the door behind him. He smiled inwardly at memories of a young girl barging through a front door with school bag and scarf, slamming the door behind her. And there she was now, part of his home no longer, married to a stranger, inviting him in. She put her arms round his neck and kissed his cheek.

'Come on in.'

Dressed in an ankle-length housecoat and trailing the fragrance of a recent bath or shower, she led the way into a kitchen that had none of the warmth or clutter of an impending meal.

'Where did you get that?' She pointed at the bruise on his face.

Rhys instinctively felt it gingerly with two fingers. 'The boom caught me,' he said. 'Getting a bit slow in my old age.'

Sian smiled. 'Cup of tea?'

'No, thanks. I just popped in to see . . .'

'We're just on our way out, actually, Dad. Going out to supper. With Tom – he plays rugby with Roger – and Jennifer. Known as Tom and Jenny.'

They both laughed shyly.

'In fact, Dad, you can do me a favour. Go and get Roger in to have a bath. He's out in the garden. I'll go and put my face on and I'll be back.'

Rhys's and Roger's synchronous 'hellos' cancelled themselves out in their weight of guarded friendliness. Both men still wondered what to make of the other. If Rhys had not been his father-in-law, Roger would have respected him as a surgeon but would have had little time for him otherwise. If it were not for the fact that he must be polite to the man whom his daughter had chosen to marry, Rhys would never have sought the company of this earthy young buck whose professional self-assurance only brought back painful memories of himself at that age.

'Your wife says you've got to go in and have a bath,' Rhys smiled, 'and, if I might say so, I can see her point.'

Roger looked down at his hands, at his filthy, torn trousers, and laughed. He had been laying concrete and his large, capable hands were roughened and grey.

'It'll all come off when I scrub for the first aortogram on Tuesday,' he grinned. 'I often wonder what the patients would say if they saw us at weekends sometimes.'

Their chatter was friendly enough, like good neighbours talking across a hedge in the early twilight, but both were relieved when Sian appeared at the kitchen door.

'Roger, come on; we'll be late.'

Back in the kitchen, Rhys made a conscious effort to feel at ease, and failed.

'Are you sure you won't have that cup of tea, Dad?'

'Quite sure, thank you, Sian.'

'Can of beer then?'

'Right.'

Rhys perched on a stool. The beer was fridge-cold and he found it difficult to swallow. He tried politely to conceal a painful belch.

'Have you heard from Mum?' Sian asked.

'Yes. Spoke to her on the phone late last night. Said she didn't enjoy the meeting much but she found the dinner interesting.'

'Why didn't you go with her?'

Rhys found he could not return his daughter's direct look – there had been a time when no one could stare him down.

'What, me? Go to London? You know me. I hate the place.' He forced a laugh.

'That's not the point, Dad, and you know it. You should have gone with her. No doubt you could have gone to the dinner as – ' she hesitated as mentally she changed 'her' to 'a' ' – a guest. You should have stayed up today, gone to a show. What have you done with yourself today?'

'Been for a sail.'

'On your own?'

'Yes.' Rhys paused, hoping to attract sympathy without appearing to complain, straining to the last not to breach the facade of unity that he and Alex had always kidded themselves they had maintained in the presence of their daughter. 'What makes you so certain your mother wanted me to go with her?'

Sian had no answer for him, merely another question.

'Why do you do it, Dad?'

'Do it? What d'you mean? Do what?'

'Take it the way you do. Let people push you around, walk all over you.' There was a mixture of affection and suppressed irritation in her voice. 'Why are you always so bloody soft, Dad?'

'I'm not,' her father laughed.

'Yes, you are,' Sian said, more forcibly. 'Don't you realise how it drives everyone mad, anyone who loves you, that is? D'you imagine I haven't seen you and Mum? The more she lashes out, the more you curl up. Like a hedgehog; no, not like a hedgehog; that at least had got spikes. Don't imagine I haven't felt for you; I have. But don't imagine I haven't felt for Mum either.' Rhys suddenly realised how like her mother Sian was becoming as a strong, forceful character angrily searched for words. 'Arguing with you is like – like – punching your way out of the proverbial sack.'

Sian saw on her father's face the look that she had seen her mother produce a hundred times. She softened, walked over to him to put her hands on his shoulders and kiss him.

'We all still love you, you realise that, don't you, you great daft thing, you.' With a smile, she wiped a trace of her lipstick from his cheek. 'Better get rid of that, hadn't we, or people will be wondering what you're getting up to while Mum's away.' She paused, looking concerned. 'What are you going to do for supper? Let me make you something quick. We can ring Tom and Jenny, tell them we'll be a bit late.'

'Certainly not.' Rhys drained his beer as he stepped off the stool, pushing Sian backwards. 'Your mother has left enough food for a month. I must go. Enjoy your meal.'

'All right.' Sian was careful not to show her relief. 'But we're expecting you for lunch tomorrow; you haven't forgotten, have you?'

In the hallway Sian shouted to Roger than her father was leaving. Rhys also called up the stairs to ask at what time the Off Licence at the end of the road closed, to be answered by a naked, red hairy torso that appeared, still dripping, on the landing.

'Nine o'clock,' Roger grinned as he dried his crotch, oblivious to the furious looks from his wife. 'Watch it now; none of this solitary drinking, it's dangerous. Why don't you call in the Star just after ten? We'll probably be there for a jar after supper.'

And Rhys, embarrassed, lowered his eyes, murmuring 'Goodbye' to the daughter from whom he had always hidden his own nakedness.

Four men in the Off Licence peered at the rows of bottles with the silence of loners thumbing through pages in a dirty book shop, their skin pale jade under the strip light. Rhys joined their ranks. A bottle of Rudesheimer he chose almost at random but he took his time to select one of the château-bottled clarets, all his actions now those of someone driven by a calm certainty, a comforting inevitability.

Balaclava Crescent looked the same as it had for fifty years, a little more attractive perhaps in the dusk, only the very peak of Mynydd Bychan still catching the evening sun. The old man's welcome was unchanged – in his timeless existence, measured only by the clock's remorseless countdown, he showed no surprise at a Consultant Surgeon calling to see a patient late on a Bank Holiday Saturday evening. The atmosphere, tanged with tobacco smoke, was still as warm and peaceful. The chair sagged its welcome once more. A half hour of strolling conversation was marred only by the winks and nods as the old man told of the regular visits of Paddy, someone from the hospital, someone who was so good to the children, taking them swimming at the leisure centre in Avonport. Hearing how the old man welcomed Paddy's visits only added to Rhys's possessive longing. The gel should have a man about the place, the old man argued; it wasn't natural, a lovely gel all on her own like that. Rhys was wondering just how much longer he could justifiably stay when he heard the sound he had been waiting for. The kitchen door opened and shut and there was a momentary clatter of dishes. Then, in a few strides, the tempo was raised from andante to presto by a bouncing, generous spirit.

'Where's our hero, then?' She held up her *South Wales Echo* for them to see. 'I saw the car outside. What have you been up to then, getting your name in the paper?'

Rhys stood up awkwardly while the old man turned in his chair to smile his love. Rhys looked at the paper Nansi held towards him and saw the small headline halfway down the front page – 'South Wales Surgeon in Sea Rescue'. She turned the page round and began reading, her face flushed. 'Mr Rhys Wynne – ' her head came up momentarily '– they've spelt your name wrong; typical – Mr Rhys Wynne Owen, one of Avonport's senior consultants –' she paused again to look at Rhys and purse her lips in mock deference.

'Get on with it, gel,' the old man wheezed.

'– was involved earlier today in a dramatic rescue in the Bristol Channel when a child was carried out to sea in his inflatable by the strong tide. Mr Owen, who was sailing in the area at the time, was able, singlehanded, to drag eleven-year-old Mervyn Wragg, of Lon-y-Deri, Pencoed, into his boat, having himself been in difficulties on the treacherous Craig Ddu reef in the process. Both Coastguards and the RNLI were full of praise for Mr Owen's prompt action and warned against the dangers, in the Bristol Channel's strong tides, of the use of toy inflatables which . . .'

Nansi's voice trailed away as she handed the paper to a beaming father.

'What were you doing out there on your own?' she asked.

Rhys shrugged his shoulders but it was obviously not going to be enough for Nansi. 'I promised Hannah I'd show her my boat.'

'You promised Hannah you'd show her your boat,' Nansi repeated, shaking her head. 'You men are all the same, just want to show off. And what's that?'

The hand that pointed at Rhys's bruised face stayed up as she came round the table to put cool fingers gently on the swelling, her other hand coming to rest equally gently on his shoulder. When Rhys judged she was about to take her hand away, he laughed shyly.

'I've got another one round here,' he said, leaning his head towards Nansi as her hand searched behind his ear.

'That one is even bigger,' she said beneath a caring frown. 'How did you manage that?'

'Truth is, I made rather a cobblers of the whole thing,' Rhys grinned, 'and got a bit knocked about in the process.'

A bubbling laugh came from alongside them as if the bruises had taken someone back to a match he had played at Pontypool more than a generation before.

'Have you put anything on them?' Nansi asked.

'No. They'll go down on their own.'

'Again, typical.' There was a perceptible lift to her voice as if she already anticipated the answer to her next question, as if she was anxious to give strength to a small hope that was beginning to excite her. 'And what about Mrs Owen? What does she think of all this?'

'She doesn't know. She's in London for the weekend.'

There was now certainty in both minds, excitement in both voices.

'Have you had supper, Mr Owen?'

'No.'

'When did you eat last?' Nansi asked.

'I had some sandwiches on the boat.'

'Nothing since then?'

'No.'

Her eyes glowing, Nansi turned to her father. 'Dad, you've got your paper. Your biscuits are in the kitchen and the hot milk's in the thermos. You've got your whisky?' The old man smiled and nodded. 'Don't forget your tablets. I'll see you in the morning. 'Night, *cariad*.' She bent to kiss her father's forehead. 'I'm just going to give Mr Owen some supper.'

Rhys shook the old man's hand and wished him 'Good night', to be answered with eyes that also danced with mischief, one of them twitching in the merest suggestion of a wink.

Nansi led Rhys out of the kitchen, through the ragged breach in the old brick garden wall and into the mirror-image house next door. The ground floor of the old, solidly built house had been converted into one large, comfortable living space, the coal fire replaced by a modern gas fire. Nansi whisked away some underwear draped over a radiator.

'These old houses take a long time to warm up,' she said, as if apologetic about the cosiness. 'If you find it too warm, please take your jumper off. I'm sorry it's such a tip but it's usually worse then this – the children are away for the weekend.' She managed to impart the information with her back to Rhys but her voice was too nonchalant. She turned, looking nervously at Rhys. 'If I'd known you were coming, I'd have got some steak or something. All I've got is something from the freezer. Cottage pie – will that do? Some potatoes and peas?'

'Sounds great.'

'Sit down then while I do the potatoes. I'm afraid I don't have a drink to offer you. Since . . . I don't keep drink in the house any more.'

'I have a bottle of wine in the car,' Rhys said. 'Which do you like, red or white?'

'First time I've heard of a car with a cellar, Mr Owen.' Nansi glanced at him out of the corner of her eye. 'Always keep a selection in the boot, do we?'

'Only when I'm lonely,' Rhys grinned. 'You never know your luck.'

'Well, perhaps your luck is in, Mr Owen. Let's have both.'

Five minutes later, Nansi leaned over the sink unit, peeling potatoes while Rhys, with his back to the unit alongside her, struggled with a rusty corkscrew to extract a crumbling cork from a bottle of lukewarm Rudesheimer. He paused in his efforts.

'Staff Nurse Rees,' he said, softly, still gazing studiously at the cork. 'May I kiss you?'

'I was beginning to think you'd never ask, Mr Owen,' was the equally soft-spoken reply.

Their hands fixed in front of them, they leaned their heads and shoulders sideways and drew the moment of silk-cool contact out as long as they could. As their necks began to ache, Nansi broke away to quickly dry her hands and place herself appealingly in front of Rhys.

'More, please, Mr Owen.'

'On one condition, Staff Nurse.'

Nansi raised one eyebrow.

'That you call me Rhys.'

'Wouldn't that be rather forward of . . .'

The last two words were spoken into Rhys's mouth as they kissed more fiercely. She felt his arousal as she pressed him against the unyielding unit and did not back away when he bent her backwards to place the bottle on the table behind her. He winced as her fingers found the bruise behind his ear. Nansi felt the jerk and reacted with a surge of *maldod.* As Rhys's hands crept inexorably lower, his pelvis beginning to grind, Nansi stood back. This was too rushed, didn't fit into the sequence the sight of his car had triggered off in her imagination. She laughed at his look of tantalised dismay.

'Easy,' she murmured. 'There's no hurry.'

The wine poured, the potatoes boiling, they returned to the living room, glass in hand. Nansi sat at Rhys's knee, her forearm warm against the inside of his thigh, almost purring as his fingers explored her neck. The second glass saw her kneeling between his legs with Rhys sliding down the chair to feel her warmth as he held her against him. At the kitchen table, Rhys said little as Nansi prattled on, putting up a flimsy barrier of hospital gossip to keep themselves apart at least long enough to finish their meal. Rhys scarcely noticed the crunching pie crust and overboiled potatoes as he tastelessly gulped his claret to slake his dry mouth. The fresh air and excitement of his sail, the seductive warmth that surrounded him, the wine with little food, all had rendered him dull-witted and it took him some time to realise that Nansi also now was quiet. He looked at her to see her stand, smile slowly and hold out her hand.

'Come on, *cariad*.'

Nansi led him to the stairs which stood along one wall of the living room, so narrow that she had to turn half-sideways as she climbed, to keep her hold on Rhys. In the dimness of the bedroom, yellow tinged by a distant street lamp, she guided him past the foot of the double bed, scarcely a shoulder's breadth from the opposite wall. The space between bed and chest of drawers was cramped and Nansi's head struck Rhys gently as she bent, swiftly, unhurriedly, undressing to stand naked, inviting his gaze in the shadows. Laughing softly, she helped pull his shirt over his head, ran her fingers over his chest before loosening his belt. Rhys heard the rasp of his zip and felt his trousers sag. He was still shuffling out of his trousers, shoes and socks as Nansi slid beneath the bedclothes, holding up the thick duvet, inviting him in. There was neither foreplay nor savage thrust but a slow gentle coition, a fusion of needs that left them blissfully silent. As Rhys began to move, so Nansi began to softly croon her love as she encouraged him, enfolded him. Her eyes did not leave his face, her 'Yes, *cariad* – there, *cariad* – there – and there – and there' sounding like words of comfort for a child, but, as her own needs, her own self-love, began to take control and her body began to drive against his, they lost their sharp focus until, for all she could see through the climactic glaze that clouded her cornea, the man who humped and jerked above her might have been some total stranger. But her awareness of his physical onslaught returned as what had started like the crescendo of animal excitement became a ferocity that seemed out of his control, his short, barking shouts that came faster and faster through tightly clenched jaws, filling the tiny bedroom as he reduced Nansi to mute, frightened submission. As he rolled away, sobbing his release, there was a silence between them that Nansi finally, wonderingly broke.

'Are you all right, *cariad*?'

There was no reponse as Rhys, his eyes still closed, groped within the black emptiness of mind and spirit that still surrounded him. Nansi left him in peace for a while longer.

'Is it always like that for you?' she whispered.

This time Rhys opened one eye and the corners of his mouth twitched.

'I can't remember,' he said.

'Oh, *cariad*, *cariad*; come here.'

And Nansi held him close until she felt the regular breathing of sleep.

The window was set low in the bedroom wall, the deep sill between the thick stone walls no more than a few inches above the dark stained floorboards. Without raising his head, Rhys, in the early morning light, could see halfway up Mynydd Bychan and he watched an elderly man climb the steep slope beyond the children's park towards a row of ramshackle pigeon lofts. The window was closed, light filtering through the drawn, unlined curtains that matched the voluminous duvet. Rhys tried to find more air in the still, cloying atmosphere by pushing the duvet away from him but, each time, the yielding warmth surged back. He began to put together in his mind the events of the previous day, trying desperately to recall each detail. He found himself frustrated in his attempts to mentally re-enact their lovemaking, like someone frantically trying to crystallise the details of a dissolving dream. While guilt was never far away –it was the first time he had been unfaithful to Alex – he felt the pleasurable excitement once more as his reflexes fed on the pictures of Nansi's nakedness his mind was only too ready to provide. He consciously wiped the self-satisfied smirk from his face as he heard the stairs creak. He struggled to the sitting position and pulled the duvet round his waist as Nansi, in a thick, quilted gown, zipped from ankle to neck, kicked open the door and walked in, carefully balancing a cup of coffee in each hand.

'Good morning, sir.' There was mock deference in her smile as she sat on the bed alongside Rhys, handing him one of the cups. 'I trust sir slept well?'

'Good morning, Nansi. Thank you.' Rhys took the cup, trying to act like a man of the world and only succeeding in looking sheepish. 'I slept like a log.' He accentuated the appearance he always had of looking from under his upper lids. 'I trust I didn't follow what I understand is the classical pattern and snore afterwards, did I?' he asked anxiously.

Nansi threw her head back as she laughed delightedly. 'Haven't a clue,' she said. 'I went out like a light myself. Something stirred and woke me when you began to get a bit frisky in the early hours again but you were fast asleep and I didn't have the heart to wake you. And you needn't look so proud of yourself. That's one you owe me.'

Rhys laughed. 'What about your father?'

'He's all right. I've seen to him; given him his breakfast.'

Rhys's eyes flickered towards the window. 'I was thinking about my car,' he said. 'I imagine everyone in the street has seen it by now.'

'Crescent, if you please,' Nansi said, smiling. 'We don't like it called a street round here. Yes, they'll have seen it; hardly miss it, posh car like that. Does it bother you?'

Rhys hesitated before he lied. 'No, not really.'

'So now they know I am a scarlet woman.' Nansi shrugged her shoulders and it flashed through Rhys's mind that perhaps there had been previous occasions that had given them cause for suspicion. For a blindingly jealous moment, the picture of Paddy's lean, tattooed body lying where he was refused to be ignored. 'But you needn't worry. They're a funny lot, nosy as hell, but not a word will go beyond the Crescent, you can depend on that. There's a strange loyalty amongst Welsh mining families; they'll probably take a sort of pride in it. Not often they have a big Consultant Surgeon calling.'

Rhys's gaze returned to the window as he sipped his coffee. He could see two men now, a flurry of pigeons around them. He began wondering whether any of these people would be patients of his; there might even be others nearby who worked in the hospital. How would they react the next time they saw him? Avonport was not that big; it was bound to get around. And Alex? How much simpler it would have been if he had gone straight home the previous night! Life would have been much less complicated that morning. But all such guilt-ridden anxiety was brushed aside as he looked at Nansi again, saw the small crinkles around eyes that seemed to be reading his thoughts.

'Don't worry, love,' she said, quietly. 'I'm not going to ask you to marry me.'

The gentle statement left a soft, generous mouth open just enough to reveal the tip of her tongue moistening her lower lip. The coffee did nothing to prevent Rhys's mouth go dry as he watched the glistening lure trace her upper lip. He found great difficulty in co-ordinating his tongue, mouth and jaw to make his words sound flirtatious, not simply reflect the sudden surge within him that would know no reason.

'You mentioned I got a bit frisky in the night. I'm not sure but I rather think . . .'

Rhys left the rest unsaid.

Slowly, Nansi took his cup from him and placed it, with hers, on the bedside table.

'Perhaps sir would like me to check for him? After all, you do owe me one.'

Their lovemaking was, after a few delicately hesitant passes, devoid of embarrassment. Freed from the clinging duvet, unspoilt by lust, their appetites met and were satisfied by acts of giving and taking, taking and giving, deliciously drawn out into sensations that Rhys would scarcely have considered possible. Nothing was demanded, nothing refused. While there were no wild protestations of love, Rhys was conscious of giving his body with more affection than he had thought himself capable of, had ever shown for Alex, had ever been given the chance to bestow on Helen.

His mind transiently set free from dragging guilt and time-engrained self-reproach, Rhys fell back into a peace that he knew would soon begin to be eroded once more by all the old whirling self-censure. Added now would be thoughts of Nansi; that he would be taking once more, giving little in return. What joy was there going to be in it for her? What was going to happen to what little self-respect he had left? And the respect of others; he had no illusions how much he valued that. They were worlds apart, he and Nansi. There was to be no joy for either of them. And he hadn't used anything. And she hadn't asked him to. Why not? Perhaps she was on the Pill. If so, why? All he knew for certain was that, whatever his doubts and anxieties, he would be back. Sooner or later his need for affection would blot out all reason and, once more, he would seek out this generous heart and body who, he knew, would never refuse him. It was the final outcome that obstinately refused to come into focus.

Nansi saw the small furrows between the closed eyes, outward and visible signs of the ripples that were already reclaiming the serenity she had produced in him. She kissed him gently.

'Don't worry, *cariad*,' she whispered. 'It'll be all right.'

Alex swept aside the heavy brocade curtains. From the seventh floor windows she looked across Park Lane, taking its Sunday morning breather after the frenzy of the week. Hyde Park was making its usual brave attempt to look like the English countryside in the kindly early morning sun. Alex stared, without seeing, at what little movement there was; the small, neat couple who had travelled halfway across the world from one capital city to take photographs of another; the two joggers in such breathless intimacy as to have no time for the bum who had slept rough, earnestly picking for lice amid the thick, filthy layers of his clothing like someone who can't find his train ticket. The inner excitement that rendered her so impercipient was the aftermath of a long, wordless, almost gruelling sexual encounter that had been a struggle, as yet unresolved, for supremacy rather than lovemaking. The sheer joy of the contest had blotted out any smear of conscience that Alex might have had. If she had thought of Rhys at all, it had been in the context of comparison, and Alex had found enough affection for Rhys to drive such thoughts from her mind. She had enjoyed it. Firm honesty tightened her mouth as she admitted to herself that she had damn well enjoyed it. There was little doubt the man in the bed behind her, strides away across the thick pile carpet, half his powerful torso rearing above a crowded breakfast tray, had enjoyed it too. Her lips relaxed again into a small wry smile as she heard him push away the plate, grease slicked from the bacon, egg and sausage, to reach for the toast and butter. She knew that one suggestion of compliance or submission on either her or Gordon's part and the excitement, for them, would be over. But it wasn't over and her only worry was a nagging doubt about her ability to hide the fact. And Rhys, not the most insensitive of men, would know it. Well, he would just have to come to terms with it – or do something about it.

15

She really was the most beautiful girl. Virginally seductive was the nearest description Yousef could find as, later, he recalled how she had looked when she had opened the door. The white silk blouse, high-necked and long-sleeved, revealed Clare Drury's breasts more surely than any plunging neckline, the large gold cameo at her throat seeming to stand guard like a seal on some unopened document. She blushed slightly as, with an elegant, unembarrassed bow of his head, Yousef gave her the flowers as if in tribute. Her flat was exactly as he would have predicted, warm, comfortable, lived in, but still neatly sophisticated and bright.

He would have liked to have taken a closer look at the books that crowded the long shelf, looking more like old friends than decoration – it might have helped him divine what went on in that Saxon head – but he sank into the depths of the armchair. She stood over him.

'Am I allowed to ask you if you would like a drink?' she asked.

'Looking like that, Clare, you are allowed anything,' he smiled, 'but I'm afraid I have got to refuse. But, please, don't let me stop you having one. Perhaps I could have a soft drink of some kind to keep you company. Then you can tell me what to expect tonight.'

'I only wish I knew, Yousef.' Clare spoke over her shoulder as she poured the drinks. 'I've no previous experience.' She handed him his glass and sat opposite him. 'Few people have. Rhys is a poppet to his juniors, always is, but it's very rare for them to be asked to dinner like this. I think he has become very fond of you, Yousef,' she said, earnestly. 'I've only been asked along to make up the numbers.'

'I reckon it's the other way round myself,' Yousef answered.

'No, I've watched him when you are together.' There was no trace of sentimentality in her voice as Clare's grey-blue eyes held his. 'He treats you like the son he never had.'

'Nonsense,' Yousef said, though he showed no sign of displeasure at the suggestion. 'And Mrs Owen? What's she like?'

'Formidable, by all accounts. I've never met her; not exactly looking forward to it. I'm so glad you are going to be there to hold my hand.'

'Pretty dedicated career woman, by all accounts.'

'And what's wrong with that?' The words had tumbled out before Clare saw the smile on Yousef's face. She heard the quiet laugh long before she had finished the sentence, kicking herself for taking the bait. 'Pig.' She stuck the tip of her tongue out at him. 'Good thing you're leaving in the morning. What time do you go?'

'First thing.'

'And taking Rhys with you?'

'Yes. He's coming for three or four weeks.'

'During which time, who do I ring if I find myself faced with a torsion of the gall bladder again?' There was a look on her face now as if she wanted to talk of things that would link them, not of tomorrow when she would not see him again. 'I don't suppose you'd have any use for a very inexperienced junior out there, would you? I don't suppose I could come too, could I?'

'Can't think of anything I'd enjoy more,' Yousef said. But, inwardly, the image of that flaxen hair, instantly transposed amongst the dark uniformity of his people, suddenly brought home to him the polarity of his two worlds. He was surprised at the pang of regret that swelled within him, annoyed with himself at its strength. He thought he was over that.

Clare and the Mercedes blended as one. She seemed not to give it a second look, stepping into it with the cool indifference of someone who never thinks of travelling in anything less. Yousef felt the excitement of a beautiful woman and a powerful car as he drove to the Owens' house. As they got out and slammed the doors, Yousef smiled as he looked round at the undulating garden with its few salt-burned shrubs and crumbling wall that marked its boundary. Beyond the wall and coastline gleamed the Channel. They stood for a moment, side by side, before ringing the door-bell.

'Why is it you British always feel the need to fence yourselves in?' Yousef asked. 'At home . . .' He paused before correcting himself. 'In America, all the gardens sort of run into one. Seems more open somehow.'

'Comes of being invaded,' Clare laughed. 'You ask the only real Americans, walled up in their reservations there. You wait until America has been overrun a few times by the odd Viking or Roman.' She pulled at her hair. 'I don't imagine I would be here but for a bit of looting and pillaging a few centuries back. And I'm still a bit of an invader in this part of the world, you realise that, don't you?'

'Difficult to imagine anyone fighting for long to keep you out, Clare.' Yousef walked to the door. 'Let's ring the bell and see if they'll lower the drawbridge, shall we?'

Twenty minutes of polite conversation and it became obvious to Clare and Yousef that they were to be the only guests and, suddenly, a long evening seemed to stretch before them. It was confirmed, almost in passing, by Alex.

'We had hoped Sian and Roger would be coming tonight but Sian was admitted to Singleton this morning.'

Clare's genuine concern was immediate.

'Oh, I'm sorry. I hadn't heard. Is she all right? Nothing . . .'

'She had a miscarriage in the early hours of this morning. She's all right.'

Yousef looked at Rhys to find his face inscrutable, his eyes almost closed as he played with his drink. He almost winced at the matter of fact tone of Alex's final remark on the subject.

'At least it puts off the evil day of becoming a grandmother, I suppose.'

Yousef exchanged the briefest of glances with Clare before turning his sober gaze back on Alex. He began to wonder whether she had been drinking, felt more certain of it as he saw the careless way in which she poured herself another gin. Yousef felt hungry but there was no sign of a meal and he watched, fascinated, simply fuelling the conversation with a few remarks of his own, as Alex's tone became more aggressive, her attitude more and more isolated. She gave the impression that she was with them but not of them, just fulfilling a courtesy that had been forced on her, not really enjoying the charade, that her heart and mind would be elsewhere. Rhys said little or nothing as Alex seemed to delight in putting herself at a distance further and further from them, never quite agreeing with any opinion expressed, never conceding a point. Yousef got the feeling that, with a few more gins inside her, she would be telling them what a trio of soft-hearted, featherbedded idealists they were and that they should try the hard world of private enterprise outside and see how they got on.

The meal was superb. Course after course was produced, seemingly out of thin air, with effortless competence, all offers of help from Clare being refused firmly, almost curtly. Clare smiled her thanks to Rhys as he poured her a glass of Benedictine.

'And you're off to foreign parts with Yousef tomorrow, Mr Owen. Are you looking forward to it?'

'Very much so, Clare; yes.' Rhys answered, taking his seat at the top of the table once again.

'He can't wait to get away.' The voice from the other end of the table did not specify what Rhys could not wait to get away from.

Clare looked towards Rhys. 'I wish I was coming too. It sounds fascinating.'

'What's this?' Alex broke in again. 'Someone else anxious to get away?'

'Oh, no,' Clare said, hastily, glancing at Rhys in case he had taken the remark wrongly. 'I'm more than happy in Avonport. It's just that, from what Yousef has told me about his country, it sounds an enchanting place to visit.'

'Really?'

Alex made scant effort to conceal her contempt, not for Shahin – it was a country of which she was ignorant and, therefore, supremely indifferent towards. What she was doing was throwing her cap in the ring. Here was another man who, like her husband, delighted in surrounding himself with bogus mystery, always holding something back, always stopping short of putting everything up front. But Alex suspected a worthier adversary beneath the suavity of his American good manners. She stared at him as if daring him to take up the challenge, while Clare, sensing the conflict of wills, joined Rhys in the background.

'You lived in America for a while, Alex, I understand?' To Clare, it sounded as if Yousef had made his choice of battle field. 'When was that?'

'Long ago. Too long.'

'I get the impression you enjoyed it?'

'God's country.'

'I suppose one might argue that depends on who or what your God is,' Yousef said with quiet intensity. 'Whereabouts in America did you live?'

'Washington. My father was on the staff of the Embassy there. We were out there for two years until he had some heart trouble, had to come home.' She made it sound like a crime for which there was no forgiveness.

'What did you like about the States particularly?'

Alex squinted at him as if looking into the sun, as if she did not want to see too clearly how well dressed, perhaps too well dressed, he was, how totally in control of himself he appeared. She resented his early use of her Christian name in that friendly, American manner of his. She wasn't taking too kindly to being treated as an equal by someone who had, after all, only come there to learn, someone junior to Rhys.

'I thought it really was the land of opportunity,' she said.

'Just so long as you are blessed with the ability to take advantage of those opportunities.'

'Oh, sure.' Alex waved the coffee pot at Yousef but he shook his head. She put it down again without looking at Clare or Rhys. 'What's wrong with a system that rewards ability and hard work?'

'Perhaps you should ask that of someone who has had the misfortune to be born unable.' There was no fear in Yousef's face as he turned his head to look directly at Alex, the merest tremor in his voice the only evidence that Alex was getting to him.

'Unable to do what?'

‘Anything; anything, that is, to protect themselves from the predators in their own tribe. It’s quite accepted, isn’t it, to call someone able and leave it at that; considered a compliment. It’s not too bad to be disabled these days, virtually an honour if you’re a Veteran. But unable, that’s different; we still have very little time for them.’

‘Stupid, you mean.’

‘No, I don’t mean stupid.’ There was an even emphasis on each word that was born of an inner conflict between passion and self-control. Both Alex and Yousef flickered their irritation as the crack of a cheese biscuit from Rhys’s end of the table broke into their awareness. ‘Stupidity to me is the misuse of ability. The fact that you are intelligent doesn’t mean that you are immune to stupidity. You’re an intelligent woman, Alex; do you mean to say you are not capable of doing something stupid from time to time?’

Rhys looked up briefly, glancing across the table as if he would be interested in the answer to that question too.

‘Of course I don’t; but one thing’s for sure, I would never have been so stupid as to leave the sort of job you had in America. What possessed you to do that? To leave your wife and – two children, is it?

‘Please, Alex, don’t get me wrong. It wasn’t an easy decision to make. I love America; I love Americans. I owe them a great deal – my education, my surgical training.’

‘All I can say is, you have a strange way of expressing it,’ Alex retorted, scathingly, but Yousef took little notice.

‘They are the most generous, warm-hearted people in the world. Always the first in line with their money when there’s been an earthquake or flood or famine or whatever. It’s just that they are a bit slow in taking the hint when they’re not wanted. I have every reason to be grateful to them and I don’t think for a moment I would have left the States if I had not gone back to Shahin to see my father when I heard he was so ill.’

‘Your father?’ Alex asked.

‘The Sultan. My father is Sultan of Shahin,’ Yousef replied, simply, feeling the upsurge in interest all round the table.

‘And what does that mean exactly?’ Alex was striving not to show she was impressed.

‘It means my father is Shahin’s leader, both religious and secular; like any truly fundamentalist country, we do not recognise any distinction. He is our Imam, our religious leader, as well as our Head of State. And you were quite right, I was possessed, possessed by my father’s hopes and dreams for his country that I had forgotten about in my quest for a bigger swimming pool, a more powerful car. I was overcome by, what do you

Welsh call it, *hiraeth*? No, Shahin is now my home.'

Alex heard the steel return to his voice and welcomed it. For a moment she had thought he too was backing away to hide behind that smug, self-righteous screen so beloved by Rhys whenever she tried to involve him in an argument.

'I don't imagine for a moment that you've given up your American citizenship? Still carry an American passport, do you?' Alex taunted.

Yousef, for the first time, looked uneasy. 'Yes, I do.'

'Want a foot in both camps, do you?' Alex almost sneered and didn't give him a chance to answer. 'And is your wife going to join you in your country – what do you call it – Shahin?'

'No.'

'Can't say I blame them either; you'd never get me to move from America to some place in the desert. I imagine that makes you a Muslim, Yousef?'

'I am, yes.'

Alex's laugh was short and mirthless as if she wasn't really expecting anyone else to share the joke. 'Perhaps you have a family home and abroad then?'

Clare suddenly shuffled in her seat as if trying, overawed as she was, to indicate to Alex that she had gone too far. If Alex registered the gesture, she showed no sign of it as she poured herself another brandy.

'No.'

The one word was spoken with the tranquillity that reflected Yousef's sudden change of emotion. He saw an intelligent, strong-willed woman, swayed by passion to the point where there could be no return to the accepted pleasantries of hospitality, driving herself to goad him into some sort of reaction. And why? She had no reason to feel so strongly about America or Shahin. She would have no more than the usual British condescension towards Islam. It could only be that she equated him with Rhys. He was only taking the full brunt of her alcohol-freed repressions because he was, to her mind, so like her husband. And what should he do? He was not in his own country now, where such behaviour between host and honoured guest would be unthinkable. He was being deliberately provoked. Should he withdraw behind a bland smile of apparent indifference, retracting his idealism from Alex's attack, join Rhys in his retreat? Or should he put his dreams on display, test them in the heat of Alex's inevitable scorn? 'I still love my wife and children dearly,' Yousef said, quietly. 'And I haven't given up the hope that perhaps one day, when the children are grown up, they'll come and join me. I still hope to see them from time to time. I will never marry anyone else. But now I have another love for which I am prepared to make sacrifices.'

Clare looked near to tears but, by the tone of her voice, Alex was not so impressed.

'And what's that?'

'We have a dream. It is that Shahin will become a haven for all those who wish to live out their lives peacefully according to the fundamental principles of the Faith.'

'With public executions and amputations and floggings; that sort of thing?' Alex was now openly contemptuous.

'No. We must try to make the punishments more humane without necessarily changing the law that is broken.'

'What's this, fundamentalism and compassion? Something of a contradiction in terms, isn't it? You've got a job on if you're hoping to convince the West at the moment that you Muslims are a compassionate lot. Mention the, what do you call them, Shi'ites? – ' Yousef nodded ' – and anyone in this country would immediately think of a terrorist.'

'Islam is the most tolerant of all the monotheistic religions,' Yousef argued back. 'We recognise both Christian and Jew. We are not all terrorists. In any case, it depends on what you call a terrorist.' Yousef had no feeling of anger, just a realisation that Alex was only tracing out for him deeply etched prejudices that he had dedicated himself to erase. 'One country's terrorist is another country's patriot.'

'I wondered how long it would be before that old platitude was trotted out. That's what the IRA say. You know that's nonsense.'

'Is it? Frenchmen take great pride now when they talk of their part in the Resistance as they called it. They went round blowing things up and killing people, innocent people at times, and are proud of it, but I'm sure the Germans saw them as terrorists.'

'That's not the same thing,' Alex retorted, scathingly. 'They were at war. They had been invaded by the Germans. Not the same thing at all.'

'No? The Shi'ite so-called terrorists in South Lebanon, they, as old men, will tell their grandchildren of their part in their struggle against the invader. They will be honoured just like the French Resistance fighters. Don't tell me you couldn't see any resemblance between the Israeli Iron Fist raids on the Shi'ite villages and some French village being shot up by the SS for harbouring some of the Maquis?'

For the first time, Alex had no immediate answer with which to fend off the next thrust of Yousef's argument.

'The Arabs of South Lebanon, they were peaceful farmers until Israel invaded their country, an invasion America could have stopped any time it liked, and they more or less welcomed the invaders if it meant ridding themselves of the PLO. They were as peaceful as the farmers of Southern Ireland. Can you imagine the reaction of the Irish and of Senator Kennedy if the British Army invaded Southern Ireland saying they were protecting their border from terrorists? Is an Arab not allowed to react too? Is he some sort of second-class citizen who must smile and say "Thank you" when he is forced, with a gun at his head, to watch some Israeli soldier tear up and walk all over his beloved Koran? And you forget, we Arabs were never taught cricket, so, if you don't like the rules, don't play the game.'

During the silence that followed, Clare did not take her eyes off Yousef's face.

'It all depends where your sympathy lies,' Yousef added quietly.

'What you mean is that you sympathise with terrorism?' Alex came back. She was not finished yet. 'Does this country of yours support terrorism?'

'No more than you do.'

Alex looked puzzled at Yousef's reply, as if amazed that anyone could consider the possibility of it.

'You no doubt look on the CIA as a bunch of clean-cut, all-American boys defending the American way of life but, believe me, seen through the eyes of an Arab, they are the most efficient terrorist organisation in the world. When they train Lebanese Intelligence men in the techniques of urban bombing, with the full approval of their President, does it really matter who ultimately pulls the firing pin?'

Alex said nothing.

'No, we never actively support terrorism however much we sympathise with the cause; at least, not actively.'

Alex came back sharply.

'Not actively? What d'you mean, not actively?'

'We offer sanctuary.'

'To terrorists?'

'Yes.'

'You mean you are harbouring known terrorists?' Alex, though tiring under the combined influence of weariness and alcohol, did her best to make it sound a biting condemnation.

Yousef answered with no suggestion of either shame or pride.

'Yes. Shahin is the Arabic name for what you, in this country, call the peregrine falcon. It is a migratory bird in our part of the world and to tame this bird of prey so that it will settle peaceably with us, requires endless patience in teaching and feeding. No, we will never refuse sanctuary to anyone who observes the true Faith and turns his back on terrorism.' He looked vaguely, dreamily at somewhere near the centre of the table. ' "Your muddled masses yearning to breathe free, the wretched refuse of your teeming shore, send these, the homeless, tempest tossed, to me" . . .'

'Romantic poppycock,' Alex cut him short.

'I'm surprised you should think that, Alex,' Yousef slowly turned his head to look at her, 'seeing they are words carved into the Statue of Liberty.'

And Rhys joined in his triumph with a laugh.

'She really is a thorough-going, 100 per cent, copper-bottomed bitch.'

Yousef took his eyes off the road for a moment to smile at the venom in the normally serene profile alongside him.

'She's not so bad. You mustn't be too hard on her.'

'How can you say that after the way she was needling you?' Clare stamped her foot as she gave a little grunt of pent-up fury. ' "This country of yours," ' she mimicked. 'What business was it of hers, the vindictive old bitch.' Yousef put his head back and laughed outright, delighted in the transformation in this ice-cool paragon. 'How Rhys copes with that every day, I can't imagine.'

'Fifty–fifty, Clare. It's alway fifty–fifty. Wait until you get married; you'll find out.' He sensed Clare's dissent. 'Yes, it is. Don't get me wrong; my heart goes out to Rhys but I shouldn't think he's the easiest man in the world to live with. And Alex was a bit drunk – ' he paused, adding thoughtfully ' – and, I think, a bit guilty about something.'

'Oh?' Clare sat up, turning her body towards him, beginning to show her love for him. 'Psychiatrist as well as brilliant surgeon now, are we?'

'You bet. Seriously, I don't think she gives a damn about me or Shahin. It was only my likeness to Rhys, my rapport with him, that got under her skin. She wasn't lashing out at me – what does she care about Shahin? – I was just standing in for Rhys. Poor Rhys. He's showing all the signs of the battered husband syndrome, I'm afraid.'

'Oh?' Clare laughed. 'How can you tell?'

'It's not easy. There's more than one method of battering and mental bruising doesn't show. But there has to be a reason for her wanting to hurt him like that; that's not just marital boredom. I reckon that's guilt. I suspect that, deep down, our Alex is not too proud of herself either for some reason.'

Clare's stage whisper was directed at Yousef's left ear. 'You mean another man?'

They were still entwined in bright chatter when they stood at the door to Clare's flat. Beneath her levity there was a desperate urgency that Clare tried to keep out of her voice. She suddenly felt almost ashamed of her virginity. A twenty-five-year-old, not unattractive, thrusting, career-bent doctor and a virginal survivor of medical student gropings and the aftermath of wild Resident's parties? No one would believe her, not in this liberated day and age. There had been plenty of offers to initiate her into the art but she had never wanted to feel the length of a man's body against hers like this before. And whom had she picked? – a man who made no pretence about still loving his wife and children and was to leave the next day for good. She felt ashamed of her stammering ineptitude.

'Can I interest you in a c-cup of coffee? I know I can't ask you in for a drink.'

'I'd love one, Clare.'

Yousef followed her in.

'Sit down for a moment, Yousef; or put a record on, if you like. I won't be a moment; I must just comb my hair.'

As she disappeared into the bedroom, Yousef walked to the bookshelf, pulling one of the hardbacks out at random. It was only a small cry but, across the silence between them, Yousef heard in it fear and hurt and disgust.

'Clare?'

There was no answer. Yousef replaced the book carefully and, unhurriedly, walked into the bedroom. Clare did not turn from where she stood, staring at her dressing table. He looked round the room, saw the neat femininity, the only concession to disorder being the tousled, battered old rag doll propped up on one of twin bedside tables, standing sentinel beside the immaculate, single bed. He stood behind her, was about to put his hands on her shoulders when she turned and pressed herself against him, her arms folded against his chest like a child. He put his arms around her, pressing her head to his shoulder, feeling her silent sob.

'What's the matter, Clare?'

'Someone's been here.'

'What d'you mean?'

'Someone's been here,' she repeated. 'Since we left this evening.'

'Are you sure? How d'you know?'

'I'm sure. I don't like clutter,' she said, as if it was something to apologise for. She drew her head away a little and turned it towards the dressing table, turning Yousef with her as she struggled to stay close to him. 'I like to be neat and tidy and I know where everything is to a fraction of an inch; I'm sorry, but I'm that sort of person – and those have been moved.'

Yousef looked over her shoulder to see the heavy polished silver frame that enclosed heads and shoulders of proud parents, handsome and strong in their declining years.

'And look . . .' Clare freed herself and led Yousef by the hand to the bedside. 'That clock's been moved too. Daddy gave me that when I started my first house job.' She sounded as if she were giving away her deepest secrets to a lover. 'It's been moved. I always prop it up by putting that little catch on the case into the bottom of the clock itself.'

Yousef looked where the lower edge of the folding travelling clock rested in the velvet-lined hollow of the case. Clumsy, that; sloppy workmanship. Had they needed to go through all her things like that? Or was it just some wet-lipped, heavy breather who enjoyed an assignment more if it happened to involve being alone in a young girl's bedroom, leaving his mark on her vestal underwear? They had left no such traces in his apartment. And now he must be careful what he said; the tapes would already be turning.

'Are you quite sure?' he asked, to be answered with a vigorous shake of her head.

'I'll go and see if there's any sign of a break-in.' Yousef left the bedroom and made a show of examining the door lock, looking for the tell-tale marks he knew would not be there – they would hardly have been that clumsy. As he looked at the windows, he made enough noise to carry to the bedroom. When he re-entered the bedroom, Clare was just closing a drawer with her fingertips as if fearful of some contagion. He felt her relief as he put his arms round her once more.

'Yousef, I'm frightened.'

'There's no need to be. You're quite safe.'

'But, I tell you; someone has been in here tonight.'

'You can't be sure, Clare. Perhaps you brushed against these things when you were dressing.'

'No.' Clare was adamant.

Should he mention the police? The last thing he wanted to do, but wouldn't Clare expect it?

'Would you like me to call the police?'

'Oh, no.' Clare reacted quickly. 'They wouldn't believe me. You obviously don't so why should they? But, please, Yousef, stay with me. Please don't go.'

Yousef felt the hypocrisy of the kiss he slowly placed on her forehead. A Judas kiss setting the seal on his betrayal. He wondered where they'd put the bugs. He could not search for them though they would not be hard to find if you knew where to look; it hadn't taken him long in his own rooms. Those he had left untouched; to have removed them would only have been evidence to confirm their suspicions. It had been a damned nuisance, the calls to prearranged public call boxes in London from random, draughty boxes around Avonport, but it had been worth it if only to visualise the boredom of some audio lab technician listening to miles of useless tape. But they might have left him alone here. Did they have to touch this girl's life with their grubby feelers? What had they hoped to achieve? Some vital piece of information let slip by passion? Some foolish indiscretion picked up by the marvels of modern electronics at the moment of defloration? Anyway, how does a Ministry stenographer transcribe the sounds of sexual intercourse?

'Clare, I must go. I can't possibly stay. We leave early tomorrow morning and I haven't said goodbye to Hannah yet.' Each reason sounded more fatuous than the last.

'But you're leaving tomorrow; I shan't see you again.' The ache was back, obliterating for a moment even her fear.

'All the more reason why I should go now.'

'But I want you. I want you to make love to me. Please; do I have to beg you?'

She kissed him, at first to cover the embarrassment at her own sudden shamelessness, then deeply, pleadingly, only to feel him hold back. In one step backwards, Clare changed from soft, supplicating femininity to impenetrable frigidity.

'In that case, I think you had better go, Yousef. Have a good trip, as I believe they say in your country. But, of course, it's not your country any more, is it?'

'I really am sorry, Clare. Perhaps, in time, you'll come to understand.'

'Oh, sure. In the meanwhile, your country needs you. Don't let me keep you.'

He was backing away through the living room, flinching at her taunts, longing for release from the look of withering scorn that had replaced all trace of fear.

'If you're still worried tomorrow, perhaps you had better give the police a ring. They'll keep an eye on you, I'm sure. In the meanwhile, put the chain on the door and don't let anyone in. You'll be quite safe.'

'Sure thing, Yousef. No doubt they'll send Starsky and Hutch round and then everything will be OK. If I'm lucky, they'll bring Huggy Bear with them – he always was a favourite of mine.'

She shepherded Yousef through the door and, in an appalling attempt at an American accent, gave full and final vent to her fury.

'OK, lover boy; get lost.'

Before turning away, Yousef hesitated for a second, gazing at the door slammed in his face, gritting his teeth against the sounds of rending heartbreak that came from beyond it.

16

The farewells at the Owen's front door were awkward and short. In the brief space of time it took for Yousef to put the luggage in his car, Alex and Rhys had kissed and said goodbye, their only other physical contact being a brief holding of hands. Though emotionally distant by nature, they had not been physically apart for more than a day or so since they were married and a surge of mutual affection, rapidly suppressed, left them with a certain shame in their inability to do better in front of a stranger.

Neither man spoke much as the car sped along the M4, Rhys trying to analyse the inexplicable sadness he felt at parting from Alex, images of Nansi making the task virtually impossible. The process became a confused struggle for supremacy, Rhys finally succumbing, putting his head back, his eyes closing around fantasies of Nansi's warm nakedness. His mind was too full of his own thoughts to detect, in what little conversation took place, a subtle change in Yousef's attitude. It was only at Heathrow's Terminal 3 that Rhys became aware of it. At Avonport, Rhys had been the patriarch, Yousef the honoured guest, the favoured son. But there was a new brisk sense of purpose about Yousef that left Rhys standing amongst the luggage, like some third former going back after the holidays, while Yousef returned the hired Mercedes. After passing through Passport Control, a place to sit and a cup of coffee were both found as would be expected from a worldwise son for an honoured father.

As they sat, their conversation uneasy and clipped in the subtle tension of an airport lounge, Yousef changed seats to turn his back on the unpleasant scene that was being enacted two rows of seats away. An Arab, gross even beneath the forgiving folds of his robe, had entered with an airline official. The whiteness of his dress relieved only by the gold on his fingers and wrists, he had stood aside, silent and impassive, as another passenger, complaining volubly, had been escorted back out through Passport Control by the politely adamant official. Yousef was unable to meet Rhys's inquiring gaze, his whole manner embarrassed and apologetic.

As they boarded the Gulf Air Boeing, Rhys registered mild, pleasant surprise as the chief steward personally showed them to their seats. He settled in the window seat, courteously offered by Yousef, and looked round, trying to analyse what it was that was so different from other planes in which he had flown. The contrast in dress between Arab and Western was obvious. Some of the Brits, with their pin-stripe suits and briefcases, might have stepped off the 8.30 at Victoria. Others, big men, many with beards, wore shiny suits with pale blue shirts, open at the neck; Rhys could imagine the tattoos. But, of course, that was it; there were no children. Rhys screwed his head round to look between the seats; no women either. There were no young, female faces, suffused with excitement above polo-necked ski jumpers; just poker-faced men thrown together for a while as they went about their business. It was against this background that Rhys began to notice the bowing, unsmiling deference one or two of the Arabs showed towards Yousef.

The jet descended from a cloudless sky to give Rhys his first sight of Shahin. As the plane flew parallel with the coast, the wakes of ships on the rippled sea, far below, led his eye to the large coastal town, the natural harbour to the west of it looking to be a deep water port, judging by the size of the ships moored alongside. Anchored in the lee of an island a mile or so offshore, were smaller craft, some carrying a sail that Rhys, even from that height, could see was of a shape never to be sighted in the Bristol Channel. Yousef stretched across him to point through the window.

'Amal,' he said, 'our capital. It is Arabic for Hope. Unfortunately, a name now more likely to conjure up pictures of street fighting in Beirut.'

Rhys felt excitement as he picked out the buildings, crammed into every available space between the sea and the sharply rising mountains. The streets looked narrow between the flat roofs but a broad, busy highway ran eastwards from the docks along the water's edge. A few minutes later, the airport came into view, a long runway built on a rocky headland so that the approach from either end would be over the sea. The airport buildings, as far as he could see, looked modern, half a dozen or so jets parked neatly in front of them, but, as the plane banked to make its final approach, Rhys was surprised to snatch a glimpse of a military aircraft dispersed around the far end of the runway.

Rhys had imagined their arrival would be essentially a reversal of the procedures at Heathrow and was totally unprepared for what occurred as they emerged from the plane into a searing heat that made him cringe. The large, black Mercedes, parked a few yards from the bottom of the steps, shimmering in the tarmac's fierce reflection, was surrounded by a group, strange to Rhys's eyes in their dress, one young man, upright and alert, carrying an automatic weapon that hung from his shoulder like an extra limb. He searched amongst those crowding around him at the plane's exit, wondering who was so important as to warrant such a reception, only to see Yousef emerge, descend alone and walk to the car. By the time Rhys felt the heat of the ground through his shoes, Yousef had returned to speak to him.

'I must leave you now, Rhys,' he said, in the tones of a Consultant telling his Registrar he has been called away. 'Salim here will look after you.' He turned his head to indicate a man whose dark, lean features stared unsmilingly at Rhys from under his *shamag*. 'He has a car waiting for you and he has instructions to help you in any way he can while you are with us. Take a day or so to get used to us, Rhys. Do a bit of sightseeing. I shall be busy for a few days but I'll be in touch with you as soon as I can and then perhaps we can get down to some work.'

As the car drove away, Rhys fought down a feeling of being abandoned as he took his place in the shuffling queue towards Passport Control. He tried a few tentative smiles at Salim, standing impassively at his shoulder, but got no response. One or two questions in the kind of English that foreigners are expected to understand were equally unrewarding. Outside the airport buildings, Salim, without a word, threw the case into a battered Chevrolet and took to the dual carriageway that had been visible from the air. The excitement Rhys had felt in Yousef's company had evaporated with his sudden disappearance. He tried to fight off a sudden depression by forcing himself to take an interest in his new surroundings but he found no great comfort in the palm trees that stretched along the central reservation of the six-lane highway. All the cars seemed to be Japanese though he twisted his head rapidly as he saw a Jaguar XJ6, incongruous amongst the tiny yellow Mazdas, speed by in the opposite direction. The atmosphere in the car was stifling and his mimed complaint to the driver only produced a few twiddles of the air-conditioning controls and a defeatist shrug of the shoulders. Rhys could not believe it could be any worse with the window open, but it was. He fell back in the seat. He suddenly felt vulnerable, his immediate future seemingly in the hands of the mute stranger at the wheel, and he longed for a chirpy London taxi driver and the haven of a pre-booked hotel room. He had lost all sense of direction when the car jerked to a halt and Rhys followed Salim through the door of a two-storey building that carried neither name nor number. A simple desk and an old-fashioned telephone switchboard were the only furniture in a cool, whitewashed hallway. Salim deposited Rhys's case in front of the desk and turned to him, his face an unintelligible mask.

'I am to serve you during your stay with us. Tomorrow I will return. May God's blessings be upon you.'

By the time Rhys had conjured up suitable words to reply, Salim had shuffled his way through the door and was gone. In contrast, the face behind the desk smiled an immediate welcome. Yes, he was expected. Yes, there was a room for him, a nice room; there had been instructions. But the friendly human contact lasted no longer than the time taken to show him into the room on the first floor, the feeling of isolation returning as the door closed on him. Rhys walked out on to the balcony and into the blistering heat of a huge courtyard enclosed on all sides by balconies identical to his own. He looked down at the deserted, blue-tiled swimming pool, the chairs and tables around it silent in sunshine that made his eyes ache if they stared at any one point too long. While there was neither sight nor sound of life, Rhys sensed his fellow man behind the rows of wide open balcony doors. Motivated now by no more than basic animal instinct, Rhys turned back into the room, stripped to his underpants and, without a thought to unpacking, unsure whether the water was fit to slake his thirst, not knowing where or how next he would eat, he curled up on the bed and gratefully accepted the asylum of sleep.

'Hullo. May I come in?'

By the time Rhys had opened his eyes, blinked at the strange surroundings and run his tongue round an arid mouth, the man had crossed the room, introduced himself as Tom Bowdler, crushed Rhys's grip, feeble with sleep, and folded his great height sufficiently to sit in the chair against the wall. His hair was straight, thin and faded but the bushy moustache was still fiery red. His clean-shaven cheeks showed the coarseness produced by years of desert sun beating down on skin unprotected by native pigment. His khaki bush shirt and trousers, worn and loose fitting, looked freshly laundered and ironed and the soft-soled 'brothel creepers' completed the picture of an officer left behind after one of Montgomery's desert campaigns. Alongside him, Rhys felt grubby and naked.

'Just arrived, have you? Feels a bit strange at first, doesn't it?' The sixth former seeking an acolyte in the new boy. 'How long are you here for?'

'Not absolutely sure,' Rhys replied, now sitting with his legs dangling over the side of the bed, his face still screwed up against the brightness. 'About three to four weeks, I think.'

'Oh.' Bowdler sounded disappointed. 'What are you?' The question did not sound inquisitive. 'All the Franks have something to do out here. No such thing as a tourist. What do you do?'

'Surgeon,' Rhys answered and Bowdler looked impressed. 'Franks?' Rhys raised one eyebrow.

'It's what the locals call us Europeans amongst themselves. They have a name for everyone who's been here any length of time. Me? I'm Taweel; the tall one.'

'I see,' Rhys said. 'And what do you do?'

'Engineer.'

'Oh?' Rhys began to take an interest. His morale began to improve. It would be a change to meet people who were not doctors. 'What sort of engineer?'

'Roads. I build roads.' Bowdler's tone was dismissive, as if his job was of little importance compared with Rhys's. 'Very dull. Have you eaten?'

Rhys shook his head and Bowdler immediately banged his broad, bony hands on the arms of the chair. 'Come on then. I expect you could do with something to eat. I'll leave you to get unpacked and have a wash. I'm next door but one, on the right. Give me a shout when you're ready.'

In his mood of resentment at Yousef's sudden abandonment, Rhys would have welcomed any form of human contact but he had found no difficulty in talking to such an open, friendly character and had been surprised how freely the conversation had flowed throughout the meal without recourse to the subject of medicine. Bowdler had taken him to his favourite restaurant, the International, run by friendly, white-toothed Pakistanis. Rhys had tasted camel meat for the first time but had declined Tom's laughing offer of a goat's head. Now, fed and hydrated, he sat in the darkness that had fallen like a shutter, chatting to Bowdler and watching men bathing beneath the lights around the pool. From somewhere nearby came the unmistakable slamming, slapping sounds of a squash court.

'Did you say you'd been given a car and a driver while you are here?' Bowdler asked.

Rhys nodded.

'I'm impressed. Not many get that sort of VIP treatment here. Still, if you're friendly with the Sultan's son, I suppose it's only to be expected. He sounds a fascinating chap. I'd be interested to know what you think of him. I've never moved in those sort of circles myself. As I saw on my report in the Army once – "unlikely to reach Field rank".'

'You were a Regular?'

'Does it show?'

'Only in the nicest possible way.'

They laughed quietly, in complete rapport.

'Yes,' Bowdler said. 'Came up from the ranks. It was my whole life until we – shall we say – mutually agreed to go our own ways.'

Rhys said nothing but looked at Bowdler sympathetically as if he knew there must be more to come.

'I have this drink problem. That's why places like this suit me so well. Just have one sister in Acton, so no real home ties. And this is the nearest to Army life as I can get without the demon drink.'

'How long have you been in Shahin?'

'Two years. Been in the Middle East for over ten now, in four different countries altogether.'

'And you enjoy it?'

Bowdler thought for a moment. 'Yes. I must do. I certainly can't imagine myself living back home again now. And, I don't know – ' he lifted his shoulders as if putting on a cloak ' – it gets to you. Even if you don't have a problem like mine. Particularly if you're a Brit somehow. They keep coming back, especially the old sweats. They've no time for the Westernised Arab – you know what the Army thought of Farouk – but the Regulars always have had a tremendous respect for the tribesmen. Bloody marvellous fighters.'

'A touch of the Lawrence of Arabias, you mean,' Rhys laughed.

'If you like.' Rhys stopped laughing as he saw that Bowdler was quite serious. 'I served a couple of years not too far from here. Didn't see much action, mainly repairing roads that promptly got blown up again, but I was caught in an ambush for one night once. Very unpleasant, I assure you.'

'I can imagine,' Rhys said, politely, though Bowdler looked as if he doubted it. 'But is that much of a problem now?'

'Not really. But the tribes still block the road at times if they reckon it crosses their land, expect a sort of toll if you want to pass, usually in kind rather than money. Sometimes they rather overdo things and we have to go and clear a way again. It wouldn't do for you to go wandering on the Jebel without someone who knew what he was doing.'

'Jebel?' Rhys asked.

'Mountain range up to the north. The tribelands. Independent bunch of bastards like all highlanders; think the plainsmen down here the lowest form of life. You'll soon pick them out when you see them; always got a rifle sticking out somewhere.'

'Where are you building your roads, then?' Rhys was now fighting off the tiredness of the journey, the excitement, the disappointment, the heat and now the gentle, soporific conversation. He stifled a yawn, loath to exchange Bowdler's open protection for his room's encapsulating loneliness. 'I imagine there is plenty of scope for your job out here.'

'We're mainly site clearing at the moment. I work for an American construction company laying the service roads for the new University complex and the huge new hospital and Medical School they are going to build out beyond the airport.'

Rhys became more interested, more alert.

'Hospital? Medical School? I understood there was a new Medical School here already.'

'They may have got a few medical students for all I know,' Bowdler said, 'but the hospital here doesn't look much cop. I've never been inside, thank God, but I know for a fact that, if any of the ex-pats get a pain in their guts, if they can possibly hang out, they're on the next plane back to Blighty or Germany or Holland or wherever.'

'Really?' It conjured up a picture in Rhys's mind into which he was finding it difficult to fit a modern Dialysis and Transplant Unit. 'That's interesting.'

'Yes. I took it you were here to advise them on something to do with the planning of the new hospital. Was I right?'

'I don't really know, Tom. For my sins, I run a Dialysis and Transplant Unit back home and I understood I was to advise them on setting up one here. From what you've said, it doesn't look too promising, does it?'

'It must be for the new hospital,' Bowdler reasoned. 'Got to be.'

'And is your company building that too?'

Bowdler put his head back and laughed, leaving Rhys with the feeling he had just said something very naive.

'That's the $64,000 question, or rather the £300 million question. There are companies all over the world who'd like to get their hands on that contract.'

'And it hasn't been signed yet?'

'No.'

'And there'd be a lot of wheeling and dealing going on over it?'

'You can say that again.'

'And, no doubt, the inevitable corruption?'

Rhys sounded smug, a reflection of his general attitude as he sat back. He was still smarting from Yousef's defection and saw an opportunity of cementing his new friendship by mutually vilifying the Shahinians. It would comfort his wounded pride to spend a while with someone who also saw all Arabs as two-faced, insincere bastards. But he was to be disappointed.

Tom Bowdler was too much the gentleman to disagree forcibly with Rhys. He inclined his head between shrugged shoulders before answering.

'No; not really. I'm not saying there isn't any. God knows there has been enough in the Arab world to make it impossible to get rid of overnight. It has always been accepted that it is one of the perks of being in authority that you took a slice off the top, especially the ruling families. But here – ' once again Bowdler gestured his regret at having to disagree ' – I must say, they are trying. They really are, Rhys. I have the greatest respect for what they are trying to do here in Shahin.'

Rhys was surprised at the intensity of feeling shown by someone he had judged to be a pleasant but ineffectual boozer who was capable of holding down a job only in some such God forsaken part of the world. Once again, he felt rebuffed but found it impossible to be at odds for long with such a kindly man.

'So, what are you going to do tomorrow?' Bowdler asked.

'I don't really know. Any suggestions?'

'You must go and see the suks. Just make sure you don't get ripped off. They expect you to haggle so for God's sake don't accept their first offer. You can take your pick depending on what you want. There are carpet suks, gold suks, camel suks. And there's the port. You mentioned you were a sailor. You'd be interested in the old trading boats. Just one word of advice, don't be tempted to use your car to get up on the Jebel, not on your own.'

'Oh?'

'You'd be all right though you might find the tribesmen's attitude a bit frightening. But here in the towns, you can walk round quite safely, day or night. There's no such thing as mugging or rape. You'll find they are either very friendly or they'll ignore you completely.'

For four days, Rhys strove hard to maintain his lonely interest in the strange sights, sounds and smells around him. At first, the muezzin's intonations, seeming to vibrate in the heat above the rooftops, had sent a shiver down Rhys's back but, as the days went by, he became less tolerant of Salim's frequent calls to prayer. After his first visit, the docks looked like any other docks and the booms he had seen seemed to prefer their diesel engines to their graceful sails, modern inflatables lashed incongruously to their decks. He had enjoyed the bargaining over the hand-embroidered scarf he had bought on the first day for Alex but came to resent the constant haggling as he sought the solution to the problem of Nansi's present. He found himself snapping at the youngsters trailing after him, urging him towards their particular merchant. The smell of coffee and goats lost its charm and the sounds from an Arabian transistor radio became as tiresome as that from any other. Hours of enervating siesta did nothing to raise his morale. Even the companionship of Tom and the rest of the ex-pats began to pall. Rhys's patience reached breaking point the morning after he had been obliged to share the sweating, sniggering, flickering blackness as the men had gathered behind locked doors to see the latest blue movie that had been amongst the less official items in some diplomatic bag.

'I must speak with Dr Yousef,' Rhys demanded. Salim had been waiting with the Chevrolet as usual but seemed in no way put out by Rhys's manner. He merely shrugged his shoulders.

'It is not for me to arrange such things.' He opened the car door. 'Where would you wish to visit today, the suk?'

Rhys closed the door without getting in as if things had gone far enough.

'Today, you will take me to the hospital,' he said, firmly. It had little effect. 'You know where the hospital is?'

Salim considered the point before slowly nodding his head but still did not move.

'I insist on talking to Dr Yousef today.' Rhys repeated.

'The Sayyid would not be there,' Salim countered.

'The Sayyid?'

'Sayyid Yousef. He is a man with much power. By the will of God, I am but a humble man. We are of one country but two worlds.'

'But you know where to find him?'

Salim again gave the question due consideration before nodding.

'Then take me to him,' Rhys growled as he opened the car door and got in. As Salim slowly settled behind the steering wheel, their eyes met in the small, cracked mirror.

'We will go,' Salim shrugged, 'but what will happen Allah alone will decide.'

Half an hour in the stifling heat of the car parked outside a large, square, unremarkable building, breathing the dust kicked up by tyred wheels, animal hooves and sandalled feet, did nothing to improve Rhys's mood. He was wondering whether he would go looking for Salim when that emotionless face appeared at the window to emit but one word.

'Come.'

Salim ushered Rhys into a room, bowed and withdrew. It took a moment for Rhys to recognise the man behind the desk as Yousef. It was not just the clothes. To say that he was dressed in open-necked shirt and belted trousers might suggest a man at leisure but the shirt was of strong khaki drill with pockets and epaulettes. As Yousef stood to offer his hand, Rhys saw the loops and buckles on the thick leather belt, the patches worn smooth in the brown corduroy of his trousers by the equipment that had hung from them. The transformation from the urbane Westerner was striking but as nothing compared to the change in Yousef's face.

It was not that Yousef's welcome was in any way unfriendly. The respect and affection in his look was unchanged but it was no longer transmitted with the elegant charm that had won over so many hearts in Avonport. The sensitive features that had reflected his mood as he had reacted to Rhys's arguments, Hannah's truculence, Clare's uncertainty, were now set with a stern intensity, his eyes half-closed as if in perpetual anger. Only Alex had produced, briefly, such a reaction. Rhys could not believe one person could genuinely present two such contrasting miens. One had to be false. Was the man shaking his hand play acting? Or had the enchanting visitor to Avonport been the total sham?

'Good morning, Rhys. How are you?'

No apologies. No sign of embarrassment. No excuses for his sudden abandonment.

'Brassed off, Yousef; and disappointed.' Rhys sat to face Yousef across the desk. 'I understood I was coming out here for a purpose. I didn't come just to sit in the sun. I could have done that in the Canaries and had a beer too. What the hell's going on?'

'It is very difficult, Rhys,' was the only response and it came home to Rhys that no longer was he dealing with a visiting American surgeon but a true Arab. He waited for an explanation that was not forthcoming.

'I'm supposed to be advising you on setting up a Dialysis Unit and I haven't even seen the hospital yet. What's the matter? Are you so ashamed of it that you don't want me to see it?'

There was little room for any other emotion in the dedication that controlled Yousef's features. Even so, Rhys saw that he had got through to him.

'This isn't Avonport, Rhys.'

'I didn't expect it to be. I wasn't quite sure what to expect.' Rhys felt his anger rising. 'But I always thought the Arabs prided themselves on their hospitality. Did we treat you so badly in Avonport that you're getting your own back, leaving me alone for days in a strange country?'

Yousef shifted uneasily in his chair but there was no suggestion of an apology, just the merest impression that there was an explanation that he had no intention of giving.

'I can only repeat, it is very difficult. But you will be shown the hospital tomorrow. I have arranged it.'

'And you will be there?'

'No, Rhys, I won't. I have other responsibilities – ' Rhys was fuming inwardly at Yousef's new deviousness when he heard a knock followed by the noise of the door being opened and closed behind him. Yousef did not take his eyes from Rhys's face, as if the man crossing the room had been expected ' – but I will make sure someone is there to show you anything you want to see.' He turned in his chair to wave at the man who had taken station behind him, massively erect, muscular, hairy forearms crossed in front of his chest. 'Rhys, this is Alistair Robertson, another of our advisers.' This time, a twitch of the lips gave a hint of the Yousef of yore.

There was absolutely no response to Rhys's brief 'Good morning'. Yousef had made no attempt to explain to Robertson who Rhys was but, from the intense interest that the man was showing in him, Rhys got the feeling that he was already known to the man, that he had been called in to have a good look at Rhys. Rhys returned the inquisitive glare. He saw a huge man at the peak of his physical power, wearing clothes so similar to Yousef's as to suggest a uniform. Very little skin of his face was visible, a strong beard rising up his cheeks almost to his lower lids, merging in the V of his open shirt with the matted hair of his chest. Luxuriant curls, as black as the hand gun that hung in its holster from his belt, emerged from under the bright red scarf that was wound round his head, Arab-style.

'And what do you advise on, Mr Robertson?' Rhys asked, none too kindly.

Robertson showed no inclination to answer and Yousef responded for him.

'Security. Robbie is our Adviser on National Security. He works with our Defence Forces.'

For the first time, a small thrill of fear passed through Rhys. Until now, his emotions had been a mixture of disappointment, disillusionment, frustration and anger. But now fear took its place amongst them. For the first time, he felt threatened. He had been lonely over the previous few days but had always felt secure in the knowledge that Yousef was there to protect him. Now he was not so sure. He sensed his impotence, his vulnerability in the presence of two such powerful young men, two men with minds closed to him but visibly in accord with each other. What had Yousef become that this man of force seemed happy to stand deferentially at his shoulder?

Yousef stood up and walked round the desk, now the senior who had decided the interview was ending. There was some of his old affability as Yousef accompanied Rhys out along busy corridors between offices resounding to the clatter of typewriters, like the nerve centre of some vast administration. No, Rhys thought, more like the battle headquarters in some World War II movie. In the midst of the activity, Yousef looked equally at home as he had in the hospital milieu of St David's. Rhys was not to worry, Yousef reassured. Salim had been given instructions to take him to the hospital in the morning. Dr Ahmed would be waiting for him and look after him, show him anything he wanted to see. And, when Rhys was ready, they would meet and talk again. In the hall, as Rhys was handed back into Salim's silent care, Yousef put the final touch to his transformation as he said quietly, almost shyly, 'Go in the Grace of the Merciful.'

17

Rhys would never have allowed it in St David's – but then, he wasn't in St David's. The swarthy young man with the open-necked shirt and jeans beneath his white coat, was not one of Avonport's junior staff, but a local doctor dressed to the local standards. Though he found it irksome in the heat, Rhys had no intention of doing a ward round anywhere not properly dressed and his tie would stay, come what may. He wasn't very impressed with Dr Ahmed's attitude either. Stocky and powerfully built, there was a restlessness about Ahmed that suggested a personality of dissent and dissatisfaction. He had introduced himself without a smile, as if he wanted Rhys to know that he had more important things to do and there was a ferocity in his eyes as if he was permanently looking for a fight. An otherwise striking head was marred by a thick-skinned nose, wide pores and pock marks on his cheeks giving him the inevitable unwashed appearance.

Ahmed found Rhys a white coat which was too small for him and, if left to the young man, Rhys's tour of the ward would not have lasted half an hour. They were joined by a young, smiling Arab who spoke no English and seemed content to be totally ignored by both. Though nursing staff moved amongst the beds, Rhys saw no sign of anyone resembling a Ward Sister. There were no students. The wards themselves were large and airy with high ceilings and gleaming floors and there was a cathedral-like peace that contrasted with the chattering bustle of the wards he knew at home. The patients sat or lay in a fatalistic calm in the all embracing whiteness. No flowers, no get well cards, no new Marks and Spencer striped pyjamas.

During the next two hours Rhys saw a wider range of surgical problems in one ward than he would ever see at home. Well over half of the patients were the result of road traffic accidents and he felt stretched to talk intelligently about a branch of surgery he had not been involved in for several years. The urological problems were lost amongst the remainder that ranged from piles to paediatrics. He felt the loss of communication with the human beings that bore disease with such a wary calm. Few of the patients had so much as a word of English and Rhys's smiles, nods and gestures were returned with polite suspicion and frequent glances at Ahmed for reassurance. What discussion took place was ground out of Ahmed who seemed anxious to be away, as if there were more important matters going on elsewhere. There seemed to be no question of them visiting the women's ward and Ahmed's farewell was gruff and ill-mannered. With an audible sigh of fatigue, Rhys sank into the chair in what he took to be the Ward Sister's office to smile in delighted surprise at the trim figure stretching at the mirror. Generous vermilion lips had to be relieved of hairgrips before they could form the friendly 'Hi' they directed at Rhys. The blonde highlights in the hair to which the grips were attaching a small, lace-edged cap, cheered Rhys, their frivolity in such delightful contrast to the surly austerity he had experienced all morning.

'Good morning,' Rhys smiled back.

'I'm Angela. Cup of coffee? Sorry I missed your ward round. 'Fraid I overslept.' And she pulled up her shoulders as if she knew she had been a very naughty girl. Her accent could have been from anywhere south of Manchester, and the silver buckle from one of Birmingham's major hospitals that clasped the broad blue band round her tiny waist was not one that Rhys recognised. It took a while for Rhys to adjust to the fact that such a pert, young girl could be a Ward Sister.

'And how long have you been working here, Angela?'

Widely varying emotions flitted across her face before she replied.

'Three months to go. Been here nine. Murder, isn't it?' She laughed. 'I did two years in Riyadh and then went home but I couldn't stick nursing at home for the peanuts they pay. So, here I am, back again for the money, putting up with Dr Ahmed's funny little ways.'

'Hm.' Owen said no more, his reluctance to criticise another doctor in front of a nurse extending even to Dr Ahmed.

'I just wish his brother would come back; he was working here when I arrived. He was smashing – but then you'd know – he's been working with you back in UK, hasn't he?'

'Who?'

'Yousef.'

'Yousef? Yousef is Dr Ahmed's brother?' Owen sat upright in disbelief.

'Well, yes. Didn't you know? Half-brother really, both sons of Sultan Faisal but with different mothers. Didn't they tell you?'

'Strikes me, Angela, there's a lot they haven't told me about this place.'

Owen settled back into his chair and did something he would not have dreamed of in Avonport, unashamedly tap an inexhaustible source of hospital gossip, scandal and local politics. He listened, fascinated, as a quick, shrewd mind explained to him how Yousef's efforts to improve the hospital had gradually been abandoned as he had involved himself more and more in politics.

'Everyone knows he spends days at a time with his father, out there in the old fort, out along the coast.'

Owen heard how Ahmed was not a patch on his half-brother as a practical surgeon and that Ahmed's jealousy of Yousef was an open secret. There was another brother, a mental defective of some kind, and at least one sister somewhere though neither of them was ever seen. It was accepted throughout Shahin that Yousef was the favourite son and almost certain to be the next Sultan.

Owen shook his head in wonder. He waved his hand vaguely in the direction of the ward outside.

'So; what about this Dialysis and Transplant Unit? It doesn't sound as if he's going to have the time for that and, frankly, Ahmed doesn't strike me as being up to it.'

'No chance, Mr Owen. Mind you,' Angela was quick to add, 'I think it will come. I'm sure Yousef is keen to have one here eventually but he's found there's a hell of a lot of other things to do first. But, at the moment – ' She smiled brightly ' – I'd do what I do, take the money and get a sun tan.'

'Actually, I'm not being paid for this,' Owen explained.

'More fool you, then.'

The girl behind the Gulf Air desk at the airport had the sharp, Americanised 'Have a good day' attitude common to her calling the world over. Her bright face did little to raise Owen's spirits except as an indication that he was on his way home. She had sounded just as friendly when he had rung her the day before as his disenchantment had become complete, driving him to bring forward his return flight. He had tried. He had fought to maintain some sort of rapport with Ahmed, a struggle made more difficult by a complete lack of respect for Ahmed's surgery which was, at best, adequate, at its worst, blatantly incompetent. His frustration had been almost unbearable, seeing pathology on the wards beyond the ability of Ahmed to cope with, and he had been given no opportunity to operate himself. Despite the obvious futility of the exercise, he had tried to obtain figures from the Health Department in his effort to make a true assessment of the dialysis problem. On the matter of transplantation, he had not bothered to try, considering it was a waste of time to explore the immunological backup. With a little help from Ahmed, Owen would have been prepared to discuss the possibility of getting specialised help from a neighbouring, more advanced Arab state, but none had been forthcoming. Tom Bowdler and Angela had done their best to prop up Owen's sagging morale as his disillusionment had soared on failing, time and time again, to get through to Yousef. It had been the hint of 'Oh God, not again' in their honest, cheerful faces at his approach that had been the final straw. In bitter frustration he had picked up the phone as the first stage on his return to Avonport and to what appeared to him now as honest, open relationships.

'There you are, sir. Your flight will be called at 11.45.' Owen smiled as, with her 'Have a good trip, Mr Owen' she did not let him down.

He watched his case trundle away on the conveyor belt and, with ticket and passport in his hand, he approached the Passport Control gate. Keeping his ticket, he slid his passport under the glass screen. As the official examined it, Owen was concentrating on sliding his ticket into an inside pocket and instinctively put his hand out as, out of the corner of his eye, he saw the man move. His lips were framing his thanks when he realised there was no passport there to pick up. He looked through the glass, startled, as he saw it being passed back to a second man standing behind. The man scanned the pages, looking up at Owen menacingly before turning and emerging from the back of the kiosk. He stood and beckoned, making Owen come to him. Though there was a feeling of unreality as Rhys turned on rubbery legs, there was nothing unreal about the bulging holster at the man's waist.

'It is regretted, Mr Owen, but your flight has been cancelled,' said the man, looking not in the least regretful.

'What d'you mean, cancelled?' Owen found his mouth had suddenly gone dry.

'Your seat is required.'

He had been told by Tom how the Franks were sometimes 'bumped off' a plane if some influential Arab wanted a seat at the last moment.

'And what am I supposed to do?' Owen felt too lonely, too far from home to be too angry.

'You already have a flight booked, Mr Owen.'

'But that is not for another week,' Owen complained, too confused to wonder how the man knew that. 'Can you get me on another flight?'

'That is not possible. You would do well to return to your villa and wait.' Dumbly, Owen held his head out for his passport only to see it disappear into the man's breast pocket. 'Your passport will be returned when you leave.' Without another word, the man turned and disappeared through the barrier, leaving Owen to wander, dumbfounded, back to the airport entrance. It was only when he saw Salim, still standing beside the Chevrolet, Owen's case at his feet and showing no surprise at Owen's return, that the reality flooded in. It was Salim who bore the early brunt of his anger and anxiety.

'You knew all about this,' Owen snapped, finding someone, at last, he felt he could dominate. 'You knew this was going to happen. You knew I was going to be turned back.'

'I am but a humble servant. It is God's will that I do as I am told. And now, I must suffer your anger.'

'Who told you? How did they know I'd booked my flight? Why have they stopped me going home?'

'I have told you. It is enough for me to see that you are well, to take you to this place, to take you to that place.'

'And spy on me?' Owen growled, bitterly, as Salim's hangdog face drooped lower.

'It is odd,' Tom Bowdler agreed later that evening. Owen was sitting in the seat beside the pool that, in even the short time he had been there, had become accepted as his. 'Of course, it's possible you were bumped off the flight because one of the local nig-nogs wanted a seat. But it has been much less frequent recently and, when it happens, they usually give the chap another seat on the next flight – and there are at least two or three flights a week home now. No; very strange, I must say. Keeping your passport too. Very odd.'

'D'you think I should go to the Embassy or Consulate or whatever they have?' Rhys asked.

'Haven't got one, old boy.'

'What?'

'No. Didn't they tell you before you came out?'

'No.'

'There's never been any trouble,' Tom explained, 'but the British Government still doesn't officially recognise Shahin. All a complete sham, of course; they're quite happy to trade with them still; most of our equipment has been imported from the UK. I've often wondered,' he laughed, cynically, 'what would happen if they offered us a naval base here or wanted to buy a dozen Tornadoes or Harriers. I've no doubt those devious bastards in Whitehall would find a way round it. But, as things stand, the Portuguese Consulate looks after us if we're in trouble. Americans are the same. Ever since Shahin took in some of the Shi'ites after those explosions in the Lebanon. The Yanks would give their eye-teeth to get at them of course, find out a bit more about the Jihad. The trouble with Britain goes much farther back, however.'

'How's that?'

'The Sultan led the uprising that finally kicked us out. Must be getting on for seventy now, I suppose. Said to have been personally responsible for killing some of our lads.' Tom broke off to laugh. 'Must be difficult for our Government. There are at least two British firms competing for that contract for the University and Medical School, yet they can't bring themselves to recognise a regime that kicked them out by force. They actually had Faisal in gaol once only the tribesmen bust him out, killing several guards as well as losing quite a few of his own followers in the process. They worshipped the guy; still do. I don't think it's even the usual sort of religious fervour; they seem to adore the man himself.'

'It's for you, Rhys.'

Owen had heard the phone, seen the man detach himself from the group playing poker to answer it, but ignored it. Except for one stilted, shouted conversation with Alex, he had come to accept that any phone that rang was for someone else.

'For me?' he asked, surprised. 'Who is it?'

'Didn't say.' The man looked as if he didn't care either as he picked up his hand.

They had never spoken on the phone before but Rhys instantly recognised Yousef's voice. The sound released in Rhys a flood of recrimination that left him drained of emotion, standing unable to find further expression of his feelings to pour into the seeming void at the other end as Yousef stayed silent. It was as if Yousef was waiting for the storm to blow itself out for there was neither explanation nor apology as Rhys stuttered to a halt.

'Rhys, I know everything that has happened. And now, I want to show you something which I hope will make amends. Tomorrow, about seven, be ready. I will pick you up at your villa. Bring enough clothes for two, maybe three nights.'

'Where are we going?' Rhys asked, bewildered and submissive.

'We're going to a wedding.'

18

Dressed in black gown and turban, Yousef sat, proud and erect, at the wheel of the dark blue Range Rover. As Rhys climbed in beside him, he noticed a similar vehicle further down the street. Yousef stretched across him to help close the door, a loose, gold-embroidered sleeve brushing Rhys's knees, the gown falling open to reveal a brilliant magenta sash from which protruded a jambia's ornate handle. The two men exchanged guarded smiles but said nothing as both vehicles began to pick their way considerately through the backstreet evening traffic. By the time Yousef reached the highway, the darkness of a moonless night was complete. To Rhys's surprise, they pulled off the open road a mile or so to the east of the airport. As they bumped their way down a track leading to the beach, Yousef smiled across at Rhys and broke the silence.

'Privilege of rank, Rhys.'

Rhys sat like a hurt child, bursting with curiosity, feeling a growing excitement, but refusing to show it. Yousef and his countrymen had treated Rhys badly, humiliated him, and he was not going to forgive them just because they were taking him to the seaside.

The Range Rover found the level sand and its wheels began to make a whirring sound on the small ridges, the engine note purring higher as Yousef accelerated into the backness. 'This used to be a very popular pastime until they had a series of horrendous head-on crashes. Now it's officially forbidden but I find it irresistible. I only do it at night.'

Silence fell between them again but Rhys was man enough not to let his resentment spoil the hour as they hurtled towards the black wall that seemed to retreat ahead of their headlights. Yousef's only means of holding course were the faintly luminous breakers from a swell conceived in some tropical storm far south in the Indian Ocean. Rhys watched, fascinated, as bright yellow crabs scuttled away from the high-pitched whine of the tyres. Lulled and mesmerised by the sensation of speed within an unchanging cocoon of light and sound, Rhys had no idea of how far they had travelled when he was blinded by the instant brilliance of a searchlight. He put his hand to his eyes as the beam picked them out and followed them. Yousef, who showed no surprise, decelerated, finally braking as three men, waving torches, came within range of the headlights' beam. One, an Armalite rifle cradled lovingly in his arms, stood staring at Rhys while Yousef, leaning from the driver's window, spoke in Arabic to the other two. Voices were not raised and it was not long before one man stood back and waved them on. Rhys learned the true meaning of being plunged into darkness as the searchlight was doused. Yousef set off once more, cautiously, his eyes straining.

'Doesn't do much for your night vision, that sort of thing, does it?' he said.

'What was all that about?' Rhys asked. Both seized the opportunity to break their silence.

'Guards,' Yousef said. 'But there was no problem. They were expecting us. Hang on a moment and I'll show you.'

Rhys suddenly remembered the other Range Rover, turned and looked out of the rear window. There was no sign of any lights following them. A mile further on, Yousef slowed, edging up the beach. He peered through the windscreen.

'There,' he said and pointed.

Rhys could just make out a vague shape in the starlight. Irregular and forbidding against the northern sky, the outlines of an old fort stood proud, two or three of its windows dimly lit. 'You can't see it at night but it still shows where your twenty-five-pounders made rather a mess of it. What walls are left have bullet holes all over them. It's the one fort you British never took – perhaps they didn't think it worth the bother – but it's his favourite place.' Yousef was quite unashamed of the note of reverence which softened his words. 'His Highness rarely leaves it now. It is my father's wish to die there, and, with God's grace, that wish will still be granted. Allah kareem.'

Yousef continued to drive cautiously until more guards further along the beach waved them through without stopping. Another half hour and lights appeared ahead.

'Dar al-Islam, the old capital,' Yousef explained. 'An interesting place. Amal we plan to develop as a modern city and port but the old capital we hope to preserve as it has been for hundreds of years. Perhaps we can stop for a while on the way back.'

A mile or so short of the outskirts, too far away for Rhys to see anything with clarity, Yousef turned inland, bumping and jerking between the rocks to cross the coastal road and head inland. For an hour or so, the surface was tolerable, the track recognisable in the headlights, but it was a particularly spectacular lurch that made Rhys remark, 'I sincerely hope you know where you are going.'

'We must be in the mouth of the wadi now. That's why it has suddenly got worse. It's impossible to maintain any sort of track in a place like this as it gets washed away each time the rains come. The wadi is several miles wide here but it is fairly flat and we should be seeing the lights soon. Keep an eye out for them, would you?'

'What lights?' Rhys asked.

'Where we're going to camp tonight. The others went on ahead along the coast road to get things ready. Shouldn't be far now.'

Another half an hour and Rhys began to sense a growing uncertainty in Yousef but he rapidly assumed once more his calm confidence when Rhys called out, 'Light, there, over to the right.'

The other Range Rover Rhys had seen in the street came into view as the headlights swept round. There were cries of 'Ahlan wa Sahlan' as three young men, each carrying a weapon, each dressed in that combination of Western paramilitary uniform and Arab dress that Rhys had come to accept, greeted Yousef with a mixture of affection and deference as he stepped out. More shadowy figures moved in and out of a rough stone shelter illuminated incongruously by the light from two small camping gas lamps. For their meal, already laid to await their arrival, they ate what Rhys decided must be mutton until Yousef told him it was goat. It took a little time for Rhys to get used to tearing the meat from the joint and accepting some of the choicer portions picked and offered by his companions. The rice that he learned to knead into balls soon filled his stomach and he was the first to stop eating. As he sat, warming himself in the strength of such young, vigorous men around him, he sipped scalding coffee that tasted strongly of ginger, regretting the language barrier that divided them. He listened, absorbing himself in the moods around him that swung from joking, horseplaying banter to passionate oratory and back again.

'Where would you rather sleep, Rhys?' Yousef asked. 'The Bedu have lain blankets in the shelter and the men will sleep there; it is much warmer. But the shelter is also used by the animals; one gets used to the smell, but Abdullah here – ' he dug one of his grinning companions in the ribs ' – he tends to snore a bit. So I usually sleep under the stars. It is very cold but we have a sleeping bag for you if you would prefer it.'

The lamps extinguished, the chatter from the shelter died away and the stories about Abdullah's snoring proved unfounded. Rhys had often pictured himself drifting at sea alone under a night sky but his dreams, even at their most vivid, had never approached the brilliance of reality. Flat on his back, he stared into lucid, black, star-studded space. Enveloped to his neck in the sleeping bag, he felt the cold night air etch at his face. In a silence he could almost hear, he sensed that Yousef, wrapped in a blanket alongside him, was also wide awake.

'Yousef, are you awake?'

'Yes, I am.' After a pause that almost took form in the silence, he added, 'Fantastic sight, isn't it? Are you cold?'

'No.' The sleeping bag's embrace triggered a memory of Nansi's enfolding warmth but with it came the cloying atmosphere of a small room and billowy bedclothes. He moved his head in the desert night, sucking in lungfuls of the crisp freshness as if searching for some inner purification. It was a time for the confessional.

'I have news for you, Rhys, which is not good news.' Yousef gave Rhys time to catch his breath. 'It's about Hannah.'

'What about her?'

'She has had a transplant and I'm afraid it has not been successful.'

'What? Is she . . .?'

'No, she is not dead.'

'When?'

'About forty-eight hours after we left.'

'Who did it?'

'Johnson.'

For a while, Yousef did not intrude in Rhys's jumbled thoughts. Johnnie had done just what Rhys had searched his soul over. He had jumped Hannah up the queue and probably not given it a second thought. Rhys felt embittered as jealousy welled up. He could almost see the grin on Johnnie's face. Or was it possible that Johnnie had done it as a favour to Rhys? He would have known, like every one else, of what Hannah meant to Rhys even if he had no means of knowing the reason why. And Hannah? Yet again he felt he had let her down. He should have been around. Would she blame him for the failure? Would she feel it would have been successful if only Rhys had done it? He could imagine her face.

'How d'you know, Yousef?'

'I still have . . .' Yousef hesitated over the word '. . . contacts in Avonport.'

Rhys imagined he meant Clare Drury and pressed him no further, only feeling guilt at his own flimsy contact with his home; that one duty phone call to Alex and recurrent fantasies of Nansi. He hadn't really felt concern for Hannah until now, so involved in his own troubles had he been.

'Do you know any of the details?'

'Not really, Rhys. I just know that the kidney has not functioned at all to speak of and she has already developed quite severe signs of rejection. She must have a high antibody titre.'

'Which probably means they will remove it.'

'I imagine so. She has been in considerable pain.' Yousef paused only long enough to take in a long slow breath. 'Why is Hannah so special, Rhys?'

Rhys wondered why he had found it all so impossible previously to put the story into words, but there was a cleanliness, a selflessness, about the affection he felt for the young man that lowered the stubborn, silent defences which, he knew, hurt Alex so much. To the man he now knew he loved as a son, he poured out all the guilt that he had never been able to confide to Alex, knowledge of which no level of intimacy with Nansi would ever extract from him. He left nothing untold, from his shame at the loss of Helen and her child to the self-contempt for a marriage so empty of affection, let alone passion, that he could stand aside and do nothing about his wife's affair save look for easy, cheap male assertiveness in Nansi's bed. And, as if to confirm the love as mutual, the confidences, murmured into the darkness, drew their due response. Unashamed confession that Hannah, to Rhys, represented Helen's reincarnation opened a door as Rhys was also made privy to a passionate young man's dreams.

'My mother is dead, as is Ahmed's,' Yousef began, slowly, as if feeling his way. 'Both had strong personalities and my father loved them both, but my mother, as my father still is, was outward-looking, anxious for me to be educated abroad, to learn to live with other creeds. Ahmed's mother was different. He was sent to Cairo where he qualified and he has never travelled as I have. I admit I was attracted to the Western way of life and forgot my roots. I must have been a great disappointment to my father at that time though he has never spoken of it, but Ahmed has both envied and despised me for it. It was only when I came home to see my father, when His Highness developed his renal failure and looked as if he might die, that I realised just what I had turned my back on.'

Yousef's voice was steady, full of conviction.

'I have no need of the status that wealth brings. I am a Sayyid, a descendant of Mohammed, an Ibadi, a survivor of the Kharijites, one of the earliest followers of Mohammed who rose against the cruel Omayyads. It was we who showed the Sa'udis the true path.' There was pride and passion in each murmured word. 'This is my country now; my people. There is so much to do, Rhys. At first I thought I could help most as a surgeon but, in the light of His mercy, I have been shown where I can serve best. But it is not easy, Rhys.'

Rhys said nothing for fear of snapping the thread.

'They are so far behind, Rhys. The women you will meet tomorrow, not one will be able to read or write; and they are not stupid. Intelligence and enforced ignorance; can you think of a more intolerable combination? And the bride; thirteen. Thirteen,' he repeated. 'It's not uncommon for the bride to be no more than nine or ten. The little girl tomorrow will probably have been in purdah since she was ten. Dressed all in black, a child of ten. Her wedding dress will be the first colour she has worn. No pretty dresses. Just imagine my daughter . . . Difficult isn't it, when you hear all that, to believe that the Koran was a great step forward for Muslim women? Before the Koran, they were mere possessions to be bought and sold, with unwanted female babies buried alive. How are we to move forward and, at the same time, preserve what is best?' Rhys heard Yousef move restlessly beneath his blankets. 'They are proud people, Rhys. Who are we to tell them what is right, what is wrong? What do we want to change all this for, drugs and abortion? The Bedu over there, in the dark near the water-hole, they are nomads. Try to imagine them in a tower block of apartments! Offer them a transistor radio and they'll ask you if you can drink it. A country's wealth should be shared equitably by all, not just spent on palaces and airport buildings. But give the Bedu possessions and you kill them. To them worldly goods are useless burdens. So, how can we help them? They will submit to the will of God and to the desert but to nothing else. If we were to become rich, suddenly find oil, what would become of them? Would we do to them what the Australians have done to the Aboriginals? And yet, can you stand by and watch children die if the rains fail?'

'I envy you, Yousef,' Rhys spoke softly. 'At least, I think I do. At times I wish I had a faith as strong and as passionate as yours. And, again, there are times when it frightens me; I sometimes think what a peaceful world it would be without religion. I am sure you have guessed by now that I have no beliefs. And I hope I didn't say that as if I was proud of it.'

Yousef laughed affectionately. 'Don't worry, Rhys, I am no evangelist. I am not trying to seduce you into the Faith. We are an army of volunteers, not conscripts. We need to be because it is going to be a long hard battle, starting from so far back.'

So pervasive now was the intimacy between them that Rhys's feelings of abandonment and humiliation over the previous weeks blurred. He was in the mood to forgive Yousef anything. Try as he might, however, there was sharpness to his voice as he asked Yousef why, with problems as basic as those he had described, he had bothered to ask him all that way to advise on dialysis and transplant.

Some of the Arab's fencing with words returned.

'That was not straightforward, Rhys. I was not alone in that matter. Mistakes were made for which I was not solely responsible. I still have dreams of such a unit but perhaps you will now appreciate how difficult it is to decide priorities in a developing country.' For the first time, his reasoning became tortuous, opaque. His words became faster, more slurred, as if there was something he did not want to reveal. There was already a hint of the politician as he led Rhys away from what was obviously an awkward question. 'It is up to us educated, the professionals and the academics, to lead our people with understanding into the next century. But first it is necessary to give our country an identity. We are looking for some sign with which to unite the cities and the mountains, the tribes within those mountains, perhaps to explain even to the world outside what we are trying to do. We are not understood. We are a small, backward country. The reason why we are so peaceful is that we are so poor. No one bothers with us. But – ' Rhys was wondering at the train of thought that had produced such a response to his question about dialysis when he felt a veil being drawn between them once more as Yousef began to speak precisely, choosing his words carefully ' – if we were suddenly to find the wealth to do all the things we want for our people, we would immediately find ourselves the victims of international greed and corruption. And then, we would have to demonstrate to the world that we had the strength and the determination to defend our peaceful way of life even if we have to fight to do so.'

Yousef stopped and laughed, partly at his own passion, partly at the subdued silence he had induced in Rhys. 'So, Rhys – if we have treated you badly, you must forgive us. If you have found us a little – preoccupied – it is my heartfelt hope that you have not taken offence. I hope that what you will see tomorrow will give you pleasure, heal any wounds.'

In the morning, Rhys found that he had paid for the night's experience with a stiff back. He found more tribesmen than he had expected around the water-hole, a few yards from the shelter. He smiled at a young Bedouin girl, barefoot and clad only in a torn black shift. Having examined him with the haughty disdain only to be expected from a member of the desert's aristocracy, she continued on her way to fill her goatskin. Rhys washed as best he could with his companions but stood aside to listen to the soft moan of morning prayers. Later they resumed their journey and, by mid-morning, after several hours of bouncing along the ever-narrowing wadi in the Range Rover, Rhys was tired and hot again. He ran a finger around his shirt collar. Yousef smiled at his obvious discomfort.

'Another hour, Rhys, and there will be shade. Those tight clothes are a trial, aren't they?'

'I was going to ask, Yousef.' Rhys hesitated. 'I felt a bit of a fool this morning and I imagine everyone will be dressed up for the wedding. Would it be possible – I mean, would they be insulted if I were to put on Arab dress; if you could get me some, that is?'

Yousef put his head back to roar with laughter. 'Of course not. They'd consider it a compliment. And you needn't worry; I won't tell anyone back in Avonport.'

He stopped the Range Rover in its tracks, turned and rummaged on the back seat. To the impish delight of those in the second vehicle, Rhys felt the sun scorch his bare back as, self-consciously, he changed in the open desert. Back in his seat, enjoying the freedom of an Arab's dress, he watched the rocks and thorny trees gradually give way to more lush cultivation with patches of maize and barley and the darker green of palm trees. They came upon the village very suddenly, its tall, tapering, sand-coloured houses camouflaged against the sheer face of the wadi. Through the village and beyond, they came to a whitewashed house set in a garden overhung with quince and mango. Water tinkled in a pool surrounded by a terrace pillared in cool shades of green and blue.

Overall was an atmosphere of excitement. Groups of women, sitting in the shade of the courtyard, gossiped in an animated, undulating monotone. Rhys was entranced by the unfamiliarity of what he saw: the long faces, high cheek-bones visible above veils. Some women did not wear veils, but if they saw Rhys looking they would draw their headscarves shyly across their faces, hiding from view the stone transfixed to one nostril by its silver ring. Drums sounded from somewhere in the house.

They were welcomed by the bride's father, dignified and solemn against the background of buzzing anticipation. Rhys followed discreetly behind Yousef, watching and copying as he slid off his shoes and shook hands with all those guests already there. For what seemed an age, they waited quietly in a large bare room. All men, they stood patiently, no one seemed the least embarrassed by the absence of conversation. Yousef edged nearer to Rhys and whispered, 'Sorry, Rhys, but I'm afraid we're a day late.'

'Really?' Rhys looked surprised. 'But surely . . .' He indicated all the activity.

'This has been going on for days. The wedding lasts a week or so but the bride and groom slept together last night. We would not have been allowed to see her before they'd slept together – only the family and intimate friends are allowed that. The bride would be locked away in a room upstairs at that stage. But we are to be allowed to see her in the bridal chamber, and that is a great compliment, Rhys. They will have spent the whole morning washing her and painting her hands and feet. It is only because I am a Sayyid and you are my friend that we are being allowed to see her. But say nothing while you are there, just leave this on her bed as you leave.'

Rhys felt money being pressed into his hand as he followed the group that now climbed the stairs.

There was so much Rhys wanted to remember of what he saw. It was overwhelming and he came away with no more than a blur of impressions of two older men standing beside the couch, behind them, the bridegroom, poker-faced and resplendent in orange and green and red, his white headscarf large and precarious. And the motionless child bride, hands and feet henna daubed, her eyes modestly downcast. It was only as Rhys bent to lay the money in her lap that he saw the swollen eyelids.

Rhys was close to emotional exhaustion as he lifted himself to sit, shoulder to shoulder with Yousef, on a low wall that surrounded the courtyard. Dark red bougainvillaea hung from the pillared arches above them; the air was heavy with the scent of jasmine. Their faces flickered in the light of a large wood fire that crackled and spat. He felt he could take little more of this exotic disorientation, coming so swiftly after the psychological battering of the previous week. Far enough from home, he was light years away from his culture and roots. For weeks he seemed to have been travelling, making superficial friendships, being buffeted between excitement and disillusionment, frustration and exhilaration. He had found within himself the ability to love once more. But soon, he and Yousef would be living in cultural worlds so divorced as to be separated by interplanetary space. He had just coped with the protocol of an Arab wedding feast, the hand-washing, the strange courtesies, and he suddenly longed for the informality of a village pub. But they had not finished with him yet. The endless shrill cries and ululation of the women still stimulated him. The drummers, like wrinkled and aged black witches, came out into the courtyard to excite his mind. In twos and threes, the women, in their blue and green cloaks, danced, the air around them still warm in the flame-lit darkness. The drums became more urgent, demanding more and more of the dancers until they gave way to a solitary young woman. Within a few strides, she had imposed her authority on the drummers, making them slow to her rhythm. Urged on by the ululating women, she gradually increased her tempo, moving towards Rhys and Yousef. As she came closer, Rhys saw the silver belt that held the short black dress to her tiny waist, the multicoloured decoration at her breast. With a stamp of her feet that brought sound from silver bells tied to her ankles, she tore the orange scarf from her head, two plaits of jet falling to her waist. With an upwards tilt of a jaw and a defiance that took Rhys back to a bedside thousands of miles away, the dancer swirled away from them to drive the drums faster and faster. The cries of the women now frenzied, she returned to look challengingly at Yousef. In two defiant movements, she removed the pearl combs from her plaits to shake her hair into a cascade over her shoulders. Grunting with the physical strain it called for, she swung her hair round her like some fisherman casting his net.

Rhys felt his throat constrict. He fought back tears with clenched fists and jaw, blinking furiously. In the firelight, he prided himself on his self-control, ashamed of the reaction of an emotional Welshman, and forgetting he was sitting alongside an equally passionate Arab. He felt the gentleness of Yousef's hand on his shoulder.

'Don't grieve, Rhys. She will be well again, your Hannah. I feel it. God is merciful.'

Rhys's passport was pushed towards him by an unsmiling clerk at the Control desk. Rhys had bid farewell to Salim who, in his own morose way, had seemed genuinely sorry to take his leave of Rhys. This time, Rhys had watched him slam the door of the faithful old Chevrolet and drive away. Before passing through into the Departure Lounge, Rhys had searched, just once more, for the man he hoped might have come to say farewell. But there was no one and he failed to get a window seat on the crowded plane for that last saddening look.

19

To Rhys's great relief there was no reaction from the bored young man behind the Passport Control desk at Heathrow. Heaving his case from the rumbling carousel, he walked through the Customs, his face showing that controlled apprehension that even the most innocent can't suppress. He flushed and his heart thumped as the uniformed man near the far door stepped slowly into Rhys's path.

'If you wouldn't mind, sir; would you take your luggage to that officer over there?'

The face behind the counter spoke rapidly as it looked over Rhys's right shoulder and Rhys nodded vaguely as a card was held in front of him. Disconcerted, Rhys's hand shook as he found the key to unlock his case, his feelings giving way to anger at the thoroughness of the man's search, pushing Alex's scarf and Nansi's gold brooch aside as if of no consequence.

'That seems in order, sir.'

The case, its contents jumbled, was pushed back towards Rhys, the Customs Officer watching impassively as Rhys struggled to close it again. Rhys had just turned the key when the man asked Rhys if he would please come with him. Now completely bewildered, Rhys followed him into an office, his case scraping the varnished door as he floundered into the room. From the corner of his eye, he saw the Customs Officer shake his head and leave, closing the door behind him. Rhys's attention now swung to a man sitting at a cheap, modern desk. Behind him, lounging with one shoulder against the wall, his hands in his trouser pockets, stood another, staring as if he found the very sight of Rhys nauseating. The man at the desk was picking his teeth with what looked like a sharpened matchstick. He stopped long enough to point to a chair.

'Sit down, Mr Owen.'

Rhys's dislike for the man was instantaneous. 'Now you,' he said, sitting slowly on the hard, straight-backed chair, 'do really frighten me.'

'That so, Mr Owen? Why should that be?'

'Perhaps you could tell me,' Rhys replied, surprised at how cool he now felt. 'These chaps with their flat hats and uniforms – ' he jerked a thumb over his shoulder ' – at least you know where you are with them. But somebody with no uniform, someone who knows your name, starts interviewing you with a witness standing behind him. Who the hell are you, KGB?'

'Something like that.' The man glanced appreciatively at what he had just found between his teeth, snapped the stick and threw it in a tin ashtray. 'Name's Ledgerman; sort of policeman, I suppose you might say.'

'Shouldn't I ask to see some form of identification?' Rhys asked.

'You've been watching too much Kojak, Mr Owen. Enjoy your trip, did you?'

Ledgerman looked as if he cut his own hair. Recently washed, the greying tufts stuck out at all angles. Unusually for a man with such heavy features, his face was lively and intelligent, his hands constantly on the move, scratching, probing, brushing. A powerful man, he was also fat, his chair pushed well back from the desk. The grey flannels and hand-knitted jumper bulged beneath the open Harris tweed sportscoat.

'Yes, I did,' Rhys replied, defiantly.

'Business trip, was it?'

'I suppose you would call it that, yes; business and pleasure.'

'And what did you get up to then, altogether?'

'I don't see why I have to tell you. Why should I? Of what possible interest is it to you?'

Ledgerman sighed, brushing at his jumper as if something there offended him. 'Look, Mr Owen. If you want to be on an Inter City heading for the land of your fathers in an hour or so, just answer my questions like a good little surgeon. If you want to play the proud Britisher, that is your privilege, but you had better be prepared to spend the night here or somewhere less comfortable. Take your pick.'

Rhys stayed silent so Ledgerman repeated his question and got Rhys's sullen reply.

'I went out to advise them on setting up Dialysis Units, possibly renal transplantation.'

'And were all the good people of Shahin pissing to your satisfaction when you left?' The sneer in Ledgerman's voice could only have been born of intense hatred. 'Mission accomplished, was it?'

'Not entirely.' There was no fear in Rhys's reply, all such emotion replaced by his deepening dislike for Ledgerman.

'Would you say you had any success?' Ledgerman's eyes shot up to catch Rhys's immediate reaction and saw what he had wanted. 'No, I thought not.'

There was a pause as Ledgerman considered his next question and the man standing behind him shifted his weight to the other leg.

'Why do you think they really asked you to go out there then?'

Rhys could hardly object to a question he had put to himself so many times. He shook his head but said nothing.

'Come, Mr Owen, you must have thought it strange, an intelligent, thinking man like yourself?'

'No,' Rhys lied.

'Must have talked it over with your friend Yousef.' Rhys's head came up sharply at the mention of Yousef's name. 'Did you see a lot of him while you were over there?'

'Yes and no.'

'Don't be cryptic, Mr Owen. Leave that to us coppers. Did you see friend Yousef while you were out there?'

Over the next half hour, Ledgerman milked Rhys of all his reactions to Shahin and Yousef. On one side of the table, Rhys experienced for the first time the discomfort of unrelenting, hostile questioning, while, on the other, Ledgerman marvelled at the stubborn passion such a grubby little country could rouse in the breast of this stolid, middle of the road, pillar of the establishment.

'You were fortunate to have such an influential friend, Mr Owen.'

'I value Yousef's friendship, yes.'

'Becoming quite a power in the land, they tell me.' Ledgerman's sneer was back. 'Swapped the hospital wards for the corridors of power, I understand. That so?'

'I wouldn't know,' Rhys answered.

'Wouldn't you now? And you and him being so close and all. Does he do much operating these days?'

'I didn't see him operate but that doesn't mean . . .'

'Quite so. So how do you think he occupies his time then? Not the type to walk out on his family just to sit on his arse in the desert doing nothing all day, d'you think?' Ledgerman paused and Rhys got the feeling he was coming to what he really wanted to know. Up till now, Rhys had found his questions for the most part rhetorical. 'I don't suppose you got to meet His Highness when you were out there?'

'Who?'

'The bloody Sultan, Mr Owen. Who else?'

The words were spoken with such venom and Ledgerman became so physically agitated that it had a strangely calming effect on Rhys.

'No.'

Ledgerman looked closely at Rhys as if he believed Rhys could lie about that one.

'Not even professionally?'

Rhys laughed. 'Certainly not.'

'Why do you laugh?' Ledgerman picked up the matchstick as if he had found further work for it and regretted breaking it. 'Not in the best of health, His Highness, so we understand.'

'There are rumours in Shahin, certainly amongst the ex-pats, that he is ill. But I have no way of knowing.'

'Didn't get invited out to the fort, then?'

Rhys didn't answer but sat, wondering at the extent of Ledgerman's knowledge of Shahin.

'So,' Ledgerman sounded as if he had suddenly lost interest, 'you'd better be on your way. You're well shot of that lot, doctor.'

'That's not the way I look at it, Mr Ledgerman.' Rhys was not inclined to be discarded just like that. 'I came to have considerable respect for what they are trying to do out there.'

'Doctor,' Ledgerman stood up and Rhys realised for the first time just how vast he was, 'go home. You've got a good job, nice family, other interests.' Rhys felt as if Ledgerman was stripping him, layer by layer.

'You've had your fun. Go home and look after the good people of Avonport. Leave that bunch of wogs to me.'

'But that isn't altogether possible, Mr Ledgerman.'

Rhys had the satisfaction of seeing Ledgerman's attitude harden. He was not going to be dismissed simply on the fat man's terms.

'How's that, Mr Owen?'

'Because we are having another of their surgeons, a Dr Ahmed, at Avonport shortly and my son-in-law may be going out to Shahin on a sort of exchange – if he wants to, that is. They hope to have a very modern teaching hospital soon and we hope to arrange a series of exchanges in this way.'

'Your suggestion or theirs?' Ledgerman's voice was terse and incisive.

'Theirs,' Rhys answered, proudly.

For the first time, Ledgerman looked at the man behind him.

'Now that,' he said, 'I find very interesting.'

PART TWO

20

Rhys recognised the urgency in Sister Vaughan's voice. Over the years, he had come to know and respect its tone. One of his patients was at risk; it could mean nothing else. Sister Vaughan's loyalty to the patient had overcome her loyalty to the Registrar. It happened now and again, resulting in a few words from her over the phone. Owen would then 'happen to call in as he was passing'.

This time it was slightly different. Never before had she told him that if he didn't come in and sort his Registrars out, something awful was going to happen.

'Soon as you can, please, sir.'

Even so, on impulse, Owen swung his car round and reversed into his parking space, switched the engine off and settled back to gaze down over the undulating common to the road below and the deserted beach beyond. Within seconds his view was blurred by the rain on his windscreen. It had to be the wettest August he could remember. It seemed to have been raining for weeks. It all added to his gloom. He hated rows; would do almost anything to avoid one. Not that he felt particularly proud of the fact. In some ways he envied people like Johnnie who could tear strips off some luckless House Surgeon without batting an eyelid. Rhys himself had worked for chiefs who had tried to instil loyalty through fear and he knew the futility of it. It simply didn't work. He favoured the soft sell. Some minor mistake, some forgotten investigation, and he would resort to the silent look of reproach and disappointment. Make them feel they had let him down. He found it got results with most people.

But not, it seemed, with friend Ahmed. Sheikh Ahmed al Said. Owen should have known he spelt trouble after seeing his work in Shahin. He should have made sure someone else came over but Yousef had been quietly insistent, and the fact that Ahmed was his half-brother had not helped. He could hardly have refused. But the contrast with Yousef had been complete. Why was it, Owen mused, that, to him, all Arabs were either romantic, handsome men of mystery or greasy, shifty bastards? There seemed to be nothing in between.

Ahmed had started off badly, insisting on a room amongst the Residents while Yousef had found his own accommodation. His surly introversion had alienated the rest of the Registrars and his lack of ability had become something of a sick joke around the hospital; the nurses, those most forgiving of creatures, had turned their backs on him. Roger had refused to go out to Shahin after hearing his father-in-law's description of the place, deciding he'd wait until they had built the new hospital, saying they were anxious to start a family. Owen had failed to find any other volunteer. The Professor had shown no interest; there was no place in any of his schemes for such a backward, impoverished country. And Ahmed's disastrous presence had culminated, two days before, in a call from the Hospital Administrator. There had been complaints from the other Residents about the noise from Ahmed's room; sounds of passionate argument going on late into the night. The maids had reported that someone had been using an upturned electric fire for cooking and there were food scraps all over the floor. They had failed to remove Arabic graffiti daubed over one wall. His room was constantly full of strange Arabs, Ahmed arguing with the Administrator that they were students from London, staying with him for a few days. Rhys had wondered whether he should object to the sight of so many of them wandering around the hospital.

Owen sighed. He had been hoping to get away without any bitter confrontation – it must be getting close to the time for Ahmed to go home even though there had been no mention of him leaving – but it sounded as if whatever was waiting for him up on the ward was not going to be resolved peaceably. He couldn't put it off any longer.

He slammed the car door behind him and ran, ducking his head in a futile attempt to save himself from the rain. Up the lift and through the swing doors of his ward and he could hear the voices. Walking down the ward corridor, he found Sister Vaughan standing sentinel in the doorway to a single-bedded room. *Ils ne passeront pas*. The defenders of Verdun must have looked like that.

When he walked into the Sister's office, Patel stood up and Ahmed did not. Both were flushed and agitated. Anger superimposed on hatred. Rhys closed the door behind him. In all his years of working with overseas graduates, Owen had never encountered problems over religion.

Christian, Hindu and Moslem, the occasional Buddhist, all had always worked in harmony. But now there was in their faces malice he had not encountered before, enmity that had little to do with surgery. Owen had known passions roused by surgical differences but never to produce the transformation in Patel's normally gentle features. At the sight of Owen, relief spread over Patel's face while the Arab scowled from where he sat at the desk. Rhys had to stand over him before Ahmed relinquished the chair.

'Now then,' Rhys said, trying not to look at one more than the other. 'What the hell's going on?'

Both began to speak loudly and Rhys was forced to make a choice.

'Mr Patel. What's the problem?' He almost felt Ahmed's sneer as he gave Patel the courtesy title of someone with his Fellowship.

'The oesophagectomy, sir.'

Owen had guessed as much. He had known which patient Sister Vaughan had been protecting out there but his heart still sank. The removal of a malignant growth from the gullet was one of his favourite operations, one in which he took great pride. But it was one that returned the patient to the ward with a variety of tubes and bottles and their management required great care over the first week. It was accepted that nothing was adjusted without his personal approval.

'What's the problem? If that's the latest chest film,' he nodded towards the viewing box behind Patel, 'it looks all right to me.'

'There is no problem, sir. But I am having trouble explaining to Dr Ahmed here the way you like to manage these patients after the operation. I am telling him that you like them to have a Dionosil swallow on the ward before we are giving them anything by mouth. But Dr Ahmed says that if they are going to leak then they are leaking; that there is nothing you can do about it. He also wants to take up the Ryles tube and I am having trouble preventing him doing so. I am afraid to leave the ward, Mr Owen. And – ' a thousand years of bitterness chilled Patel's gentle voice ' – he is saying things about my country and my family.'

'And you, Dr Ahmed?'

'He is too timid,' Ahmed sneered. 'The chest X-ray is good. To leave the tubes in any longer will cause infection. She should be given fluids now. If your suture line is good, it will come to no harm. If it is not, then she will leak. And if she leaks, well, she will die.' He closed his remark with a shrug of his shoulders.

Rhys felt his teeth clench in anger. There were many aspects of Arab life that under Yousef's influence, he had come to admire, but not the will of Allah.

'And, if you had had your way, would you have taken the Ryles tube up?'

'Yes, I would.'

'Without asking me?'

Ahmed did not answer, his powerful shoulders hunched forwards, radiating aggression. Without taking his eyes from Ahmed, Rhys spoke quietly.

'Mr Patel. Go and tell Sister I shall be along in a minute to see the oesophagectomy. And,' he added, as Patel began to leave, 'please close the door behind you.' He turned to Ahmed. 'Sit down, Dr Ahmed.'

'I take orders from no one.'

'While you are on my ward, you will.'

'No one commands me to sit or stand like a dog.'

'But you will do as I say when it comes to my patients.' Rhys fought to control his desire to shout. He could imagine the heads already turned their way, hoping to hear what was going on. 'Differences of opinion I do not mind; I'm ready to discuss the management of a case with anybody at any time. When it comes to the final decision on treatment, however, I insist on making that myself. At the end of the day, I carry the can for everything that goes on on this ward and therefore I get the last word on everything. Is that quite clear?'

'And did that go for my beloved brother too?' Ahmed turned and, in his own time, slid insolently into a chair. 'Did he have to refer everything to you?'

Owen didn't answer him directly. 'Would you have taken that Ryles tube up, as Patel said, without asking me first?'

'I am not afraid to make decisions like Patel. He is a servant. He will always do as he is told. He does not know how to lead.'

'Would you have taken that tube up?' Owen persisted.

'Yes.'

'Even though you had been told that, with these particular patients, nothing like that is done without my consent?'

'Yes. It is of little importance.'

'In that case, Dr Ahmed, you will take no further part in the clinical management of patients in this hospital. I will make sure the staff know that you are no longer allowed to operate or order treatment. I must say, I am very disappointed. The standard of your work has been poor and lacking in judgment, you have upset many members of staff and, I don't mind telling you, it will come as a great relief to everyone when you go home.'

Rhys found himself shaking, with fury. He was amazed to see that Ahmed was smiling. 'In fact,' he continued, 'I think it would be a good thing if you were to arrange to go home as soon as possible. I can't remember how much longer you were meant to stay – it can't be much longer – but I think the sooner you leave the better.'

This time Ahmed laughed out loud.

'What's so funny?' Owen snapped.

Still sniggering, Ahmed heaved himself out of the chair. Putting both hands on the desk in front of Owen, he leaned forwards, his face twisted in contempt. 'To think, at one time we allowed you to be our Lords and Masters. You are such little people.' He straightened, turned and walked out. As Rhys listened to his footsteps receding down the corridor, he heard Ahmed's parting words.

'Au revoir, Sister Vaughan.'

For a while Rhys sat, the familiar surroundings of the empty room cooling down after such unfamiliar hostility. This was where he and Yousef and Clare Drury, Sister Vaughan and young Jones used to enjoy each other's company in a job they all loved. Ahmed had smeared the memory. It had been a mistake, he reflected sadly, bringing such an aggressive, incompetent bastard to Avonport. Yousef had been a one-off. That time would never come again. He'd better write to Yousef and try to explain.

Rhys walked across the corridor to see the patient who, tense and anxious, sensed that his management had been the subject of a flaming row. Switching on the professional look of infallibility that he knew would be expected by someone so ill, for several minutes he worked hard to erase any doubt in his mind that the noise of argument might have caused. As he left, the optimism drained from him, only to be pumped up once more as, with a subdued Patel and Sister, he carried out a quiet, clipped, no-nonsense ward round on his remaining patients. With a nod, he left them to walk slowly through the dialysis unit in search of Nansi but found her cleaning vomit off a thin, pale teenager who looked at him, distressed, wide-eyed and apologetic. An appealing 'Not now' smile from Nansi and he moved on.

'What was all that about, then?' Hannah asked before Rhys was two strides into her room, somewhere he now seemed to seek as a haven with an unfailing release of tension it never occurred to him to question. 'What was that barney with Ahmed all about?'

'What barney?'

Hannah clucked her irritation. 'Come on. Everyone knows about it.'

Rhys shook his head in disbelief. It was little more than half an hour since his showdown with Ahmed, and Hannah, in her self-imposed exile at the far end of the corridor, already knew about it. Any such news spread through the ramifications of a District Hospital with computer-like speed and Hannah, in her fourth month in that small room, was now an integral part of that gossip circuitry. Sitting in the chair beside her bed, she wore clothes Nansi had bought and which Owen had paid for, but nothing ever seems to fit the chronic sick. A volume of *The Lord of the Rings* lay on the bed beside her. Owen picked it up, was about to ask her how she was enjoying it, when she snatched it teasingly from his hand.

'Well? What was it all about?'

'A slight difference of opinion, nothing more. It happens to everyone.'

'Have you given him the sack?'

'He's going home very shortly.'

'That's a relief. He's such a pig.'

'Hannah, you mustn't talk about people like that. I've told you before.'

A frown creased the skin between her black eyebrows. 'And Yousef was a pig in his way too.'

Rhys had long since given up showing surprise at anything Hannah said.

'Going away like that; so much for his promise to write. And you going with him, leaving me to that Johnnie. I wouldn't have had to have my kidney taken out again if you had done it.'

'Now, Hannah,' Rhys sighed. How to rationalise her misfortune? 'You're not only rude but unfair as well, and you know it. You know enough about your condition to realise that your kidney was rejected. It had nothing to do with Johnnie – Mr Johnson. The operation was done perfectly. He is a very good surgeon.'

Hannah pulled a face. 'You doctors always stick together. You wouldn't have let them use a lousy kidney like that if you hadn't been enjoying yourself with Yousef.'

'You can never be certain even with what looks like a good match on paper, you know that. That was just bad luck.'

'I will get another chance, won't I? I don't think I can stand this much longer.'

Her eyes turned to watch the rain run down the window, imagining the feel of it on her face. 'You did promise.'

Rhys knew that her battles with him were only a vain effort to keep depression at bay. Her spirits were so fragile.

'Hannah, I have never promised you anything, only that I will do my best.'

'Your girlfriend was in this morning; called in for a chat.'

Rhys had become used to Hannah's wayward mind but this threw him completely. He felt his colour rising and a feeble smile loosened his lips. 'What d'you mean, girlfriend? Who's that?'

Hannah looked at him out of the corner of her eye and giggled impishly. 'Everybody knows about it. Nansi. She's brill. Does your wife know?'

Rhys's jaw sagged as he struggled for a reply. His immediate reaction was to walk out, try to preserve his dignity, pretend nothing had been said. A moment of regret swept over him that he had allowed his relationship with a patient to get so far that she could talk to him like that. But Hannah was more than a patient and he was surprised by a sudden feeling of release. So everyone knew about it. Had he really kidded himself that they didn't in a place like St David's? In some ways it was a relief to have it confirmed. Hannah broke into his thoughts with a softness he had not heard before. 'It must be very difficult for you.'

As he looked down on the wasted frame, the muscles of her neck standing out like a surface anatomist's dream, Owen realised how wrong he had been. He had only seen the courageous, spirited teenager, the spoilt long-term patient to be indulged to salve his guilty conscience. He had completely missed the soft-hearted, hard-headed woman adversity had produced long before her time. It dawned on him that during the last four months it had been to her refreshing, sharp-tongued friendship that he had turned so often, when seeking refuge from Alex's rebuffs, even Nansi's enveloping softness. His visits had not been simply to bolster her morale. He realised now just how often he had drawn strength from this emaciated waif.

'Is she coming with us on Sunday?'

'Who? Where?'

Again Hannah showed her irritation at Owen's bewilderment. 'Nansi. Sailing. You promised to take me sailing on Sunday.'

'No, of course she can't. And I didn't promise. Only if the weather is fine and – ' Owen looked over his shoulder ' – the forecast for the weekend is for more of this. This time I'm determined to have a nice, peaceful Bank Holiday weekend, not like the last one. And I don't know that you are quite fit enough yet for a sail, even in good weather. You wouldn't want to let another kidney go by just because you had pneumonia, now would you?'

'I'd be all right. I watched a TV programme the other night, all about people on dialysis, showing what they could do, running, swimming. They even had one girl riding a horse.' She looked accusingly at Owen. 'You know I'd be all right. You're just afraid to let me out in case I run away, aren't you? Well, I can run away from here if I want to – you won't stop me if I really try.'

'It's not just that, Hannah. You know the administrators have been after me to get you out into some sort of residential accommodation. You are ruining their figures. That's an acute bed you're occupying. Patients are not supposed to lie there for months on end. If they catch you using this place like a hotel, going out sailing, I won't really have a leg to stand on.'

'You're the boss, aren't you?' Hannah pouted.

Rhys laughed. 'Only up to a point.' He knew that, not for the first time, the Records Officer, as a favour to him, was turning a blind eye to this long-stay patient, conveniently omitting a figure that would distort Owen's 'throughput' statistics.

Hannah stood and moved the two steps to stand beside him at the window. He turned with her. It was as much as he could do not to put his arm around her bony shoulders. 'When I get my kidney, can I go back and live with Dai and Jessie?'

'I don't see why not,' Owen replied, quietly. 'At least I'd know where you were; keep an eye on you.'

'And, if it fails again?'

'It won't. Worry about that if and when it happens. But it won't. I'll make damn sure it won't.'

Hannah looked out through the distorting raindrops at the distant waves, white-topped by wind over tide, as if attracted by the muddy waters. For a moment she let her defences drop, to speak with the soft, appealing voice of the confessional. 'Because I don't think I could take it again. I really couldn't.'

21

Roisin Dineen turned and paced the length of the room once more. She found herself in a large room, filled with student clutter: junk, books, clothes all competing for space with the double mattress on the floor. The waiting was the worst part. She jerked her head contemptuously at the Madonna poster. Despite the plethora of books she couldn't concentrate on reading. Another day, cooped up in that room, with no one to talk to, would drive her mad. There had been one brief respite, the night Eamon Dickens had taken her out of the city, along the M4 and into the timeless anonymity of a service station. There, for a while as Eamon had pitted his reactions against the Space Invaders, she had talked with a pro – as tough and ice-cold as herself. She had done the job of quartermaster once herself and she knew a pro when she met one. At least she could be sure there would be no slip up; everything they had asked for was ready, waiting to be picked up.

She pulled the one armchair into the large bay window, widened the gap in the dust-laden curtains a little and resumed her lonely vigil. Cathays Road was a long, straight thoroughfare within walking distance of Cardiff's University buildings. Normally busy with light commercial traffic, the road was quiet. The occasional car swished through the puddles of a wet Bank Holiday Saturday afternoon. Parked on both sides of the road were rusting saloons that would never know another new tyre. A faceless community, too transient and multi-racial to have an identity. Perfect for going to ground, she had to admit. A population of students, immigrants, inadequate intellectuals, and old folk whose children had bettered themselves and moved on. On one corner, she watched an Asian boy in his astronaut's cap, playing ball against the red brick wall of the boarded up Presbyterian church. Opposite, a light glowed in the corner shop and she saw Dickens come out. She hooked a finger around the curtain to take a closer look but let it fall back as she saw him wave.

Eamon Dickens watched the curtain fall back and his smile faded. 'Hard-faced bitch,' he muttered as he climbed the echoing stairs. The smile was back as he entered the room. He was about to tell her proudly what he'd bought when she turned on him.

'What the hell d'you mean, waving at me like that? Why don't you just put a notice up, saying I'm here?'

'For God's sake relax, woman. Who the hell's to notice? And what does it matter now? Another couple of days and won't you be on the front page of all the newspapers?'

'There's no point in taking any risks. Have you been using that shop regularly?'

'I have so. And why shouldn't I? I live here, don't I? Wouldn't it be more suspicious if a nice friendly boy like myself behaved like a recluse now?' He unloaded the plastic bag on to the table. 'If anyone is going to get us into trouble, it's you. Sure and you're a bloody sight too uptight. I'd say you're more likely to do something bloody stupid than me, the way you're behaving. Anyway, as I say, it doesn't really matter here now. From what you tell me, they'll never be able to send me back here again.'

Roisin detected the relief in Eamon's voice and despised him for it.

'Dickens.' She curled her lips around the word. 'Who ever heard of an Irishman called Dickens? Where did you get a name like that from?'

'It's an English name.'

'I know it's an English name. Where does it come from?'

Eamon took a time to answer. 'My grandfather or great-grandfather or someone like that; he was English.'

'That probably explains it,' Roisin dismissed the subject witheringly. 'What have you got to eat?'

Eamon rummaged amongst the packages and tins. 'Got some eggs and some bacon, a tin of baked beans. There are some potatoes left over from yesterday; thought I'd fry those up as well.'

'You realise this could be the last meal we have for some time?'

'And haven't I thought of that as well? I thought we'd make some bacon sarnies and I've got a couple of pork pies. A couple of cans and we'll be laughing. But we'll have to get going. I want to nick this van in daylight.'

'Why do you need to do that?' There was nothing but mistrust in Roisin's voice.

'Because it looks far less suspicious if a man in a white coat goes up to a van and drives it off in broad daylight. Hardly the thing someone does at two o'clock in the morning. Anyway,' Eamon added as he went to work with a can opener, 'in daylight, perhaps they can see you but you can also see what's around. We can have a scout round first; make sure there's no filth about.'

'And you're sure you can get one of the vans? Everything fails if you can't.'

'No sweat. I tell you, the whole thing's a piece of cake. You're talking to an expert.' He couldn't resist wasting a beguiling smile on her. 'You drive me where I tell you and drop me off. You don't hang around, d'you hear? You bring the car back here. Safer than abandoning it anywhere. It could stand here for a year and no one would take any notice. Then walk round the corner. I'll pick you up outside the old Forum cinema. You won't have to wait long; I'll be right on your tail.'

A half hour later and they sat at opposite ends of the kitchen table, stealing guarded glances at each other between mouthfuls. Eamon was mulling over his disappointment. They might have sent someone more appealing, rather than this flat-chested alley cat. He looked at her hair, hacked short as if she hated the sight of its fiery colour. Her pale cheeks bore freckles that spread down on to her upper lip above a pinched and vicious mouth. He watched her eat with short jabbing movements of her knife and fork as if her anger with life even extended to her food.

She was even more disappointed. Dickens certainly did not fit the bill for an urban guerilla. She had been landed with a Danny Boy from the Emerald Isle, not a dry eye in the bar after his rendering of Mother McCree, a throwback to the old amateur days of the People's Army. He had no place in the fighting commando she had been trained to command.

She began to wonder about the great build-up she had been given, all the talk about how important this mission was, so important that her orders had been delivered to her direct by the Chief of Staff himself. An opportunity for the IRA to show its ability to co-operate in international terrorism, he had said. She knew that Dickens was only a sleeper but, if the operation was to be that important, she would have expected someone with a bit more spunk. The last time she had been in the UK she had been one of a pack of wolves, snarling in watchful defiance of a hostile environment. Now she had a spaniel for company. He'd probably faint if he cut his finger.

Roisin was proud of her toughness. Back home, the flint-eyed, shadowy leaders had made sure she was made of sterner stuff before sending her over alone, insisting on her presence at the execution of the two informers. The man's death had been quick and clean but Roisin had helped corner the fleeing woman, had seen her final terror before the shots that left her brains dripping and slithering down the stones of the wall against which she had finally spreadeagled herself. They had watched Roisin closely and not been disappointed. But even they had had no way of knowing. They had not been there the day they had shown her what an Army of Occupation's bullet had done to her man's face. They had done nothing, before screwing down the lid, to hide the blood-caked cavity where his eyes had been, but she had shed no tears beneath the mourning Balaclava as the pistol volleys had rung out, only silently, with one black-gloved hand caressing his coffin, made him a promise, a vow.

Roisin's paranoid reverie was broken by Eamon Dickens. 'Come on; time to go.' He grinned. 'I don't think I'll bother to do the washing up.'

Outside, Roisin threw her duffle bag, now also containing Eamon's luggage of razor and underpants wrapped in a T-shirt, into the back of the rusting Cortina. She saw him eyeing her anxiously.

'You can drive a car, now, can you?' he asked.

'Get in,' was her only reply but his sudden doubts were justified as she let the clutch in with a jerk. He saw the car parked in front shudder as she clipped its wing. 'Mother of God.' He looked sideways, saw her back straight and tense, inches away from the seat. 'Bloody marvellous. Are you trying to tell me you drove off the ferry in Liverpool like that and they didn't stop you to ask for your licence?'

By the time Eamon had guided her through the side streets to within sight of the towering dockland cranes, Roisin was sweating with the concentration of a learner driver. They were now within the boundary of the new South Moors industrial estate, its service roads dividing the coarse grass and rubble of old dockland warehouses into a mottled patchwork moonscape. Here and there, seduced by the blandishments of the Welsh Development Agency but still clustering around the periphery as if afraid to venture alone into the barren wasteland, stood new, light industries. Eamon pointed to one of the squat, russet-coloured buildings.

'That's it. Now drive on past and round the next corner. Not too slowly.'

Newton and Russell, wholesale pharmacists, were obviously thriving. The modern building, clad in corrugated metal sheeting, had already been extended by two tiers of Rentakabins. Separated from the road only by a low grassy bank, the forecourt was traversed by a row of gleaming white Transits and Lutons reversed up to the main building. The staff car parks in front of the offices were empty. The only obvious security were two red boxes high under the overhanging eaves.

'Right. Carry on round the block and drop me off on the road as near to the vans as you can.' Eamon's words emerged jerkily as he pulled on a white overall. 'And don't wait, d'you hear? You're a wife, dropping her husband off for an emergency delivery, aren't you? She wouldn't wait, would she? Glad to get rid of him, most likely. Can you find your way back?'

'Hell of a time to think of that, isn't it?'

A grin spread over Eamon's face as the car came to a halt. He leaned towards her. 'Give us a kiss, then. Make it look real. The wife would be bound to give hubby a kiss, going out to earn all that lovely overtime like this.'

Reluctantly she pushed a cheek sideways. Laughing, Eamon waited until she was forced to turn her head but felt no warmth in her rigid mouth. 'Don't you ever . . .' he began but took one look into her eyes and simply shrugged his shoulders.

As he walked purposefully, unhurriedly, across the grass towards one of the Transits, she waited and watched long enough for a glimmer of respect to glow momentarily. Perhaps it took a different kind of bottle to be a sleeper, over here all on your own with no one to turn to. Perhaps, in some ways, it was easier to be a front line fighter than a spy. She doubted whether she could do it. Perhaps, after all, they had known what they were doing. She cursed as the car jerked and almost stalled as she pulled away but there was no one to notice.

Eamon was as good as his word. Roisin did not have to wait long at the Forum Cinema. He reached across to close the door after her. 'In the back with you and keep your head down,' he grinned.

The van was empty and Roisin, sitting on the floor, was grateful for what little comfort her duffle bag provided. Even so, she felt every bump and rattle over the next twenty minutes. The car breaker's yard was a modest affair, tucked away at the end of a cul de sac of three-up, three-down terraced houses. No one had bothered to declare their ownership to any passerby and it appeared deserted as Eamon drove between the heaps of eviscerated car bodies towards the large corrugated iron shed at the rear, but, at a flick of the Transit's headlights, the heavy metal doors rolled up. Eamon drove in and, with the rattle of pulley and chain, the door descended behind them.

Mrs Phillips got up from her desk and walked across to the window. August Bank Holiday Sunday morning; the families should be streaming down to the beach by now from the municipal car park over to the left. But the bay was deserted save for two intrepid windsurfers riding the rollers that were breaking over the end of Craig Ddu in the stiff westerly breeze. It was only a few months since her promotion to Nursing Officer and she couldn't get used to being called by her new title. She had been a Ward Sister so long. And there she was, sitting at the desk of the Director of Nursing Services, taking her weekend on duty in charge of Avonport's nursing staff. Director of Nursing Services; she smiled to herself. Time was when that would have been Matron's Office and woe betide anyone who put a foot inside it without permission. Not that she was complaining. She had begun to find the ward work hard going. Now she wouldn't be quite so tired at night, be able to look after her husband a bit more. He hadn't been well and there were only the two of them.

She had just finished supervising the transfer of a head injury to the neuro-surgical unit at Cardiff and had begun reading the reports from the night staff, looking to see which wards were particularly busy. She had not realised just how tricky it was to spread out the nursing staff fairly amongst the various departments and staffing the wards on a Bank Holiday was particularly difficult. They tried to give time off to as many of the girls as they could but they could never be quite sure just how many patients would be in the hospital over the weekend. The Casualty Department would welcome the bad weather – not so many road traffic accidents – but acute disease knew no holidays and she would have to keep the Intensive Care Unit fully staffed. And that acute poisoning on emergency dialysis up on the Unit, that had been unfortunate with all the nurses part-timers. She was a good girl that Nansi Rees; fair play to her, she had been the first to volunteer. Myra Phillips couldn't bring herself to believe all those things they were saying about her and Mr Owen. Not Mr Owen. He was such . . .

Her attention was distracted by a white van as it passed from right to left in front of the window. Apart from Mr Patel and Dr Drury arriving a little earlier, it was the only sign of movement she had seen. Glad of the diversion, she got up and went to the window once more. By the time she got there, the van had been reversed up to the pharmacy at the end of the block and she saw the driver get out, straighten his white jacket and walk round the van, out of her sight. Without opening the window and pushing her head out, she could see only the front half of the vehicle and the last two words of the sign – and Russell – must be Newton and Russell; they had been supplying Avonport General for years. Must be some urgent delivery, maybe to Pharmacy. More likely dressings. Yes, dressings, Mrs Phillips decided, and probably Maternity; they were always running short. They might have let her know.

She suddenly remembered the little girl on the Children's Ward, the one who had been admitted in diabetic coma, the one they were having difficulty stabilising. She had promised Sister she would go to the kitchen and make sure about the diet. Glad at last to have something purposeful to do, Myra Phillips left the office, crossed the corridor and walked into the cheerful, noisy kitchen. The harassed duty Catering Officer, with several hundred meals to produce in the next couple of hours, Bank Holiday or no Bank Holiday, was in no mood to talk to a bored Nursing Officer with not enough to do. But, who knows, Nursing Officers could be useful at times, so she submitted herself grudgingly to ten minutes of hospital gossip. Myra Phillips only broke the conversation off when she felt another of her flushes coming on.

Back in her office, she went straight to the window, opened it and put her head out. The flushes were bad enough but it was the sweating that was so embarrassing. If it went on any longer, she would have to go and see someone about it. She couldn't go and do her ward round before lunch looking like that. That was strange, that van still there. The driver would be up on Maternity having a cup of coffee, no doubt. Well, she smiled, she'd done it often enough. When she did her round, she'd leave the Midder Ward until near the end, give the driver time to have his coffee in peace.

With her head out of the window, she didn't hear the door open. It was only when it slammed shut and the Yale lock snapped closed that she turned and saw his grinning face. Even when she looked down and saw the rifle he was pointing at her throat, it was still in her mind that this was some kind of prank. But the jabbing movements he made as he advanced towards her, quickly convinced her it was not. She tried to do something she had never done in her life before, scream, but it wasn't as easy as it looked on TV. Her throat seemed to be clamped in a vice. It was when Dr Ahmed said, his thick-lipped grin intensifying as he did so, 'If you make any sound, I shoot you,' that Mrs Phillips fainted.

The large manilla envelope, propped up against the milk bottle, mocked him. Rhys looked again at the address, printed in pencil in thick, crude lettering. He could almost see someone licking the pencil stub between each word. He should have known better than to open it with a knife. He remembered, as a child, being told it was bad luck to open a letter with a knife, that it always brought bad news. He leaned forward on the kitchen stool to sip his coffee, brewed in the unwashed mug he had used earlier that morning. The remainder of his breakfast dishes were partially hidden behind the envelope but the saucepan, yellow-streaked from the previous night's scrambled egg, lay only too obvious on the draining board. He dragged his attention away to the world outside, anything to put off taking the contents of the envelope out yet again.

He was glad the weather was really bad. He had been doubting the wisdom of his promise to Hannah to take her sailing, she was still so frail. He would not have minded if the weather had been perfect and there was no problem with it blowing the way it was; no one with any sense would be out today. What Rhys had feared was weather just good enough for Hannah to nag him into going, just bad enough for him to worry about it. But he must go in and see her, perhaps take her something, a book. Then there was the problem of feeding himself at midday with no staff dining room to go to.

Concern for how Rhys was going to feed himself was probably the ultimate constraint that Alex had had to overcome in her final decision to leave him. The problem had even featured in their last cold, heartaching discussion ten days previously. Rhys could remember, word for word, snatches of their conversation.

'But how will you manage?'

'I'll manage. It's kind of you to show such concern, I must say.'

'You can't boil an egg.'

'I imagine I'll have to learn, won't I? Breakfast is easy. I can have lunch in hospital and, in the evening, well . . .'

'But it's useless. We're killing each other, Rhys. You've got to admit, this can't go on, can it? I don't know what it's more, a tragedy or a farce. I can't stick it any more. I've got to get out.'

He remembered with shame how he had simply shrugged his shoulders. Any man worth his salt would have shouted, cursed and sworn, demanded who the other man was, but any anger he might have felt had been overpowered by a weight of sadness, a feeling of guilt. There had been no need to ask who the other man was. There had been an unspoken compact, he would not mention Baxter's name and she would not ask whose cheap perfume she had smelt on his clothes, characteristic of the unbridgeable, icy crevasse between them. Looking back, they had been doomed from the day Sian had left home. They hadn't been able to communicate even in anger.

'I can't stick your withdrawal any longer, Rhys; it's killing me. We don't even touch any more.' She had smiled a fleeting, perverse glimmer of affection. 'And you are sitting there, saying to yourself you can't put up with my bossy, domineering ways either.'

'Where will you go?'

'I've rented a flat in Cardiff.'

'All fixed up. You must have decided a long time ago. Bit cold-blooded, wasn't it, even for you?'

'You're a fine one to say that. How long has it been since there was any warmth in this house?' She had folded her arms around herself and faked a shiver. 'Let's at least give it a try, Rhys. A couple of months. Who knows, miracles happen; perhaps by that time you will have found you have missed me and asked me to come back, or I might be knocking on the door, pleading to let me in.' She had tried to smile.

'D'you really think so?'

There had been no reply.

Rhys reached for the envelope once more, slowly inserted a finger and thumb and took out the five colour enlargements, now smudged by the countless times he had shuffled through them. He pushed his coffee mug away and spread them on the table in front of him. Rhys was no photographer but it was clear to him that the man, whoever he had been, had not possessed the skill to do justice to the camera. He had obviously used a zoom lens but the focus was poor, his aim worse. Even so, there had been no mistaking Alex and Baxter, coming out of a pub. There was another of them walking together somewhere, could be a park. Another showed them getting into a car. In each, Alex was dressed differently. He must have been following them. Should he tell Alex? Or the police?

Rhys was honest enough to ponder the poses he and Nansi might have presented to this photographic peeping Tom over the last few months, when he was startled by the phone as it shattered the house's silent void. His first impression, vivid and immediate, as the person the other end began to speak, was of abject terror. Rhys spoke to frightened people over the phone often enough – the GP ringing about the lump in the breast his wife has just shown him; the Registrar who has ventured out of his depth in some emergency operation – but this was sheer gibbering terror.

'Please come, Mr Owen.'

'Who is that?'

'Mrs Phillips.' She was having trouble articulating her own name.

'Mrs Phillips?' Rhys tried to sound polite, his forehead furrowing as he struggled to think of any Mrs Phillips he knew.

'Sister Phillips. Oh, please come, Mr Owen. Please.'

Now Rhys remembered; one of the Sisters on the medical wards.

'Now, calm down, Sister. What's the problem?'

The only reply he got was a strangled squeal, a tiny spike in the pitch of her voice, as if someone had just prodded her in the ribs. Rhys found himself being carried along into a sense of unreality.

'Sister!' he called. 'Are you still there? Are you all right?'

When Mrs Phillips finally replied, the terror in her voice was replaced by the sound of despair. Though still fearful and tremulous, the tone was lower, like someone who has accepted the inevitability of some dreadful, imminent catastrophe.

'Please, Mr Owen. Please come at once.'

'Where are you, Sister?'

'Matron's Office.' There was a final surge of fear before the line went dead. 'Please be quick.'

Owen had been in the game long enough to know that there were only three things worth running for, fire, respiratory obstruction and torrential bleeding. He couldn't believe that Sister Phillips's call had related to any one of those. In spite of that, he found himself strangely flustered. He was heading for the door when he remembered the photographs. Hurrying to put them back in the envelope, as if that would put them out of his mind for a while, he dropped one of them, face down, on the floor. With a small tut of annoyance, he picked it up and tenderly smoothed Alex's face with his handkerchief. With one foot in his car, he remembered about a book for Hannah, hesitated, but decided he had better get on. The roads were deserted and he soon found himself on the approach road to the hospital across the common. Matron's Office; he smiled. Funny how people revert when under stress. He scarcely noticed the van parked outside Pharmacy but he registered Patel's silver grey Honda and Clare Drury's red Mini. Must be in for an appendix. No. Had to be more than an appendix for both of them to be in.

Through the doors and hallway, he turned right into the main corridor. Sniffing at the smell of food, he wondered whether he could scrounge some up on the Unit later. His left hand was already turning the door handle as his right gave a small, polite tap. As he walked into the room, he saw Myra Phillips sitting at the desk with terror in her eyes. But they were not focused on him. As he closed the door behind him, he turned to see what could possibly produce such a mesmeric effect.

It was probably fortunate for Rhys that Ahmed hesitated while he relished to the full his moment of savagery. As a result, Rhys was already swaying back in startled disbelief at the sight of so much hatred when the rifle butt hit him. If he had been standing still or going forward, it must surely have broken his jaw. As it was, as he fell to the ground, cracking his head on the desk, his tongue was already forward, searching, protecting. He heard a scream from Myra Phillips cut off by a loud slap encompassed in hissing obscenities he could not believe could come from a female voice. His upper lip was numb and yet already gave him the impression of being three times its normal size.

In a daze, he struggled to sit up but was too slow to avoid the kick Ahmed aimed at his lower ribs. The soft trainers Ahmed wore took some of the momentum out of the blow but there was still enough force to knock the wind out of Rhys. Striving to breathe, some blood and saliva caught the back of his throat, making him cough. A fastidious if untidy man, Rhys viewed the blood and saliva on his shirt with dismay. Seeking refuge in the normal world, he told himself he must get his laundry problem sorted out, now that Alex had left him. He groped for his handkerchief and put it to his mouth. He felt something hard, loose in his mouth and pushed it with his tongue out into the bloodstained cloth. With almost academic interest, he saw a tooth he diagnosed as one of his incisors, confirming the fact with his tongue. As he felt the gap, he also discovered the deep, vertical split in the mucosa of his upper lip. With his finger he was glad to feel the skin intact. Still, that split ought to have a catgut stitch in it.

He saw Ahmed draw his foot back for another swing at him and he rolled away. He raised the hand that did not hold the handkerchief to his mouth.

'All right, all right. You've made your point. There's no need for any more of that.'

Ahmed leered down at him, his Armalite hanging loosely over Rhys's lower abdomen.

'The master surgeon; one of the master race,' he said, before pursing his lips to spit in Rhys's face.

22

As Rhys struggled to the sitting position, propping himself against the desk, he became conscious, for the first time, of the woman hovering menacingly over Mrs Phillips. She must have been standing behind Ahmed when he came in. Rhys was used to being popular, particularly with women; people seemed to get on well with him. As a result, he was puzzled by the intensity of hatred with which the woman looked at him. What the hell had he done to make her look at him like that? That is if you can call a pinched little red headed drab in creased trousers and anorak, holding a 9 mm Uzi submachine-gun, a woman. Owen was excited to find he had reacted with hatred, not fear, and he realised the feeling was mutual. He enjoyed the discovery. It helped. He was delighted to find he was not afraid. It had all been so sudden that he had had no time to be scared but had derived a perverse exhilaration from the physical pain of Ahmed's blows. He had suffered so much emotional pain recently that physical hurt came almost as a relief. Somehow he felt Ahmed could do no worse, short of shooting him. He looked from Roisin Dineen to Ahmed as if trying to decide who he was going to hate more.

'Get up,' Ahmed said. 'I have much work for you.'

'And if I don't choose to?' asked Owen.

Ahmed did not answer but took a pace forwards, raising his Armalite above his head. Owen stood up hurriedly, gasping at the sudden pain in his side. There must have been more weight behind Ahmed's foot than he had thought; maybe he had cracked a rib. He looked at Ahmed who suddenly seemed overcome by nervous uncertainty. He was swinging and jabbing recklessly with his Armalite as if uncertain what to do with his newfound power. Not a man to be provoked any further, Rhys decided.

'What do you want me to do?' he asked.

'That's better.' Ahmed calmed a little. 'First you will clear the kitchens over there and then you will clear A and B Blocks.'

'I'll what?' Owen regretted his astonishment as it drew a jab of pain from his side.

'You'll . . .'

The noise of the telephone ringing took them by surprise. For a moment all four looked at it as if they had never heard the sound before. Ahmed waved the butt of his rifle in Mrs Phillips's direction.

'Answer it.'

Myra Phillips's only response was to shrink further into her chair where she began to sob. There was vicious delight in Roisin Dineen's face as she swung her free arm, giving Myra Phillips a slap that jerked her head sideways.

'Answer it, you stupid great cow.'

A coarse shaking spread over Myra Phillips's body, jerking her shoulders and neck, and her eyes took on a distant, detached, glazed look. The phone continued to ring insistently.

'You,' Ahmed snapped, his head jerking from Owen to the telephone. 'Be careful or I shoot you.'

Owen recognised instantly the voice on the phone even though it was agitated with a mixture of fear and anger.

'Is Mrs Phillips there, please? Quickly, please.'

'Nansi; it's Rhys here. What d'you want?'

'Rhys? Is that you? It doesn't sound like you; you sound funny. What are you doing there?' Her voice began to shake. 'What's going on?'

'It's all right, Nansi.' Owen glanced sideways as Ahmed came close, the muzzle of his rifle now at point-blank range and pointed at his temple. 'What's the matter?'

'Rhys, there's a man with a gun. He's out on the landing. I've just been out to go up to Theatre for something and he won't let me pass. He just pushed me back into the ward. What do I do, Rhys? Do I ring the police? Rhys, I'm afraid. He's real. It's a proper gun. I don't think it's a joke.'

'No, Nansi, I'm afraid it's no joke. There's another of them down here. Don't be frightened. Just stay where you are. Don't do anything and don't ring the police.' He saw Ahmed nod his head as he repeated, 'Do not ring the police. I'll ring you back as soon as I can.'

He put the phone down.

'That's good,' Ahmed said. 'Now ring kitchens, tell them get out. Tell them there is IRA bomb at the front of hospital. You will not mention me. You will tell them it is IRA bomb, you understand that? Tell them get out through back of hospital.'

'IRA?' Owen had learned now to control his astonishment and saved himself some pain.

'You'd better believe it.' Roisin Dineen's voice was low and spiteful as Owen turned his attention to her. 'You can tell them there's enough explosive in that van outside to bring this end of the building down and it's on remote control.'

Owen remembered the van parked outside Pharmacy. He found the internal number of the kitchens and was halfway through convincing an incredulous Catering Officer that he was serious when he heard a sound like a distant chattering magpie. It took him some time to realise it was a sound made commonplace by TV, that of automatic gunfire. For the first time, he felt fear, not for himself, but for others. He looked up from the phone at an exultant Ahmed.

'Residents,' Ahmed sneered. 'Time they got up. You British spend much time in bed, I think.'

They stood quietly for a while, listening to the clamour outside as the kitchens were evacuated. They heard a scream, someone fall. The sounds of confusion gradually died away. Ahmed took one hand away from his weapon to search in the breast pocket of his denim jacket. Owen noticed the dark, wet stain in the front of his pale blue sweatshirt. He thrust the scrap of paper in Owen's direction.

'Now we start work on A and B Blocks,' he said, 'but, before that, you make telephone get me that number.'

It took some time for the girl on the switchboard to answer. Her voice conveyed the panic rising within her. She calmed under Rhys's influence and gave him his line, promising to answer immediately if he rang again. Rhys dialled the London number Ahmed had given him and waited until he heard a gruff voice answer unintelligibly. He offered the phone to Ahmed who pointed to the desk. Owen put the phone down and Ahmed prodded him towards the window before picking it up. Ahmed spoke a few words in Arabic, putting the phone back without waiting for an answer. It was during the confusion of Owen trying to explain to the telephonist that she must ring all the wards in A and B Block, telling them to evacuate their patients, that Owen heard the first wail of a police car getting rapidly louder.

Ahmed elbowed Owen to one side as he came to the window, still open from the time when Myra Phillips's flushes were all she had had to worry about. They all heard the distant squeal of tyres as the car screamed round and up the common towards the hospital. As if living a nightmare, Owen saw Ahmed take careful aim at where he guessed the police car would appear. The driver must have been told where the trouble was as he swung to his right towards the front of the Ward Block rather than go, as they invariably did, to the Casualty entrance. The fingers of Ahmed's right hand blanched as he began to squeeze. As Owen, with a small cry, hurled himself at Ahmed, the Armalite fired and the car's windscreen crazed, seemed to hold for a moment and then disintegrated. Owen clung to Ahmed's back until a blow from an Israeli weapon, wielded by an Irishwoman in defence of an Arab, split an innocent Welshman's scalp and brought him to his knees.

The car's crew had abandoned it in a hurry, leaving both doors wide open, headlights on, the two blue lights still flashing, as they dashed for the cover of the Casualty Department.

'Now,' Rhys heard Ahmed mutter, 'I think we show them how near they come.'

And with two single shots, he shattered the two blue lamps.

Normally, at this stage of Shahinair Flight 136's progress across Europe, there would be nothing but friendly chatter against the background of professional calm on the flight deck. They had done the trip so often they had almost worn a groove along Upper Amber One. Still within the Milano Control Area, they would shortly be coming to the point where they would be handed over to Geneve Control, a simple enough routine for Jack Barclay and his crew, but there was a level of tension that kept them quietly attentive in their seats. They each had to make conscious efforts not to keep glancing at their HF panel, as if that might help speed the message they were awaiting with such rapidly increasing urgency. If they did not get their instructions to divert soon, Barclay was going to have to make a decision.

Having to cross at least one international boundary, Barclay had had to file his flight plans back in Shahin – one from there to Rome, another from Rome to Gatwick – just as he had done so many times before. But he had known, this time, there had been no possibility of their landing in Gatwick. He had been told to expect his orders to divert from Alitalia, their handling agent in Rome, but they had not materialised. They still had not received them. He knew he couldn't land in Gatwick and he dared not divert on his own initiative without confirmation that all had gone well the other end. That left but one choice if the message did not arrive soon; he must turn back to Rome while that was still a reasonable option.

They had refuelled at Rome's Ciampino airport as was their routine on their regular freight runs from Shahin to London Gatwick. Barclay had flown C130s in the RAF, a beautiful plane to fly, but for a pittance compared with what he was being paid now. And, after what they had been promised for this particular flight, they would all be able to retire. Not that the three of them would not have done it for far less. There was something about the Shahinians that got to you.

Barclay turned to his co-pilot. 'Scared, Tony?'

'Let's just say I'm glad I put my brown underwear on.' Anthony Telford, ten years Barclay's junior, grinned, trying to make anxiety look like excitement. They had flown together for five years and there was little that could be hidden between them. 'Joking apart, Jack; what d'you think? D'you reckon there'll be shooting?'

Barclay shook his head. 'I don't think so. We know we have nothing really to worry about from that lot back there and as long as I can play my part right, I don't see that they are going to send in the SAS, or anything like that.' He did his best to encourage the younger man. 'I reckon you're more likely to die of boredom. How long did they say it might take, anything up to two weeks?'

'Yep,' Telford answered, trying to sound relaxed. 'We've got enough food and drink stacked away back in the hold for at least a fortnight.' Slowly, the strained smile on his face was replaced by something more honest. 'To tell you the truth , Jack, I'm shit scared. Let's be honest. I just hope I don't let you down. I think I'll feel a lot better when . . .'

The Selcal bell rang and the HF light flashed. They had received 'company' messages over the Selcal system often enough but none quite like this one. Co-pilot and flight engineer held their breath as they listened to Barclay acknowledge his instructions. Within minutes, their anxious tension replaced by genuine excitement, they were informing the Torino controller of their diversion and, ten minutes later, over the Saint Prex beacon, thanking him as he handed them over to Geneve Control. A few words in the emotionless verbal shorthand of flight control with the new Controller who would work them across the Geneve sector, and Jack Barclay relaxed a little. He turned to his flight engineer.

'Harry, you'd better slip back there and tell them it's on, would you? They must be wondering what's going on. They've been very good, I must say. I rather expected one of them up here with us, keeping an eye on us. Tell them we've had the signal; things seem to have gone all right the other end.'

He had only landed at Cardiff-Wales once before; he had been diverted there once when RAF Brawdy had been closed by fog. He smiled. Strangely enough, that had been in a Hercules too. No problems there. A good airport; come a long way from the old Glamorgan (Rhoose) days. He reckoned they would probably hear of the diversion first from Dan Air, their handling company at Gatwick; it would probably raise a few eyebrows but no more. West Drayton would have been informed as their new flight path was passed from Controller to Controller, but London Control would probably not let Cardiff know until a half hour or so before their ETA.

Barclay, while complying with the ritual submission of his flight plans, had decided his route long before he had left Shahin; he would go 'up the ambers' in much the same way as he always did until he got into London controlled airspace and then, at Biggin, get clearance for Upper Green One. Easier and much safer than crossing Piccadilly Circus on foot. At each control point, however, he found that he was consciously preventing his voice from rising with excitement and, at Lyneham, he discovered his mouth had gone dry. West Drayton had put him over the beacon there at 7000 feet and informed him that, as there was a lull in the holiday traffic going in and out of Bristol, he was to contact Cardiff direct. He noticed with irritation that his hand was sweating as he stretched to change to Cardiff's frequency.

With a quiet curse, Barclay changed his course by thirty degrees. Though his aircraft was equipped with the necessary transponder, Cardiff did not have the Secondary Surveillance Radar necessary to give that comforting indentifying squawk alongside his blip on the radar screen. Although many would have taken London's range and bearing as sufficient identification, this radar controller was not going to; the weather was pretty foul, there had been a lot of traffic and he was making sure the blip on his screen also changed course by thirty degrees before he accepted him. Reassured, the controller transmitted the local weather conditions and, as Telford made his instrument corrections, Barclay began his descent through the eight-eighths cloud on a course that would bring him at 1500 feet in line with the ILS, eight miles from runway three zero. He was referred by the radar controller to the tower, was given their clearance to land and broke through the dirty, ragged cloud base to see the muddy waters of the Bristol Channel breaking against the cliffs of Steep Holme below. Barclay took his eyes from the cross wires of the ILS for a second to conjure up a reassuring grin for his co-pilot.

'And the best of British luck to us all.'

'I'll go along with that, Jack,' Telford replied and there was a quiet 'Amen' from the engineer behind them.

Though there was no real need to do so, Barclay used the whole length of the runway, turning right into the taxiway at the far, western end. That was how he had imagined doing it and he felt happier to keep to the plan he had gone through in his mind time and time again. The controller saw it, showed his surprise but made no remark to his assistant. Jack Barclay taxied slowly the length of the apron in front of the terminal buildings. Even at that stage, he could not resist a glance of professional admiration for the lines of the Aerospace 146 alongside. Stand twelve, allocated to him as he taxied, was round the eastern end of the terminal, near the Servisair freight terminal and out of sight of the controller in the tower. A marshaller, his 'bats' hanging from his hands, stood waiting for the aircraft to come into sight.

It was probably the marshaller who reacted first. The tower controller was watching an Air Europe 737 charter flight arrive from Corfu and missed the stage at which the marshaller began to wave his 'bats' impotently. The charter flight safely on the ground, something unusual registered in the controller's peripheral visual field, striving for attention. He looked left.

'Christ Almighty. Where's he going?'

The controller shot to his feet. His assistant was no more than milliseconds in following him. They reached for their binoculars but there was little need. They saw the Hercules make no attempt to turn left behind the terminal but carry on up the taxiway back towards the eastern end of the runway over which they had just landed. Increasingly urgent calls on the RT produced no response.

The more frantic the controller's voice became, the broader spread the grin on Jack Barclay's face. He looked at his co-pilot, saw the tongue moistening dry lips.

'Excitable, isn't he? Not to worry, Tony. Piece of cake.'

Three to four hundred yards from the end of the terminal buildings, the taxiway passed within fifty yards or so of the airport's fuel farm, a fenced-off compound of fuel tanks and petrol bowsers. At this point, Barclay applied his brakes and switched off his engines. He turned to the flight engineer.

'Right, Harry. Get back in there and tell them – go. And, Harry – ' half out of his seat, the engineer hesitated ' – wish them "Good luck".'

The tower controller was still trying furiously to raise Barclay on the RT when he saw the aircraft's ramp come down. He couldn't believe his eyes. Some kind of armoured vehicle emerged, followed by a large, black limousine, to speed back down the taxiway and disappear at full speed from his view behind the terminal buildings.

Both vehicles turned unhesitatingly towards the perimeter fence. Alongside the freight terminal stood one of the emergency break-out points for the airport's fire and rescue services, known locally as a crash gate. It was a simple iron framed affair, covered in mesh similar to the perimeter fence and topped by two meagre strands of barbed wire. The one small brass padlock proved no match for a ten ton Saracen armoured personnel carrier travelling at twenty miles an hour. By the time the astonished controller was reaching for the button that would connect him with Airport Security, the vehicles were already out of his sight, accelerating westwards, out of the airport complex and on to the open road beyond.

The sight of Rhys kneeling on the floor, blood streaming from his scalp wound, had brought the instinctive reaction of the born nurse from Myra Phillips. She had risen from her desk, found some tissues, moistened them at the hand basin and knelt to staunch the bleeding. Ahmed's reaction had been less compassionate.

He had stood over him, silent and almost motionless, as if willing Owen to do something positive so that he could club him about the head once more. For nearly two hours, the motley quartet had said nothing, listening to the distant sounds of confusion. Owen had still been wondering whether the telephonist had been sufficiently calm to understand his instructions when Ahmed suddenly dug his rifle barrel into his shoulder.

'Now, you, great surgeon, you sit at desk.'

His stomach feeling like the early stages of sea-sickness, Owen sank gratefully into the chair.

'I think now we ring police, give them instructions. You fix it.'

'What d'you want me to say?' Owen asked, spraying bloodstained saliva as he spoke.

'You will tell police to make sure Blocks A and B empty. They must do this quickly. This way no one is hurt. This must be done in one hour. Tell them.'

'Impossible.' Owen found the word difficult to say through the gap in his teeth and split lip. 'They can't possibly do that in an hour. The best they could hope to do is to empty B Block in that time.'

'Tell them they must do it. Tell them they must do it,' Ahmed repeated excitedly as he began to pace up and down the room. 'Tell them there is one of my men on each floor and more are on the roof. In one hour they will go into wards and shoot if patients are not gone. There are not many patients. It is your holiday. You always have holiday. You British do not know how to work.'

'What about the wards above here?' Owen pointed up at C Block above them.

'They stay. For now, they stay.'

'And theatre? There has obviously been a case going on in theatre.'

'Watch him. Don't trust the bastard.' Roisin's voice came from the window where she was keeping watch. 'He should be more afraid. He's too cocky. I don't like that. Perhaps we should shoot this one now – ' she laughed contemptuously at Myra Phillips ' – just to keep him honest.'

Ahmed seemed to be considering the idea for a moment before turning to Owen once more.

'You; phone,' he snapped. 'Do it.'

Owen picked up the phone. He heard a few whispered words at the other end before a confident male voice came over clearly.

'Inspector Harris here, Mr Owen. Can you tell me what the hell's going on, sir?'

'Not exactly, Inspector, no. All I know is that, at this moment, I have a gun pointed at my head by someone who wouldn't hesitate to use it. Now please, please, don't do anything rash. Do as they say.'

'What do they want, Mr Owen?'

'All I know is that they want all the patients out of A and B Blocks, in a hurry. I have told them that is not possible but that perhaps you can clear B Block for them at least to start with, by moving patients across the corridors into A Block. It might be a good idea to get them out of there too; as many as you can anyway.'

'What the hell for?'

'I don't know, Inspector.'

'Is it the IRA, sir?'

Rhys hesitated before answering and he saw the rifle's muzzle raised.

'There is someone from the IRA here and they say there is a large bomb in the van you can see parked against the end of the building. I think you would be wise to take that as the truth. I don't think these people are bluffing.'

'You mean there's more than one there with you, doctor?'

'Yes,' Rhys replied, quickly.

'All IRA?'

'No.'

'What you say?' Ahmed hissed.

Rhys went on hurriedly. 'So keep out, Inspector, please. Let them clear B Block. Don't go in. They have got a gunman on each of the landings between B and C and at least another one on the roof. I imagine the ground floor is covered too.' He saw Ahmed nod. 'So there's no point. If you show your face amongst the patients on B then I don't think they will hesitate to shoot.'

'What about the patients in the other block, Mr Owen?'

'That I just don't know. I imagine . . .'

Owen got no further as Ahmed tore the phone from him and dropped it back on its rest.

'That is enough, I think. Now we wait.'

Owen was forced to sit on the floor once more, alongside Mrs Phillips, his back propped against the wall, his side and head stiffening with pain, already conscious of the smell of his own dried blood and sweat. The office had its own small private toilet and a terrified Nursing Officer begged to use it. Though there was no means of escape from it, Roisin insisted that she leave the door open and Ahmed, lolling in the seat at the desk, his Armalite resting on the top, laughed at the sound of her pitiful few drops. Roisin Dineen added to the gruesome picture by pulling on a rough knitted balaclava as she watched and listened out of the window. From where he sat, Owen could see nothing but he heard sounds of shouting, wailing sirens and revving engines. Above it all he heard the rhythmic slap of a helicopter. He could only sit and wonder what possible reason anyone could have to hijack a hospital.

'What exactly are we waiting for?' he asked.

'Wait and see, great surgeon,' Ahmed grinned. 'We have a surprise for you.'

*

Great Britain's first line of defence against the invasion of its sovereignty was a solitary police constable, standing four square in the middle of a country road, the clean-cut, unarmed epitome of the British bobby so beloved of foreign tourists. The local police frequency had been fairly buzzing with some sort of flap on over in Avonport. He had heard all available patrol cars being diverted there; there had been reports of shooting. Far enough away for him not to worry. But the call on his car's radio had changed all that. Some sort of military vehicle followed by a large black vehicle, possibly a Mercedes. Known to be heading west from the airport. Thought might be making for Avonport. Not known whether proceeding along coast road or may have turned towards the A48 at Llantwit Major. To report any siting and follow at safe distance.

PC David Evans raced for the junction where the road from Llantwit Major joined the A48. Half a mile down the minor road, he reversed his little white Escort into a farm gate, got out and waited at the end of the only straight stretch for miles. He did not have to wait long. He saw them through a gap in the hedge as the road wound down a slope some distance away. He braced himself, drew himself up to his full height and raised his hand high above his head in a futile gesture of authority as the armoured vehicle came into view. Moments later, he was diving for the hedge as both vehicles swept by. By the time his message had resulted in bringing the helicopter overhead, they were approaching the outskirts of Avonport. One last hasty attempt at setting up a road block before they were in amongst the streets only resulted in a wrecked patrol car. It was only the sheer weight of police vehicles already blocking the road below the common that finally brought the strange little convoy to a halt.

Several of the police now carried hand-guns, their forearms out stiff before them across car bonnets and roofs. The Saracen's turret traversed, its Browning machine gun waving, Dalek-like. A swarthy young man in leopard-spotted fatigues and flak jacket looked along the sights of another heavy machine-gun mounted on the rear.

It was a stand-off.

It was also watched from the hospital by Ahmed. He shouted from the window words that were blown away before they got twenty yards. Agitated, he paced the room, returned to the window, shouted again, and fired a burst of automatic fire into the air.

'And what good d'you think that will do?' Roisin asked. 'You didn't really think the pigs would let them through, did you?'

'Then we must make them.'

Owen now learned what it was to look into the eyes of a murderer. A gentle man who spent his life striving for compassion, he had never seen a face so abandoned to the desire to inflict pain. The ferocity the hostage must see the second before the terrorist bullet rips through him blazed at Owen and he was certain he must die. He was so sure of it that he was slow to believe what Ahmed was saying to him and his sluggish reaction resulted in a kick in his groin that left him pale and sweating.

'I said, you get on phone again,' Ahmed screamed at him. 'You tell them I shoot you one by one if they don't let them through. You tell them watch if they don't believe me.' He turned to Roisin. 'You stay and see he does that.' With one hand grasping her collar he hauled Myra Phillips forward. 'You; you come with me.'

Doubled up in pain, Rhys made a token movement to stop Ahmed but found himself pushed to the desk by Roisin, while Ahmed dragged a defenceless woman, incontinent and whimpering, out through the door.

There was no need for Rhys to spell out their despair, the agony in his voice was sufficiently convincing. Neither was it necessary to explain to the police surrounding the two vehicles what Ahmed was trying to say as, standing outside the door between B and C Blocks, he shook Myra Phillips like a rag doll and fired his rifle in the air.

The road was cleared and the Saracen and the Mercedes, its passengers concealed behind closed curtains inside opaque windows, edged their way through and up the slope.

Roisin replaced the telephone and motioned Owen back to sit against the wall. He lost track of time as he came to terms with the fact that he was a hostage; not watching it; not reading about it; but being it. He sat, sick and degraded, wondering what sort of patriotism could so twist anyone gifted with any human intelligence, when he heard a soft movement, felt someone's presence. He looked up to see someone framed in the doorway.

It was Yousef, a gun in his hand. A handsome young warrior, a predatory god. For all the pride in his bearing, there was also gentleness in the hand that helped Rhys stand and sadness in the eyes that saw what Ahmed had done to him. For the first time in his life, Rhys almost yielded to the rough tenderness of a man's embrace. But soon his anger and his pride returned, swelling to bursting point.

'No,' he shouted, pushing himself away from Yousef so violently that he found himself back against the wall. 'Get away from me. Leave me alone.'

23

The newsreader, elegantly upright, professional to her fingertips, put on her neutral expression to cope with the newsflash she had just been handed. As she read, she replaced it gradually with her grave international look.

'News is coming in of a shooting incident at a South Wales hospital. While details are, as yet, hard to establish, it is understood that evacuation of a number of patients is already under way, while part of the hospital has been surrounded by armed police. It has not been confirmed as to who is responsible for the shooting, though there are rumours of a car bomb being placed in the vicinity of the hospital and that several of the staff and some patients are being held hostage. Avonport's St David's Hospital is the £20 million showpiece only recently opened. It is not known as yet whether there have been any casualties.

'An incident is also reported to have taken place at Cardiff Airport this afternoon, though whether this is connected in any way with what has happened at Avonport is not yet clear. It is understood that vehicles, at least one of them armoured, which had just arrived in a transport plane from the Middle East, broke through the airport perimeter and were seen to be proceeding westwards. It is not known whether this represents some form of terrorist attack but efforts, including the use of helicopters, are being made to halt the vehicles and question the occupants.

'Any further details we will bring you in our nine o'clock news. In the meanwhile, this is . . .'

Sian Morgan stood up, the *Sunday Times* slipping from her lap. She ran out to the garage.

'Roger, something's going on at the hospital. It was on the BBC news.' There was no response so she kicked the feet protruding from under the car. 'Roger! You know I don't like you getting under the car like that. Come out.'

'What's the matter?' he grunted as he struggled into view.

'St David's. On the news. They said there has been some shooting. And they mentioned hostages.'

'Shooting? Hostages? Don't be daft. In Avonport?'

Her husband looked inclined to disappear again so Sian kicked him on the foot once more.

'I'm serious. I'm worried about Dad. What if he's there?'

'Bank Holiday Sunday evening? He's not on call, is he?'

'No, but you know what he's like, especially now he's on his own.' Her voice began to tremble. 'I'm going to ring him.'

By the time Roger had joined her, still soaping his oily hands, Sian had kept the phone to her ear far longer than she would have normally to decide there was no one at home. She slowly replaced it and pressed herself to her husband's chest, ignoring, in her concern, the oil-slicked drops on the carpet as he put his arms around her.

'Don't worry, love. He's probably down on the boat.'

'On a day like this? No; I have a feeling. It would be just like him, the silly old nitwit, to get caught up in something like this. I don't suppose it would do any good to ring the hospital, would it?'

'I doubt it, but I'll try, if you like.'

Ten minutes later, Roger gave up trying.

Sian took the phone from him. 'I'd better ring Mum, just in case she didn't see the news. Where's her number? Where's that piece of paper?'

She listened to the calling tone almost as long as when ringing her father before replacing the receiver.

The plastic table top was cold and unforgiving under Rhys's forearms. He shifted his position but his trousers still stuck to the seat of the tubular framed chair. He decided he must try and keep some idea of time. He looked at his watch; seven o'clock. Once again he wondered what others were doing; Sian, Nansi. What had happened to Nansi after he had talked to her on the phone? Had she got out? And Hannah. No one had had any food since the morning. Would they allow her dialysis? What was going to happen about that? What about everyone's dialysis for that matter? What about the clinic? What about those booked after the holiday?

And that poor youngster over there, the acute poisoning, lying in the bed in the corner, blissfully ignorant, in her deep coma, of the drama going on around her; were they going to be allowed to look after her?

And always Alex. Wherever his mind wandered en route, it always seemed to return to Alex. Shadowy in outline, her features perplexed, she was the only one he could not put a picture around.

He swept his hand over the hard, comfortless formica. He must have passed that table a hundred times and never noticed it. Lying as it did in the middle of the dialysis ward, it was usually covered in disposable equipment in their plastic bags. Now it was the limit of his tangible world, his only possessions the commonplace items in a man's pockets. There was no airing cupboard with its neat pile of clean shirts, no freedom to walk down the road and take his bloodstained jacket to the cleaners. Not even the freedom to walk out of the room. He looked at the terrorist, now accepting him to be nothing more, who had been posted at the door. He decided that, if anything, he was more scared of this one than Ahmed. Obviously given orders not to let any one of them move, he was going to do just that. Any slight shifting of position and his rifle swung that way as if by reflex action, the fingers around one of the hand grenades that hung from a strap over his shoulder twitching in sympathy. He was jumpy, dangerously unpredictable, reacting to any shout from outside the room.

Rhys looked round at the men held with him. Paddy Moore, Kumar the anaesthetic Registrar, a couple of male nurses, a theatre technician and two theatre porters. Paddy seemed calm enough though the skin over the lean muscles of his neck and forearms glistened as he sweated profusely. It was Kumar, sitting rigidly upright, who showed the fine, total body tremor of deep fear, genetically engrained by generations of murderous religious confrontation. Though some were obliged to sit on the floor, no one lay on the vacant dialysis couches, as if to do so might prove some evil omen. They all glanced at Rhys from time to time as if expecting some sort of leadership.

Rhys raised his hand rather like a child asking to use the toilet. It resulted in the rifle being pointed directly at him.

'I need to see to that patient over there,' he said. 'Her drip needs changing. The bottle is running out.'

'You stay,' was the only response.

Rhys tried again. 'She is very ill. If she is not attended to she will die. I must change that bottle.'

There was no response and the man seemed to derive comfort from caressing his grenade once more, as if, when faced with a decision, he gained confidence from the feel of the only thing he knew anything about.

'What will the Sayyid Yousef say if I tell him you have let a woman die?'

The man thought about that for a moment before jerking his gun. 'You go,' he said.

Rhys found he still could not walk upright; any attempt to do so only brought back that sickening pain in his crotch. There was a window above the head of the bed and he took his time over changing the drip bottle and fiddling unnecessarily with every tube and tap he could find while he stole repeated short glances at what was going on outside. The first impression he had was of a beautiful evening. The cold front had obviously passed through and the evening sky was full of fluffy white clouds racing in on the fresh westerly that was following behind it. The common and the road below it were the scene of utter chaos. Three floors up, he could not see the immediate front of the building but he could see the police car which had been first to arrive, its doors still wide open, its headlights still blazing. He wondered how long it would be before the battery died. A Wessex helicopter had just landed in the municipal car park to his left and Rhys saw men in dark berets crouch as they ran from it, long, awkward-looking bags under their arms. Across the lower common, men were putting up scaffolding and one short length of the coast road was already screened from his view by sheets of plastic that flapped in the breeze. Further along, there was more scaffolding, tower-like, which had Rhys confused until he just made out the cameras. Where the hell had all the stuff come from so quickly, he thought. There must be some people who made their living just sitting round waiting for something to get hijacked. Fascinated, he stared for just too long.

'You. You come back now.'

Rhys took one last look at the patient.

'I said, you come back now.'

Pressing hard over the inner end of the patient's eyebrow, Rhys saw no flicker of response. She wasn't going to make it, that one. He heard Kumar give a little whimper as their guard shouted and started to move towards Rhys. Raising his forearms, showing the palms of his hands, Rhys returned to his seat. At least the sight out of the window had given him something else to think about other than his aches and pains and that subtle combination of nausea and hunger. He was running his tongue over the split in his lip, wondering how it would heal without a catgut stitch, when the door opened.

Another Arab Rhys had not seen before came in and Rhys wondered just how many must now be in the hospital. Quite at random, a rifle was pointed to two of the hostages. 'You; you; you come with me.'

One of the theatre orderlies, sullen but composed, rose and went towards the door. Kumar tried to stand but his legs buckled under him and he slumped back. He began to sob and looked piteously towards Rhys. 'I cannot go. They will be killing us. I know these people. Always they are hating us.'

'What do you want them for?' Rhys asked.

'We have work for them.'

'I think I am being sick,' Kumar whined as Rhys looked around, wondering whether there would be any volunteers to take Kumar's place. But no one would meet his eyes.

'All right, I'll go instead of him,' Rhys said, beginning to rise, only to be forced back into his seat by the pressure from the butt of a rifle on his shoulder.

'No, you stay. He comes.' The barrel was then used to lever Kumar out of his seat and propel him unsteadily out through the door where the Arab turned once more. 'We are going to get food. Soon you will eat and then you would be wise to sleep. Do as you are told and no trouble will come to you. But we will shoot if you do not help us. There are many of us now. Do not look for help from anyone. We are in control now. We are masters but we mean you no harm. Help us in our mission and no harm will become you. Help us and Allah, in his Mercy, will see us all safe.' Fleetingly, his features softened. 'Eat and then sleep. We are not cruel but we are determined.'

It is difficult to locate exactly where the heart of a District General Hospital lies. To say it has no heart, that it is not a living system, is to belie the experience of anyone who has worked in a DGH for any length of time. But where is it placed? The wards are widespread, the Outpatients closed at night, the X-Ray and Path Lab shadowy with on call staff only after five. Even Casualty, that most capricious of departments, perhaps quiet at midday, sometimes a teeming frenzy in the small hours, is peripheral, most of its patients never reaching beyond the department's confines.

Probably nearest to the heart of a hospital are the General Surgical Theatres. Centrally placed, they may doze from time to time but never sleep, their corridors brightly lit every second of a hospital's lifetime. Those who work in them consider themselves an elite as any visitor, even one of their closest colleagues who has suffered their indulgent, slightly condescending smiles, will testify. Anyone on entering, even a surgeon from another hospital, is conscious of an individual, vital atmosphere.

This was probably why Yousef handed his rifle to the gunman on the landing outside the theatre before going in. To have carried a weapon in would have been to him akin to sacrilege.

It did not prevent him, once within, from disregarding the ritual of changing before entering the 'clean' side and he was still in his battle garb as he walked up the main corridor. Through the door of the Surgeons' Room he saw Patel trying to use the phone, while, out in the corridor, two nurses scuttled out of sight to leave him facing Paddy Moore who had put himself defensively in front of Clare Drury. A burly theatre orderly hovered behind them. For a moment there was silence, broken by Paddy Moore.

'Mr Yousef, sir.' Paddy nodded, still prepared to be respectful. 'What in hell's name is going on?'

'Hullo, Paddy.' Though he replied to Paddy, his eyes never left the troubled face behind.

'We've heard what sounds like gunfire, we have not been allowed outside by some guy with a gun on the landing and we can't get through on the phone. What the hell's happened?'

'You will understand in time. Everything will be explained. In the meanwhile I ask you to do as you're told. Do as you're told and no harm will come to you. A week or so and we will leave you in peace. But you must realise we are totally committed; nothing will stop us now.'

In his surprise, Paddy Moore completely missed the hardening in Yousef's voice.

'A week or so?'

Yousef chose to ignore completely Paddy's amazement. 'Now go and find all the staff on duty up here and take them into the Surgeons' Room so that I can talk to them.' Paddy looked inclined to discuss the matter further but Yousef snapped, 'Now, Paddy.'

Paddy's departure left Clare Drury and Yousef face to face. Neither found words for the other, Yousef's features inscrutable, Clare's those of someone longing for an answer. She lowered her eyes and walked into the Surgeons' Room to wait for the others. Ten minutes later and the Arab out on the landing had escorted most of them down to join those on the floor below, leaving a nurse to look after the patient in the Recovery Room and Clare to face Yousef with no possible escape.

Yousef waited for the last sounds to die away. He waited again until he was confronted by angry grey eyes, half-closed as if to prevent any further hurt. Dismissed from their minds were such trivial things as guns, police sieges, fear of death. For the moment, Yousef could only see and hear once more the slamming of an apartment door and the sounds of sobbing beyond.

'Your apartment was bugged,' he said, softly. 'That's why I left you that night. I couldn't explain.'

'It was what?' Clare's eyes now opened wide in astonishment, in disbelief.

'Bugged. I am sure it was. Just as mine was. I could hardly tell you that then but perhaps it helps to explain things now.'

'But why?'

'Because of me.'

'Why you then?'

‘That, I must admit, puzzled me; it still does.’ They leaned towards each other slightly in their chairs, their body language already in harmonious dialogue. ‘Not that they didn’t have good cause,’ Yousef laughed, ‘but what I still don’t understand is how they got on to me. I thought I’d given quite a good performance as a visiting surgeon, just here to learn. I know they have had their agents out in Shahin but I don’t exactly know why.’

‘Who’s they?’ Clare asked.

‘Your lot. Your Security Service. Why should they be so damned interested in us, as far as they’re concerned a small, unimportant Middle East state? I wouldn’t have thought they would go to the extent of bugging every visiting Arab surgeon’s apartment, certainly not his girlfriend’s.’

He smiled as he saw her face soften.

‘I don’t imagine you would have wanted a tape recording of what we had in mind that night, now would you? Am I forgiven?’

His answer was to see her anger melt to be replaced by the same mixture of bewilderment and fear she had seen in Patel, Paddy and the rest.

‘So what are you doing, dressed like that, frightening everyone out of their wits? Was that really gunfire we heard?’

Yousef nodded. ‘Only one person has been hurt.’ There was nothing bogus about the sadness in his voice as he went on, ‘Unfortunately, that, of course, had to be Rhys, of all people.’

Clare Drury gave a little cry as she sat upright.

‘He’s all right,’ Yousef reassured her. ‘Nothing to do with the shooting. But I’m afraid Ahmed got to him before I could be here to look after him.’

‘Ahmed has always frightened me.’ Clare gave a little shiver. ‘That man is evil; I’m sure he is.’

‘Let’s try and forget Ahmed for a moment, shall we?’ Yousef looked round the room. ‘We spent a few hours here, didn’t we, talking.’ He smiled. ‘Perhaps it’s as good a place as any to start winning a few hearts again, not to mention a few minds. I suppose it is just conceivably possible we might be able to do what we have planned by fear but I hope that, when you have heard what I have to say, you will help us. Perhaps you will help me earn Rhys’s forgiveness too. I want that with all my heart but it is also true that, without his help, things will be very difficult.’ He looked appealingly at Clare who was already prepared to forgive him anything. ‘Will you help me?’

Clare nodded.

‘Then sit back and listen, just like you used to.’

*

Roisin surveyed her small flock of nurses and domestics, scattered around the room in varying degrees of crumpled fear. Sheep. Placid, submissive sheep. That menopausal old bitch at the far end had snivelled for the last hour non-stop, however much Roisin had sworn at her. Those two huddled together on the floor in the corner, like a pair of Lesies. They made her sick. Sheep. Happy to go here, go there, in a man's world. She pitied them. Content to work for a pittance, then go home and look after some bum too bloody idle to go out and look for a job, as like as not. No fulfilment in life except the joy of giving his rights to a maudlin husband on a Friday night. Poor sods; never to know the love, the hard, unsentimental thrust, of a fighter you knew might meet a violent death the next day.

She had seen the helicopter land, had noted the rifle cases, had thrilled to the subliminal mental image of a blue-black barrel and a telescopic sight. The real world.

She looked up as the door opened. A dark-haired woman, not much taller than herself, came in, recovering from a slight push she had received from someone outside. Without a word, the door closed behind her again. Another one, Roisin decided. Or was she? Beneath the bewilderment and fear, Roisin detected anger in Nansi's eyes. The first faint trace of something Roisin could respect.

'Sit down.' Roisin waved towards the wall with the Uzi.

Nansi had been alone with the unconscious patient in the Dialysis Unit when the Arabs had burst in. She had been busying herself by doing her back, changing her sheets, trying desperately to pretend everything was as usual, that she had not seen the man with the gun outside, had not had that strange telephone conversation with Rhys. They had not hurt her, simply told her to move further up the block into the Urology Ward, almost as if they were clearing a path for someone. Instinctively, she had gone into Hannah's room and closed the door. Like excited voyeurs they had watched what was going on below them, trying to behave as in a dream, not as part of what was a terrifying reality. Mouths agape, they had listened behind the door to the sounds of activity, punctuated by terse, fervent Arabic. There had been the noise of a bed being moved in the next room. They had heard the dry creak of a mattress. The bustle had subsided, the door had opened and Nansi had been ordered out, leaving Hannah to climb back into bed, alone, frightened but defiant.

As Nansi settled against the wall, tucking her legs under her, she looked around her. Even as she began to assess who was there, who wasn't, two more were pushed through the door, Sister Ferguson from Theatre and another, identifiable only by the stripes on her cap as a first year nurse.

'Who's looking after the patients? Is there anyone left on the wards?'

The first human voice to be heard for more than an hour sounded muffled in the crowded small room.

'So we've got at least one bloody Florence Nightingale amongst us, have we? All these cows have been worrying about has been their own skins. Welcome.' Roisin bowed in mock salutation. 'What's your name?'

'Nansi. What's yours?'

Roisin gave a little start of delight. 'What's this? Something that passes for fighting spirit in this part of the world?'

'When are the patients going to be fed? They have had no food all day.'

'Three meals a day. You people think the end of the world has come if you don't get your three meals a day.'

'You have to feed patients. You can't leave sick people without food for long.' Nansi found her anger made her less frightened. She had coped with worse than that skinny bitch coming home from school along coal-dusty back lanes. Put that gun down and she'd scram her eyes out.

'Is that so, Florence? You couldn't stand aside and watch one of your beloved patients starve to death, could you? Just wouldn't do in this country, would it? But it's all right in some other poor bloody country, isn't it? Some poor black bastard can watch her kid die. Just so long as your patients get their couple of thousand calories. And you don't look as if you go short, darling.'

She gloated over Nansi's submission.

'It is all being arranged,' Roisin added, as if to dismiss the subject.

'But not by you.'

And in one unconscious, intuitive claw, Nansi got through. Show our ability to co-operate in international terrorism, they had said. Get this one right, the man from the Army Council had stressed, and they would be through to limitless funds, an ample supply of weapons. Roisin sensed already that they had been wrong. She had believed it for a while, just so long as Ahmed had been in charge. He thought and acted in terms she could understand, simple, direct action channelled by guidelines of hate against the tyranny she saw all round her. But that other one, the one they called Yousef, he was not one of them. She hadn't been impressed. He did not have the eyes of a man who would put a Black and Decker through a man's knee joint. It was always the eyes that gave them away, the weak ones. To her he looked a man who might commit violence with passion but not with honest hatred. He might be driven to kill someone who stood between him and his ideal but he would never lie in wait and kill someone whose face he would never see. And it was he who had told her to go and stand guard over the women, like some faithful, old, toothless sheepdog. She had complained and looked at Ahmed for support, only to find dumb resentment. That had been after Yousef and Ahmed had quarrelled bitterly in Arabic, glancing at her throughout, as if Yousef had not expected to see her, didn't quite know what to do with her. As Yousef had turned his back on her, she had realised that, as far as he was concerned, she had played her part and he wanted nothing more to do with her.

But she had plans of her own. They had promised to get her and Eamon out with them and she knew her usefulness on the mainland was over. There would be no possibility of further active service. America had been mentioned. Just another Irish patriot to be paraded to raise money in sleazy New York bars. But not before she had taken out just one. Just one of the bastards. She'd made him a vow; just one; for him.

Cold food, prepared hours before, helped restore a modicum of morale. There was even a subdued buzz of conversation round the room as Rhys tried painfully to get some tepid, stale tea past his split lip. Kumar, who had appeared for a while, pushing a food trolley, had overcome his fear sufficiently to show his disapproval of being made to carry out such a menial task with one of the orderlies. The first fine tendril of a bond had developed as their guard's hand left his grenade long enough to drink a cup of tea with them. Patel came to sit beside Rhys.

'Are you all right, sir? You do not look well. Can I look at that lip for you?'

Rhys smiled and shook his head.

'They are violent men, sir. What are they wanting, Mr Owen?'

'I don't know, Patel. No doubt we will find out in time. There's got to be a reason.' He had always been fond of Patel and appreciated his ability but there was now an added respect as he saw how he had conquered his fear. Another six months and he would be back in India, another fading face, just another of a string of excellent registrars he would never see again. 'What was that case you were doing when this happened?'

'Internal strangulation, sir, from a band.'

'Bad one?'

'Yes, it was very bad. There was much gangrene. I'm afraid I was resecting most of his small bowel. He is very ill.'

'I rather thought it was something like that when I saw your car and Dr Drury's outside. Did you have enough blood?'

'Fortunately yes, sir; just before they came in.'

'And Dr Drury? Was she still with you?'

'Yes. She was in the Surgeons' Room with Yousef when they are bringing the rest of us down here.'

'And the patient?'

'He is in the Recovery Room in Theatre.' A caring frown crossed Patel's face. 'He was still not fully conscious when we are leaving.'

For a few moments there was a companionable silence as two surgical minds escaped from their fears to picture what they knew best; loops of black, inert bowel, a suture line at an apex of pulsating arteries, blood pressure, fluid replacement, blood transfusion. Their escape was short-lived.

When Yousef came in, breaking up their lines of thought, he still carried a gun, his face still stern and commanding. He looked down at Rhys.

'Would you come with me, Mr Owen.'

Rhys made no move. There was no apparent change in Yousef's mood though his voice softened a little as he added, 'Rhys, please.'

Though there was defiance in every movement as Rhys rose, he was not prepared to meet Yousef's gaze before Yousef turned and led him out into the corridor. They left the ward and, out on the landing, Rhys saw the man on guard, the open door into an empty ward on the other side. Yousef had seen Rhys's pain as he walked and, although they were only going up one floor, he opened the lift gates. On the short journey, they looked blankly at each other though there was the trace of a smile as Yousef said, 'Let's hope they don't decide to turn the power off on us in the next couple of minutes.'

Again on the theatre landing, Rhys saw another guard posted at the open door to another empty ward. Yousef held the Theatre doors open for him. In the Surgeons' Room, Yousef turned and smiled as if he felt, at last, he was free to do so.

'Rhys, your lip. Let me do something for your lip. And you're limping. Can I do anything to help?'

Rhys gave one silent shake of his head.

'A shower then? I'm sure you would like a shower; clean yourself up.'

'I'm all right, thank you.' Rhys stood frigidly in the centre of the room.

'At least sit down. You look exhausted.'

'Good of you to be so concerned.' Bloody insolence, to be asked if he would like a shower, care to sit down, in his own Theatre. But suddenly he felt weary and old. He sat trying to look as if he was doing it on his own terms, not as a result of anything they had done to him.

'Shall I make you a cup of coffee?' Yousef asked.

'And will you be making coffee for all those down on the ward?' Rhys waited but got no answer. 'In that case, I won't bother, thank you.'

Yousef sat opposite him, leaning forward like a parent trying to coax a child out of a bad mood.

'I deeply regret the injuries you sustained, Rhys. There was no need for that and it certainly was not part of our plans. There have been several aspects of the operation to which I did not agree. In fact things have happened of which I knew nothing. Please believe me when I tell you I had no idea that Ahmed had involved the IRA in this.'

'What makes you think I should ever believe you again, you and all your fine words under the desert stars?' The scorn in Rhys's voice was fed by contempt and total disillusionment. 'I imagine all this – ' Rhys waved his hand vaguely around him ' – whatever this madness is all about, this was all being planned when you were here, working and living with us?'

'Yes.'

'While accepting our hospitality?'

'Yes.' There was no hint of remorse in Yousef's face or voice. 'It was necessary. That does not mean I enjoyed the deception. I loved my time here in Avonport; I mean it. It was unfortunate that I also had a duty to my country.'

'Balls.'

The vehemence Rhys put behind the words hurt his lip but it was worth it. He put his head back. He had an overwhelming desire to walk out, to go home, have a bath and go to bed. He wondered what would happen if he simply got up, strode out of the front door and into his car. Would Yousef, gentle, caring Yousef, become another Ahmed and beat him back with his rifle butt?

'What's happened to the Nursing Officer, Mrs Phillips?'

'She was allowed to leave with the patients.'

'There's a very sick man here in the Recovery Room, Patel tells me.'

'He's all right. I'm keeping an eye on him.'

'What other patients are left?'

'All the floors in B Block are cleared and I imagine they will have cleared A Block soon though I don't think it would be absolutely necessary. We have barricaded the doors on to the landings between A and B; that should give us a big enough *cordon sanitaire* as I believe it is called.' Yousef tried to get a smile from Rhys but failed. 'And there were very few patients on Eyes and ENT down below and they were all walking cases. They are cleared too so, now, we are isolated up here in these theatres and in your ward downstairs.'

'What about the Residents up on the roof? There was some gunfire from up there.'

'All cleared too. No one was hurt.' Yousef laughed. 'Apparently one or two of the lads thought it was a hoax, told my men to get stuffed and needed a bit of persuading it was for real.'

'All worked out to the last detail.'

Yousef thought for a moment. 'I reckon if Hitler had really wanted to invade this country, all he would have needed to do was sail up the Thames on a Bank Holiday afternoon. Mind you, the bad weather was a bonus we hadn't looked for; that I must admit.'

'And the patients downstairs in Urology? Have you let them go? I know there were not many in there over the weekend and there was no one that ill that I can remember.'

'No. Those patients we have kept.'

'Why?'

'It was necessary.'

'More hostages, you mean?' There was no reply. 'Keeping the staff wasn't enough, was it? Impress them more if you kept a few sick people as well, would it? Does that include Hannah? Have you kept Hannah?' Rhys was now on the edge of his seat.

Yousef nodded. 'She will come to no harm, believe me, Rhys. You have my word.'

'You cold-blooded bastard.' Rhys spat the words out. 'What makes you think I would take your word for anything any more? Coming in here with your guns and your bombs.' His eyes narrowed as a thought struck him. 'That van down there; is there really a bomb in it?'

'Yes.'

'You bastard.' Rhys was now on his feet, looking down on Yousef his hands opening and closing. 'That van must be damn near under Hannah's room.'

'I give you my . . .' Yousef stopped as Rhys gained the ascendancy, forcing him on to the defensive. 'That again was not planned. We had no knowledge of that. That was not of our doing. The deal was for guns only. But she will be safe, I promise you.'

'If anything happens to Hannah as a result of all this, whatever you are up to, then,' Rhys slowed his words, 'I will kill you, Yousef; and you have my word on that.' He turned slowly towards the door. 'And now,' he said, with bitter weariness, 'I think I'll go back to my friends, unless, that is, you have other plans for me when, no doubt, you would call up Ahmed to knock a few more of my teeth out to help me change my mind.'

'Please stay up here, Rhys. Let me get them to fix a bed for you in the Recovery Room. Get you a bit of privacy. Clare is here.'

'Is she here?' Anger flared again for a moment. 'You're holding her here, apart from the rest? Why?'

'She is quite safe.' Yousef gave a short, sad laugh. 'If anything, she had less cause to forgive me than you did but, somehow, I have had rather more success with her than with you. At least with her, I managed to get her to listen for a moment to what I had to say. That is just not possible for you at the moment. I can see that you are very tired and I understand your anger. Perhaps tomorrow, after you have had some sleep, we can talk again. Perhaps you will understand a little better what we are trying to do.' He pleaded for the last time. 'Please, Rhys, have a shower and let me fix you a bed.'

Rhys felt the surge of temptation but doggedly shook his head, standing back to allow Yousef to escort him downstairs again.

There was nothing Gordon Baxter enjoyed more than a long, hard beat down Channel except, perhaps, the struggle for personal domination. Where others might sit, cold and sick, he revelled in the feeling of fighting something which, he knew, he could never overcome, something that would always hold the final card. A powerful, deep-chested man, the law did not allow him to subdue by physical violence, and sailing hard in adverse weather was the nearest he could come to dissipating his frustration. That and domineering sex. Having been done out of the one, he had no intention of being denied the other.

The fresh, invigorating air that Rhys had noticed from the window in Avonport, followed Baxter also as the 39 foot Nicholson surged up the Solent. By the time they had turned into the Hamble, a pale and wan Alex had put her head out of the companionway. She managed an apologetic smile.

'Where are we?' she asked.

'Twenty minutes from dry land,' Baxter answered with the best he could do towards a smile, knowing he had no intention of letting her put a foot on it before the morning. 'Feeling better?'

'Yes, thanks. Much better. I did warn you. It's the same whenever I go out with Rhys and I've never been out with him in wind anything like that.'

'That wasn't much. We must try again when things are a bit quieter, gradually get you used to it.' He swore as a small dinghy, cutting across the fairway in front of him, also cut across the thought that that was the first and last time he would take her sailing.

A man with few friends, Baxter depended for crew on a bunch of bronzed, good-looking waterside bums who knew he paid well and were only too glad of a weekend piss-up in some French port. Safely moored alongside, he watched them laugh and jostle their way up the pontoon before he turned and went below.

Alex stood, a confused picture of defiance and inquiry.

'And what now?'

'Now I think you can cook me a meal that will make me forget the French cuisine you've done me out of – ' someone other than Baxter could have used the same words and made it sound bantering ' – while I open a bottle of claret. What d'you say?'

'I suppose I owe you that much,' Alex said grudgingly. 'I can cook. That, at least, I can claim to be good at.'

'You don't do yourself justice, darling.' Baxter leered up from where he was stretching into one of the lockers. 'I can think of one other thing you're good at without much trouble.'

Alex cringed inwardly at his crudity, trying to occupy her mind with thoughts of what she could manage to cook in the way of a meal. The bottle of claret opened, she smiled her thanks for the gin and tonic Baxter slid her way over the galley before taking his twelve-year-old Scotch out into the fading light. Alex tried to draw around herself the aura of the devoted couple finding comfort in each other's company after a hard day's sailing – and failed. She wondered if, however long they stayed together, a bond of affection would ever form – and doubted it. She was sufficiently feminine to want affection, sufficiently vain to feel herself capable of instilling it, but, looking at Baxter through the companionway, seeing the lounging, macho confidence, she muttered to herself, 'Alex, my girl, you're a bloody fool.'

She turned, wondering whether to switch on the small TV fitted into the panel in the corner, but decided against it, as if whoever would appear would be witness to her guilt-ridden excitement. But before a clear, legal mind gave way to blinding instinct, her feeling of guilt pushed one small worry to the surface.

She wondered what Rhys had had for his supper.

24

Nansi was smiling and winking grotesquely at Rhys from under Paddy Moore's shoulder as he made the couch beneath her rattle and creak. She was enjoying it. Rhys tried to reach them, to prise them apart, but it was not so much Ahmed's rifle that held him back as a leaden immobility that anchored his feet to the floor. He tried once more only for Ahmed to smash his rifle into his face again, though, this time, Rhys felt no pain. Now Paddy turned his head and all three laughed at the agony of Rhys's enforced voyeurism. Ahmed caught Rhys by the shoulder and shook him, speaking to him with an eerie, soundless snarl.

'What are you going to do about it, great surgeon? Good, aren't they, great surgeon? Look as if they have done it before, don't they, Mr Owen? What do you say, Mr Owen? Mr Owen, sir; Mr Owen.'

The voice changed, took substance. 'Wake up, Mr Owen. You've been dreaming, sir.'

Rhys opened his eyes to find Paddy Moore leaning over him, his hand still on his shoulder. 'Paddy?' he said, trying to focus more sharply.

'Sorry to have to wake you, sir, but you seemed to be having a nightmare.'

'What time is it?'

'About half past seven, sir.'

Rhys became conscious of Moore's sour body smell, saw his haggard face with cheeks even more shrunken than usual beneath a greasy stubble. He managed a smile as he struggled through the aches and pains of sitting up on the hard couch.

'Do I look as bad as you do?' he asked.

'With the greatest of respect, sir, a bloody sight worse.'

Rhys looked around at the shapes, some lying, some sitting, on the other couches. 'What's happening?'

'Not a lot, sir. The guard has left us but he's only just outside the door; I had a look out just now. He was on his knees, pointing east, and seemed to be looking for something on the floor, if you know what I mean.' Paddy jerked his head in the direction of the patient in coma at the end of the room. 'She's not very well, I'm afraid. Mr Patel has had a look at her a couple of times in the night, reckons she won't last the day. Had to put her back on the respirator.'

Guilty that he had slept through it all, Rhys got to his feet and walked over to the patient, followed by Moore. He watched for a moment the stillness of the chest between the movements produced by the respirator and made the token gesture of feeling for the carotid pulse before pursing his lips in a grimace of hopelessness. He went over to the window and looked out. It was going to be a beautiful day. Strange, he thought, how the weather always improves at the end of the school holidays. The ground between the building and the police barricade was deserted except for the abandoned cars and he could just see the top of the van below. Between the plastic sheeting of the barricade, hanging limp in the early morning stillness, he glimpsed men walking to and fro. He tried to picture the scene from down there, to imagine what he looked like, standing in the window. Perhaps the cameras were already at work, transferring him to an unidentifiable black smudge on the front page of tomorrow's *Telegraph*.

He returned to the couch to sit, his legs dangling, his trunk bent forwards as he leaned his forearms on his thighs. He had not cleaned his teeth for twenty-four hours and his mouth felt furred. His searching tongue lifted his upper lip and he smelt the infected blood clot. Too late for a stitch in that laceration now. He moved one hand to palpate gingerly through his trousers for the swollen testicle.

'Oh, shit.'

The obscenity startled Paddy Moore as he watched Rhys roll over and try to get back to sleep.

An hour later and the door opened. The food, this time, was wheeled in by two tear-stained women, followed by Nansi. With no thought now for what others might think, Nansi placed herself in Rhys's arms, brushing his swollen lip with her fingers before kissing him, gently. Sensitive that he probably smelt vilely, Rhys pushed her away, equally gently.

'Are you all right?' he asked.

She nodded. Her forehead creased in concern as she pointed to his lip and the wound on his head. 'I seem to remember you doing something like that to yourself once before. What happened this time?'

'I fell foul of Dr Ahmed and his friends. But I think that's all over now. I get the impression they need me in some way for whatever they're up to. I don't think they'll let Ahmed put the boot in again.'

'Why? Did he . . .'

'Let's just say that, if we get the chance to make love again in the next couple of weeks, we will have to do it very, very carefully.'

Nansi bit her lip and tried to enclose herself in his arms again but he held her away.

'What's going on outside? Where are they keeping you?'

'We're all together in a room down the corridor. There's a right bitch of an Irish girl guarding us but the others have been no trouble. They have let us out to see to the patients from time to time. Hannah's all right.'

'How many other patients are there?'

'Just five. They're OK; taking it all very well, considering. No, six,' she corrected herself. 'They've brought the case down from theatre. He's still quite ill. And, of course, Hannah.'

'Where did you get the food from?'

'The kitchens.'

'Anyone down there?'

'A guard came down with us in the lift and I saw at least another two on the ground floor. There must be dozens of them. What do they want, Rhys? Do you know?'

'No. But I think we're bound to find out today.'

At that point the women were herded out by an Arab who, minus his rifle, could have been any smiling teenager in a Beirut back street with his open-necked shirt, denim jacket, jeans and trainers. An hour later and Rhys found himself confronting Yousef once more in the Surgeons' Room on the floor above.

'Time for explanations, Rhys. Did you manage to sleep at all?'

'I slept well, thank you.'

Yousef smiled at the pride in the reply.

'Have you had something to eat?'

'Yes, thank you.'

'It's going to take some time to explain everything. Can't I talk you into having a shower first, perhaps get you into some clean Theatre clothes? I'm sure we could find you a razor.'

Rhys shook his head and Yousef sighed.

'Very well. Where shall I start? Perhaps in the middle. Rhys, we want you to do a transplant for us.'

'Bloody funny way of going about it, isn't it?'

'Perhaps you will understand a bit better when I have explained.'

'Try me. Who's the patient?'

'His Highness.'

'His who?' Rhys saw that his flippant irreverence had hurt Yousef and he took satisfaction from it.

'We have brought my father with us. He is in the room next to Hannah. Rhys, he is a very sick man.'

'No sicker or older than I feel at this moment.'

The same look passed over Yousef's face and Rhys realised that, now, he was as much the subject of Yousef's compassion as had been the Sultan a few moments before. It helped lift him from the trough of self-pity where he felt he had just touched rock bottom.

'But why me?' he asked. 'Why this place? Why like this?'

'It was necessary.'

Rhys sighed. 'If you are going to answer like that again, we are not going to get far. I repeat; why? All you had to do was bring him to London, bring a donor with you. Happens every day. All you need is money,' he added, bitterly.

'Because, Rhys, he is under sentence of death.'

'Oh, come on, Yousef. You can forget that load of crap.' Rhys was scathing in look and voice. 'What are you, some romantic novelist or a surgeon? We both know that, if we pull the plug on these people, they have nothing to do but die, so don't try that one on me, there's a good chap.'

'I'm not, Rhys. I mean exactly what I say. He really is under sentence of death.'

It slowly dawned on Rhys that Yousef was serious and his derision was gradually eroded by curiosity that had him leaning forward towards Yousef for the first time.

'What d'you mean?'

'When you decided to abolish the death penalty in this country, you rather forgot to extend the courtesy to some of your lesser colonies, including what is now Shahin.' The hardening in Yousef's American accent faded as he went on. 'When the tribesmen freed His Highness from your jail, he was within a few days of being hanged by a British rope in his own country. When you were driven out shortly after, that sentence was extant and, as far as we know, still remains on your files to this day.'

'Good God,' Rhys murmured, his lower jaw flabby beneath his swollen mouth.

'Although they would be loath to admit it, I imagine this is the reason why they are finding it difficult to recognise us diplomatically.' Yousef laughed. 'And, of course, they would give anything to be able to do so now.'

'Why?'

'We've found oil, Rhys.' There was no hiding the excitement in Yousef's voice.

'But you've had oil all along.'

'Yes, but not like this. We've struck it in enormous quantities, Rhys, offshore. We are going to be rich; relative to our population, perhaps one of the richest countries in the Middle East; so rich we are going to find ourselves with friends we never knew existed. And, of course, your country will be the first in line. Embarrassing for them, isn't it?'

'Do they know about it?' asked Rhys, his flapping lip and aching groin forgotten for the moment.

'Oh, I rather think so. British Petroleum have been doing the drilling and the signs have been very promising for a long time. Difficult to imagine Her Majesty's Government not getting to know. Witness the loans for equipment over the last year or so with no questions asked. Where do you think the money came from for the site preparation for the new University? You have been traders too long, Rhys, for me to believe you would hand out that sort of money without expecting some sort of return. And there have been other signs of increasing interest,' he smiled.

'Oh?'

'Things like bugging my apartment when I was over here, feeling I was being watched the whole time; though I still don't quite understand what they hoped to gain. And, of course, your friend Bowdler.'

'Tom Bowdler? What about him?'

'Alcoholic engineer he may have been; one of your MI6 agents he certainly was.'

'Tom? I don't believe it.'

'Do you really imagine he was so friendly to all your ex-pats? No, I'm sorry, Rhys; I was the one he was interested in and he knew we were close. He'd been briefed all about you, I'm quite sure. He's gone now. We got tipped off about him and we put him on the next plane home.'

'Well, I'm damned,' Rhys muttered. 'But what the hell has all this got to do with a renal transplant, for heaven's sake?'

'To understand that is to understand Islam,' Yousef smiled affectionately, 'and I don't suppose I am going to be able to teach you that in five minutes. You would have to understand the principle of the Caliphate, what his followers are prepared to do for their religious leader. If only the West could bring themselves to understand that, to us, our Caliph is an infallible Imam in whom works a devine charisma.' Fervour drove his voice higher. 'You must realise, Rhys, that, with us, state and religion are indivisible – we see no difference – and we are prepared to give our lives for the Sultan, not just out of our love for him, which is strong, but as a dedication to the Faith.'

Yousef paused and, when he spoke again, there was a change in his voice and manner, as if he had put aside his passion to deal with the practicalities of the moment.

'That is the belief that drives us to do such things as this, but there is also a crucial practical reason for ensuring our Imam has his transplant. Under his rule there has been peace within and around our borders. He is loved and respected, not only as our Imam, but also as a man, the man who threw out our oppressors and gave us peace and dignity. But we are afraid, afraid that without him to guide us, our new wealth could bring with it greed and corruption, set townsman against Bedouin, tribe against tribe. We need him, Rhys, to lead us from poverty into plenty, to keep the international financial vultures away, mainly, I regret to say, America. All we ask is to be allowed to work out our own destiny. If only we could get them back in the States to understand that the Islamic fundamentalists are no more cold-blooded, murdering, religious fanatics than any other patriots fighting for their right to independent existence; that the Marines killed in the Beirut bombing were no more murdered than your British soldiers who died in the bombing of the King David Hotel.'

'You'll be trying to tell me shortly there's no such thing as a terrorist.' Half an hour previously and Rhys would have said it with a sneer. Now he spoke with the intensity he might have engendered when debating some surgical technique with a respected colleague. 'You'll be telling me next that Munich and Bogota never happened.'

'No. We deplore senseless loss of life like that as much as anyone. But I see nothing inconsistent in deploring the mindless slaughter while totally supporting the cause. We do not support terrorism. It does nothing but make matters worse. We will never be understood while that sort of thing continues.'

'So why all this? What's so different about all this nonsense? You have come with a gun in your hand. You are imposing your will on others by force. Try convincing me that Ahmed is not a terrorist, starting with my left testicle.'

There was nothing contrived about the look of pain and sadness that passed over Yousef's face. He put his hand out but found Rhys too far away to touch.

'I'm afraid my brother sees himself as another Hamza.'

'Hamza?'

'A young leader of several hijacks and a militia commander with tremendous charisma in the Islamic revolution. But I'm afraid Ahmed lacks the Hamza mystique. What he doesn't realise is that we are here to win minds, Rhys, not to kill. Believe me, Rhys, no one here is in any danger.'

'You could have fooled me yesterday.' Rhys couldn't prevent some of the old bitterness from creeping back.

'We certainly owe you an explanation of how you came to be involved in all this,' Yousef hesitated as if he was marshalling his thoughts. 'We ruled out the States for the Sultan's transplant from the start, the last thing we wanted was to appear to align ourselves with either the East or West. So the original plan was to carry out just such an operation as this and I was sent to this country, one, to find a surgeon we could trust, and two, to find a hospital out of the city centre, not too far from an airfield, that sort of thing. Avonport was not the only hospital I looked at but, as soon as I saw St David's, provided the surgeon came up to scratch – ' he grinned ' – I knew I need look no further; the architects seemed to have designed it with a siege in mind. But it was only after I had been working here for a week or so and had had time to think about it that I decided the whole plan was just not feasible. I reported back, saying so, and it was then decided to ask you out to Shahin and get you to do the operation there.'

'And if I'd refused?'

'Somehow I don't think you would have, Rhys.'

'But why not let me in on what was going on?'

'We were afraid you would have told someone about it and been stopped from going.'

'Stopped? Why should I be stopped? Who would stop me?' Owen asked angrily.

'The same people who stopped the donor, my father's only sister. She lives in this country, has done for many years.' Yousef laughed. 'An amazing lady. In terms of fundamentalism, she makes the Ayatollah Khomeini look like President Reagan. She runs a small private school in South London, mainly for the children of embassy staff. She was on her way to Shahin when she was stopped and interviewed in Heathrow. She wasn't exactly forbidden to leave but she got frightened and turned back.'

'Why?'

'They left her in no doubt that she might have difficulty getting back in and, while I am sure she would have been prepared to do so if ordered to by His Highness, she was very loath to leave her children. It wasn't altogether unexpected; she's been harassed more than once, you know, just a few signs left to show someone's been in the house while you've been out. We've never been able to understand why; after all, there are thousands of Arabs in this country, over 7,000 Libyans alone. So why pick on someone who has been living here quite peacefully for years? Someone, somewhere, seems to have a particular interest in us. It happened to me while I was here. And Clare.'

'Clare?' Owen looked astonished.

'Yes,' Yousef replied. 'They bugged her apartment, at least I'm pretty sure they did.'

'Good God.'

'So, there we were with no donor, arguing what to do about it, when you decided to walk out and go home. We stopped you only because we were confused and didn't know where to go next.'

'But still, why this country? What was wrong with France or Germany? Why not Lyon, let us say? Why not take him there?'

'Because the same problem would have arisen. The donor would still have had to leave this country. No; we decided that, if we couldn't get the donor to the patient, we must fall back on the original plan, with all its problems, and get the patient to the donor. And then we made our biggest mistake. We sent Ahmed to arrange this end. We had no idea of his links with other terrorist organisations. It could still wreck the whole operation for if one life is lost in this operation – ' Yousef spoke with deliberation ' – then we will look on it as a failure.'

There followed a silence during which Rhys's emotions found neutral ground. While there was none of the deep affection he had felt for Yousef, neither was there the disillusioned antagonism of the previous day.

'One of the objects of the original plan was to give two signs, one to our own countrymen, one to the rest of the world. Perhaps you may remember, I hinted at it when we talked in the desert. Our tribesmen will only unite behind a leadership that is strong and there have been mutterings that Faisal is old and weak and that there is no one to succeed him. We are also anxious to show our determination to the rest of the world to be our own men, to make it clear that, when the oil starts to flow, we will not simply sell ourselves to the highest bidder.'

Yousef clenched his fists.

'And we must succeed. Our people have always been rich in the dignity of their own culture and it is going to be difficult to use our new wealth to improve their standard of living without destroying that culture. We have already done that to some extent. Do you remember that visit we made to that wedding?' For the first time, they smiled at each other. 'When I was in full Arab dress?' Rhys nodded. 'And drove a Range Rover?'

Yousef shook his head sadly. 'We should have paid them the compliment of going on camels. Fifty years ago and we would have been obliged to. Another fifty years and will they be keeping just a few camels for the tourists? We want to avoid that if we can, Rhys.'

Yousef looked up to see the trace of a smile on Rhys's face. 'I know, I know,' he said, raising his hands. 'I'm sorry. But it's so exciting to be a part of it, to be able to help. Do you really think I could go back now to working my butt off for a few extra bucks because my neighbour has a bigger swimming pool than me? I want to be there, Rhys. There is a great surge in the desire to return to the basic values and self-discipline of the Faith and it's not only amongst us, the academics and professional class, but amongst the young too. Can that be bad, seeing what seems to be happening to the young in the rest of the so-called civilised world? But we are also part of a modern world and finding our true place in that world is not going to be easy. We have no more wish to become a nation of extremists than a nation of Farouks.'

Yousef sank his head in his hands like a tired, dispirited youngster who can find no one to share his passion. For a while he stared at the floor between his feet but the feeling of excitement stirred once more as he raised his head to sense in Rhys a degree of cautious understanding.

'I think I'll have that shower now,' Rhys said, slowly, painfully levering himself out of the chair. 'I need time to think.'

'Of course.' Yousef leaped to his feet. 'Your lip – can I . . .'

'Go away.' Rhys did not smile but the spite had gone from his voice. 'Ahmed's wounds are no problem, it's only a matter of time before they heal. Your wounds go deeper. Go away; leave me alone. I need to think.'

As Rhys searched for a disposable razor, enjoying his new, limited freedom to wander from room to room along the Theatre floor, a Jaguar sped north across Salisbury Plain, neither of its occupants with eyes for the splendour of the rolling countryside. When they had finally got round to switching on the boat's radio, the cultured tones of the newsreader had brought both Alex and Baxter abruptly to the sitting position, sweaty and naked. Now they had thoughts only for themselves. At least Baxter had a wheel in his hands and pedals under his feet on which he could thrash out his ill humour. Alex could do nothing but sit and fume, willing the journey to end. Superimposed on a basic stratum of concern for Rhys's welfare were layer after layer of guilt, resentment, anxiety and downright pique; guilt at her duplicity, resentment at how Rhys and his damned hospital had, once more, asserted their influence over her, anxiety at the thought of the media finding out where the devoted wife had been at the time of her husband's greatest peril, and downright pique that Rhys, with no conscious effort on his part, was going to get more fame and notoriety than she could ever hope for, however hard she worked her guts out.

Commander Brian Ledgerman's early years as a young copper had passed rapidly on a groundswell of intelligent enthusiasm. The gradual disillusionment of the middle years had been made bearable by the challenge of rapid promotion. But all attempts to groom him into the acceptable stereotype of senior rank had failed and he knew that his manner and appearance grated on his silk tied bosses. It was policy not to leave anyone longer than two or three years as head of C13, and the best he could expect shortly was to be shunted sideways to await his retirement in benevolent obscurity.

He closed his eyes, shamming sleep as the helicopter carrying him towards Avonport, slammed its way westwards. Pictured in his mind was the committee meeting he had just left in the Cabinet Briefing Room, the famous COBRA. The Home Secretary had presided, sitting at the head of the table, trying to look like some latter day Churchill. Amongst the members had been a wary Director General of MI5 whose department had, for months, been dismissing Ledgerman's field reports on the Shahinians as paranoid rubbish. Those who had impressed Ledgerman most, however, had been the absentees. There had been no sign of the Cabinet Secretary, and the PM, on holiday in Florence, had not found it necessary to return to London. The Foreign Secretary, fishing in Scotland, was being kept informed.

Ledgerman's briefing had been straightforward – get down to Avonport and take over from the local police – and the Permanent Under Secretary for Defence had given him the latest situation report.

Avonport's Prince of Wales Hospital had been taken over by terrorists at gunpoint at approximately 11.00 hours the previous day. The hijack had been led by a Dr Ahmed who had been working in the hospital for some weeks. There were known to be other Arab terrorists in the building but there was no accurate estimate as to numbers. They were heavily armed and were being assisted by at least two members of the IRA, one male, one female. There was every reason to believe that a bomb with remote control was placed in a van in front of the hospital. The information had been obtained from the one hostage released so far, one of the nursing administrators.

Later the same afternoon, a C130 Hercules, ostensibly on a routine freight flight, had landed at Cardiff-Wales Airport and two vehicles, one an armoured Saracen troop carrier, the other a large Mercedes estate car, had broken out of the airport perimeter and had joined the terrorists in Avonport.

The present position was that the two Ward Blocks not occupied by the hijackers had been completely evacuated, the last patients being got out in the early hours of the morning and either sent home or transferred to neighbouring hospitals. The hijackers had allowed the two lower wards in the block they controlled to be evacuated also, thus leaving the end block in question as follows – the ground floor with offices, kitchens and Pharmacy, two empty wards above that, a ward with staff and patients held hostage above that and, finally, the operating theatres on the top floor. The building was now surrounded by police. Members of the Special Patrol Group had taken up position though it was impossible to overlook the hospital from any real vantage point. An SAS unit was already deployed but was being kept out of sight in the local golf club. An open telephone connection had been established with the terrorists and, up to that time, no demands of any kind had been made. The negotiator appeared to be American.

From what they had been able to learn from the nurse, apart from the man Ahmed and the two Irish, there must have been three or four more already in the hospital. The Saracen could have been carrying twelve all told. Suggesting for argument's sake, there had been six in the Mercedes, then there was a possible hostile force of twenty-five or more. They appeared to be well armed with modern automatic weapons, also having at least one heavy machine-gun which they had taken from the Saracen. There was absolutely no reason to think they were bluffing over the bomb in the van parked outside.

'And the number of hostages?' Ledgerman had asked.

In the confusion after the evacuation, many of the staff on duty had gone straight home without thinking to report to anyone, and all the duty rotas were still in that part of the hospital under siege, but the best estimate they had was – one Consultant Surgeon, two other surgeons and an anaesthetist, nine nurses and four technicians and orderlies. The Nursing Officer had been very distraught but she had been fairly sure there were just eight patients left inside, two of them seriously ill.

The Home Secretary had put his pen to work – fifty souls.

'And the airport?' the DG had asked. He had trusted that the agreed policy of shooting out the tyres and then sitting it out had been adhered to? No, the tyres had not been shot out, proximity of the fuel stores; one ricochet; useless loss of life; pilot's passionate pleas for no shooting; crew's vehement assertion that they were in no immediate danger.

Ledgerman had suddenly had a vision of the PM sitting behind the Home Secretary, pulling the strings.

When Ledgerman next looked out of his window, he saw below him the muddy turmoil of the Bristol Channel. Not long to go now; soon he would be facing the local police who would see him as a reflection on their ability to handle the siege. Explanations that he had specialised knowledge of the hijackers, the fact that he had just come from being briefed personally by COBRA, nothing would prevent them resenting his official appointment in overall command.

Not that there was such initiative to take, as far as Ledgerman could see. Storming the hospital had been ruled out by COBRA except with definite evidence of a dead hostage. They could not be starved out – a middle grade Civil Servant on the fringe of COBRA had had the figures at his fingertips; a hospital kitchen was likely at any one time to have food for three meals a day for 500 for four or five days – but Ledgerman had raised an eyebrow when instructed that any request for fresh food, milk, vegetables, things like that, should be immediately complied with. With seriously ill patients amongst the hostages, Ledgerman knew he could not turn off the power and, without access, they had little to hope for in the way of surveillance. Those laser things had proved a disappointment in the Libyan Embassy siege; someone only had to draw a curtain and the damn things were useless.

As the helicopter crossed the coast just to the west of Avonport to sink agonisingly slowly into the far corner of the vast municipal car park, Ledgerman had his first sight of the hospital. He would have liked to have leaped to the ground, giving the impression of someone ready to inspire, impatient for action. As it was, he stepped gratefully on to solid tarmac, wondering how best to conceal his feeling of impotence. But it was going to be interesting. He had always been fascinated by his fellow man and there was likely to be a wide range of personalities boxed in there together. Out of range of the slowly swishing blades, Ledgerman stood straight, turning his back on the group he could see waiting for him, to stare fixedly up at the tall building where, if he could trust his intuition, lay evil incarnate in the form of the man to whom, in his wildest dreams, he had never hoped to get so close. He swung round to walk towards the peaked caps and silver buttons, his jaw set, his eyes unblinking. Essentially a kindly man, he was having difficulty in fighting back a vicious hope that someone would get shot and give them the excuse to rush the place, give him the chance, at last, to see the bastard, face to face.

25

Shaved and showered, Rhys looked at himself in the changing room mirror. He was trying to comb his wet hair around the scalp wound which had not turned out to be as bad as he had thought. They always bled like hell. He managed to grin at himself, albeit lopsidedly, and regretted he could no longer go and show his wounds to the old man by the fireside. The old charmer had died two weeks previously, stealing away quietly with the 'old man's friend', old fashioned, untreated pneumonia. He breathed in, cautiously expanding his chest to its utmost. The pain was better; perhaps he had not cracked a rib after all. There was little to encourage him, however, as he slid his hand beneath his waist band, gingerly feeling the tenderness and the swelling. He pulled on a white coat over a theatre shirt and wriggled his shoulders, enjoying the crisp cleanliness. Except for a slight limp, it was with almost the same businesslike briskness that he normally assumed in hospital that Rhys returned to the Surgeons' Room. He felt clear-headed, aware once more of what was going on around him, no longer befuddled by anger or confusion. He brightened further at the sight of Clare Drury. Almost as tall as he, she leant one hand on his shoulder and gently kissed his cheek.

'Sorry about this,' he said, running a finger across the stubble over his swollen lip where it had still been too tender to shave. Sufficient sensation had returned for him to exercise some degree of control over it and he tried to keep the lip lowered to hide the gap in his teeth. 'Are you all right?'

'Perfectly all right, thank you.'

Rhys saw her smile, not only at him, but also at Yousef, giving Yousef a look of utter trust that said it all.

'You haven't been hurt?'

Her only reply was a slow shake of long fair hair as she stepped back, leaving Rhys and Yousef centre stage. Each man stood, silently regarding the other, both proud, Rhys grim and unsmiling, Yousef tensely expectant.

'I've decided I'll see your father.' Rhys held his hand up at Yousef's obvious relief. 'I said I'll see him; now that's all I've promised. When it came to the crunch, I found I couldn't turn my back on a sick man. Anyway,' he added hastily, sensing the pomposity of such a statement, 'the sooner things are brought to some sort of conclusion, the sooner, I suppose, we'll all get out of this madhouse.'

'Thank you,' Yousef said, simply. 'You have no idea what a relief that is to me.'

'I've agreed to see him, nothing more.'

'That's good enough for me.'

'How old is your father?' Rhys asked, habit engrained by years of history taking bringing out the first basic question.

'I'm not sure,' Yousef laughed.

'Not sure? Your own father?'

'It's his only vanity. Late sixties I would say; maybe just seventy. Do you mind waiting until tomorrow to see him? I realise there is a certain urgency about all this but His Highness is on dialysis today.' Yousef saw Rhys's look of surprise. 'We have brought the nurses who normally look after him. And, naturally, he is very tired after the long flight yesterday. But I know he is looking forward to meeting you too. I'm sure you'll get on well together. You are very alike in many ways; both pillars of the Establishment.'

'Oh?' Rhys could not prevent himself from showing interest.

'Yes, My father is perhaps the biggest Anglophile I have ever met.'

'He's what? After being sentenced to death by us?'

'It's happened before,' Yousef laughed. 'My father lived in this country for many years when he was an impressionable young man. He trained at – what is your equivalent of West Point – Sandhurst?'

'Well I'm damned.'

'That's not all.' Yousef, in spite of increasing weariness, was now openly enjoying Rhys's amazement. 'He still holds an honorary commission in one of your oldest infantry regiments. He was never asked to resign it even after being sentenced to death and he has always valued that, as if it was the Army's tribute to him as a fighter. I know you will never believe it, but he admires this country enormously.'

He braced his shoulders back while audibly taking a deep breath.

'And now, that only leaves the most frightening task of all, the one I've been putting off as long as possible.'

Both Rhys and Clare looked at him enquiringly, both realising for the first time just how tired Yousef really was, as if the nervous energy that had kept him going had drained away in the relief at Rhys's decision.

'Hannah. I haven't been to see her yet and I can't put it off much longer. I imagine I'm going to get a pretty hostile reception – I think I would rather face the SAS. I don't suppose you'd come with me, Rhys; hold my hand?'

'On one condition.'

'The patients and staff downstairs. We need to explain to them what's going on, to reassure them. They can't be kept under guard in a room like that any longer. They have to be given more freedom of movement. That's more important than Hannah at the moment.'

'Agreed. Shall we go down together?'

They moved out into the corridor as if to begin a ward round as they had done so often before. But now, instead of Rhys striding ahead with his Ward Sister, he and Yousef walked side by side, both with too much respect for the other to seek arrogant domination, each too proud to be led. All three hesitated for a moment at the door where Yousef picked up his rifle. There were cautiously friendly nods from the guards on the landings now and Rhys felt relaxed enough to go across to the open door that led into B Block. At the far distant end of the ward corridor he could see the beds and tables piled high.

'I only pray they don't decide to try and come for us through there. That's our one blind spot,' Yousef said, standing beside him. There was a mixture of fear and determination in his voice. 'I just can't imagine what would happen if they did. Anything this end, I know I can control. What worries me is if they do anything unexpected out there.'

Rhys found himself reassuring his captor. 'I wouldn't have thought that likely. They tend to sit it out, don't they? I seem to remember, in the Iranian Embassy siege, they only sent the SAS in when they were sure someone had been killed. I'm sure they won't use force as long as no one gets hurt. Even when that poor girl Fletcher was killed, they didn't storm the Libyan Embassy.'

'And yet your Government was amongst the first to show their support of the Egyptians in Malta when sixty people died.'

'But there too, hostages were being killed, if I remember correctly – one every hour, wasn't it – and being thrown out of the plane? I really don't think we need worry about them storming us just so long as we can convince them no one is going to get hurt.'

When they reached the door to the Dialysis Unit, Rhys hesitated and turned to Yousef.

'If,' he said and paused to repeat the word, 'if we decide to go ahead with your father's transplant, it is not going to be possible without the total co-operation of the staff in there and the nurses. What happens if they refuse?'

Yousef gave a tired grin. 'I have a feeling if you ask them, they'll do it. His Highness is not the only Imam around here.'

The men in the Unit stood, showing their relief as they sensed a degree of rapport between Rhys and Yousef and saw a smiling Clare Drury follow them in. A few words of reassurance from Yousef and Rhys found himself smiling inwardly at the riveted attention with which they listened to his explanation of the Arab's demands and to his plea for their co-operation. If only he could have got that reaction to every lecture he had given. Most still looked dazed and there were no questions, but a few heads nodded when Rhys finished. Silently, like a well-behaved sightseeing group, they allowed themselves to be led down the corridor to where the women were being kept and Rhys felt moved by the whispers, tears, handshakes and hugs as the men and women mingled, much as members of a family might behave on meeting again after some terrifying ordeal they had not expected to survive. A few more words of explanation and Clare Drury was left with the task of arranging a twenty-four-hour rota of what staff was available as Yousef and Rhys headed in the direction of Hannah's room. As they passed the door of the room next to Hannah's it opened and a tall, athletic man emerged, nodded to Yousef and, seeming to change his mind, turned back and closed the door behind him. He would have been noticeable if only for the Heckler and Koch MP5 hanging from his shoulder but Rhys was startled by his incongruously long, blond hair. Rhys showed his surprise and Yousef laughed.

'One of His Highness's personal bodyguards. Born in Newcastle. I can't understand a word he says.'

Yousef had expected a verbal lashing as soon as he put his head through the door but Hannah sat upright, a picture of mute, bristling hostility. She took one look at Rhys's face as he followed Yousef into the room and turned her gaze back to Yousef with added intensity. A woman's instinct softened her features for a moment as she saw Yousef's utter fatigue but she overcame it as if she considered it a weakness. She waited for one of them to speak.

'Hullo, Hannah,' Yousef said, limply. 'How are you?'

Hannah ignored him and turned to Rhys. 'What have they been doing to you? Is that another cut on your head?'

Rhys smiled ruefully as he touched his scalp. 'One of those things, Hannah; no problem now.'

Hannah screwed her face up. 'And is that a tooth missing?' She turned her attention to Yousef without waiting for an answer. 'Is this the way you pigs treat your friends? If it is, God help your enemies. What do you want back here anyway? We don't want you. Is that the only way you feel brave enough to come back and see me, carrying that thing?'

She pointed to Yousef's rifle and he looked down at it as if he had only just remembered he had it. Smiling apologetically, he moved to prop the weapon against the wall near the door. When he returned, Hannah was sitting, her chin jutting as if she was owed an explanation, but looking more and more puzzled as she saw the two men in total rapport at the foot of her bed, much as they had looked when they had come to see her months previously.

'Somehow, I feel she's more likely to accept an explanation from you, Rhys, than from me at the moment,' Yousef said and stood back, watching with delight the excitement that softened her face as Rhys described the events that were transforming her dreary existence.

'And you mean he's a real Sultan?' she asked, breathlessly, as Rhys fell silent.

'Yes, Hannah, a real Sultan.'

'In that room there, next door?'

'In that room next door. He is also Yousef's father.'

'Your father's the Sultan?' Hannah turned to Yousef, wide-eyed. 'The one with the horses?'

'Yes, Hannah; except the horses belong to the nation, as I told you.'

She suddenly remembered to look cross again. 'I still think you are a pig. And I hate you.' But there was now a tone to her voice that told Yousef he had been forgiven. He gave an audible sigh of contentment.

'Thank goodness that's over. Now, perhaps I can go and have a few hours sleep, now I've made my peace with the three I love most in Avonport.'

'Three?' Hannah was quick to ask but added an 'Oh, her,' with a jealous, dismissive toss of her head as if she had worked it out for herself. 'I'm going to be a doctor one day too. I've decided.'

Hannah looked at them, expecting some reaction to her sudden statement but saw nothing but fatigue.

'Well I am,' she added quietly, as if regretting that she had given away her secret.

'That'll be nice,' Rhys said, adding, 'but, in the meanwhile, shouldn't you be on dialysis today?'

Hannah nodded.

'And it's already very late to start,' Rhys said, looking at his watch.

'Who cares,' Hannah said out loud while, inwardly, she heard the words, 'I love you both.'

'I do,' Rhys replied over his shoulder as he turned for the door. 'If Nansi's not too tired, I'll ask her to come and give you a hand.'

'And I'll call in again later,' Yousef added as he turned to follow, only to be rewarded with the sight of a dry, coated tongue protruding from a grotesquely twisted face.

As their footsteps faded, Hannah buried her head in the pillow, near to tears, wondering whether she would ever be able to let go, to tell anyone, people like Dai and Jessie, Rhys and Yousef, that she loved them.

Nansi, too tired and preoccupied to gossip, had come and gone. Hannah had been handed a plate of almost unedible food by some good-looking Irishman who had stayed to chat, had almost broken through her guard and made her laugh. For all too short a while, she had slipped into that penumbra of existence that passes for sleep in someone tethered to a machine by lengths of tubing. Back to the misery of full consciousness again, she knew there would be no further escape from the hours of crashing, joint-stiffening boredom that lay ahead. She stretched her neck to look out of the window but could not quite see the activity below. The ennui of a long hospital afternoon enveloped her like a pall. Across the silence, she strained to hear a slight rustle from the next room, the low rumble of subdued, desultory, male conversation. She heard a door open and close and the terrifying, sepulchral silence returned.

She twisted her head upwards and sideways as if to confirm the presence of the wall behind her bed head, as if measuring the distance. Slowly, tentatively, she stretched her right hand above her and found she could not quite reach. Digging her heels in and wriggling her bottom, she managed to sit more upright and she had to wait until the rattle of her tubing gave way to silence once more. She felt the cold plastering under the knuckle of her middle finger but withdrew it again at the last moment. Finally, holding her breath, she tapped, twice. She held her breath until she could do so no longer, letting it out in a long sigh of disappointment. She tapped twice more, slightly louder, but heard nothing in reply. She gave the wall one final rap, a single, defiant reply to her rebuff, like a full stop. She was about to slide back into the bed to mull over her failure when she heard muffled sounds that had become all too familiar, the creak of a bed and the dull chink of plastic tubing against stainless steel. She listened and heard the answering knock, faint but distinct above the thumping of her heart. She tapped again and, this time, her answer came more quickly. Two taps were answered with two, three with three, and Hannah slid back down into the sheets, her gaunt cheeks aglow with the unique beauty of a young girl contemplating the joy of a new love affair.

Rhys hesitated before knocking, his hand hovering in front of the door. If they were to dispose of the body that day, better it was done in daylight. And yet he was anxious that Yousef should have as much sleep as possible.

He made up his mind, knocked and opened the door. He found Yousef already awake.

It had been shortly after midday that Patel had asked Rhys to look at the patient in coma. He had found Nansi by the bedside. They had said little to each other, communication being mostly by nods and facial expressions. At a gesture from Rhys, Patel had turned the respirator off and they had watched the inert body for a while in silence. Rhys had gone through the motions of raising and dropping the flaccid limbs, looking for the slightest reaction to the most painful of stimuli. He had looked at her eyes, already those of a corpse, with the wide, black pupils behind the lustreless cornea. He had even taken the trouble to look at her retinae through an ophthalmoscope though he knew that, with her heart still faintly audible, he would be unlikely to see 'trucking', the break-up of the blood in the retinal veins that occurs after death. There had been no chance of the clinical comfort of an EEG to confirm brain death; Rhys alone had been obliged to make the decision. It had gone through his mind that here was another potential kidney donor but had felt that that would have been just too much to take. He had given one final, curt nod in Patel's direction.

'Pull it out.'

He had watched Patel's almost ritual movement of pulling the plug out of its socket, had heard it rattle to the floor. Rhys had taken one last look at a beautiful face pulled ugly by the obscenity of the endotracheal tube. He had seen the traces of lipstick, now strident against the blueness of her lips, and had wondered at the mental agony of a young girl who makes up her face before taking an overdose. He had imagined two grieving parents, denied the last farewells, and, for a moment, he had stood silently, no longer a doctor, as if in proxy. He had motioned towards the endotracheal tube.

'Take that thing out. Let her die with a bit of peace and dignity.'

Nansi saw the pain in Rhys's face. She told him to go, that she would stay with her.

'We have a small problem, Yousef,' Rhys said. 'That young girl with the overdose has died. What do we do with the body?'

Yousef sat up, stifling a yawn.

'Did you sleep?' Rhys asked.

'Yes, I'm all right. When did she die?'

'A few hours ago. I thought I'd wait for you to get some sleep but, if we are going to do something about the body, I imagine we had better do it before it gets dark. We can't leave it,' Rhys added, as if he was expecting

Yousef to raise difficulties. 'If this is going to go on for at least a few days, we can't have a body lying around all that time.'

'Of course not,' Yousef agreed. 'Does Ahmed know about this?'

'No. He's been round a couple of times, checking the guards, but he seems to spend most of his time, as far as I can make out, up on the roof.'

'No trouble?'

'Not really. Doesn't say a word; just looks like a man who regrets having missed the opportunity of kicking me on the other side,' Rhys grinned.

'And the Irish woman?'

'Seems to spend most of her time on the roof too, thank God.'

'Won't be far away from Ahmed, that's for sure.' Yousef swung his legs to the floor. 'I'd better let him know what's going on. Then I'll talk to them and come back to you, Rhys. Any idea why she did it?'

Rhys shook his head.

'Poor kid,' Yousef muttered as he picked up his rifle, his thoughts flashing momentarily to a sunlit garden thousands of miles westwards.

An hour later, Yousef and Ahmed stood aside and watched as Rhys and Paddy Moore pushed the shrouded trolley from the ground floor lift to the front door. Ahmed made a great display of cocking his weapon.

'Not you, great surgeon; you stay. And you,' he pointed the gun at Paddy. 'You don't think of running, you understand? You would not make it; I see to that.'

Rhys ignored him long enough to help Paddy manoeuvre the trolley through the door but turned and, at a prod from Ahmed's gunbarrel that brought a tightening to Yousef's lips, joined them in the Nursing Office alongside the hall. Through the open window they watched Paddy struggle to steer the yawing trolley, with its clacking wheels and juddering load, over the uneven surface. Paddy's back was bent but he tried to keep his face in the direction of where he was sure the cameras were whirring, blissfully unaware in his moment of stardom of the fact that Ahmed's threat had been no empty one. The cameramen must have been in a dilemma whether to concentrate on Paddy and the shrouded body or the rifle barrel so blatantly levelled through the window on his back. As Paddy, with some reluctance, relinquished his charge at the edge of the car park alongside the abandoned police car, and returned, Rhys watched, fascinated, as a subtle change came over Ahmed. At the sight of the two policemen emerging from a gap in the plastic sheeting, their empty hands well away from the sides of their bulky, bullet-proof jackets, the whole of Ahmed's body seemed to be taken over by slow, sinuous movements, like a cat about to strike. In contrast, his head was rock-still, his eyes wide and unblinking, his whole attitude suggesting the desire that the men did something, anything, to give him cause to close that right hand that caressed the stock of his rifle so lovingly.

So preoccupied with Ahmed was Rhys that he failed to notice Yousef, standing back, his rifle cocked, where he also could watch Ahmed.

In one respect the hijack was not going according to plan. The hostages had gone through the initial phase of shock and excitement as their adrenalin had surged and they had certainly shown depression and fatigue earlier in the day as their adrenal exhaustion took its toll. But the classical final stage of disillusionment and terror had failed to develop. Amongst those sitting and standing in the Sister's Office, watching the TV propped on her desk, there was something of the wary, homesick excitement of the new boys at boarding school. They wished with all their hearts that they were at home but there was no denying the thrill of fear as they wondered where exactly they would sleep and what the next day would bring. There was also the distinction of belonging to an elite, experiencing events they couldn't wait to relate to their families whenever they saw them again. Their excitement increased as they saw two women, chador-clad, come in and stand silently to one side. Their guard, lounging against the wall near the door, they now thought of as no more than an indulgent prefect. A small group of sixth formers, Rhys and Yousef amongst them, came in to hover loftily at the back, just in time for the late evening news.

As the familiar fanfare died away, they were pleased to see they still took pride of place. No President had been assassinated, no town devastated by earthquake or volcano, to push them down the ratings. They found it fascinating to see what was happening out there, grasping at any evidence of the normal world outside. They were silent as they watched general views of the hospital with the untidy litter of barricades, policemen and vehicles, cables and cameras. More briefly, they were shown the scene at the airport, with pictures of Army scout cars and a distant view, shimmering in the heat coming off the tarmac, of the Hercules' crew taking, in the shade of the fuselage, the few uncramping steps allowed them by hooded, armed terrorists.

They listened respectfully as the Home Secretary was interviewed. The whole matter was being handled by the local police assisted by the anti-terrorist squad according to a well-established policy planned to concede nothing to the terrorists and to starve them of the publicity they no doubt desired. No; they had received no demands from the hijackers and, as yet, the reason for the hijack was still a mystery. Yes; this had come as a complete surprise from a nation that had been, until now, utterly peaceful. No; there had been no reports, so far, of anyone being seriously hurt and there were no threats to kill hostages. Without evidence that anyone had been hurt, there was no question of resolving the situation by force of arms. Of course, the Prime Minister was being kept up to date with events but there was no reason for him to return at this point in time; matters were being handled according to a well-established plan.

Human interest took over. There was a subdued cheer as Paddy Moore appeared with his trolley but he was on screen for a disappointingly short time before there were pictures of the body being loaded on to an ambulance. Someone recognised the ambulance driver and there was even a quiet boo from the burly theatre orderly as the cameras panned to Ahmed at the window.

The excerpt was to end in embarrassed silence. The senior member of staff known to be amongst the hostages was Mr Rhys Owen, a General Surgeon at the hospital with a particular interest in kidney surgery. The picture flicked with the speed of light to a garden gate and a drive beyond which half a dozen press photographers jostled around a black Escort that was trying to force its way between them. Mrs Owen was not available for comment – a tense face was glimpsed through a closed window as she stared fixedly ahead – and one was only left to conjecture what the feelings of the hostages' families must be at this time.

Rhys's eyes narrowed to slits. At least Alex had gone home. He wondered why.

As the news switched to a Royal visit to the industrial North-East, those sitting near the TV moved nervously, looking around as if unsure whether they were allowed to go on watching. Rhys and Yousef were turning to leave when they were brushed aside as Roisin Dineen stormed through the door behind them and with a dramatic flourish, turned off the TV. She swung her Uzi wildly and, for a moment, looked as if she was about to fire into the now silent screen. She turned her attention to the small crowded room and stark fear returned, with a tightening around mouths and eyes, and with hands searching for others to hold. She began to harangue captors and captives alike, that it was not permitted to watch such Government propaganda, that it was nothing but lies. It was not permitted to watch TV again, anyone caught doing so would be instantly punished. As she tore into Yousef, the first frail strand of hope they had been given was severed. She taunted him: 'You are a bigger fool than they are. Don't you see what they are doing to you? They are leading you on. They will make you soft. You are weak.' She pointed at Rhys. 'They are getting the upper hand.

They are not hostages any more, you will be theirs. Another day of this –' she waved at the room in general ' – and can you be sure you will bring yourself to shoot them if it becomes necessary?'

She stood, untidy in her drab anorak, her face shiny with sweat, as the Arab shifted his position, looking anxiously at Yousef for leadership. Yousef did not move until Roisin, with a snort of disgust, walked briskly towards the door.

Yousef brought her up short, grabbing her and holding her at arm's length. She found herself gazing into green, uncompromising eyes.

'I think it is time we got something clear.' Yousef made sure he could be heard by all in the room. 'You have no further part to play in this operation. If it had been left to me, you would not have been involved at all. We want no part of your philosophy. We are not here out of hate. No one –' he looked at the anxious faces turned his way ' – no one will get hurt if they do as we ask. All we ask is everyone's co-operation for a few days and then everyone can go home. Who knows,' he added on an afterthought that was plain to see, 'perhaps we might be able to help St David's in many ways in the future.'

'Nobody –' Roisin wriggled free from Yousef's hands ' – Arab or English pig gives me orders.' In a parting act of defiance, she turned. 'And, if you think there is no one here with the courage to take any one of you, male or snivelling female, out and shoot him, if the time comes, you have never made a bigger mistake.'

26

It was Tuesday morning. Commander Ledgerman stood with his back to the sea, looking up at St David's through a gap in the plastic sheeting, oblivious of the movement around him. The early confusion had settled down. Police, Special Patrol men and Army personnel were queueing at a mobile police canteen. A group of reporters and cameramen, apart and to one side, played cards, not too far from zoom lenses and directional microphones permanently focused on the top corner of C Block. Ledgerman scanned the rows of windows of the top two floors. He had studied the scale model built for the SAS to the architect's plans but there was no way of knowing the disposition of the hostages and hijackers within those rooms. There had been no intelligence gathering of any kind to help them, no demands, no threats, the only contact so far being their request for fresh food. He had called them on the open line an hour or so before dawn, the classical time to detect any weakness, but there had been no evidence of fatigue in the response, no hysteria, nothing to suggest a fall in morale. Even the orderly who had pushed the body out the day before had not looked frightened.

A protracted telephone conversation early that morning with the Home Secretary had given Ledgerman little cause for encouragement. Once again, Ledgerman had got the impression, even over the telephone, that he was talking to a man not in complete possession of the facts. He had been able to confirm for Ledgerman that the Irish woman was Roisin Dineen, no swashbuckling adventuress like Leila Khaled, but a vicious psychopath, wanted for her part in mainland bombings. The Irishman's name was not known but he was thought to be a sleeper, caught up in the action, out of his class and almost to be discounted. After this short burst of constructive information, the Home Secretary had fallen silent as if in no hurry to ring off, as if seeking reassurance. Ledgerman had felt obliged to say something.

'A strange business this, don't you agree, sir? Not the usual hijacking, is it? Nothing in the least opportunistic about it. With notable exceptions, these are not wild, unstable personalities with no clear picture of what the next day will bring, the type who see ultimate victory only in death. Nothing so far has been left to chance and, if you accept the premise, it must be inferred that whatever they have planned to do from here on will not be left to chance either. Which must make one wonder if there are perhaps aspects of this whole mystery of which we are being kept in the dark.'

Ledgerman had paused and had taken the Home Secretary's silence as evidence of agreement.

'I have given the matter some thought, Home Secretary. I find the whole thing fascinating, especially when you consider the true meaning of the word "hostage". "A person given to another as a pledge", that's how the *Oxford Dictionary* describes a hostage. Given, Home Secretary, not taken. If you accept that at its most literal, then one might argue that the ones who are the hostages in the hospital in Avonport are not the patients and staff but the Arabs. Anyone on the outside, looking at the whole thing objectively, might be excused for thinking of them in that context, as men who have voluntarily given themselves as our hostages. But, if that is so, what is the pledge, a simple copper like myself asks? As I said, I find the whole thing fascinating.'

'Thank you, Commander. It has been most interesting speaking to you.' The Home Secretary's voice began to fade. 'Please keep me informed. I will see to it that you have direct access to me at all times. No detail too small.'

Rhys was remembering the times he had stood like this before – outside his headmaster's door, waiting for viva voce examinations at Queen Square and the Royal College, trying to anticipate what he was likely to be asked by some appointment committee. Leaning against the wall outside the Sultan's room, he felt just as dry-mouthed and nervous. It hadn't helped to be kept waiting. Yousef had asked him to be there at nine-thirty and it was now after ten. During those thirty minutes he had seen all the signs of controlled urgency that, to the cognescenti, mean only one thing, a sudden, life-threatening emergency. The Arab women who hurried in and out of the room, the rustle of their robes reminding Rhys of the nuns at some Catholic nursing home, carried bowls and trays of soiled instruments and Rhys was slowly putting the diagnosis together from the discoloration of the swabs when Yousef came out. He showed the subtle combination of anxiety and relief that goes with a sudden emergency resolved at least for the moment. He managed a tired smile.

'Sorry, Rhys. I didn't have a chance to come and explain. His Highness suddenly got worse about an hour ago. I've suspected for some time that he had a pericardial effusion but he developed tamponade. I've just aspirated it.'

'He's that ill?'

Yousef nodded. 'As I said, under normal circumstances I don't think anyone would touch him. And he knows it. Will you still see him?' Yousef asked anxiously.

'Of course.'

As they turned to enter the room, the door opened in front of them and Ahmed burst out, his rifle striking Rhys painfully on the elbow as he brushed them both aside. They watched his back recede down the corridor and Yousef gave a short, weary laugh.

'I am not sure if he came out of concern for His Highness or just to keep an eye on me.'

The Sultan's room was a mirror image of Hannah's next door. Not a large room, it seemed small and cramped under the influence of the giant of a man confronting them. With his back to the light, he was not instantly recognisable to Rhys.

'You've met Alistair before, Rhys,' Yousef said. 'It's all right, Robbie; Mr Owen has come to see His Highness.'

Silently, reluctantly, Alistair Robertson turned sideways to allow them both to pass. Overawed by such physical power, Rhys smiled timidly at the eyes that glowered from above the strong, black beard and from below bushy eyebrows and brightly coloured headscarf. Beyond him, Rhys was still denied his first view of the Sultan by the back of an Arab woman who was devotedly putting the finishing touches to his dress. Her final duty was to hand the man a book which he immediately clutched to his body as if he were a child seeking comfort from a favourite toy. No doubt the Koran, Rhys thought. With good-natured, if impatient, waves of his free hand, the Sultan dismissed the woman who left the room, her head bowed demurely. The Sultan looked up as if, now, he was ready.

Rhys had never been able to put together a clear mental picture of what the Sultan would look like but nothing he might have imagined would have come close to the real thing. He saw, sitting in a chair, a small man, made to look tiny by the redundant folds of a black gown and Arab head-dress. Incongruously, from below the gown, protruded the trousers of a dark, pin-stripe suit. Bare, skeleton-thin ankles disappeared into highly polished black shoes. An open-necked, white cotton, theatre shirt was immaculate except for a stain where some serum had leaked through the dressings taped over the spot where Yousef has inserted his needle.

An angry voice growled behind Rhys with all the fierce pride of the Gorbals, 'Ye'll no be staying long. His Highness canna stand a great deal. D'ye understand that?'

'Alistair, Alistair.' Rhys's first impression was that of the gentleness in the reproof. 'Mr Owen is our guest.' The Sultan turned bright eyes on Rhys. 'You must forgive Alistair, Mr Owen, but he suffers from an exaggerated opinion of my importance.'

'Your Highness,' Yousef said, 'may I present Mr Rhys Owen? Mr Owen, this is His Highness, Sultan Faisal bin Hamoud.'

'I am pleased to meet you, Mr Owen,' the Sultan said, simply and unhurriedly, and Rhys found himself tongue-tied.

'Now go away and leave us alone.' Again there was the flutter of the hand that did not hold the book. 'But before you go, would you move me nearer to the wall, Alistair?'

Handing Yousef his gun, Robertson, with a tenderness that surprised Rhys, leaned to lift man and chair like a baby in a carry-cot. He turned to leave with Yousef, and, as the door closed behind them, the Sultan waved Rhys to a chair in front of him.

'So, at last we meet, Mr Owen.' His speech was sedate, his manner gracious. 'But already I feel I know you well. Yousef has spoken so much about you. He has a great affection for you.'

'And I for him, Your Highness.' Rhys, by nature iconoclastic, was surprised he felt no mental reservation in using the title.

'An affection that has, no doubt, been under some considerable strain in the last day or so. And all because of me. Please accept my most humble apologies.'

Rhys tried and failed to find words to reply, overawed by the simple gentleness of manner. He had expected the oblique attitude of mind of the Arab that he thought he had begun to detect in Yousef. The simplicity of the truly modest man confused him.

'I can't imagine what you must think of . . .' Faisal stopped abruptly, turned his head and listened. The smile on the small wizened face deepened as he moved the book from right hand to left. 'Forgive me, Mr Owen, but I think my friend wants to say "Good morning". I heard her trying earlier this morning but I was too busy to answer at the time.'

Fascinated, Rhys listened, watching the delight on his face as both he and Hannah strove to give some form of intelligence to their tapping. As the Sultan stretched one spider-veined hand to the wall, the heavy volume slipped to his lap from the other. The hand-worn cover lay flat. The *Collected Works* of Rudyard Kipling. The tappings stopped.

'I understand her name is Hannah?' There was sadness in the quiet voice as if he felt that few such moments of joy were left to him. 'An intelligent child. I can tell.'

'I suppose the correct answer to that would be "Yes and no".' Rhys found himself relaxing under the influence of the old man's charm. 'Intelligent, yes, but uneducated, I'm afraid.'

'Ah, yes; a problem Yousef and I have discussed many times.'

'But a child, no. She is a young woman. Although she frequently acts like a child, I sometimes wonder whether she ever had the chance to be one. We know very little of her background but I suspect that, where she came from, young girls grow up very quickly if they are going to survive. Childhood is very short-lived. And, of course, she is very sick. Having the same sickness, I'm sure you can appreciate better than most what a burden her uraemia must be to her. You have the compensation of a long and eventful life to look back on; she has had no life to speak of so far. You can find refuge in an educated mind – ' Rhys pointed at the Kipling volume ' – she has only the same waspish defence of the lonely child that has probably served her well over the years.'

'And what are her chances of complete recovery?'

Rhys shrugged his shoulders. 'She already has had one failed transplant.'

In the ensuing silence, unwittingly, Rhys's gaze returned to the book.

'Perhaps you enjoy Kipling too?'

Rhys had read of eyes twinkling but, until now, had never really believed it possible. 'Er – no,' he admitted, apologetically. 'East is East and West is West – that's about it, I'm afraid.'

'You English . . .' The Sultan raised his hand and closed his eyes momentarily. 'I do apologise – Yousef did warn me – you British. Someone has to be dead for at least a hundred years before you accept him as a great writer. And it is such a shame that someone who loved the British Army so much has been murdered by so many barrack room orators. Do you know, Mr Owen, how the rest of that verse goes?'

With genuine shame, Rhys shook his head.

'Then that is a great pity,' Faisal scolded, gently, 'for it is more relevant today than ever.' He began to recite. ' "Oh East is East, and West is West, and never the twain shall meet, Till Earth and Sky stand presently at God's great Judgment Seat; But there is neither East nor West, Border, nor Breed, nor Birth, When two strong men stand face to face, though they come from the ends of the earth." '

He spoke with quiet ferocity, lingering at the end of each line. Rhys found himself responding to this man's quite blatant integrity, his mesmeric charm, longing to earn his respect.

Faisal, silent and level-eyed, studied Rhys's face. Apparently satisfied, he asked, 'What made you agree to operate on me, Mr Owen?'

'Before I answer that, Your Highness, are you sure I am not tiring you? Yousef has told me how ill you were earlier. You must still feel very weak. I can come back later.'

Faisal shook his head.

'In that case, I must tell you that, as yet, I have not definitely agreed to do so. My only promise to Yousef was that I would come and see you.'

'I see. Tell me then, Mr Owen, under normal circumstances, if I was not who I am, would you operate on me?'

'Probably not.'

'Why not?'

Rhys paused thoughtfully for a moment before answering. It was not that he did not have a ready answer so much as his desire to be utterly honest with a man who already commanded his respect. 'I think I can say truthfully that it is a question of supply and demand. So long as kidneys are scarce, then we are obliged to make choices and – ' his apologetic smile was answered with an understanding nod ' – I'm afraid you would appear rather a long way down the list. However – ' for the first time, Rhys moved uncomfortably in his chair ' – in the unlikely event of kidneys becoming abundant, I like to think that we would offer transplant to everyone irrespective of age or likelihood of success, but we never know just how we would behave in a hypothetical situation, do we? Everyone with the power to do so must have fallen for the temptation to act as God at some time or other, haven't they?'

Faisal turned his head through a few degrees so that he could look at Rhys from the corner of his eyes. 'As when ruling a country, do you mean, Mr Owen?'

Rhys sat forward, embarrassed. 'No, Your Highness. I didn't mean to . . .' He stopped as he saw Faisal laughing gently and realised that he had been equally gently teased.

'And you would be operating on me of your own free will?' The tone was serious again. 'Or would you feel forced to do it against your wish? With all that has happened to you, I could well understand such feelings.'

'If you had asked me that, at gun-point, twenty-four hours ago, I like to think I would have had the courage to refuse. But, since then, I have been worked over by a very persuasive young man whose dreams have done more to me than any rifle butt.'

'I do not look on Yousef as a dreamer so much as a man of vision – there is a difference, Mr Owen – sent by the Prophet in His wisdom, to guide our people in the use of their new wealth. He has so much knowledge of the new, so much love of the old. No; I am the dreamer. My dream is that Allah, in His mercy, will allow me to see the hospitals and universities that Yousef has so set his heart on.'

Rhys gave the smile and nod that indicated that the Sultan's confession was safe with him. 'But to go back to your transplant,' he said, 'there is still one point on which I would need to be convinced.'

'Yes?'

'The donor. I would need to be reassured that the donor has agreed to this without any form of pressure.'

'It is my younger sister who will be giving her kidney. But it is not possible to say that she has not been subject to pressure.'

Rhys raised his eyebrows inquiringly.

'You have my word that she is giving her kidney freely, but to say that she is not under pressure is not true. She is driven by the tenets of her faith about which I can do nothing. It is her belief that she must do everything possible for her Imam, her religious leader, to the point of giving her life if need be. It is one of the strengths, and, perhaps, one of the weaknesses, of our religion. It is one of the burdens that Yousef will have to bear.'

Faisal laughed at Rhys's frown.

'Mr Owen, we may have come from the ends of the earth to meet here, alone, in this room, but we know, do we not, that there is no difference between us that has not been devised in men's minds? Kipling was right. There is no barrier of border, breed or birth between us that has not arisen out of man's fear and greed. We have much in common, you and I. I am as much a hostage of my people as you are, perhaps more so. If all goes according to plan, in a few days you will be free. I will never be free. We are both thinking, caring men, Mr Owen; I know it worries you, whether you are being coerced into an ill-advised operation, if not by force, then by skilful persuasion. Perhaps then it will help you to know that, under normal circumstances, I would never allow you to operate on me and, thereby, put my sister at risk. But men have died for me, Mr Owen, and I owe them.'

Rhys, the perfect listener, said nothing.

'I believe Yousef has told you about our new wealth?'

Rhys nodded.

'And, no doubt, that the reason for this rather dramatic interlude is the unification of our people, the desire to give them an identity, a pride to fend off the predators our new wealth is bound to attract. I expect the term "people's minds" has cropped up, that we are here to impress just how far we are prepared to go to fight for a peaceful cause. Perhaps Entebbe and the Falklands have been mentioned.' Faisal paused, looking distantly as if considering each point. 'All true. But only part of the truth.'

'The real reason being?' Rhys asked.

Faisal paused, thought and did not answer directly.

'We give sanctuary to terrorists and therefore it is difficult to convince the world that we do not condone terrorism. But we give them sanctuary only so long as they take no further part in terrorism. We supply a haven for burnt-out or disillusioned terrorists; where else can they go?' Faisal's voice hardened with contempt. 'They can't all be like Menachem Begin and go on to win the Nobel Peace Prize.' The Sultan became quieter, almost as if he was talking to himself. 'I stayed in your country too long. I also abhor any killing that is not done face to face on the field of battle. I am like those commanders of yours in the last war who did not approve of sending raiding parties behind the lines to kill enemy officers in their beds.' He laughed. 'You might say that you see before you a blue-nosed Colonel Blimp, Arab-style, someone who has outlived his time, someone who thinks the Japanese didn't quite play the game at Pearl Harbor. But the days of the professional war are over, fought to the Geneva Convention like good sportsmen. Terrorism is here to stay, is only going to get worse, certainly so long as the world finds it more convenient to shoot them on sight than to stop and listen to their despair.

'That is why it is so important that Yousef is the next Imam, to prevent Shahin becoming embroiled in active terrorism at least for another generation. It is the people who will decide who their next religious leader is, not I; he will be democratically elected as all truly Islamic Heads of State should be. That is why Yousef must return from this with the image of a strong man of peace; why the loss of so much as one life in this operation will doom it to failure. We now have many men of violence in Shahin. So far we have been able to keep them at peace but there are those striving for leadership who, given the chance, would turn our country into a training camp for the Hizbollah or Jihad, the Da'awa or Jundallah. For this mission to become a blood bath would only strengthen their hand and my country could become another Libya. We have always been a peaceful nation, Mr Owen, only rising to arms to throw out invaders. But we have no intention of allowing what has happened to our brothers in Southern Lebanon to happen to us.' The wrinkles of his face deepened as his facial muscles tensed. 'That is why we need a strong man who dreams of peace. That is why we need Yousef and not Ahmed, need to show to our people that Yousef is capable of controlling his brother.' A hint of mischief relaxed his expression. 'And, of course, to get a predominantly Shi'ite nation to accept someone who still has American citizenship as their Imam at the moment is going to be more difficult than getting the Church of England to accept a black Archbishop of Canterbury.' From deep inside the recesses of his head-dress, there came a sound very close to an impish giggle. 'When I lived in London, I was always quietly amused how the English seemed to find it convenient to forget that Jesus Christ was born in the Middle East. I used to enjoy your Evensong but I always got the impression that, in their hearts, the congregation knew that Jerusalem was somewhere in Surrey.'

They both laughed softly and their mutual joke at the expense of the English strengthened their bond.

'But it is such bad manners for a guest to poke fun at his hosts especially when he holds them in such high regard.' The Sultan saw the look of doubt on Rhys's face. 'Your face tells me you do not believe that, Mr Owen.'

'I find it difficult to understand, Your Highness; a country you have fought so bitterly, one that has passed sentence of death on you?'

'But we fought with respect. There were atrocities on both sides but then there always have been in every war, and an Arab is a passionate animal. I am a tribesman; street fighting was new to me and I found it difficult to control those who would now be given the grand title of urban guerillas. Terrible things happened between the young men of both our countries but I think the British soldier has always had a respect for the Arab as a fighter. And I am sure the same holds for the Arab. You have been a great nation, Mr Owen, and I still hold this country in great respect even though it seems to have lost the two qualities that, I think, made it great – style and discipline. You had such style, Mr Owen. There was nothing small about you; everything was done with such a grand manner. When you come to think of it, you were probably the biggest hijackers the world has ever known. We only play with it in comparison, a few aeroplanes here, a liner there. You; you hijacked whole subcontinents, took hostages by their millions, held them for nearly 200 years, shot them in their thousands. And still you managed to keep so many countries' respect.' He paused to laugh as if a thought had only just occurred to him. 'I suppose you might say the British Commonwealth is the biggest manifestation of the Stockholm Syndrome one could possibly imagine.'

Faisal leaned his head back as if his talking had tired him. He raised one frail hand. 'You must forgive me for rambling on so but I do not have many opportunities for conversation these days and you are an even better listener than Yousef. Young men are so impatient. And we have rather strayed from the point, have we not?' He now spoke as if conserving his energy. 'I am a dying man, Mr Owen; I know that, you know that. But I could still, with your help, give one last service to my people, some of whom gave their lives for me. Yousef is strong and honest and, I'm sure, a fine, experienced surgeon, but, as yet, he is very inexperienced when it comes to dealing in the murky shadows of international politics. He is learning fast but he needs a guiding hand for just a year or so more if he is not to suffer the same fate as my old friend, Anwar Sadat, and pay the price of trying to walk the tightrope between orthodoxy and Western progress. The question is, will you help me render this final service?'

Rhys did not answer directly, but he nodded slowly. 'Today is, let me think, Tuesday. I have lost track of the days. If we take bloods today, we should have the results by this time tomorrow, providing, of course, we can negotiate that with those people out there. With a live donor, ideally we should do a lymphocyte culture but that would take too long and Yousef assured me that has been done already. Let me think.' His voice dropped almost to a whisper as he mentally ticked off a list. 'Blood urea, electrolytes, donor's CSU, blood group, tissue typing, Australia antigen and a lymphocyte cross-match.' He spoke up once more. 'I suppose, at a pinch, we could get all that done for you in time for later on tomorrow – the sooner it's done, the sooner the whole problem is resolved – but I think, to allow time for anything unexpected, we had better aim for Thursday morning, 9 a.m. Well then; shall we make it Thursday morning?'

Rhys leaned forward as if to offer his hand to seal a bargain but Faisal's head was back, his eyes shut, his 'Thank you' scarcely audible.

27

'Don't worry, great surgeon. I will watch over you.'

Ahmed patted his rifle as he grinned at Rhys. Together with Paddy Moore, they stood in the hallway, waiting, Owen holding a plastic tray on which rested an assortment of specimen containers. A sheaf of pathology request forms protruded from the breast pocket of his white coat like some newly qualified Houseman.

'When Yousef is sleeping, I will be here always.'

They turned to look out of the door, across the car park and down the slope to the plastic sheets of the police barricade. There had been surprisingly little discussion over the open line, no attempt to strike any sort of bargain over their requests. A time had been agreed and that time was now approaching. The first man to emerge from a gap between the sheeting looked, from that distance, more like some passerby wandering on to the scene while out walking his dog, but there was no mistaking the uniformly dark beret, jumper, flack jacket and trousers of the man carrying a heavy cardboard box in his arms.

'You go now. But no tricks. I watch you.'

After a few strides, Rhys closed his eyes and took a deep breath, sucking in the luxury of clean, fresh air like someone emerging for the first time after a long illness. They passed the shot-up police car and had reached the grass before the four men met, Ledgerman and Owen face to face, Paddy and the policemen at their elbows. Owen, long past being surprised at anything, showed no emotion at the sight of Ledgerman.

'Good afternoon, doctor. I see you've been having a bit of dental treatment since we met last.'

'Fell on a rifle. Nothing serious.'

'I see.' Ledgerman looked as if he was studying the attitude more than the man. 'All pals together in there, are you?'

'I've been in worse company.'

Ledgerman nodded as if some deduction had been confirmed and turned his head to the policeman. 'Hand that stuff over and get back.'

Paddy Moore stepped forward, his forearms out before him like a fork lift truck. As they passed beneath the heavy box, his arms tangled with those of the policeman and, between them, they almost dropped the load. When Paddy turned his head towards Rhys, there was an anxiety on his face over and above the strain of the weight he carried.

'All right, Paddy; you get back too. I'll follow in a minute.'

'You're taking all this very calmly, doctor, I must say. Doesn't it worry you that there are rifles trained on you at the moment?'

'Depends which ones you mean, yours or theirs.'

'A foolish attitude to take, Mr Owen, if I may say so. Now we haven't much time. These investigations you want carried out, I understand from your colleagues they are the routine tests carried out before a transplant, correct?'

'Yes, that's true.'

'So we can safely deduce from that that they want a transplant performed. There has been . . .'

The sound of helicopters, flying to and from the municipal car park alongside the hospital, had become so common as not to be noticed but this time it was different. Approaching from the other side of the building, the noise of the engine had been muffled and the roar and down-draft exploded above them as the helicopter appeared directly overhead. It hovered for a minute before passing on to hammer away eastwards without landing. As it had hung above them, Rhys had hunched his shoulders, partly against the noise and turbulence, partly from what he had read somewhere, that an assault often started with some sort of noisy diversion, like flying helicopters overhead. But he had looked up to see a smiling Ledgerman, his windblown, ill-cut hair the only sign of disarray.

'Just keeping them on their toes, doctor. Taking a few photographs while they were at it.' Ledgerman dismissed the matter as of no further consequence. 'To get back to what I was saying. We haven't much time. There has been no demand for a kidney so I take it they must have brought their own donor with them.' Ledgerman brought out the sentences like statements already logically worked out, not like a man exploring new territory. 'And there is only one man they'd go to those lengths for. Which means he's there, isn't he? He's in there somewhere.'

Owen stood, silently watching the transformation in Ledgerman's face from its usual look of down to earth, cynical intelligence to suppressed fury. His fascination was blunted, however, as he wondered just how long Ahmed would allow this to go on. It would only need a few warning shots from Ahmed and a couple of trigger-happy policemen to start shooting from both sides. 'I don't know what sort of hold they have over you, doctor; you strike me as not being sure whose side you're on. But have no illusions about those people in there; you are keeping company with murderers. Your friend Ahmed has been known to the CIA for some time. Medicine is not the only thing he studied in the Middle East. They don't think it any coincidence that he was out of the country about the time a Libyan stray dog was found murdered in an Athens backstreet. How he was ever allowed to practise medicine in this country amazes me; Immigration must have known about him. Just another little mystery. And that Irish hellcat you're harbouring, she's been around when some of our lads have been killed, here in the UK as well as in Ulster; may not have pulled the switch, but she was there. But the biggest butcher of them all, he's there too. Something I've dreamed of. There, so close I can almost smell him.' Ledgerman raised his head, focusing his bulging eyes roughly where he estimated the source of his hatred lay.

'Faisal.'

His shout came from deep inside his chest and was held until he had no more breath to sustain it, his face red and bloated, the name spattering the saliva that bubbled from the corners of his lips. It sounded to Owen like the challenge of one Biblical champion to another to single combat in front of their followers.

Slowly, reluctantly, Ledgerman lowered his eyes again to look at Rhys. 'You look somewhat perplexed, doctor. No doubt you are wondering why

I should have such hatred for a man I have never met. Well, I'll tell you, Mr Owen. I had a brother, my eldest brother, Jack. I don't remember a mother or father, just Jack. Fed and clothed me as a kid, he and his wife. Always there if I was in trouble. He was a Regular. I was brought up in married quarters. He was one of the last troops in Shahin and they ambushed him, him and another Sergeant. And they butchered them both, doctor. No nice, clean soldier's death from a bullet. They butchered him. And they paraded my brother Jack's head on a stake around a village square, doctor, that's what they did. So how d'you expect me to feel?'

'I'm sorry. I had no . . .'

Owen's voice trailed away in astonishment at another abrupt transformation in Ledgerman's appearance. The look of hate had been wiped clean, erased by intense concentration on something high above Owen's head. Owen was about to turn to see what had happened when he saw heads and shoulders appear at the corner of the Casualty Department and from windows in the Pathology Department above and to his right. One man ran, crouching, to take cover behind the police car. All carried rifles aimed in the direction Ledgerman had been looking in. Owen turned. High against the parapet of the Ward Block stood something, someone, pale against the blue sky. Owen had to widen his stance against the vertigo of small, white clouds moving above the high building. He put his hand to shade his eyes and slowly made out a head and trunk, naked pink, with frilly white cap on blonde hair.

'My God, it's a nurse; they've got a nurse. What are . . .'

He was cut short by a rapid, rhythmic, clacking sound and the shape above began to disintegrate as they watched, the white cap fluttering downwards. A pause and another burst of gunfire hurled a blur of arms and legs into the air and Owen stood aghast as his frenzied vision picked out briefs, suspenders and white stockings on a whirling, now headless human form as it plummeted in front of the Ward Block facade to crush the roof of Clare Drury's Mini. The first feeling of reality returned to Owen with Ledgerman's voice behind him, terse and commanding.

'Stay where you are, doctor. Just don't move.'

Still staring in horror, Rhys heard Ledgerman speak into his hand set.

'No firing. It's a dummy. No one's hurt. I say again, no firing. Back off.'

In spite of his command, the armed police seemed reluctant to withdraw.

'I rather think they were trying to tell us something, doctor, save us the bother of developing those pictures. Not much doubt now where that machine-gun is. Just a warning, I think, of the reception we would get if we tried to get in through the roof.'

He looked round at his marksmen who had not moved, still staring at the roof as if inviting someone to come out firing. He was just about to repeat his order to withdraw when he saw them stiffen and take aim once more at another shape that slowly, triumphantly, appeared at the parapet. From where they stood, Owen and Ledgerman could only pick out the grey anorak and the red hair. With a leisurely arrogance, Roisin Dineen raised her arms until they were spreadeagled above her head, one fist clenched, a gun in the other, as if baring a chest that ached for the blackness a bullet would bring.

'No one fires, d'you hear me? No one fires unless she fires first.' Ledgerman hissed the commands into his hand-set. 'Stand still, doctor. One sudden movement and that thing up there could go off like a time bomb.'

The words Roisin shouted in the final surge of defiance before her macabre thrill subsided, did not reach the men below. They only heard an unintelligible cry before she reluctantly lowered her arms, turned her back and disappeared.

'Perhaps that little episode will convince you, doctor, more than anything I can say, just what sort of people you are dealing with. I think you had better get back now. Take care, doctor. We will let you know when these results are through.' He took the tray from Rhys and crumpled the request forms into his jacket pocket. 'I imagine that will not be until tomorrow.'

Owen nodded, looking longingly for a moment at the road, the beach, the sea, and suddenly felt loath to leave Ledgerman's protective influence. He turned and walked back inside.

The Consultant Surgeon kissed the Staff Nurse behind the closed door of the linen room. But there were no hurried gropings or passionate grunts, simply two sensitive people, with love for each other, exchanging a moment of comfort. Nansi kept her eyes closed to delay a little longer her return to the outside world. They managed to sit awkwardly amongst the fresh-smelling sheets and blankets. Another time and they would never have contemplated doing such a thing, but now there was no danger of discovery; everyone knew they were there and, with the forgiving tolerance that now bonded the hostages, would leave them in peace. Rhys took her hands in his and Nansi saw that look that was all she asked for.

'How's it going, Staff Nurse Rees?'

'Not too badly, Mr Owen. How are you?'

'Coping, I think, just.'

‘Rhys, what’s going to happen? Are we going to get out of this?’

‘Of course we are, Nansi,’ Rhys smiled encouragingly. ‘I genuinely think they mean us no harm.’

‘I wish I could be as sure. That firing this afternoon. I knew you were outside but we couldn’t see as the guards made us come away from the windows. Is it true that Dr Drury’s car is all smashed?’

‘That was just Ahmed and that Irish woman’s idea of a joke after that helicopter buzzed us. They’d obviously seen the dummy. According to Patel it had been stolen from the School of Nursing for a party the Residents had last week. They’d put it in one of the Housemen’s bed; my guess is the one they think is a bit of a fairy. I can’t imagine where they got the clothes.’

Nansi giggled. ‘That seems like another world now, doesn’t it? What exactly do they want, Rhys? As far as we’ve been able to make out, their Sultan is in that room next to Hannah, there is a donor amongst the Arab women and they want you to do a transplant. Is that right?’

‘Absolutely right. We hope to do it on Thursday morning. By the looks of it, we will need you in Theatre.’ He smiled. ‘Think you can remember enough to take table again?’

‘I’d manage. But we’ve got a Theatre Sister with us.’

‘With a live donor it would be nice to run both operations at the same time; not essential, I know, but I’d like to give His Highness the best chance we can.’

‘His Highness is it now? How come you’re so chummy all of a sudden?’

‘Nansi, I don’t know what the man has or has not done in the past. To be honest, I am getting so confused, I couldn’t care less any more.’

‘I never thought I’d ever hear you say that, Rhys,’ Nansi said, sadly.

‘Say what?’

‘That you couldn’t care less.’

‘I didn’t quite mean it like that. What I mean is that all I see now is a very sick old man who needs a transplant and I just wish people would let me alone to do what I do best, operate, and stop buggering me about.’

Rhys had never sworn to her before. It made her look more closely at him and see just how strained he was. He saw her lean towards him and forestalled her sympathy.

‘What about the children? You must be worried about them.’

‘Not really. I know they’ll be looked after. I’m only worried that they’ll be anxious about me.’

‘At least you don’t have your father to worry about now.’

‘No, bless him. I think you miss him too, in your own quiet way. He was very fond of you, you know. What about your wife? She must be worried too.' There was genuine concern in Nansi's look with no hint of sarcasm in her voice.

'She'll survive.' Rhys's tiredness allowed bitterness to come to the surface. 'If anyone is going to come through this unscathed, she will.'

'Rhys, I feel I've been the cause of so much trouble. It's wrong, isn't it, what we do? I can't help feeling responsible for you splitting up like that.'

'You didn't cause that, Nansi. That had been coming a long, long time. A question of the old irresistible force and the immovable object, I'm afraid. You were one of the results, not the cause. Mind you,' he added, smiling as if to lessen any disappointment Nansi might feel at not being cast as a *femme fatale*, 'you haven't exactly helped.'

'She's gone back to your home, hasn't she? We all saw that on the news.' It was not difficult for Rhys to follow her train of thought. 'Why d'you think she's done that?'

'There could be all . . .'

The tap on the door was discreet but it opened before they could say anything. As Yousef appeared, there was none of the embarrassment when someone discovers the Chief holding hands with a Staff Nurse.

'Rhys, can I see you a moment?'

Yousef saw the flicker of weary resignation in Rhys's face. 'Well,' he said, hurriedly, 'I'm sure Nansi would like to hear the news too. Rhys, they've got another kidney for Hannah.'

Rhys stood, dropping Nansi's hands, all weariness gone.

'Where? How? Will they let us do it? Can we do it?'

'Slowly now, Rhys, slowly. Maggie's on the line. Go and talk to her.'

Nansi watched Rhys's joy, but her look of pleasure was tinged with a sad understanding of the frailty of her hold over him as he turned and, without a backward glance, hurried away from her.

'Maggie.'

'Hello, Rhys. How are you? Are you all right?'

'Yes, of course. We're all fine.'

'Naturally, we're all worried about you.'

'We're all right, Maggie. You just keep them calm out there, don't let them do anything silly and there won't be any problem.'

'The rumour is that they just want you to do a transplant. Is that right, Rhys?'

'That's right, Maggie.'

'Funny way of going about it, I must say.'

'Never mind about that, Maggie. What's this about a kidney for Hannah?'

'Yes. Good news, isn't it? Blood group's compatible and, of course, that is all we can say with any certainty as yet. But, under the circumstances, we have done something a bit out of the ordinary; I hope you won't mind. We've had the donor's tissue typing carried out on his peripheral blood. As you know, this isn't ideal technically and, of course, we will repeat it on his spleen. We had Hannah's tissue type on computer and the match is not bad, Rhys, not brilliant by any means but not bad. We will just have to keep our fingers crossed about the lymphocyte cross match. We wondered whether we should tell you anything about it – we felt perhaps you had enough on your plate at the moment – but then we decided you'd probably be very cross if you found out about it afterwards. Can you cope with it, Rhys?'

'Of course I can. There will be no problem this end.'

'That's one of the odd things, Rhys. There's no problem this end either. I thought, in situations like this, they tried to isolate hijackers as much as possible, but there's no objection to this from the word go. I wouldn't go so far as to say they were falling over themselves to help but they are certainly not making it difficult.'

'Where's the donor, Maggie?'

'Singleton, so it's very convenient. Young student, Australian, fell off a cliff. Fractured base of skull with brain damage plus plus. He's been on a ventilator for a week. Carried a donor card. He's had his brain stem tests done, all negative. The parents are in Australia and have been contacted. Singleton are just waiting for us to say the word, really. Johnnie says he'll go and take the kidneys. We'll offer the other one to Bristol. What d'you say, Rhys?'

Rhys stopped to think.

'We're doing the transplant here first thing day after tomorrow. You'll need tomorrow to tee things up so we'll do it after the other one on Thursday. If you ask Johnnie to take the kidneys tomorrow afternoon – he hasn't got much else to do, I suppose, at the moment – then you could get the typing and cross-matching completed by late evening and we could do the transplant as soon as we can the next morning. I think we would have to leave it until the morning; everyone is pretty tired here, as you can imagine, and it would be better to operate after a night's sleep. Can you manage that, Maggie?'

'Don't see why not. Normally we try to fit in with them but I'm sure they will understand the difficulty this time.' Rhys heard the change in Maggie's voice. 'This is not a brilliant match by any means, Rhys, carried out on peripheral blood; you appreciate that, don't you? The picture might change when we have his spleen. And you know the level of Hannah's antibodies, 90 per cent. At best it is only likely to be marginally a better chance than her previous transplant. You must be prepared for it to fail again.'

Maggie Rix waited for a reply but there was none.

'Rhys, are you there?'

'Yes, Maggie, I'm here.'

'You mustn't be upset if she rejects again. Would you rather wait and see what comes up on the SOS scheme?'

'And how long would we have to wait for that?'

'Well, she's only just gone on the scheme; who knows how long we would have to wait.'

'We can't, Maggie. I really don't think Hannah will wait much longer. I'm afraid she'll go and do something stupid.'

'All right then, Rhys. Let's go ahead and I'll be in touch with you again sometime tomorrow evening. We can make a final decision then. It might be a wise thing not to tell Hannah anything about it in the meanwhile. Take care, Rhys. Goodnight.'

'Goodnight, Maggie.'

28

Gordon Baxter swore as the elderly driver in front of him did not give the exact toll and had to wait while the man in the booth handed back his change. With tyres squealing, Baxter accelerated eastwards, away from the Severn Bridge, glaring his hostility as he caught up with and passed the family saloon.

'Bloody peasant. Shouldn't have a car.'

'What's the matter with you, Gordon?' Alex was slumped down in the seat, her chin on her chest.

'Nothing. You're a fine one to talk.'

'What are you so upset about?'

'I'm not upset.'

'You are. You've been like a bear with a sore head ever since we left.'

'I've got toothache. And indigestion.'

'Why don't you go and see a dentist then?'

'I have. It's only about ten days since I had a check-up with my quack up in Wimpole Street. He reckoned my teeth were perfect, and for one of those boys not to find something to do is nothing short of a bloody miracle. Charge you an arm and a leg just to clean your teeth for you. Bloody quack; I'll ring him in the morning, tell him what I think of him.'

'I don't see why you can't go to one of the local dentists like everyone else. Which tooth is it?'

'I don't know.' Baxter drew back his lips and clenched his teeth together violently several times. 'Not even sure which jaw it's in; bottom one, I think, but it's difficult to say. Seems to be both sides.'

'Gordon, must you drive so fast?'

'Yes, if you insist on going somewhere so far away. And I need a drink.'

'You know how I like that place in Bath.'

'With, of course, the added attraction of not being known there?' Baxter shifted his position in the hope of relieving his dyspepsia. 'Wouldn't do for the hero's wife to be seen going out to dinner with another man while the hostages go in fear of their lives, now would it?'

'You saw what a palaver I had to go through to get away from those photographers. There was nowhere we could go even in Cardiff. And I needed to get away; I was going mad in that house.'

'Why did you go back there then?'

And Alex did not reply because she could not. It was an unanswered question she had put to herself so many times. What possible reasons could she have had? Had it been the instinctive reaction of the loving wife, so that Rhys could draw strength from the knowledge that she was there, waiting for him after his ordeal? Balls. Or was it that she had wanted a piece of the action, a jealous rage at a spineless husband who had suddenly walked into the limelight? More like it. Or was it that, rather than coveting publicity, she had had visions of what a feast the Press would have made out of her affair with Baxter?

'Got a bit lonely, did it? Got a whiff of what it's like to live alone, did you?' Baxter took his eyes off the road ahead just long enough to laugh at

Alex. 'Got hungry for something as well as food, did you?'

Alex's mouth tightened as she turned to look at Baxter. She saw the heavy gold bracelet and ring on powerful wrist and hirsute finger and wondered at her ambivalence. At the same time as she felt a sudden longing to see gentler hands emerging from less expensive sleeves, she craved the feel of Baxter's hands, searching, exploring, skin on skin. An elegant childhood, an expensive education, the pride of upper-class breeding, none of these had come to her aid when this boorish man had crooked his gold-ringed little finger. But, with no real affection between them to fall back on, she knew that her strange attraction to this perfect caricature of vulgar wealth had almost run its course. Just one more night. Tomorrow, she would tell him to go to hell.

Baxter did not have his usual luck with parking the car and they had a long walk to the restaurant which was full. Anxiety over the fate of the Avonport hostages did not seem to be putting any of the diners off their food. As they waited, Alex looked disapprovingly at the second large whisky Baxter gulped noisily. She did not doubt her ability to drive the Jaguar but wondered whether she would be able to get the keys from Baxter. The table they were given was private enough in an alcove within the rough stone wall but it was near the door and noisy. They did not enjoy a superb meal.

When the old man, his smiling, gentle face framed in flowing, white hair, stopped at their table on his way out, Baxter was about to ask what the hell he wanted when, in a quiet, cultured voice, he spoke to Alex.

'Mrs Owen, how nice to see you.'

Alex's coffee cup rattled in the saucer as she put it down. Her face flushed, she stammered, 'Good evening, Sir Malcolm.'

'You've had a good dinner I trust? I do so enjoy coming to this place, don't you? Worth travelling the distance for food like that, isn't it?' He frowned as if cross with himself that his memory was not as good now as it was. 'But, of course, you have been having a most anxious time recently, haven't you? Your husband is amongst those poor hostages being held at Avonport. What's this then, a celebration dinner?' His eyes turned to Baxter as if anxious to share good news. 'You must forgive an old man – I'm getting a bit slow – but I hadn't realised it was all over. I'm so pleased you did not come to any harm, Mr Owen.'

'Name's Baxter.' The whisky and the best part of a bottle of claret had done nothing to improve the dyspepsia.

Alex half-stood in her agitation. 'Sir Malcolm, may I introduce Gordon Baxter, an old friend. Gordon, this is Sir Malcolm Gedrich.'

'Pleased to meet you, I'm sure, Sir Malcolm. Had a good meal?'

'Quite excellent, yes, thank you.'

'More than can be said for us then. 'Fraid things are a bit stressed at the moment if you know what I mean.'

'I can quite imagine, Mr Baxter, and I'm sure it is very kind of you to bring Mrs Owen away from it all for a few hours.' His smile was understanding enough when he turned his head back to Alex, but eyes that had been looking into men's souls for fifty years had hardened. 'I hope, my dear, that your anxiety will be over soon. It is my sincere wish that you and your husband are reunited safely before long. I wish you both goodnight.' He had spoken with the easy grace of someone who cherished his language and the slight bow he gave did not seem out of place.

Unable to speak, choking with vexation, Alex waited for Baxter to open the car. She got in and slammed the door. Baxter got in beside her and laughed in spite of his pain.

'Better be my place, hadn't it, darling? With all those Press photographers around, you don't want to end up on page three, do you?' Baxter was surprised that his remark had produced no reaction and looked sideways to see Alex head down, furiously kicking at the floor. 'What's all that for then?' he asked.

'Of all the people to meet.' She gave the floor another vicious jab.

'Who, that white-haired old git?'

'That white-haired old git, as you so delicately put it, is no other than the Honourable Sir Malcolm Gedrich, one of Her Majesty's High Court Judges, that's all.'

'So what?' Baxter sniggered as the surging power of the Jaguar just squeezed him passed traffic lights he had completely misjudged. 'The old bastard looked in his dotage. He won't remember a thing about it in the morning.'

'What, with one of the sharpest brains on the Queen's Bench? Don't you believe it.'

'Hasn't been your night then, so far, has it? Never mind; hang on a bit and I'll take your mind off it; we'll make it a night to remember yet.'

By the time they had reached the M4, Alex, brooding silently in the darkness, had made up her mind. More than anything she had ever wanted before, she must be free of this man on her right. It was not a decision made from any sense of superiority – false pride did not figure amongst her confused emotions as she scourged herself with the truth that there was little basic difference between herself and Baxter. It was not simply a matter of coming to terms with a sexual appetite she had found difficult to accept as proper in someone of her background; Baxter had at least taught her there was no shame in that, had given her a feeling of liberation for which she was grateful. But Baxter at least was honest with himself, accepting the fact that he lacked qualities for which money was no substitute. His vulgar, rich lifestyle was an honest one, no sham facade put up out of fear of 'what people would say'. He spoke out loud with the same voice, the same language, as he used in his mind. Alex knew that she sounded quite different on the telephone or at a party than when talking to herself through the maelstrom of her thoughts. Driving ambition had made her a poseur and it had been the generous simplicity of the gracious old man in the restaurant that had brought her to her senses. She suddenly longed to look that old man straight in the eyes once more, having done something to earn the approval of someone who, she knew, had the ability to listen to what people were thinking, not to what they were saying. With a breathless urgency she now wanted to get home, to make her peace, first with Rhys, then with herself. She must tell Baxter to go to hell. No, not go to hell, just go.

'Will you take me home, please, Gordon?'

'Whose home, mine, yours or his?' Baxter sniggered self-confidently.

'Ours; Rhys's and mine.'

Both the words and the tone in which they were spoken meant only one thing to Gordon Baxter, he was being dismissed, and he felt his blood pressure rise. The pain in his jaw surged, spread to his throat and seemed suddenly more commanding. 'And what does that mean exactly?' His fingers tightened around the steering wheel as the pain in his belly cramped. There was another pain now, leaden and deep beneath his breast-bone, seeming to join those in his neck and belly into one dread-filled whole, making his heart give a few irregular beats that rattled against the inside of his rib cage.

'It means, Gordon, that I don't want you to ring me again. What we're doing is wrong. It has to come to an end some time or other, you know that as well as I do.'

'Nobody walks out on me just like that, Alex.' His gasping speech was not simply that of fury as his natural aggression drove him to fight against the pain that sought to overwhelm him. 'Don't imagine you're going to cock your snooty, upper-class nose at me and walk away. When we split up it will be by mutual agreement and I'm not ready yet. All right, you're tired and that stupid old git has obviously upset you though I'm damned if I can see why. I'll give you a ring tomorrow night and we'll talk . . .'

'No, Gordon, it's over.'

'Nobody . . .'

Baxter stopped suddenly and Alex, alarmed by a choking noise he made, saw a look of surprise spread over his face. He put one hand to his larynx, feeling it as if he had only just noticed it. He began to gasp and look to Alex, his eyes wide, silently crying for help. He began to panic as he felt his heart jerk and bounce, a crescendo of crushing chest pain peaking agonisingly in one last violent arrhythmia before all pain and terror was extinguished in blackness.

Baxter was dead before the Jaguar, hurtling down a long gradient, hit the central crash barrier. Though her scream was instinctive, Alex fought bravely for some sort of control but he was slumped over the wheel. She was struggling to knock the gear lever into neutral when they touched the car in the lane inside them. The Jaguar was already beginning to roll when they crossed the hard shoulder and mounted the grassy bank which deflected them in a series of rolls and slithers back to the tarmac. One final rending, grating cartwheel left the car swivelling slowly on its roof, its headlights sweeping the road like some macabre lighthouse warning the onrushing cars.

Rhys woke, confused and bad-tempered. He struggled to orientate himself in the strange surroundings. The male medical staff now slept in what had been a four-bedded ward and the unfamiliar shapes around him slowly took form. So did the man who was shaking him by the shoulder.

'Rhys. I'm sorry to disturb you,' Yousef whispered.

'What is it now? What d'you want?' For a moment they were back to the hesitant Registrar waking the irascible Consultant. 'I thought you were off watch.'

'I must talk to you, Rhys.' Yousef looked round the room with its shadowy, sleepy aura. 'Please come outside.'

Out in the corridor, Rhys saw Yousef, fully dressed, in obvious distress, shifting his weight from side to side and having difficulty in looking directly at Rhys.

'What is it, Yousef? What's happened?'

'It's the police, Rhys; they came on the line a short while ago; they wanted to speak to you but my men wouldn't let them without speaking to me first. I have bad news, I'm afraid, Rhys.'

'What is it?' Rhys showed his irritation that Yousef did not come to the point. 'If there's some problem with the bloods, couldn't it . . .?'

'It's Alex, Rhys.'

'Alex? What about her?'

'She's been involved in an accident, a car accident.'

'Oh, God. Is she dead?'

'No, Rhys. She's alive but she has a severe head injury and is deeply unconscious. Apart from that she has cuts and bruises but nothing major that they can find.'

Rhys leaned back against the wall, feeling its coldness across his shoulders. Wearing only ill-fitting Theatre trousers, he felt unclean from his stubbly chin, through his furred mouth, his aching chest and sagging belly, to his feet, bare and sweaty against the polished, unforgiving floor.

'Where is she?'

'In a hospital called the Frenchay.'

'The Frenchay?' Surprise was the first emotion to break through Rhys's haggardness. 'How did she get there? Where was the accident?'

'On the M4; somewhere the other side of the Severn Bridge.'

'What on earth was she . . .?'

They fell silent.

'Would you like to talk to them?' Yousef asked. 'Go and have a word with them.'

With no thought of dressing first, Rhys turned and walked towards the ward exit, his shoulders hunched, one hand holding the sagging waistband of his trousers. When he returned, Yousef was waiting for him.

'One more thing, Rhys. I've told His Highness about Alex. He is very anxious to see you. Can you bear to . . .?'

Robot-like, Rhys started towards the Sultan's room. The fair haired Geordie standing guard outside seemed to be expecting him and simply opened the door to let Rhys walk in alone. The room was in darkness save for a shaded lamp on the wall above the bed, its light reflected from eyes in a small head, sunk into the pillows beneath. Through his misery, Rhys realised he could not remember seeing a white-haired Arab before.

'Please sit down, Mr Owen. I do not wish to intrude into your sadness, only to try in some way to share it. I am so sorry to hear of your distress.'

Rhys rested his elbows on his knees and looked vacantly into the palms of his hands. His bleak 'Thank you' was spoken to the floor.

'We have brought great trouble to you.'

Rhys shrugged his shoulders without raising his head.

'You must want to be with her.' There was no answer and the Sultan's eyes were bright and sharp as he tried to bridge the silent shadows between them. 'Oh, you British and your stiff upper lip.' He stared at the top of Rhys's bowed head for a moment. 'If you wish to go to her, we will not stop you. I will give the word and you are free to go.'

There was a slow shaking of Rhys's head and a whispered 'No'.

'But I am sure I have read or heard that sometimes people in a coma respond to voices and sounds they love? Yousef will perform my operation; I am sure he is sufficiently capable. It is not what we planned and will place Yousef in great difficulty if I die afterwards but that is as it shall be if you wish to be with your wife.'

Rhys lifted his head and, this time, his reply was given with more certainty, as if he had made up his mind.

'No.'

It took a little time for Faisal to put it all together in his mind but there was a faint note of understanding in the long expired breath.

'I would not be so presumptuous as to think you are staying out of love for me though I have no doubt you will have weighed your surgical duty to me against your love for your wife. But you have another love. Yousef has told me about the kidney for the girl, Hannah. I also know the reason why she is so special to you. And you are a prisoner of the dogma that it is sinful to love more than one. You cannot break free of the belief that to love one makes it a mortal sin to love another, that you must abandon the one for the other. You are tortured by the feeling that to stay and look after Hannah is a denial of your love for your wife. I tell you, it is not. Would you feel so tortured if you did not also love your wife?'

'There is only one flaw in your argument, Your Highness,' Rhys smiled, self-weary.

'And that is?'

'That I have severe doubts as to my ability to love anyone.'

Faisal's smile slowly deepened.

'And to think that, in the very near future, I am going to trust my life to someone so foolish.'

29

Paddy Moore and Eamon Dickens had found the key to the cupboard. The days of the traditional hospital Christmas dinner are over. Gone are the times when the Consultants dragged their reluctant families to the wards on Christmas morning where he would ritually carve the turkey and have enough sweet sherry forced on him to ruin the rest of his day. The word has also gone out from a new, all-powerful nursing oligarchy, against the departmental Christmas parties when, once in the year, bottles of booze were brought out for one riotous evening, what little remaining undrunk being locked away securely for the next twelve months, sacrosanct in the Ward Sister's private cupboard. Avonport's Dialysis Unit, with its part-time staff and no inpatients, had, so far, managed to avoid the ban, and the temptation had proved too great for Paddy.

It was near noon the next day when Rhys, passing the door of the linen room that had provided sanctuary for Nansi and himself, heard the giggling. Without knocking, he opened the door. Two flushed, laughing faces were turned towards him from where Paddy and Eamon sat on the floor, each holding a bottle by the neck. Empty bottles littered the space between them. Moore, the nearer of the two, waved his bottle at Owen.

'Rhys. Sit down. Sit down. Have a drink.'

The change from Paddy's usual deference surprised him. Like everyone else, he had heard of Paddy's drinking but had always thought of it as something remote, something that would never involve himself. In spite of his fatigue, he kept up the charade of the aloof but tolerant Chief.

'No, thank you, Paddy; another time. Too much on my mind at the moment.'

'And hasn't he been telling me what a hell of a guy you are,' Eamon Dickens broke in. 'Lot of respect for you.'

'That's very kind of him, I'm sure.' Rhys smiled wanly.

'S'true,' Paddy slurred, his eyes slow to change focus from the bottle to Owen. 'Best bloody Consultant in the hospital. Yes, honestly, you are. Better than some of the snooty buggers I could mention.'

Rhys knew he was being drawn into what Paddy would have enjoyed, a discussion of his colleagues, and tried to change the subject. 'We are operating tomorrow, Paddy, you know that, don't you?'

'I'll be there, boss, fear not.' Paddy waved his bottle with alcoholic bravado.

'So, d'you think perhaps you've had enough of that?'

Paddy Moore turned his head slowly to Dickens and grinned. 'Got to hand it to them, Eamon, haven't you; they're clever. The iron fist in the old silk glove. "Don't you think you've had enough?" ' he mimicked. 'Hasn't the bloody guts to come and take it off me.'

Rhys was amazed by the sudden swing in mood and expression.

'Not as if it would be the first thing you've taken off me, would it?' There was no trace of respect in Moore's face now.

'What d'you mean?'

' "What d'you mean?" ' Now the lips were turned down in a snarl. 'Took my Nansi from me, didn't you? She's had no time for me since you came sniffing around. Just couldn't keep your hands off her, could you? All so gentle and polite with that little boy lost look; never fails with the women, does it? And you the big Consultant and all. But one "Boo" from anyone and you're off, aren't you? Never have the guts to just take what you want. Always got to be the perfect gentleman, haven't you? So why don't you piss off and leave two men to their drinking?' His grin returned for Dickens as he turned his shoulder on Rhys. 'As I was telling you about this time with Nansi . . .'

Rhys was surprised how light Paddy Moore was as he bent down and caught him by the shirt, feeling the lean muscles of Paddy's chest wall slip through his grasping fingers. He was able without difficulty to lift Paddy up and push him back against one of the supports to the wooden shelving, hearing his head crack backwards against it. As Paddy lifted his left hand to defend himself, whisky slurped from the open bottle towards Rhys, making him let Paddy go and step back in disgust as the reeking fluid splashed his trousers. Shaking with fury, he wondered what to do next when he saw Moore struggling to pull something from his right trouser pocket. Whatever he was pulling at was black and flat and a rounded knob on one corner had caught in the material. As Eamon Dickens watched, too glazed and stuporous to react, Moore put the bottle down on one of the shelves with exaggerated care, and took two hands to his troublesome pocket. Rhys, mesmerised, realised it was a gun Moore was struggling with long before he had freed the Browning pistol and pointed it at him. A brief mental picture of Paddy's face when the policeman had handed him the parcel of food, also answered the question before he had asked it.

'Where the hell did you get that from?'

'Well, at least one of us will put up a fight if this lot really get nasty. They're going to need someone on the inside to give those boys out there a bit of help if they decide to rush us.' Moore pointed at Eamon Dickens who was drunk to the point of being incapable of reacting and who merely smiled distantly as if he was enjoying the whole scene. 'He wants to help us. He wants to get out.'

'You bloody fool,' Rhys shouted. 'Give me that.'

Dickens found himself sprawling with Rhys in a tangle of arms and legs before he realised he had had the gun torn from his grasp. By the time he had disentangled himself, sat up straight and steadied his eyes on the door, Rhys had gone, leaving him fretting like a child who had had a favourite toy taken from him.

Swept along on the anger that had allowed him to snatch the gun without thought as to whether it was loaded or cocked, Rhys burst out of the ward and down the stairs. With the tails of his white coat flying, he had passed the startled guards on each of the landings before they could react. The man on the ground floor saw the gun and was about to stop him when something in Rhys's look made him hesitate and by the time he had recovered, Rhys was through the door and running between the parked Saracen and the Mercedes, shouting wildly as he ran. When he reached the grass, incoherent with rage, he stopped to hurl the gun as far as he could in the direction of the police barricade, lobbing it like a grenade. The obscenities he hurled after it were directed at the police in general and Ledgerman in particular and he was still shouting and waving his arms above his head as he turned and walked back.

In the hallway he was met by an anxious Yousef and a grinning Ahmed, both tensely alert. Owen pushed his way between them as if now totally unimpressed by guns of any kind. Behind him, he heard Ahmed laugh as he lurched backwards.

'I'm impressed, great surgeon. Now I am not sure who will shoot you first, us or them.'

'That was very foolish, Rhys,' he heard Yousef say, more softly.

Owen stopped and turned and looked at them both, his face white. He took a few steps back towards them, his voice hissing with anger, his lips drawn back to show the disfiguring gap in his teeth. 'Let's get one thing straight. I've just about had my gutful of being buggered about by a bunch of homicidal maniacs. Now. I'm giving you fair warning. Tomorrow I do two transplants and then I walk out of this place, right through that door there, and if you – ' he turned his head towards Yousef '– or you –' he nodded at Ahmed before jerking his head upwards '– or that Irish paranoid psychopath up there on the roof choose to shoot me in the back, please feel free to do so.'

*

It was after eight o'clock in the evening before the call came over the open line. The results of the tissue typing had arrived. There was a problem. It seemed that Maggie Rix must speak to Owen personally before a decision could be made and no one now seemed surprised when Ledgerman raised no objection. The late summer sun shone low into Rhys's eyes as he emerged from the building but that was not the reason why his head hung. His earlier outburst had left him in a trough of self-recrimination. He knew he lacked the guts to walk out the way he had threatened and he took no pride in the knowledge. Adding to his misery was a constant mental picture of Alex, naked under a thin white shift, unconscious and catheterised, her eyes blue-black and closed. He knew how she would hate to see herself looking like that. He was also recognising the truth of much of what Paddy Moore had said, that he stole people's affections rather than earned them. Now it looked as if something had happened to jeopardise the only thing about which he still retained a shred of pride, his ability to make up for his shortcomings in the only place he seemed to find peace, the operating theatre. Pray God the problem was with the Sultan, not Hannah.

He was jolted out of his reverie by the sight that met him as he walked round the Casualty entrance to the front of the hospital. From the littered, deserted no-man's land of the Consultants' car park, he stepped into a bustling scene of white police transit vans with their 'jam sandwich' stripes, strong young men in white shirts and blue epaulettes, some smoking as they gossiped, others sitting in deck-chairs, closing their eyes against the setting sun. A police Alsatian, lying at its handler's feet, eyed him suspiciously as he passed. As he turned to walk in through the main entrance, he saw, away to his left in the main hospital car park, three small, armoured vehicles, beyond them a Royal Engineers' Bomb Disposal five-ton truck and a couple of Land Rovers. At the door he was met by a poker-faced Police Inspector who led him through the hall towards the stairs to the Pathology Laboratory above. A typewriter clattered from Casualty and Rhys just glimpsed the fresh white shirt and tightly bobbed hair of a policewoman seated at a flickering row of closed circuit TV screens. Probably the other end of the open line was in there too, Owen thought.

One of the Biochemistry labs seemed to Owen a strange place to arrange a meeting but that was where he found himself as the Inspector closed the door behind him. Ledgerman was sitting at a desk facing the wall, his back to Maggie Rix. Between them stretched a work bench with its peculiar array of implements, ranging from mundane chemicals in Victorian shaped bottles to space age, high tech machines. It was obvious they had found little to talk about while waiting. Ignoring Ledgerman, Rhys walked round the bench to kiss Maggie.

'Rhys; are you all right? Your face . . .'

'That's nothing, Maggie. Do you have any news of Alex?'

'No change. We rang an hour or so ago and spoke to Sian who is with her. She's no worse.'

'Good evening, doctor. I was sorry to hear of your wife's accident.' Ledgerman did not look round as he spoke and Rhys was about to walk around the bench to confront Ledgerman when he felt Maggie Rix hold his arm. He saw her shake her head anxiously and point to a small pile of pathology reports on the bench in front of her.

'Perhaps you can tell me what happened?' Rhys asked across the bench top. 'Was anyone else involved?'

'One other, man called Baxter, died; thought to have had a heart attack at the wheel. Fortunately the motorway was pretty quiet at that time of night and no one else was hurt.' Ledgerman's voice was flat, as if reading a report, with no inflection to suggest either sympathy or censure. He turned in his chair as if now prepared to face Owen. 'It seems Dr Rix here has a problem to discuss with you. Why she could not have done that over the phone I can't imagine but I'm sure you won't object to my sitting in on your discussion.'

It was certainly strange – there had been no problem in the past that could not be resolved over the phone – but Maggie Rix's face was a mask. When she leaned on the bench, her shoulders hunched, he did the same beside her and found that she had carefully arranged the reports where they were hidden from Ledgerman behind a blood gas analysis machine. Softly she began to explain.

'So that I can hear, please, Dr Rix. You needn't worry; I'm not a squeamish man.'

'Sorry.' Maggie beamed at Ledgerman over the top of the machine as she raised her voice. 'You have got problems with the tissue typing, Rhys.'

'What, with the Sultan? That can't be right. If the donor is his sister as they claim and they have already done . . .'

Though Maggie Rix managed to keep the expression on her face unchanged, under cover of the machine she clenched one fist and shook it to give the clear message to shut up and leave the talking to her. Spreading her hand, she laid the pathology forms flat on the bench, separating them into groups as she did so.

'These in this row are the Sultan's, these are Hannah's and these are from the two donors, all of them Group O Positive, so no problem there.

As you say, there's no problem either with the Sultan and his sister. There; have a look at their HLA types. And no problem with their lymphocyte cross-match, of course,' she added, standing up a little as Rhys bent closer to read the small figures. Rhys's lips moved silently as he read the Sultan's results but the sister's findings he read out loud, 'A1, A2; B8, B27.' He nodded his satisfaction. 'First-class match.'

'Now have a look at Hannah's and you'll see that you have got a quite unusual problem on your hands. Frankly I don't think you can be asked to make up your mind on the spot – I'm sure you will want to go away and think about it – but have a look at those two.' Maggie Rix curled her middle and ring fingers beneath her thumb, stretching her index and little fingers wide to bridge two of the rows of forms.

Rhys saw Hannah's name on the form under Maggie's index finger. He began to read out loud 'A1, A2 . . .' until he felt the pressure of Maggie's substantial shoe on his instep. Silently, he went back and scanned the figures once more – A1, A2; B8, BW35. His focus moved the few inches to Maggie's little finger as she said, 'And now compare it with that.'

Rhys saw the report to which she pointed – A1, A2; B8, B27 – and, tired, confused, emotionally battered as he was, he did not need Maggie to move her little finger that fraction to point out to him that it was not the Australian student's form he had read but, once more, that of Faisal's donor.

'To add to your problems, Rhys, the lymphocyte cross-match is also confusing and you will find that, as a result, they have carried out more than one. Make sure you go through them all and compare them. It's going to take time to sort it out and, frankly, I don't envy you your decision.' Maggie stood up abruptly, shuffling the forms together. 'I think you ought to take these away and think about them. The kidney's here. Under the circumstances, we've offered the other one to Bristol. You'd better take it with you, hadn't you, and, if you decide against doing Hannah after you've studied those reports, let us have this one back as soon as you can, there's a good chap. It would be a pity to waste it.'

'What does all that add up to then, doctor?' Ledgerman ran his fingers through his hair as if it was too tidy. 'Don't tell me the whole thing's off.'

'No, certainly not. His Highness's transplant goes ahead as planned.'

'His Highness.' Ledgerman was withering in his contempt. 'His arsehole, you mean.'

Maggie Rix blushed and turned to leave. She touched Rhys's arm as he accompanied her to the door. 'Don't worry about Alex, Rhys. We'll keep a close eye on her. We'll let you know when she improves. The best of luck tomorrow.' Without a glance at Ledgerman, she left and Owen turned back to Ledgerman.

'That was a bit crude, wasn't it, even for a policeman?' Rhys looked with distaste at Ledgerman's alert features but was getting to know him well enough to see beyond the tough, traditional 'seen it all' copper's face. He saw the restless fingers, the downturned eyes and got the feeling of irritation, of frustration. Rhys felt as if Ledgerman would have liked to have apologised to Maggie for his obscenity if he had not feared the damage it might do to his policeman's machismo.

'What's the problem, then? There didn't seem much there that you couldn't have said over the phone.'

'It's never quite the same,' Owen answered. 'I might have missed the problem if it hadn't been pointed out to me like that.'

'As I understand it, the problem's with the girl?'

'Yes.'

'Will you be able to do it? I don't give a damn about His Bloody Highness but I'd be sorry if the girl missed her chance.'

'I don't know. As I say, I need to go away and think about it. We do have one other problem, however.'

'And what's that?'

'We are going to need another anaesthetist, one of the Consultants. We're going to need him eight o'clock tomorrow morning.'

'Why?'

'Because we are going to run two Theatres simultaneously and we only have one anaesthetic Registrar in there. Plus the fact the old man is extremely ill and will need someone very experienced.'

'Nothing but the best for our guests, of course,' Ledgerman said, scathingly. 'Yes, you can have your anaesthetist.' He gave a short, humourless laugh. 'You can have the bloody Lord Mayor if you want.'

Owen watched as the large, shaggy head in front of him dropped and slowly shook from side to side. He sat on a swivel-top stool, overcoming his anxiety to get away and study the forms he had put away in his pocket.

'There can never have been such a goddamn crazy hijack, doctor.' Ledgerman raised his head and Rhys saw a weariness in the eyes that matched his own feelings. 'Hasn't anything struck you as strange about this lot? You're a thinking man. Has nothing struck you as odd?'

'Well, I can't say it has fitted in with my usual weekly routine exactly.'

'Come on, doctor, you can do better than that.'

'I must admit I've been surprised at how easy it has been to get anything we want, food, investigations; no conditions imposed of any kind;

absolutely no problem about the donor who is brought to Avonport by police car, blithely walks up the common and into the hospital, just like that. I thought it was your policy to isolate and contain, cut them off from all chance of publicity, that sort of thing; keep them guessing. After all, silence can be very frightening, can't it? And that's another thing; one reads accounts of hijackers in aircraft and in that Iranian Embassy business. I thought hijackers got more and more jumpy, more nervous and threatening to kill hostages. There's nothing like that in there, Ledgerman, I promise you. If you are hoping they're going to crack, you've got a long wait ahead. They've got enough men in there to keep a duty rota working indefinitely and they're showing no sign of fatigue. We're the only ones showing the strain.'

'More than that, doctor.'

Rhys thought for a moment before slowly shaking his head.

'Hasn't it impressed you,' Ledgerman said, raising one untidy eyebrow, 'just how well it has all been planned? Must have taken months. All worked out almost to the minute.'

'Sure.'

'And still nothing occurs to you?' Ledgerman looked as if he couldn't believe how stupid some people could be.

'No, not really.'

'Do you really believe, doctor, that they would go to all that trouble to plan their way in without planning their way out as well?'

And Rhys Owen joined Ledgerman in his wonder at how stupid people could be.

'I must admit, that never occurred to me. But – they can't have planned that. That can't be under their control. That would have to be played off the cuff. They must accept there is no way they can shoot their way out. It would have to be negotiated except we've all heard the Prime Minister go on about it – "no negotiation with terrorists; cut off the oxygen supply of publicity" – or words to that effect.'

'Unless, of course, it has already been negotiated,' Ledgerman said, quietly.

It took a moment for Rhys to answer, the time it took for what Ledgerman had just said to sink in. 'Oh, come on; that's got to be bloody nonsense. You've got to be joking.'

'Have I? I tell you this, doctor; any Government that allows a policewoman's murderer to go free, to let him walk out within yards of where her blood still stained the road, is capable of anything. We even gave them a police escort to Heathrow just in case any harm came to them.

Probably travelled first class. We probably paid for their bloody tickets.'

Rhys stayed silent, impressed by Ledgerman's passion.

'There are all kinds of hostages in this affair, doctor. I am just as much a hostage as you. No doubt you wish nothing more than to be allowed to get on with your job. Well, so do I, doctor, so do I.' Ledgerman shook two clenched fists in front of him in his fury. 'But I am held hostage by my political masters. I don't go in fear of my life but neither can I hope for my freedom. Her Majesty's Government will tell you they are not permitted to direct the police, yet I'm instructed by the politicians as to how I must negotiate with these villains and told off for the "unduly provocative attitudes of my paramilitary policemen"; "likely to give offence to our friends overseas". I tell you, doctor, if I was left to do my job as I see it, none of those murdering bastards in there would get back to their mud huts again until they were so old they'd forgotten what a rifle looked like. And as for that evil man you all seem so besotted with, I'd see that he spent the rest of his miserable days rotting in some English jail.'

'I wish you could meet him, just talk to him,' Rhys said gently but saw the implacable hatred in Ledgerman's eyes and did not pursue the point. 'But what makes you say it could all be negotiated already? What possible reason could there be for that?'

'Money. Power. What else makes the world go round? The addiction to power that influences other people's lives. We all suffer from it to some extent, don't we, doctor? Doctors, policemen, evangelistic clergymen, judges. Why should politicians be exempt when they manipulate more power than all of us put together?'

'I still don't get it. Where does the money come into it?'

'How about £500 million for starters?'

'£500 million?'

'Allowing for inflation, about the tender price to build a new university, a new teaching hospital and a new medical school in the middle of the desert.'

'In Shahin?'

'In Shahin. Well done, doctor; got there at last.' Cynicism turned down the corners of Ledgerman's mouth. 'And, in the run-up to a General Election, how many votes would that be worth, how many jobs? MI6 has known of the oil strike for months and we know all about those crates that have been shipped out of Gatwick and not been paid for – yet. Shahin is in hock to us up to here, doctor.' Ledgerman drew his finger across his throat. 'I suppose they decided they'd rather be in hock to us than either the States or the Ruskis. Anyway, being one of our old colonies, I reckon they knew we'd do anything for a bit of trade; after all, that's what the whole bloody Empire was about, wasn't it, trade? They must have seen how we crawled to the Saudis over that *Death of a Princess* business just so we didn't lose the contract for a few aeroplanes. If it had been a film about female circumcision amongst the starving natives of deepest Bongoland who have never seen an aeroplane, any objections and they would have soon been told to get stuffed.'

Ledgerman looked as if he was beginning to enjoy himself, as if, at last, he had found someone with whom he could relax.

'Hasn't it struck you as strange – but then you won't have seen much TV the last few days – how unavailable the Prime Minister and Foreign Secretary have been since all this started? They've just left the poor old sod of a Home Secretary holding the fort and he doesn't seem to know his arse from his elbow, not on this one, anyway. What are you smiling at?' he asked.

'Not exactly the language you used when I saw you being interviewed on TV a few weeks ago.'

Ledgerman grinned. 'I can talk posh with the best of them, doctor, if I have to, but you forget; I started my career in an East End nick. You should have heard the language in that changing room. Made your hair curl. No, doctor; my personal opinion is that the whole bloody nonsense is a carve-up from beginning to end.'

'Well I'm damned.'

'Not necessarily, doctor. If I've read things right and everything goes to plan, you have nothing really to worry about. I don't think the murder of hostages was on their plan from the beginning and I don't think we are going to storm the place with guns blazing just because some provincial Consultant Surgeon has had his front tooth knocked out.'

'What about his testicle that an Arab decided to play football with?'

For the first time, the two men smiled in unison. 'That so? That's why you're limping? Well, that was no more than poetic justice, if what I'm told is correct.' Ledgerman became serious again. 'There is, of course, one wild card in that pack in there.'

'Who, Ahmed?'

'Two wild cards then, if you count him, though I get the impression he's fairly well under control now. No, doctor, it's that Irish woman that worries me. Works on a very short fuse, that one. The only safe place for that sort of animal is behind bars. Why they thought it necessary to get mixed up with the IRA at all beats me. They must have known they would have had no trouble getting arms in this country.'

'That was Ahmed. Yousef admits that was a bad mistake. As you can imagine, parking a car bomb under the Sultan's room was no part of their plan. They had no idea that was going to happen.'

'That, I must admit, has puzzled me, doctor. I know these maniacs have rationalised these suicide bombings as not being a sin against the Koran if their death is in defence of their Faith, but I have never thought of this as being a suicide mission. Very much the opposite; I thought they were here to save Faisal, not to put a bomb under him. And yet, no one seems too concerned about the damn thing. They have not asked to be allowed to move it.'

'I think I can explain that. I've talked about it to Yousef and he has assured me there is no danger, that the guard on the ground floor has been given orders to shoot anyone, Arab, Irish or hostage, who goes near the thing.'

'Ah now, has he?' Ledgerman's face brightened. 'Good. That means, almost certainly, the bomb is not remotely controlled as they said. There's no wire and neither has that little Irish bitch got a small transmitter in her pocket. That's a great help. Thank you, doctor. Take care now, when you get back in there.'

And Rhys knew, suddenly, what it was like to be in the hands of a skilled interrogator and felt that, in some way, he had betrayed his friends by letting the information slip out.

30

Slowly, Rhys descended the stairway leading to the entrance hall. Under his arm he carried an insulated cardboard box inside which lay the precious kidney, wrapped in a series of plastic bags packed with ice. Instinctively, deep in thought, he turned right towards the corridor that would normally have led him to the Ward Block and to the theatres. He was brought up short by the bulk of a uniformed policeman who barred his way, his thick jacket bulging under one armpit.

'Sorry, sir. Can't go that way.'

At the main entrance, the Inspector who had ushered him in, showed transient, unsmiling interest only as he left, offending Owen's new-found sense of importance. It was now almost dark, the deck-chairs empty and wet with dew. He heard a burst of laughter from one of the Transits as he turned the corner into the no man's land of the car park once again, the abandoned vehicles casting faint shadows from the tall neon street lamps that bathed the block's flat facade in a clinically even light. Rhys felt the same desolate, dry-mouthed loneliness of the emergency call in the small hours. He found Yousef waiting for him inside the door, obvious relief spreading over his face at the sight of him.

'What's the matter?' Rhys smiled. 'Did you think I might not come back?'

'No, Rhys, I was sure you would. But you were away much longer than I expected and it did occur to me they might try to stop you.'

'Really?' Rhys's tone was pitched high enough to make it sound as if he would never altogether believe Yousef any more. Yousef heard it, looked saddened by it and was glad to change the subject.

'Were there any problems?'

'With the Sultan, no. His transplant goes ahead as arranged. It's not as clear-cut with Hannah, unfortunately, and I need time to think about it. And I need to be alone for a while. I'll let you know what I decide. Here's the kidney for Hannah; take great care of that.'

Rhys turned on his heel and left. There had been an authority in his voice that Yousef had not heard before. It was born of a feeling that he, Rhys Owen, was now in command of this strange group, not these youngsters who felt so important, strutting around with their guns. For the first time he realised that everything, the very success of the mission, now depended, had always depended, on his decisions. It was a frame of mind that was going to help him in the most important decision of all. But he must have time to study the results Maggie Rix had given him.

He found the Surgeons' Room in theatre empty, went in and closed the door. He felt at home in an atmosphere where countless, last-minute decisions had been made before. He sat at a small table, normally used for writing operation notes, and laid out the forms in the same rows as had Maggie. He saw his hands tremble and told himself to slow down. He forced himself to read the HLA types first though he knew it would be the lymphocyte cross-match that would be all-important. He also disciplined himself to read and compare the Sultan's and his sister's HLA results before looking at Hannah's, even though he knew more or less what to expect. Both the Sultan and his sister would have inherited two different HLA antigens, known as haplotypes, from each parent, giving in each child four possible combinations of those antigens and a one in four chance of them having inherited identical pairings. As Yousef had led him to believe, there was a perfect match. Excitedly, he now allowed himself to compare Faisal and Hannah, consciously slowing his senses now that he had plenty of time to study what Maggie had so fleetingly pointed out. There it was, just as before – the Sultan's donor, A1, A2; B8, B27, and Hannah, A1, A2; B8, BW35 – a one in a thousand match. To a layman the difference in the last group of symbols might appear significant – and it was – but Rhys knew that in terms of histocompatibility, at least on paper, Hannah could wait indefinitely for such a good match, even on the SOS scheme. Cursorily, as if willing the match with the dead Australian not to be so close as to possibly influence the decision that was already forming in his mind, he looked at the young man's report and, almost gratefully, set it aside.

His tiredness and aches and pains forgotten, he now picked up the lymphocyte cross-match findings. Rhys's preconditioned brain scarcely registered the result between the Sultan and his donor and his heart sank as he read the result between Hannah and the Australian student. But Rhys had to read the result of the cross-match between the Sultan's sister and Hannah several times before he could accept it. The chance of such a good HLA match had been slim enough but to combine it with such a favourable cross-match was one in a million for someone with such a high level of antibodies as Hannah. Rhys gave silent thanks to some faceless technician in some distant laboratory who had noticed the HLA match and carried out the unrequested cross-match; someone to search out and thank when this was all over, perhaps.

Perhaps.

That would depend on what Rhys decided to do with his knowledge, whether what he did would need to remain a secret. There was no doubt in Owen's mind what he must do. There was going to be no equivocation, no heart-rending pacing of the room while he agonised. Somehow, Hannah was going to have the Sultan's donor's kidney, he was going to make sure of that. But how? He found that his normally high regard for the ethics of his profession no longer applied. As honourable a man as most, Owen had always believed that all men had their price and now he was certain. In a burst of inner excitement he swore to himself that he'd go to gaol to give

Hannah that kidney. An unlikely event, Rhys realised, as reason slowly took command again. He must concentrate, control his wildly undisciplined thoughts. He changed chairs for a battered easy one and lay back and closed his eyes.

Was it technically possible to swap kidneys without anyone knowing? That was the first, obvious option that needed to be explored. It was already accepted that two theatres would be operating simultaneously for the Sultan's transplant. There was nothing he could do about that now. He would be in one theatre with Faisal, Yousef in the other, performing the nephrectomy on the donor. The student's kidney would be somewhere in the theatre, in its container, waiting for Hannah's transplant that was planned to follow. No, it would not be possible to swap the kidneys himself without anyone knowing. There was every reason for bringing Hannah's operation forward before the Sultan's in view of the time factor but that obviously would not help. Indeed, it was fortunate that he had arranged the two operations in the order he had; he would have found it difficult to find a reason to change them round at that stage. There was no other way, he must have an accomplice, probably more than one. Whom should he recruit first? Rhys stood, his mind made up. He knew where he must start.

On his way along the ward corridor towards Faisal's room, Rhys met Yousef and Clare Drury. Yousef stopped as if to talk but saw the look in Rhys's face and passed on. There was also a detectable increase in the respect shown by Alistair Robertson whom Rhys found sitting, reading, outside Faisal's door, one hand on the Heckler and Koch that lay across his knees. Robertson stood up when Owen demanded to see the Sultan.

'He's trying to get some sleep. He's been on dialysis all day, ready for the morn. Are ye sure it canna wait until the morning?'

'No. I have to see him tonight. I must see him now.'

Faisal looked as if he had not moved since the last time Rhys had seen him. His head, with its shrivelled face and hair as white as the sheets, did not look heavy enough to sink so far into the pillows. Only his eyes moved as Rhys approached the bed.

'Good evening, Mr Owen.' Faisal smiled and raised one wrinkled hand to point to a chair.

'I apologise, Your Highness, for troubling you so late at night.'

The same brown hand was raised a few degrees and allowed to fall back flaccid on the bed. 'First, Mr Owen, and most important; how is your wife? Do you have any news of her?'

'Only that she is unchanged. She is still deeply unconscious but I'm told her general condition is no worse.'

'I pray her God will watch over her.'

'Thank you, Your Highness. As I said, I am so sorry to trouble you at this hour.'

'I am glad of your company, Mr Owen. Alistair is a fine man but no conversationalist and the nights are long and lonely.' He sighed. 'And my friend next door is sleeping. She does not worry about tomorrow; she is sure it will come. It is only when you get older that you begin to treasure time and are loath to squander it in sleep.'

'Hannah does not know about tomorrow yet. I thought it best not to tell her anything in case there was some last minute snag. I don't want to disappoint her.'

'I rather suspected that as she has made no mention of an operation.'

Rhys raised one eyebrow.

'We send each other letters now.' For the first time, Rhys noticed the piece of paper under Faisal's right hand. 'Alistair is our go-between and, like so many of you, has become her slave. Hannah seems to have him eating out of her hand. For the first time, I am beginning to doubt Alistair's loyalty; I can no longer be certain whom he is protecting, Hannah or myself.' The wrinkles around his eyes deepened. 'She is threatening all sorts of reprisals against you for today's extra dialysis which, she assures me, you ordered just out of spite.'

Faisal saw that there was politeness only in Rhys's answering smile, that he had smiled with his lips only, not with his eyes. He waited for Rhys to speak but Rhys only swallowed nervously.

'You have a problem with my operation, Mr Owen, and you are having trouble telling me?'

'Yes and no.' Rhys managed a short, anxious laugh. 'Or, perhaps, I should say "No and yes".'

Without moving his head, Faisal rolled his eyes upwards. 'And they complain about the difficulty of getting a straight answer out of an Arab!'

'No, there's no real problem with your operation. All the tests show that you should have a first-class chance of a good result. All the indications are that you should accept your sister's kidney very well, without any rejection that can't be coped with quite easily by drugs.'

'Just so long as I survive the operation, of course.'

'I like to think we have been quite honest about the risks at your age, Your Highness.'

'You have. So what is troubling you? It is quite obvious that something is.'

'The problem is with Hannah. You probably know she has had one unsuccessful transplant already.'

Faisal nodded. 'I suspect there are many things about Hannah that she has confided in me in her notes that you do not know. A young girl has many secrets that have little to do with ill health and operations.'

'The reason why her body rejected the kidney is that she has a very high level of certain substances called antibodies in her blood which will destroy over 95 per cent of kidneys we transplant into her. This is on top of the difficulty of finding a good genetic match, matching the characteristics she inherited from her mother and father against those of the donor.'

'Yes; I think I understand that.'

'So Hannah is on what is known as the SOS scheme. Even so, it might be months, probably years, before she gets a kidney with any reasonable chance of success.'

'But I am told you have a kidney that you intend to give her tomorrow.'

'That's the problem.' Rhys paused to take a breath before going on, picking his words as if tiptoeing through a minefield. 'I'm not altogether sure that I should go ahead with her transplant.'

'Why not?'

'Because, having had one kidney rejected already, her chances of success are reduced and the match with her donor is far from ideal.'

'And yet you have not decided definitely against operating?'

'No.'

'Why not? You can keep a patient alive almost indefinitely on dialysis, can you not? A kidney is bound to be found for her eventually.'

'A patient, yes. But Hannah is not just any patient. She has a wild, independent spirit and, if we let her go, I am afraid we would never see her again.'

'What you mean is that Shahin is not the only place that gives sanctuary?' Faisal turned his head to look with gentle understanding at Rhys. 'And is that the only reason?'

'No.' Rhys found it difficult to bring out the shortest of words past the lump that blocked the back of his throat.

'Thank you for your honesty,' Faisal said, softly. 'As you know, Yousef has told me the true reason why this young girl is so important to you and I will not ask you to spell it out, word by word. But where do I come in? I appreciate your confidence and your honesty but I get the feeling you have not come here merely to use me as a confessional. I am more than happy for you to use me as a talking block, to help put your problems into words, but I cannot see how I can assist you in making a clinical decision.' His face screwed up as he began to reason with himself. 'You said "No and yes". You have explained the "no", why there is no problem with my transplant, but you have not explained the "yes", why there is.' His words came more slowly, more certainly. 'You went on to talk about Hannah. It has got to be something to do with Hannah. In some way, the problem with my operation has to be linked with Hannah. Am I correct?'

'Yes.'

'How can that be?'

'By some incredible chance, your sister's kidney is an almost perfect match with Hannah.'

'Almost?'

'The pairing between you and your sister is identical but Hannah's typing is so close to both of you, all three of you could be siblings. Quite miraculous. If we waited for twenty years on the SOS scheme, we could never hope for a match like that.'

Rhys held his breath as he allowed time for Faisal to put it all together.

'And if Hannah were to have such a kidney, what expectation of life would she have?' Faisal asked.

'One can never promise anything, but ten, twenty years. With new drugs coming on the market all the time, who knows, three score and ten perhaps.'

'And she so eager for life.' Faisal thought for a moment. 'You want me to agree to Hannah having my sister's kidney, that's obvious. But what of the whole reason for this charade we are playing? I have a duty to my people too.' He looked up at Rhys slowly. 'You want me to have the kidney that was planned for Hannah, don't you? You had all this worked out in your mind when you came in here.'

Owen said nothing.

'And what are the chances of that kidney functioning in me?'

Owen hedged, his desire to see Hannah get the kidney at all costs preventing him from giving the totally honest answer. 'Obviously far less than if you have your sister's kidney but we have been having some remarkable success recently even with poorly matched kidneys, using the new Cyclosporin, but your chances of success would be greatly reduced.'

Faisal turned his head towards the window and the night sky. 'And, in the event of this kidney not working, would I get back to Shahin?'

'It would depend a great deal on what would be involved in getting out of here. If there was any question of fighting your . . .'

'That has been arranged.' Faisal waved his hand as if that was of no importance.

'In that case, as long as we can keep your dialysis going, I can see no great difficulty.'

'So there is no real problem, Mr Owen, is there?' Faisal, gently, unwittingly, stroked the scrap of paper under his hand as he turned his head back to smile at Rhys. 'Hannah shall have the kidney.' Faisal shook his head slowly from side to side in mock disbelief. 'And you doubted your ability to love anyone. You must still love her a great deal.'

'Who? Hannah?'

'No, not only her; the other one, the one Yousef told me of.'

'Helen.' Rhys felt his face flush as, for the first time in over twenty years, he spoke the name out loud. But he was not finished yet. For now, he must push her memory into the background. There was still one more hurdle. 'But I still have one final problem to put to you, Your Highness.'

'And what's that? I have told you, you can have your wish. I have given you my word. It means nothing to me.'

Rhys took a deep breath.

'But there is something you do not know about Hannah, something I think she is unlikely to have put in one of her notes. It's her name. Her full name is Hannah Stein. Hannah is a Jew.'

In the silence that followed, Rhys watched the fragile defence of an expressionless face crack and crumble as Faisal's turbulent emotions broke through. He saw surprise, shock, prejudice, anger, realisation and shame give way to humility and it was as if he had found peace again that he turned to Rhys once more.

'You are a strong man, Mr Owen. To think I had the impertinence to suggest just now that you were using me as a confessional when, all the time, you were quite certain in your mind that you were right in what you were doing. You are also a clever man, Mr Owen. It is I who needed the confessional. In two or three short words you have opened my eyes to myself and have shriven me of so many sins.' Slowly, as if taking an oath, he stretched his arm towards where the Kipling lay on the bedside locker. 'Was it only yesterday that, in my arrogance, I talked about no Border, nor Breed, nor Birth? And you have shown me up for the dissembler I am. I have found it convenient to forget the Jews. I have been blinkered by hatred. I scolded you for not reading Kipling and now I must go back and read it again, remembering there are peoples on earth other than Arabs and Westerners. I am not very proud of myself, Mr Owen.' He put out his arm and Rhys took the thin, dry hand in his. 'Hannah must have that kidney.'

Rhys tried to speak but failed, whereas Faisal was calm and deliberate as he went on to speak of his two sons.

'This cannot be done without Yousef's agreement; it might influence his future greatly. It cannot be done with Ahmed's knowledge; he would not stand by and allow it.' The mischievous smile returned. 'And I must speak to this Hannah of yours. I, too, wish to become a slave of this young enchantress.'

They both laughed before Faisal became solemn once more.

'And my last wish would be that, when Hannah is well again, you bring her to Shahin, show her what we are trying to do and protect her from old men's prejudices. Will you do that?'

'Yes, I promise I will do that.'

'Good. In that case I think you had now better go and find Yousef and bring him here so that we can tell him our little secret.'

'Are you a real Sultan?'

'Yes, Hannah, I am.'

'Cor.'

The clean, new light of early morning reflected off thick black tresses washed with Nansi's help the night before. Hannah's features might be wasted, her lips and eyelids pale, but her hair still shone where it fell each side of her shoulders. Faisal, clad in full Arab dress, having refused Robertson's gruff demands to use a wheel chair, sat at the foot of her bed. Hannah, alert, excited, wearing her prettiest nightdress, sat erect.

'So we are to have our operations the same day, Mr Owen tells me.'

'Yes. I hate him. Why didn't he tell me that was why I had to have that extra dialysis yesterday?'

'He was only trying to be kind. He didn't want you to be disappointed if anything went wrong at the last moment.'

'He's just like all the rest. Why does he have to treat me like a child all the time?'

'To someone as old as I, Hannah, you are a child but I know for a fact Mr Owen does not see you as one and I'm sure he must get a little cross when you behave as one.'

'He's all right really,' Hannah conceded grudgingly. 'I only do it to irritate him.'

There were a few moments of silence as they surveyed each other, their gazes fearless and direct.

'So, tell me now, Hannah; what are you planning to do with your new kidney?'

'Pee through it, I hope.'

The expression on Faisal's face did not change but somewhere, deep in the chair, a slow rhythmic shaking began which spread to take over Faisal's frail body and force from his mouth one high-pitched shout of delight which had Robertson flinging himself into the room in alarm. Without turning his head, he waved a shaking hand in Robertson's direction.

'Go away, Alistair. Have you never heard anyone laugh before?'

Alone again, Faisal said, 'Perhaps I had better rephrase that. If you suddenly found that you were quite well again, what would you do?'

Hannah thought for a moment. 'I would get dressed. I would go down and steal Rhys's car. And then I would drive as fast as I could to see Tempest.'

'Tempest?'

'He's my horse. He's a thoroughbred stallion. And I'd take him down to the beach again and we'd gallop along the edge of the sea and I'd stretch along his neck and I'd feel his mane against my face.'

'And after that?'

'After that? I'd never call anyone a pig again.' She favoured Faisal with one of her grown-up woman smiles as if to reassure him, in confidence, that all that horrid little girl stuff was only a form of defence.

'How far can you gallop along this beach of yours?' Faisal asked.

'More than a mile each way, easy.'

'How would you like to gallop over even sand for mile after mile after mile – on and on until the horse under you drops?'

Reverting to childish fantasy, Hannah's eyes had got bigger and bigger. 'Tempest would never stop,' she said, her chin jutting.

'But would you like that?'

'Would I like what?'

Hannah was not so stupid as not to know what Faisal was implying but one half of her mind wanted him to spell it out, give her something to dream of, while the other half of a mind inured to hardship and disappointment told her not to listen, to expect no favours from life.

'When you are fit and well, would you like to come to Shahin and ride the finest horses out across the desert just as far as you want? Mr Owen has promised me he will bring you if you want to.'

Hannah nodded her head, her lips half open. 'And will I see you? Will you be riding with us?'

'No and yes.' Faisal laughed. 'I'm sorry, Hannah, just a private little joke. No, you will not see me; yes, I will be with you. When you are a bit older, you will know what I mean.'

'And now you are treating me like a child too? Of course I know what you mean.'

'Because, when you are out there, riding under that hot sun, if you think hard enough, if you really concentrate, then I will be there, riding beside you.'

Throwing back the bedclothes, Hannah tucked her legs under her, raising herself into the kneeling position close to Faisal. 'I promise,' she whispered, hesitating for a moment as if wondering whether it was allowed before kissing Faisal high on one cheek.

Faisal looked at Hannah and saw her as she would be, a beautiful, strong-willed, compassionate woman.

'There is one thing you must do in return. You must do as Mr Owen says. He is a good man and you must do nothing to let him down.'

'And d'you think I would?'

'No.'

For a moment, Arab and Jew looked at each other in total honesty.

'It is considered very rude in my country for the principal guest to keep his host waiting,' Faisal said slowly, smiling. 'I think the time has come for me to put myself in the hands of the Almighty and Mr Owen.'

'Same person in this hospital,' Hannah smiled.

Faisal smiled back at such frail bravery. 'I will be saying my prayers before I go to the theatre; may I say one for you also?'

'That would be nice. And one for Rhys too?'

'Of course.' Faisal struggled to his feet. 'And you will call me?' He pointed to the wall above Hannah's head.

'As soon as I can stretch that far, I promise.'

31

There were many reasons why the theatre staff went about their various tasks with a brisk cheerfulness. They were back doing what they did best. The cold touch of surgical instruments was, to them, the sensation of reality once more. They had the feeling that they were reaching the climax of their adventure and that, busy enough to forget lingering fear for a while, after three routine operations, they would be well on their way to being released.

The theatres at Avonport had been designed in pairs, each pair sharing an anaesthetic room and a 'prep' room with its bewildering array of laid-up trolleys. In one theatre, Sister Ferguson spoke in quick, decisive bursts, moving into the other theatre from time to time to give encouragement to Nansi, frowning anxiously in her concentration. Near enough to hear the bustle and sense the excitement, the medical staff jostled and murmured in the changing room and Surgeons' Room, much like the beginning to any busy day's operating. The nearest guard was outside the Theatres on the landing and Rhys was welcoming Peter Parfitt who had been the first to volunteer his services as anaesthetist.

'Thank you for coming in, Peter. I'm sorry we're starting a bit later than we planned; a bit complicated to explain.' The sort of remark any surgeon might make to any anaesthetist, with no mention of gunmen or hostages or the gap in his teeth at which Parfitt was trying not to stare.

'Strange business, I must say.' Already changed into theatre garb, Parfitt was his usual laconic self. 'I was sorry to hear about Alex, Rhys. Have you heard anything this morning?'

'Just had a few words with Maggie on the line. Still the same apparently.'

'She'll be all right, Rhys, if she's got this far.'

'Would you mind inducing the donor first, Peter?'

Parfitt respected Owen's sudden dismissal of what he knew must be a painful subject.

'No, of course not.'

'As you can imagine, it's the Sultan I would like you to anaesthetise – he's very frail, I'm afraid, Peter – had to have a pericardial effusion aspirated only a couple of days ago. The donor is the Sultan's sister and, as far as we know, is perfectly fit but we have not been allowed to examine her. Under normal circumstances I would be more than happy to let Kumar do her, but . . .'

'But?'

'Well, Kumar is a Hindu and, while I don't think that sort of thing comes into it, it might be wiser not to take the risk. If, perhaps, you could just put her to sleep?'

'What if she finds out I'm a Welsh Methodist?' Parfitt grinned. 'Who's doing the nephrectomy?'

'Yousef, with Ahmed assisting.'

'That bastard.'

'It's all right, Peter. Yousef will keep an eye on him.'

'I wouldn't let that bastard operate on my cat.'

Peter Parfitt was amazed how calmly he took the sight of the fully dressed woman who lay on the trolley Paddy Moore pushed into the Anaesthetic Room, her dusty sandals protruding from under her full length black gown, a few square inches of skin around her eyes the only sign of life, but he came close to rebuking instinctively the other similarly dressed woman who walked alongside the trolley. He resisted the temptation to shout but his smiles, nods and gestures were sheer pantomime as he coaxed a hand out from a sleeve and persuaded the patient to allow her attendant to remove her veil. Parfitt had always imagined women who wore veils to be beautiful and was inwardly disappointed to find a face which, though smiling and serene, was downright plain. She became distressed as Paddy Moore pulled her sleeve up to compress her veins and more time was needed to show her chaperon how it was done. An injection, a few more gigantic smiles from Parfitt and she was asleep. Paddy was dismissed and Parfitt pretended to look elsewhere as the attendant and the theatre nurse struggled to undress the unconscious woman. Into the theatre and positioned on the table, her modesty was preserved once more under the surgical drapes and, as Yousef and Ahmed stepped forwards, Parfitt handed her over to Kumar to return to the Anaesthetic Room where he found Owen waiting for the Sultan's arrival.

'You'll let me know when you want to start? I don't want to put him out any sooner than I need.'

Owen nodded. 'I'd just like to make sure there's no problem with the nephrectomy first. It shouldn't take me long to explore Faisal; he's only skin and bones.'

'Faisal; that's his name is it? First names now, is it?'

'You watch it,' Rhys grinned. 'Just remember, it's "Your Highness" when you speak to him, but then you anaesthetists never speak to your patients anyway, do you?'

A friendly obscenity followed Rhys as he passed into Yousef's theatre and he was still smiling as he leaned over Yousef's shoulder to look into the wound.

'How's it going?'

'Not really down to it yet. Shouldn't be any problem.'

Rhys stayed to watch Yousef deepen the wound. In the silence that surrounded the table as Yousef passed his hand into the loin, Rhys looked across at Ahmed and saw the scowl that no mask could hope to hide. He was trying to imagine what was going through Ahmed's mind, forced as he was to play second fiddle to his brother once again, when he heard a small cry of surprise from Yousef.

'Trouble?' Rhys asked.

'Hope not.' Yousef turned towards him, his hand still deep in the wound. 'Something in the upper pole.'

Rhys closed his eyes. 'For God's sake, don't say she's got a tumour. I thought you said her IVP was normal.'

'There was nothing to be seen, Rhys, but then they weren't quite up to Roger's standards, of course.' Anxiously, they tried to smile at each other. 'Hang on a minute until I've delivered it.'

While he began to clean the pads of fat from around the kidney, Rhys was joined at Yousef's shoulder by Clare Drury. Yousef felt her presence, turned for a second, a slight shuffling of his feet the only sign of stress.

'Should have left this one for you, Clare. It's a bit stuck around the upper pole. Needs a gentle touch.' Small beads of sweat had begun to coalesce below his cap before the kidney came into view. He gave the upper part of the kidney a squeeze.

'Solitary cyst, praise be to Him.'

'Are you sure?' Rhys asked. 'Let me see.'

'Feels cystic,' Yousef said, 'and pretty deep in the substance. Do you want me to put a needle in it? Or perhaps excise it?'

Owen looked at the round, tense sphere and the glistening kidney capsule stretched taut over it. He thought for a moment. 'No, leave it,' he decided. 'Sure as fate she'll bleed into it if we aspirate it and we don't want to leave a big raw area by excising it. No, leave it.'

'What about a partial excision and sew over the cut edge?'

'No.' Rhys, acting on instinct and experience, could think of no good reason for his decision.

'Just the one for Roger's ultrasound,' Yousef said. 'Please don't tell him, Rhys; he'd never forgive us for missing that one.'

'I won't. What about the vessels? What do they look like?'

'I'll tell you in a minute after I've cleaned the hilum.'

There was another anxious period while they waited for Yousef to dissect out the kidney's artery and vein. The ureter would probably present no problem . Yousef would have to trace it down as far as he could to get sufficient length for Owen to work with but the kidney's blood vessels were often arranged quite unlike the classical pictures in the anatomy manuals. The artery particularly was subject to many variations, at times dividing into many branches as soon as it arose from the aorta. At other times a significant part of the kidney was supplied by a totally aberrant vessel.

'Nice long single artery. No aberrants.'

Rhys gave a loud sigh of relief. 'Thank God for that. We were due for a bit of luck. I think the time has come for me to go and do some work myself.' He looked at Clare, striving to control his voice. 'All ready to bring the kidney over, Dr Drury?'

Clare nodded and said nothing but Rhys saw her swallow nervously under her mask.

'Yousef will wrap it in a swab and put it in a dish. I may not be absolutely ready to work with it when it's ready so take it into the prep room and keep the swab soaked in preserving fluid until I give you a shout.' He turned to Sister Ferguson alongside Yousef and smiled. 'You won't forget to allow for the swab in the count, will you, Sister?'

Back in the anaesthetic room Rhys found Paddy standing to one side of the Sultan, a black-gowned Arab woman on the other. Parfitt sat at the head of the trolley playing with a pair of forceps. All were silent. Rhys walked up to Faisal, prepared to mouth the usual platitudes, to find him fixed eyed in a trance like stillness. A few quiet words from Rhys produced no reaction and Rhys looked at Parfitt who shrugged his shoulders.

'All right, Peter, shall we start?' Owen said and Parfitt reached for his syringe. A few minutes later and Faisal was asleep and intubated and what little was visible of the Arab woman's face showed obvious relief when they made signs that she could go.

'Only just managed to stop some bloody great bearded Scotsman from coming in here with his gun, Rhys. He's sitting outside in the corridor. How the hell you've put up with all this since last Sunday, I can't imagine.' Parfitt steadied Faisal's head as Moore and the Theatre Orderly effortlessly lifted the inert, cachectic body on to the table. 'It did occur to me – with all the top brass here – ' he jerked his head towards the other theatre ' – who exactly is looking after the shop? Who's there to stop the police if they decide now is the right time to rush the place?'

'Don't worry; they've thought of that. Every available man is on guard at the moment and there is a mad Irish woman up there on the roof with a heavy machine gun who would have something to say about it. And the man outside is ex-SAS and would happily give his life for this chap.'

Parfitt gently rubbed Faisal's cheek as if trying to bring some colour into it. 'Must be quite some character,' he said, thoughtfully, 'but they all look the same, stark bollock naked on an operating table, don't they? What position d'you want him in?'

Rhys grinned, feeling better for Parfitt's earthy philosophy.

'Flat on his back.'

When he went to scrub, Rhys found Patel standing, patiently deferential, already gowned and gloved. Patel had been disappointed when told that Yousef was going to assist at Hannah's transplant and Rhys did what he could to soothe his disappointment.

'That resection you did – the one you were operating on when all this started – he's doing very well, isn't he? I saw him yesterday. All credit to you.'

'It is very pleasing, sir, to see his Ryles tube up and he is not vomiting. Thank you, sir.'

At the table, Rhys found Faisal already painted and draped. He picked up a scalpel, looked across at Nansi and smiled. 'Now then, Staff Nurse Rees; all ready?'

'Yes, sir.' Rhys could hear her tense determination. 'All I ask is you don't shout at me.'

'I shan't do that.'

Rhys made his incision low down on the left side, rather like a left-sided appendix incision extended downwards. There was little or no fat beneath the skin and the thin layer of muscle hardly bled as he divided it. Taking great care not to enter the abdominal cavity itself, he brushed the lining away to display all the structures that lay against the muscles of the vertebral column. Meticulously, he dissected out the blood vessels he had chosen to use, taking particular care around the thin walled vein. As he did so, he explained his decisions to Patel in short, low-pitched statements.

'Good internal iliac and a single renal so we'll join the arteries end to end. The vein we can put into the side of the external iliac, as usual.'

'Yes, sir. What about the ureter?'

'Into the bladder.'

When Rhys looked up next, it was to see Yousef peering over Patel's shoulder.

'I've left Ahmed to close up. Should take him about twenty minutes.' Yousef's voice sounded thick and he was forced to clear his throat. 'Clare has had the kidney for the last ten minutes or so. Are you ready for it yet?'

'I think so. Ask her to bring it in, would you?'

As Clare Drury carried the dish reverentially towards the table, Rhys turned to Nansi. 'Leave the swab on to keep it moist, Staff, but don't forget to allow for it in your final swab count, will you?'

Rhys spent a little time placing the kidney this way and that, draping the loose ends of the blood vessels and ureter here and there, building up in his mind a picture of where it would ultimately lie most conveniently with the least chance of leaving any of his suture lines under tension. Satisfied, he began the intricate task of joining the empty stumps of the kidney's vessels to the vital circulation in the Sultan's artery and vein. It was a task that demanded total concentration if Rhys was going to avoid getting the extemely fine suture material needed for such small vessels into a hopeless, infuriating tangle. Any break in his concentration could lead to a slip which might be the first step down a slippery slope to disaster. The arterial suturing, with the thick, pulsating vessels, always looked the more dramatic but it was the vein that Rhys feared more, with its deceptively low pressure circulation and a vessel wall that was so thin that one small split led to a tear which led to a bigger tear which disappeared behind a welling pool of blood. The commitment required drove from Rhys's mind all thoughts of Arabs, unconscious wives, loves and fears, aching testicles. For three-quarters of an hour his gaze rarely rose above waist level and it was with a slow, satisfied sigh that he looked up to relax before turning his attention to the ureter.

As those standing around the table moved, shuffling their aching legs as if in sympathy, Rhys saw that Ahmed had joined them, saw him shoulder Clare Drury aside and lean over to examine more closely what had been done so far. His only reaction was to give a few grunts and intensify his aura of wary hostility. As everyone took interest again, Rhys began the process of implanting the loose end of the ureter into Faisal's bladder. After another period of total absorption in his task, Rhys had almost completed the process when Ahmed broke the silence.

'The blood supply is now good. Why no urine?'

Ahmed's query was blunt and suspicious, difficult to evade.

'Doesn't always follow. They take some time to open up sometimes.'

'But it was a good match. Why does it not work yet?'

'As I said, it doesn't always follow.' Rhys glanced despairingly at Yousef. 'About 25 per cent take up to ten days to start functioning.'

'But it was a good match,' Ahmed insisted stubbornly.

Rhys did not notice Yousef leave the table but he was increasingly conscious of the fact that, soon, he would have to remove the swab before closing up. He was startled by Yousef's voice behind him, speaking to Ahmed across the table.

'I think the donor's bleeding, Ahmed; her blood pressure has dropped a bit. I think we had better check her wound. Would you give me a hand, please?'

Grudgingly, Ahmed left and a few minutes later, Rhys had to consciously suppress a sigh of relief as he handed the swab to Nansi. 'One final swab count before we close up, please, Staff Nurse.' His voice softened. 'Thanks, Nansi, you were great.'

'Pleasure, sir. I enjoyed it; just like old times. Will you be going straight on with Hannah? Sister Ferguson has cleared the other side away and has had a coffee by the look of it. It's all laid up and she's probably ready to go.'

'The sooner the better as far as I'm concerned. How about you, Peter?' Rhys turned towards Parfitt who simply shrugged his shoulders.

'Quick cup of coffee and I'll be ready.'

'Right then; we'll press on.'

Lying on the anaesthetic trolley, her hair massed inside an ugly disposable cap, Hannah suppressed her bubbling excitement long enough to ask how Faisal's operation had gone, and it was halfway through a defiantly enthusiastic sentence that Parfitt's injection of Pentothal carried her into unconsciousness. In theatre, Sister Ferguson, leaning against one of the instrument-laden trolleys, watched Hannah being lifted into place. She saw Rhys and Yousef come in, scrubbed.

'Which side, Mr Owen?'

'Right, please, sister. Her left side will be a bit stuck down after her rejection.'

Rhys began, in total silence, what would be a mirror image operation of the one he had just perfomed on Faisal, varying only in the comparative softness of her arteries and the easier access to her wider female pelvis. For more than an hour, with the exception of small murmurs of delight at the sight of urine draining from the ureter, all four professionals around the table were lulled into that somnolent, almost narcoleptic trance that goes with the total absorption in an operation that is going smoothly, when the outside world came crashing in. No one had seen Ahmed enter and his anger startled them all.

'That kidney. Let me see that kidney.'

From where he had quietly taken up a position behind Yousef and with complete disregard for sterility, he pushed his brother aside to take a closer look into the wound. Rhys, taken completely by surprise, had no time to cover the kidney where it nestled in the hollow of Hannah's pelvis.

'That kidney has cyst. The kidney we took . . . That is same kidney; that is same cyst. I saw it. You are putting wrong kidney in.' He paused, shaking in sudden fury, to look round, scanning eyes that told their own stories.

Parfitt and the theatre sister showed their alarm and surprise but there was no trace in either Rhys or Yousef of the appalling panic that explodes within a surgeon at the suddenly discovered, irreversible mistake. Their faces showed nothing but guilt. Slowly Ahmed began to put the pieces together and for a moment he looked like hurling himself across the table at Rhys. 'This is not mistake. It is a plot. You wish to murder our Imam. You have put dead kidney into Sultan; that is why it did not work. Now he will die. And do you kill me next so you will be Sultan?' He turned to lunge at Yousef, shouting 'Filthy murderer' and, as the rest stood stunned, carried Yousef crashing to the floor. By the time Paddy Moore and the Orderly had managed to control Ahmed's flailing arms and legs, blood-stained water from a hand basin had sluiced across the floor and an instrument trolley had shed its load in a jangling cascade.

'Get him out and don't let him do anything stupid,' Rhys snapped. He looked at Yousef who struggled to his feet. 'No need to scrub again. I've nearly finished and I can manage with Sister from here. Just make sure he doesn't do anything crazy and keep him away from that Irish woman until I get out from here. We'll get Hannah off the table.' He nodded to the instruments on the floor. 'Can you manage without those, Sister?'

'I think so, Mr Owen.'

'Good.'

They closed up the wound to a background of furious, unintelligible argument from the theatre corridor.

'And what the hell was all that about, Rhys?' Parfitt asked.

'Long story, Peter; too long to tell you now.'

'But is it true? Have you put the wrong kidney in this girl?'

'As I said, Peter, a long story.' Owen looked at his colleague anxiously. 'Peter, I'm not sure just what arrangement you came to with those outside about going back?'

'They said it would depend on what the attitude was in here. I thought I'd stay until I was happy there was no post-op trouble and then get the hell out of it.'

'In that case, I'm afraid I'm going to have to ask you to stay.' Rhys was doing his best not to make it sound as if he was giving a colleague of equal rank an order. 'Better for them outside not to know anything about this, at least for the moment.'

'What makes you think I'd say anything about it?' Parfitt looked a bit hurt at the suggestion.

'Because I think you would find that the police who would interrogate you when you left would not exactly be your friendly village Bobby.

There's not much " 'ullo, 'ullo, 'ullo" about them when they're dealing with hijackers and, from what I understand, released hostages with valuable information to give don't fare much better.'

'And if I decided to go?'

'Then I'm afraid you would not be allowed to. We would stop you.'

Surprise on Parfitt's face gave way to amazement. 'Well I'm damned. It's bloody impossible to tell hostage from hijacker in here any more.'

In the Surgeons' Room bitter argument was still being waged in passionate Arabic when Rhys entered, and Yousef had to place himself in front of Rhys to prevent Ahmed striking him. Ahmed now showed none of the enjoyment that had transformed his appearance when he had bludgeoned Rhys before. There was still malice in his fury but the element of enjoyment was now replaced by fear. It was now his turn to feel threatened and Rhys realised that it made him even more dangerously unpredictable.

'Rhys, I have tried to explain to him that everything that has been done has been with the Sultan's full knowledge and permission, but he is not convinced. He will not accept that there is any chance that His Highness's kidney will function. He thinks that we have put the kidney in knowing that it will reject and that the rejection will kill him. He says that we have killed the Sultan by putting a bad kidney in him and now we will kill him too.' For the first time, Rhys saw fear in Yousef's face. 'Rhys, I am afraid he will do something stupid before we can convince him, before he can speak to His Highness.'

Ahmed backed into a corner, becoming calmer, more watchful.

'I am betrayed. You have betrayed Sultan. You have betrayed our people. And for what? For a Jew?' He turned his head to spit at Owen's feet before turning his fury on Yousef. 'What hold has this little man over you? What lies has he told Sultan? And you, my father's favourite son, have killed our Imam for Jew?'

32

Eamon Dickens and Paddy Moore looked up as the staccato fanfare that heralded the six o'clock news broke through the monotonous repartee that went with their endless card playing. They waited to hear the senior newsreader snap out the headlines before they returned to their game. The Avonport siege had been relegated to third place below a run on the pound and a Central American earthquake; time for another hand. Their interest slowly rekindled as the second newsreader's face gave way to the now routine pictures of the outside of Avonport's St David's Hospital with the cameraman trying in vain to obtain a new angle on the nurses' dummy still straddling Clare Drury's crushed Mini. Over the pictures, the newsreader's voice told them that, apart from the now routine daily transfer of blood samples required in the post-operative management of the patients still in the hospital, there had been no new major development at the Avonport siege which was now in its eighth day. There had been no further sign of the Consultant Anaesthetist who had volunteered to enter the hospital four days previously although it was generally accepted that one, quite possibly two, renal transplants had been carried out about that time. Speculation was increasing as to how the situation was to be resolved as no further demands had been made by the terrorists, little or no contact having been made over the open line except to pass news to Mr Rhys Owen, the surgeon who was understood to have carried out the operations, about his wife, still critically ill though stable in a Bristol hospital. For the latest developments in this quite extraordinary affair, Eamon and Paddy were handed over to the BBC's Political Correspondent, Anthony James.

The picture cut to the immobile head and shoulders of the reporter, who had learned to read his prompt without the flicker of an eyeball or the twitch of a hand. Only his lips moved.

'Bloody robot,' Moore growled.

'What's that?'

'Bloody robot. I reckon those fellows have got a switch in between their shoulder blades so they can be turned on and off.'

'Shut up, Paddy,' Dickens laughed. 'It's us they're talking about, you realise that? Now wouldn't you be interested in what's going to happen to you?'

They turned their attention back to the television in time to hear that there had been no change in the Government's stated policy on terrorism and that the Shadow Home Secretary, when interviewed on his farm, had been adamant that there must be no sign of weakness, with no suggestion of capitulation to political blackmail or economic interest. As for the Prime Minister, he had spend the weekend at Chequers after his holiday in Florence but had returned earlier that day to Downing Street where it had been possible to interview him and where, for the first time, he had spelt out his attitude publicly.

The black Jaguar with the high headrests came to a halt, the pin-striped personal detective opened the car door, and the well-known head and shoulders appeared. There was the smile and the wave and, halfway across the pavement, the carefully rehearsed sudden decision to have a word with the Media. Yes, he had been in constant touch with the Home Office throughout the affair but he had had no reservations about leaving everything to the police on the spot; Britain had cause to be proud of having the finest anti-terrorist forces in the world and he had every confidence that they would bring this siege, with all its peculiar aspects, to a peaceful conclusion. No, there was to be no deviation from the general principles laid down for the containment of such a situation; they would make sure that no benefit was derived from this act of terrorism, whatever the nature of the cause for which it was being undertaken, and every effort was being made to limit the publicity given to the siege, hence the low profile taken by the Government in this matter. But there were features perhaps unique to this affair. There had been, as yet, no real violence and there had been no threats to kill hostages.

The Correspondent, in his anxiety to get as many questions in as he could, made the mistake of combining a reminder of the constant threat imposed by the possible car bomb with the question of diplomatic immunity that had been such a thorny problem in the case of the Libyan siege.

Grabbing his opportunity to ignore the question of the bomb, the PM explained that, as Britain had no diplomatic relations with Shahin, there could be no question of diplomatic immunity but that, although the two countries had not gone through the formalities of exchanging ambassadors, this country wanted nothing more than friendship with such a peaceful people with whom we had been so closely associated in the past.

The PM switched on his banishing smile and turned on his heel only to be stopped in his tracks by the question of Faisal's death sentence aimed at his back; he couldn't leave that one lingering in the air unanswered. There was a stonier look to his features as he returned to face the cameras. It was true that the Sultan was still, technically speaking, under sentence of death and it was also true that it was His Highness who was central to this whole extraordinary affair. But Mr James must realise, times change. No progress would ever be made if we allowed ourselves to be shackled by the past. Shahin was full of British ex-patriots who were laying the foundation for friendly relations between the two countries, just as in other friendly countries where the political leader had, in the past, been amongst our bitterest enemies.

There was obvious doubt in the Correspondent's voice as to whether he was pushing his luck with his last question, and the mask that fell over the PM's face confirmed the fact that he had overstepped the mark. Yes, it was unfortunate that the Shahinians, in the quite inexplicably complicated method they had chosen to carry out what was essentially a perfectly peaceful mission, had chosen to associate themselves with proven murderers from the IRA. The man involved was not considered to be any great threat but the woman was a known killer and would not, Mr James was assured, be allowed to escape justice on this occasion.

'Hear that, Eamon? "No great threat", that's what they think of you.' Laughing, Paddy gave the Irishman's shoulder a push that nearly tipped his chair backwards. 'Got you dead to rights, I reckon. They must have seen you play cards. By the time we get out of here you'll have to turn to honest crime to pay me the money you'll owe me.'

But Eamon's face had become serious, as serious as his naturally pleasant features could be moulded. He put his cards down and stood up.

'I'd better take myself up to the roof and see Roisin, tell her what the man had to say about her.'

In the Surgeons' Sitting Room on the floor above them, the conversation was dour and stilted, Rhys and Peter Parfitt talking in disjointed bursts as anxiety bubbled to the surface, seeking reassurance. Each knew the final resolution of their frightening adventure could not be delayed for more than another few days, and their disquiet only increased as they each had their own mental pictures of how it might take place. The gloom was obvious to Clare Drury as she entered, Yousef following close behind her. She smiled at Rhys, hoping to lift the tension.

'I've just seen Hannah. She looks marvellous. Urine output is great and her urea is down. There's only one problem.'

'What's that?' Rhys's head jerked upwards.

'She's demanding to see Faisal. You know what she's like and it's only going to get worse as she gets to feel stronger. She says his knocking on the wall is very feeble and she says she knows he's dying and we're not telling her. Do you think you could have a word with her, Mr Owen, please?'

'Do you think His Highness would see her just for a moment, just to satisfy her?' Owen asked Yousef.

'No.'

Owen looked surprised at such a prompt, sharp reaction.

'Why not?' he asked.

'I don't know why. Who knows what goes through a man's mind at a time like this? All I know is that, when I saw him early this morning, he looked like a man preparing himself to die,' Yousef said, softly. 'He has ordered us to take him home tomorrow. Soon it will be the tenth day of Muharram, our New Year, a time of extreme penitence which he wishes to spend with his people.'

It was Rhys who finally broke the silence. 'Going home? Tomorrow?'

All three sat forward, open-mouthed, to hear Yousef's reply.

'My own feeling is that my father has been lying there simply conserving his strength for one last effort. He has no wish to be involved in any more wearying emotional clashes. He knows that, if he does not get back to Shahin soon, he may not get home at all. I have been waiting for him to say when we go and he has decided; tomorrow.'

'But,' Owen stammered, 'just like that? You can't just walk out.'

'At eight o'clock this evening,' he looked at his watch, 'I am to speak over the open line with someone from the Home Office to make arrangements for our withdrawal eight o'clock tomorrow morning.'

'Just like that?' Rhys repeated.

'We are not expecting too much difficulty. No one has been really hurt. I suspect your Government will be glad to be rid of us; to have all of us in one of your gaols would be nothing but an embarrassment to them. The only thing that will be hurt is your national pride and I'm sure the Prime Minister will find words to soothe that. Six weeks and it will all be forgotten if no one is hurt. The last thing they want is another bunch of Arab hostages in your gaols to give the Ahmeds of this world a heaven-sent excuse to go round bombing more airport lounges. That's what would happen unless they send the SAS in with orders not to take any prisoners, and there are too many of us to make that a credible option. And it would be asking a lot, even of the SAS, to shoot a defenceless, old man, lying on his deathbed. Think what the world Press, even the Americans, would make of that one. And – ' he paused ' – there are other factors.'

'Money.' Rhys spoke the word with sufficient scathing sureness to tell Yousef he knew exactly what he meant. 'It seems this country, like every other, has its price.'

'Haven't you two forgotten one thing?' Parfitt, who had watched, fascinated, as the two men had confronted each other, broke in. 'What about your Irish friends? You can't leave them here and, even if you are correct in what you say about yourselves, I don't see them letting a couple of IRA walk away. I haven't had the pleasure of meeting the young lady on the roof yet but, as I understand it, she is a wanted murderer; sorry – ' he smiled, languidly pedantic, correcting himself ' – murderess.'

Yousef wriggled in his chair, leaning forward to scratch at his ankle to avoid three searching stares. 'I admit, there we have a problem, one we did not foresee, one which would not have occurred if it had not been for Ahmed. We had no idea he still had links outside Shahin, something which His Highness forbids. He was given instructions to get weapons from other sources in this country, Arab sources.'

'Terrorist sources, you mean. Perhaps you could explain the difference between an Arab weapon and an Irish one.' Parfitt had no reason to spare Yousef's feelings. 'Try explaining the difference to someone whose son has been murdered on a Belfast street whether the rifle that killed him came from Libya or Noraid.'

Yousef took some time to answer that. 'Obviously, we will have to resolve that problem somehow.'

'Meaning you do not really know what is going to happen at the moment?'

'Meaning it will be arranged,' Yousef snapped as he stood abruptly. 'I must go and see His Highness before I speak to them. I will let you know what is to happen.'

' "Never volunteer for anything", isn't that an old Army saying?' Parfitt asked as they heard Yousef's footsteps recede down the corridor. 'It is just beginning to dawn on me what a bloody stupid thing I did, coming in here, playing the hero. But seriously, Rhys, don't you think it would be a good idea if we made a few plans of our own?'

'Such as?'

'Well, to my mind, the most effective safety catch on that bomb out there has been Faisal lying right above it. Remove Faisal and the safety catch is off. I would suggest therefore that, the moment they leave these two floors, we get everyone across at least into B Block, into A Block if we can dismantle their barricade fairly quickly. Do you think they'll take any of us with them as hostages? Isn't that what they usually do?'

'Somehow I don't think so, not this time.' Rhys looked thoughtful, considering whether to explain to Parfitt about his conversation with Ledgerman and deciding not to, as if he would have been divulging a confidence he respected.

'You mean they're just going to let them all walk out, IRA and all?'

Rhys merely shrugged his shoulders in reply.

'It's those two up on the roof that frighten me.' Clare Drury gave a little shudder. 'They're so quiet.' She turned to Rhys. 'You know they've sent everyone else down, do you? They have been up there alone for two days now, won't let anyone up. Ahmed has been down a few times for food but that's all. She hasn't been down at all.'

'I agree, Clare. They scare me too,' Rhys admitted. 'Left to Yousef and Faisal, I think that, between them, they have the intelligence and enough knowledge of just how bloody devious politicians can be, to get us all out without anything ghastly happening. But, with those two up there, I wouldn't like to predict what might happen. The Irish woman is a paranoid killer and Ahmed must now feel she is the only one he can trust. I don't know whether Faisal has been able to speak to him yet – perhaps it was a mistake not to take him into our confidence.'

'Don't be crazy.' Clare flushed as she realised what she was saying to Rhys. 'He would never have agreed. Didn't you hear him in theatre? What, Ahmed help give life to a Jew?'

'Perhaps you're right,' Rhys smiled. 'I wish I could see Faisal just once more before he leaves.'

'Have you not seen him?' Clare asked, surprised.

Rhys shook his head. 'He sees Yousef and the women who look after him and that's all. I was so sure of what I was doing before but now I talked, no, tricked, a man into having an operation which, if he gets a massive acute rejection, will almost certainly kill him.' He raised his hand as he saw Clare about to speak. 'I know what you are going to say, that he was dying anyway. That's no excuse and I would like to see him again, just once, so that I can tell him I was wrong.'

'And, if you do, you will be doing him an even greater disservice.' Peter Parfitt's voice came quietly from the corner. 'What you are doing is looking for absolution and you shouldn't be so bloody selfish. If you want forgiveness, go and see a priest or your wife or your girlfriend. Don't ask it of Faisal; to my mind, he's given enough. All you would be doing would be taking from Faisal the certainty that what he did was right. In any case you did tell him there was some hope of it functioning; I remember you saying so. It wasn't as if you told him any lies. You're being over-dramatic Rhys.'

Parfitt's words still humbled Rhys hours later as he entered Faisal's room for the last time. Yousef had told him that all arrangements had been made; they were leaving at eight the next morning and that His Highness wished to see him before he left. There had been a new expectancy in

Yousef's whole manner that Rhys had put down to the young man's excitement at the thought of going home, but he was even more surprised at the Sultan's appearance. He had expected someone *in extremis* but found him animated and bright eyed, sitting up in his bed which had been turned to lie along the wall. Owen instinctively adopted one of his standard approaches.

'Good evening, Your Highness; I'm so glad to see you looking so well.'

Faisal smiled at Rhys's professionalism. 'Good evening, Mr Owen. Yes, it seems the Almighty, in His mercy, intends to allow this old sinner to die where all tribesmen should die, under the stars.'

'How are you feeling?'

'Excited.' There was a quickness to the reply that reminded Rhys of Hannah.

'There's no feeling like going home, is there?' Rhys produced another of his standard, banal, bedside phrases.

'It is not only that, Mr Owen. They assure me that I have passed a small but significant quantity of urine this evening.' Surprise fought with delight to control Rhys's features and Faisal saw them both. 'So you must not feel guilty. Lying here, I have imagined what must have been going through your mind. Do not feel guilty, Mr Owen. I am told that Hannah is thriving, is getting more beautiful every day. I am content. I have no regret.'

'I am delighted.'

Faisal's face clouded. 'But I hear our secret is out. Perhaps we were too sure of ourselves, that we could get away with it. Ahmed's jealousy has always made him a dangerous man; now he will be even more so. I have asked him to come to me but he has not. I fear it is because he does not want to be persuaded. He now has a genuine cause for his envy to feed on and does not want to have it removed by me. It will make Yousef's task so much more difficult now, as it is impossible to predict just how Ahmed will use his knowledge.'

They were interrupted by loud tappings on the wall alongside the bed and Faisal brightened.

'My young friend can hear us talking.' He turned to return the message with one bony knuckle. 'That's why I had the bed turned this way. Otherwise it was too painful to stretch. I'm afraid I have let her down; I was so bound up in my own troubles, so miserable at the thought of the death I should welcome, may Allah forgive an old man, that I was reluctant to return her knocking, but – ' he gave one of his giggles that Owen felt he would always remember ' – it has surprised me what just a few drops of urine will do, and, of course, since she has been told we are leaving tomorrow, if I hadn't replied, I was in great danger of her knocking the wall down on top of me.'

Though they laughed together, the banter faded from Faisal's voice.

'Will you tell her what happened?' he asked.

'I have thought a great deal about that, Your Highness, and I had decided to do whatever you wished. Now, however, I think the whole thing is a bit academic. At present she does not know what you did for her but it must only be a matter of time. All the staff who are here must know about it – they won't tell Hannah while she is still one of their patients – but once this is over, knowing how gossip goes round a hospital, it must get out and there's bound to be somebody only too ready to sell the story to the Press. I can see this making headlines within a matter of days. Hannah is bound to find out.'

'I am sad. For many reasons. I was grateful to you, Mr Owen. You gave me the chance of an act of atonement for my many sins and I would have wished for that to be a personal matter between me and my God. But I am also sad at what this might do to my country; there are many Ahmeds and so few Yousefs. And, I suppose, the world, as sick as it is, might now see Hannah, that innocent, as some sort of monster. It will remain to be seen how she is treated even by her own race.' He gave a short, bitter, world weary laugh. 'I suppose some might even say her new kidney is not strictly Kosher and shun her for it, make her as much a social outcast as it was, in another race not so long ago, not to have blonde hair and blue eyes. Between us, my friend, have we produced some sort of racial pariah?'

'Or some symbol of hope for the future, perhaps?'

Slowly, Faisal brought his head up to look steadily at Owen. 'Once again, Mr Owen, you shame me.' The corners of his mouth twitched. 'I shall be quite glad to get away from you. All I could see was man's wickedness and you have shown me hope.'

'Optimism goes with the job, Your Highness,' Rhys smiled, freed of his guilt. 'Without it you soon go crackers.'

The sun was up but lacked the strength to penetrate the smoke-screen of high altitude cloud away to the east. Following his latest trip to Whitehall, Ledgerman knew exactly how it felt. He had not been to bed. He had been summoned to COBRA late the previous night and, on the trip back, his driver had grasped the rare chance of a long, high-speed journey along the M4 literally with both hands, at times making Ledgerman almost wish he was back in the helicopter. He stood, surveying the distant hospital in the early light, wondering at the quality that went to make a successful politician.

The situation showed all the signs of being resolved satisfactorily, they had been told. Agreement had been reached about the release of all the hostages in return for a safe passage back to Cardiff Airport where their aircraft had been refuelled the night before during the darkness afforded by an unexplained total power failure. Everyone would agree, the sooner they were all out of the country the better, they had not really harmed anyone and it was infinitely preferable to get rid of them as quickly as possible than have half of them lying in pools of blood in front of the cameras, the other half just a damn nuisance in gaol. No doubt some would see it as a climbdown, those who did not have to deal with the practicalities of such situations, but an official statement was to be issued by Downing Street to coincide with the beginning of the withdrawal.

Between those four walls, the voice had dropped, negotiations had been going on with the Shahinians for some time, negotiations which could not be made overt until such time as there was a new administration in that country. Meanwhile, HM Government was anxious that nothing should happen to damage long-term relations.

A light-hearted suggestion by the DG that he should organise a slight accident to Sultan Faisal on the trip home to speed up the process had been humorously received, but the professional Civil Servant had left the politicians in no doubt that, on one point, he was not joking – Roisin Dineen did not leave the country. If she did, the PM could expect the DG's resignation on his desk the next morning and his reason for doing so leaked to the Press within hours. He had been reassured that there was no question of either Dineen or Dickens being allowed to leave; the one called Yousef had given his word that arrangements had been made. One or two heads had been turned inquiringly Ledgerman's way and he had simply stared back. Any arrangements made had certainly not involved him.

Though Ledgerman's was hardly the physique of a man that felt the cold, he shivered. All he wanted now was for it to be over and done with. He was sickened by the whole affair. It was happening all over again. Like the Libyan Embassy affair, under orders from their political masters, they were going to escort out of the country a group of terrorists in whose midst was a murderer. To have come so close!

He looked at his watch; time to be moving. His orders had been direct and simple; stand back, give them space, don't crowd them. In other words, don't do anything that might hamper whatever 'arrangements' Yousef had in mind for his Irish friends. Ledgerman could only think of two possibilities; they would be shot and dumped or, far more likely, suddenly isolated to either give themselves up or be gunned down by the police. They would never put Dineen in the Mercedes with Faisal, she was bound to be in the Saracen, and they would never risk a gun fight near that car bomb or near the aircraft. It had to happen somewhere between the two. At no time during the journey must the rear doors of the Saracen stray out of rifle range. But, as he turned away, Ledgerman's greatest anxiety stayed with him, the thought that Roisin Dineen might well have made the same deductions.

Without undressing, Rhys had snatched a few hours of troubled sleep during the night. Until the small hours there had been an eerie atmosphere hanging over the groups that stood or sat around the two top floors, talking almost in whispers, unable to settle to rest. Only two were conspicuous by their absence from a fraternity bred out of concern for each other's well being the next day. Tired, homesick, motherly ward orderlies had wished gun-toting young Arabs good luck. A young, disillusioned, enlightened Irishman, with ill-defined visions of how he could get himself a short prison sentence and a new life with a new identity, had asked Paddy how difficult it was to get a job as a Theatre Orderly. Rhys had blundered into Yousef and Clare talking earnestly, with Clare in tears, before finding Nansi trying to contain Hannah's excitement. And Rhys, in his restless wanderings, had been able to think only of Alex.

Now he stood in the ward corridor unwashed, unshaven and unfed. Yousef, tense, alert and commanding, stood beside him. All the remaining hospital staff he had insisted on being shut in various rooms along the ward, together with the patients. The theatre floor above was empty. They stepped back as Faisal was wheeled past slowly, his face hidden in the folds of his gown. As the trolley disappeared through the door to the landing beyond, Yousef turned to Rhys.

'The Mercedes is virtually a small ambulance and, as soon as we know His Highness is safely inside, we will start to withdraw. You will come with us as far as the front entrance. When we have left, you will be free to come back up here and lead the others down. In the meanwhile, for their own safety, it is best they stay here. We will withdraw floor by floor. We will not use the lifts. The last to leave will be the Irish woman and Ahmed who will cover our withdrawal from the roof until the last possible moment. Please, Rhys,' Yousef took the Armalite from his shoulder, 'do as you're told.'

They stood, waiting enxiously to hear that Faisal was in the car, unaware that it was taking longer than planned. Outside the building, one of Faisal's attendants had pointed upwards and Faisal had insisted on being carried out beyond the Mercedes until he too could see and wave to the young girl with the cascade of black hair, standing at the window, shaking one arm so vigorously as to seek the support of a nurse with the other.

Rhys walked out of the ward on to the landing and stood, wondering at Yousef's thoughts as he saw the young man take one last look up the corridor before closing the doors behind him. At a shouted command from Yousef, the young Arab from the theatre landing above came down to join them. Slowly, without any further commands, they leapfrogged their way down through the guards on the stairs and landings below as in any well-drilled military withdrawal. For the first time, standing at the foot of the stairs and seeing the young Arabs in the hallway and out through the door to the vehicles outside, Rhys appreciated the size of the force Yousef had brought with him. At a nod from Yousef, they began to leave, filing through the main entrance one by one. Left alone in the hallway, Rhys and Yousef stood face to face, a flicker of doubt in their faces extinguished as Yousef closed the gap between them, spreading his arms before wrapping them around Rhys's shoulders. A moment of instinctive reserve was swept away as Rhys felt the thud of the young warrior's rifle against his back and, to his surprise, he found himself matching Yousef in the intensity of his embrace. They stood back.

'We haven't long, Rhys. They will be down from the roof any moment. May I write to you? I hope that nothing that has happened will . . .' Yousef stopped and looked up the stairs as he heard footsteps. He frowned as he saw Ahmed appear at the top of the last flight. 'Where's the Irish woman?' he asked, suddenly clutching his rifle more tightly.

Ahmed did not answer until he had joined them in the hallway. 'The Irish woman, Dineen, has plans of her own,' he sneered. 'She is coming.'

'What do you . . .'

Yousef got no further as he swung round at the sound of shouting that came suddenly from the far end of the block beyond the Pharmacy. The shouting got clearer and more demanding as the figure of Eamon Dickens flung itself through the door at the end of the corridor and began running towards them, one hand outstretched. Rhys heard Yousef cock his rifle as Dicken's words became discernible.

'She's primed it; the bomb. She's pulled the dowels. I couldn't stop her. She's . . .'

Roisin was firing even before she appeared in the doorway at the end of the corridor that was now a long tunnel of shattering noise. Eamon Dickens fell, clutching one knee, screaming in his agony as he tried to crawl towards Yousef and away from the spitting, hammering terror now framed in the doorway. With one fierce lunge, Yousef hurled Rhys to the ground and the shelter of the corner where corridor met hallway while Ahmed, a strange, vacuous, daydreaming leer on his face, stripped of both fear and reason in the suddenness of the attack, began to walk towards the hail of ricochets, raising his Armalite as if in salute.

'Wait. I am coming.'

In the shattering blur of noise and movement, Rhys, from the safety of where he lay, saw Yousef, crouching on one knee, begin firing. His burst of fire seemed endless and, when it stopped, the building above still rang with its echo. But now, there was no further firing from Roisin Dineen and Rhys watched, hypnotised, as Yousef stood, his face set, to slowly curl his finger and empty his magazine into the distant silence. He hadn't finished firing when, behind Yousef's back, the door to B Block was flung open and two black-clad, black-helmeted figures burst through, their Heckler and Kochs already traversing as they yelled to Rhys to stay down. Without thought, Rhys sprang at Yousef in a tackle that took them both to the ground and he was still trying to cover the struggling Arab with his body when he looked up to see a pair of eyes staring at him through the holes of a black balaclava. Slowly, the helmet was peeled off to show the heavy beard and bright red headscarf.

'Man, what possessed ye to do a crazy thing like tha'? You're a wee bit long in the tooth to be playing the bloody hero.' The massive head turned on its shoulders. 'Geordie, go and make sure that bitch yonder has got what was coming to her.'

As Robertson bent to give Rhys and Yousef a hand up, they became conscious of another presence in the hallway behind them. Three of the Arabs who had rushed back into the building at the sound of firing, had also stopped to look hesitantly towards the stairs, uncertain what to do. Yousef and Rhys turned to see Ledgerman, backed by two of his D11 squad, slowly descending, step by step. The two grim-faced, black-bereted policemen held automatic weapons trained on the group below them and Robertson, in similar fashion, glared back. Ledgerman, without halting his slow descent, held his hand up to show that the small black object with the barrel-like appendage was no hand-gun but his portable RT, and the steadiness of his voice as he placed it to his mouth and the discipline of the men around him prevented the bloodshed that seemed inevitable.

'Everyone stay where you are. I say again, stay where you are. Nothing here I cannot handle. Act on own discretion if any further firing but present position stable. Keep out.'

There was nothing humorous about Ledgerman's tone as his untidy head steadied itself in front of Rhys. 'Rough company you keep, doctor.' When he got no reply, he turned to Yousef. 'If this was the arrangement you had in mind, I must say I don't think much of your planning. Very messy.'

As rational thought strove to overcome the shock of what had happened so swiftly, it dawned on Yousef what had started the shooting. He hardly registered the sprawling body of his brother as he looked past the moaning heap where Eamon Dickens slumped against the wall, to the inert heap at the end of the corridor. He looked back at Ledgerman, horror-stricken.

'The car bomb. The Irish woman has made it live. That man Dickens over there shouted to tell us just before she started firing.'

'Then what the hell is everyone standing around here for?' Ledgerman bawled. He spun round to the two men behind him 'Get upstairs. Get those people out as fast as you can. Wait!' he shouted as the men began to move. Ledgerman turned back to face Rhys. 'Where are they? Which floor?'

'Top but one. They're all on the same floor.'

Ledgerman turned again to his men. 'Right; get them out. Get them across the landings and as far across to the other end of the block as you can. See if you can get one of those bloody barricades down and get them out of the building altogether if you can. Now! Move!' He brushed past the group in the hall as if they were not there.

Yousef was the next to react. He turned to the Arabs behind him. 'And all of you get out too. Go and get His Highness as far from here as you can.'

'No.'

Ledgerman was stepping over Ahmed's body when he stopped dead to shout the word. He came back the few steps to put his face close to Yousef's. 'He stays. He stays, d'you hear me? If we're all to get blown to hell by this filthy obscenity you brought with you, then, by God, he goes with us. If that car moves an inch, I'll see to it that none of us come out of this alive. And that I swear.'

Robertson looked at Yousef as if for orders but saw dumb submission and followed Ledgerman down the corridor, instinctively following a leader. They both bent over the moaning Irishman.

'What sort of bomb is it?' Ledgerman asked urgently.

His only reply was renewed moaning that spiked into an agonised scream as Robertson kicked the bloodstained leg. 'Usually jogs their memory,' he growled.

'Simple time clock.' Eamon Dickens managed to get the words out through his moanings. 'For Christ's sake get to it or we're all done for. She's pulled the dowels out. I saw her. She was crazy; just seemed to look right through me.'

'What d'ye mean, pulled the dowels out?' Robertson gave Dickens another prod with his boot but Ledgerman answered for him.

'Piece of wooden rod, used to keep the jaws of a clothes peg apart.

Probably means a simple mechanism, thank God. How long have we got?'

'Ten, fifteen minutes. No more. She wanted to keep everyone here, give time for the police to rush us; take everyone with her. She was crazy, I tell you. She just wanted to die and take someone with her. I tried to stop her.'

'Is there any anti-handling device?'

'Eh?'

Dickens looked up blankly at Ledgerman and Robertson was about to pick him up by the shoulders when Ledgerman, with a grunt of disgust, made a dash for the door at the end of the corridor. Roisin's body gave a shudder as Robertson, in his haste to follow, trod on her thigh.

For what seemed an eternity, Rhys stood silent in the hallway as the sounds of hurrying feet and frightened voices came down the stair-well from three floors up. He watched Yousef kneel beside his brother's body, straightening Ahmed's twisted limbs and closing fixed, disbelieving eyes. Suddenly the far end of the corridor was filled with the bulk of two large men, the act of stepping over Roisin's body hardly influencing the flow of low-pitched, intimate conversation that now stemmed from sharing a few minutes of sweaty, gut-cramping fear. Ledgerman spoke to Yousef.

'Better be on your way then. The good doctor here wants to get back to work.'

'Not without him.' They all turned to look where Yousef pointed at his brother's body.

'He stays,' Ledgerman said.

'No. We will take him home. He will be buried in Shahin,' Yousef replied, his face resolute. 'We do not go home without him.'

Rhys stood aside as the two men stared each other down. 'Oh, come on, Ledgerman,' he murmured. 'You've got two IRA, one dead, one wounded; you've defused a bomb that could get you a medal. What more d'you want? What is there to gain by keeping that poor bastard's body here?'

Ledgerman did not take his eyes from Yousef's face as he replied, 'It would tell us exactly which sort of bullets killed him, doctor, now wouldn't it, and they don't go in for post-mortems much back in their country, if I remember correctly?'

Ledgerman waited for a reaction from Yousef but the young man's face remained a mask. 'All right, go on,' he grunted. 'Take him. Get the hell out of here but not before I see him. I must see him first.'

'Who?' Yousef asked.

'Him!' Ledgerman almost shouted, jerking his head towards the car outside. 'Faisal.'

As Yousef and Robertson began to half-drag, half-carry Ahmed's body towards the door, Owen followed Ledgerman out ot the building. As they raised the back of the estate car he watched Ledgerman as he stood, silently glaring at the dark, shrivelled fearlessness that did not give ground before years of hatred that burned themselves out in a matter of a few seconds. As if disappointed at what he saw, Ledgerman signalled for the hatchback to be closed once more. He turned to Rhys.

'At the end of the day, it's difficult to know what all the fuss was about, isn't it, doctor?'

33

'Take care, doctor.'

It was with something close to affection that Rhys watched Ledgerman's back recede down the corridor and vanish through the door. It had been with something close to comradeship that they had made a final tour of the theatre and ward floors to make sure they were all cleared. Above them, the Bomb Squad had already begun searching the Residents' Quarters and the roof for booby traps.

'What's happened to the patients?' Rhys had asked.

'They went to Swansea.'

'To Singleton?'

'Yes, I think that was the place.'

'And the staff? You don't usually let hostages go immediately, do you?'

'I don't think there's much to be gained from keeping them this time. We've got a shrink to give them a quick look over but, if he's happy, they'll be allowed home. Most of them will be on their way home by now. Where will you go, doctor?'

Ledgerman had looked hard at Rhys but had got no reply.

Rhys made his way slowly down the stairs to the ground floor, what little noise he made echoing through the deserted building. In the hallway, he paused to look to his left, down towards Pharmacy, as if to see whether Roisin Dineen still lay there. He tried to fathom what that tortured mind had seen in the last few seconds before extinction, so filled with a blind universal hatred as to make her aim so wildly inaccurate, so indiscriminate in its toll. He also wondered who the poor sods were whose job it was to clear up the mutilated debris of urban warfare, shadowy scavengers who never appeared in identifiable form on TV. Rhys wondered who employed them, was it a well-paid job, giving the job satisfaction that seemed so important these days? He saw bloodstains where Ahmed had lain and recalled, vividly, the inscrutable look on Yousef's face as he had knelt beside his brother, showing neither the shock of bereavement nor the guilt of a latter-day Cain. Rhys heard again in his mind Ledgerman's words, 'Which bullets?', a haunting question from which, he knew, he would never be free.

Outside, two uniformed police stood guard over the Transit. The patrol car and Patel's Honda were gone, the nurse's dummy removed from Clare Drury's caved-in Mini. Rhys exchanged thumbs up signs with the two policemen as his car started with surprisingly little difficulty and, feeling the strangeness of driving in theatre garb, he began the descent down the common. The Army were gone, the barricade of plastic sheeting already being dismantled like some travelling circus. The cameramen were gone and Rhys smiled to himself; surely one of them could have stayed to record a hero's departure. As he drove through the town centre, he felt a slight resentment when no one amongst Avonport's lunchtime shoppers took a second look at a man who had just spent nine days held hostage. Not yet free of a trance-like sense of unreality, Rhys headed north to the road junction where, he knew, he could postpone the decision no longer. To the right lay the M4 and Bristol. To the left, the road to the valleys.

Rhys turned left.

Even though Balaclava Crescent looked deserted, Rhys knew better than to think he was arriving undetected. As he stood on the doorstep and rang the bell, he felt as if he was under a microscope. Nansi smiled when she saw him but said nothing, simply turning and leading the way into a kitchen full of children's chattering excitement. Pale and tear-streaked, Nansi also still wore her crumpled theatre clothes and she pushed at her hair which, she knew, needed a wash. As she slid plates of eggs, chips and baked beans in front of her children, she looked across at Rhys.

'I thought you'd have been in the Frenchay.' Too exhausted to add overtones of surprise or censure, she made it sound like a flat statement of fact.

'That's what I've come to see you about.' Rhys smiled at the children and wearily shrugged his shoulders.

'Go into the living room,' Nansi said. 'I'll bring you a cup of coffee.'

Rhys, putting on a bogus paternal look, stayed to hear about the police car that had brought their mother home before walking into the living room to sit silently in that uncomfortable ambience of someone else's home. He heard a familiar ticking sound and saw the old man's clock, also looking out of place, propped up on the gas fire. As Nansi walked in, a cup in each hand, she smiled to herself to see Rhys sitting in an armchair; a few weeks previously and it would have been the settee with one welcoming arm stretched along its back. She sat at the far end of the long, worn seat but Rhys made no move to join her. They sipped their drinks as Rhys did his best to find the right words.

'It's all right, *cariad*,' Nansi said, softly. 'Don't worry about it. I understand.'

'What?' Rhys asked. He wondered how the Baxters of this world would have handled it; just walk in, tell her to get lost, that it had been fun while it lasted? Probably a more honest approach than his, being pathetically weak, letting her put it into words for him.

'You're going back to your wife. That's what you have come to tell me, isn't it?'

He didn't answer immediately. It was as if he was still having difficulty accepting the fact and it had come as a relief to have the decision put for him in audible form. What was certain was that he was being a bastard and the sooner it was all over the better. But why? There was no question of a sudden upsurge of loving affection for Alex as a result of her accident. He wanted desperately to see her – that was one emotion, at least, he knew to be genuine – but there could be no question of rekindling a love that he now admitted had never existed. The best they could hope for was tolerant parallel existences but this now seemed infinitely preferable to cloying, sex-led intimacy. He suddenly longed for freedom from Nansi's clinging whispers, to hear again Alex's sharp tongue, to make amends.

'I must, Nansi; you must see that. But I felt I must see you first, tell you . . .' His voice tailed away feebly.

'Make you feel that at least you had done the gentlemanly thing, d'you mean? But there was no real need to explain, dear. I didn't really expect you to do anything else. After all, what would people have said?' There was now a hardness in Nansi's voice that made Rhys squirm. 'But you'll be back. Just wait until the boredom sets in again. You'll be back for your bit of maldod.' She looked at Rhys more closely when he did not reply. She stopped with her cup halfway to her mouth. 'No. I'm wrong. This time you won't be back.'

Rhys found he could not face her. He heard himself mumbling. A lot of time to think over the last few days; changed circumstances; how Alex would need to be looked after for a while; had always felt guilty; it wasn't right what they'd been doing; never any future for anyone. By the time Rhys had finished, he found himself standing, his cup on the table, only half-drunk, wondering whether he would be able to get away before Nansi began to cry. He knew he would never have a better chance, his total exhaustion would come to his defence should Nansi decide to swallow her pride and walk over to him. Another time and a few soft words, a few caresses, and he would be back, looking for comfort in the loving warmth he found so enervating. He was about to start towards the door when the noise of the telephone brought Nansi to her feet, barring his escape. He watched her pick up the phone, her eyes never leaving his face.

'Yes, he's here,' she said, and handed the phone to Rhys. 'It's your daughter.'

'Thanks.' Rhys tried to smile. 'Hello, Sian?'

'Hello, Dad. Are you all right?'

Rhys got the impression more of formality than concern.

'Yes, Sian, I'm fine.'

The formality over, there was now no mistaking the edge to his daughter's voice. 'I was rather afraid I might find you there. It's about Mum. Mum died earlier this morning. We've been trying to get you.'

No loving preamble. No few softening phrases in compassionate tones that would have made the actual words superfluous. Just a blunt statement as if he had it coming to him. Rhys closed his eyes, the sound of his daughter's voice striking him with a pain that Ahmed's rifle butt could never have matched. As Nansi saw it and came to put a hand on his arm, he managed one word. 'When?'

'Few hours ago. She just died. No question of turning machines off or anything like that. She just died, Dad; just seemed to give up.'

'Did she regain consciousness at all?'

'No, she didn't.'

'Where are you?'

'I'm still at the Frenchay.'

'I'll come over. I'll have to go home first.' Rhys looked down at himself. 'I'm not very presentable. I'm sure I smell.'

'There's no point really, Dad.' Sian's voice was already softening. 'There's not much anyone can do now. I shall be going home soon.'

'I'll come over later anyway; I'd like to see the staff and thank them.' His voice faltered. 'I'd like to see her.'

'All right, but come and spend the night with us, Dad; please. You can't go back home like that. Unless, of course . . .' She left the rest unsaid.

'I'll call and see you sometime this evening, Sian. There's a lot I need to explain.'

When he put the phone down, Rhys found himself between Nansi and the door and he backed away slowly. Nansi made no move to follow him and Rhys had to abandon all hope of immediate escape.

'Alex is dead,' he said, walking back to face her. 'Died this morning.' He felt nothing but genuine sadness and was in no mood to analyse the silent inquiry written all over Nansi's features. She put out one hand to turn his head so that he could do nothing to avoid a gaze full of down to earth honesty. She only had to look closely for a few seconds to know that the phone call had made no difference, nothing had happened that was suddenly going to transform her life. Another few minutes and she would have a bath, wash her hair, sleep and get up and go to work and do the shopping and the cleaning and look after the children – alone. Nothing had changed.

Without a word, she walked past him and opened the door to the outside world. In the tiny porch they had found so intimate before, Nansi pressed her back against the wall as Rhys sidestepped his way out. There wasn't the usual last wave after the three-point turn in the narrow road, just the frosted glass door, closed like the last page of a book.

He drove home, sick and empty, struggling to open his own front door against the heap of newspapers and letters. The house smelt deserted and unloved with dirty dishes and nine days of mould on unwashed coffee mugs. He shaved and showered, trying not to see the pink and blue bathroom clutter Alex had not taken with her. Dressed, he went downstairs, threw half a green-spotted loaf of bread into the rubbish bag and told himself he wasn't really hungry. Out of the house and in his car, he paused. He nodded to himself, a decision made, before starting the engine.

As he drove alongside Swansea Marina, his spirits gave a first, tiny surge of recovery as he pictured the little *Prelude*, patiently waiting. Out along the Mumbles Road, the sea to his left sparkled timelessly. It would look like that in a thousand years' time. He turned right and up the hill to the hospital where it stood, facing out over Swansea Bay. A few inquiries at the entrance hall, a few explanations at the Ward Sister's office, and Rhys's bearing straightened, his head came up, as if transfused and envigorated by the atmosphere of a busy hospital once more. He walked into a room so like that other one at Avonport.

'Where have you been?' Hannah asked, a new softness in her voice, her back to the window. 'I was getting worried about you.'

Rhys's face moulded into a smile, long and slow. He knew he was near to tears at the sight of the smoothness to her skin, the colour in her cheeks, the turbulence of new vitality bursting to find something on which to expend itself.

He had delighted in such sudden, dramatic transformations many times before when his transplants had liberated some youngster from the dragging shackles of uraemia. But then his joy had been born of sheer professional satisfaction. Now he was seeing a loved one reborn.

'I have had other things on my mind, Hannah. I've had some bad news. I'm afraid my wife died this morning.'

Hannah stretched one hand towards him as she raised the other to her mouth, stifling a cry with one knuckle thrust between her teeth. Slowly, she led him to a chair and pulled the bedside stool to sit close in front of him.

'Rhys, I'm sorry.'

Using words and tones no man can find, Hannah soothed and comforted until Rhys became aware just how much of a defence her brash, irreverent manner had been. Gradually, lovingly, she coaxed him away from despair until they sat quietly, the early evening peace around them.

'Hannah, will you come home with me?'

'Of course.' Her answer was quick and purposeful. 'You need someone to look after you. You're quite a helpless creature really, aren't you?' There was a trace of her old impudence.

'I mean to live with me, Hannah.'

'I know you do.' Her forehead creased into a frown. 'But what about Dai and Jessie? What are they going to say about it? The last thing I want to do is hurt them.'

'I'm sure they will understand. They love you too much to stand in your way and they know you can't go back to live in that loft. You won't be that far away; you'll be able to see them as often as you like.'

'And ride Tempest?'

'When you're old enough, I'll buy you a little car.'

Rhys sat back for a moment to watch Hannah as she struggled to subdue her excitement. 'There would be a few conditions,' he added, firmly.

'Yes?'

'You must go back to school. You are intelligent but uneducated, and we can't have that.' The words echoed in Rhys's memory as he looked at Hannah, expecting at least a few pouts but saw nothing but determination.

'I'd like that, but won't I be too old?'

'I don't mean the usual sort of school.'

Rhys's reply brought a flash of the old Hannah. 'I'm not going to any private school. No dormitories. No lights out. I've had enough of that.'

With a laugh, Rhys soothed her fears. 'I don't mean that sort of school either. You will have to go to some sort of crammer. There's bound to be one around somewhere. You may have to go to Cardiff.'

'I don't mind, as long as I can sleep at your – ' she hesitated, fighting down the old fear of any hope of happiness, and added, thrilling to the word ' – at home.'

Having surmounted that hurdle, some of her mischief returned.

'And what am I going to call you? Can I call you Rhys? I'd better not call you Dad – Sian might not be too keen on that. Father sounds a bit pompous and you don't look quite old enough yet to call you Grandpa. No, it's got to be Rhys.'

'Cheeky young hussy,' Rhys grinned. 'Any more of that and the whole deal's off. It's not too late to change my mind.'

They lapsed into silence, savouring the happiness they were bringing each other, and it was a measure of their rapport that Rhys knew exactly what Hannah meant when she said softly, 'And, one day, will you take me out there?'

'I will.'

'Soon? I want to see him again.'

'Did you not see him after your operation?'

Hannah shook her head. 'Only through the window.' She said nothing for a moment. 'But he left me a letter.'

'A letter? What did . . .'

'It's secret. But I know lots of things now I didn't know before. When will you take me to see him?'

'Hannah, he's still a very sick man. Who knows what is going to happen out there over the next few years? There's more than one Ahmed out there, I'm sure. And you've got your own life to lead now.' He screwed his eyes up as if trying to read very small print. 'I'll make a deal with you.'

'What's that?'

'The day you win a university entrance, I'll go out and buy the tickets.'

'Done.'

Again they sat silently until Hannah looked out of the window. 'And will you take me sailing too?'

'Of course, if you would like that? Would you like that?' he asked hesitatingly, afraid of so many dreams so quickly.

'If you'd only known, the hours I spent in that room, looking out of that window, dreaming of it.'

'I'll get something bigger, go in shares with someone. We couldn't manage on our own.'

'Yes, we could.' He felt her strength and vitality. 'I'll have friends. I'll bring them along. We'll have the biggest and best boat in the marina. Perhaps, one day . . .'

Rhys broke, torn asunder between so much hope and so deep a guilty sadness at what he had done to Helen and the child, to Alex and to Nansi. As he ground out the agony of a man's crying, he felt her hair against his face, her lips at his ear.

'Don't, Rhys; hush. It will be all right now.'